This book is a work of fiction. The characters, incidents, and dialogues are products of the author's imagination and are not to be construed as real. Any resemblance to actual events or persons, living or dead, is entirely coincidental.

Published by George Colton Publishing LLC

Clemons, Keith R. 1949-
     While Earth Remains / Keith R. Clemons - 1st ed.

Library of Congress Control Number: 2021911407
ISBN 978-0-9731048-7-5

Printed in the United States of America

   First Edition - First Printing

21 22 23 24 25 26 – 10 9 8 7 6 5 4 3 2 1

Note to the reader:

It is not my intent to suggest that the events portrayed in this book will happen tomorrow, or even any time soon. In reading the Old Testament we find four hundred years between Malachi, the last book of the Hebrew Scriptures, and the coming of Christ. By that time many of the Jews had stopped looking for their Messiah.

In speaking of Christ's return we find a similar scenario prophesied by the Apostle Peter when he said: "knowing this first: that scoffers will come in the last days, walking according to their own lusts, and saying, "Where is the promise of His coming?" II Peter 3: 3-4

What I've tried to do in this book is show how globalism, hyperinflation and recent technological advances, are being orchestrated by the evil one to facilitate the antichrist's rise to power. Whether this takes place now, or in the far distant future, is anybody's guess. My purpose was only to show that these things are coming fast upon us, and will shortly come to fruition.

But who knows, the Lord may yet tarry another hundred years—then again, He could come in the next blink of an eye!

Dedicated to:

Claude O'Donovan

Who, with a full white beard, is often asked to play Santa,
but in real life demonstrates how to be ready for Christ's return.

And to:
All those who believe we are nearing the end.

MARANATHA
Even so, come quickly Lord Jesus.

WHILE EARTH REMAINS

by Keith R. Clemons

To Pat

" But know this, in the last days perilous
times shall come." II Timothy 3:1

GEORGE COLTON
PUBLISHING

While earth remains,
seedtime and harvest,
cold and heat,
winter and summer,
and day and night,
shall not cease.

Genesis 8:22.

PROLOGUE

I T WASN'T SO BAD. Perhaps the unemployment numbers were too high, and runaway inflation was pushing food and housing prices through the roof. And tent cities were popping up in public parks across the nation (but that was only because it was easier to live on a government subsidy than work) and maybe neighbors who used to enjoy grilling hotdogs together had stopped talking because they held different political views—language had, after all, become more about criticism than communication, and TV couldn't be watched without involving adult sensuality—even with all that, life was good. They could abide a few minor indiscretions as long as they had access to their cellphones, the latest Twitter feeds, and Hollywood celebs telling them how to cope.

Consumed by apathy they didn't see it coming. As in Noah's day they were eating and drinking and giving in marriage, man with woman, and man with man. They were saving the planet, upholding social justice and preaching a gospel of peace. They never saw the clouds building on the horizon. They didn't know it was the beginning—*of the end.*

ONE

THE CHANT DRUMMED through the valley muted only by the tumbling whitewater of the Watalong River and the carpet of trees blanketing the wooded hillside. Men and women stood hunched shoulder to shoulder in front of a Christmas tree farm, their arms interlocked to prevent passage. No one was going in or coming out.

The police had been called but they stood off in the distance ducking flying rocks and balloons filled with urine. A sergeant in a thick wool coat that prevented the chilly December air from seeping into his bones, held a megaphone to his mouth.

"This is private property. You need to disperse. We will use force if necessary."

"Suck eggs, pig!"

"This is a free country, not a police state!"

About a dozen shoppers stood behind the police barricade waiting for the police to subdue the protestors. They had come to celebrate Christmas. It was supposed to be a season of peace. Several had already become discouraged and wanting no part of the altercation, had fled, but those who stayed were annoyed and wanted the demonstrators gone. This wasn't the time to make a political statement. It was time to decorate a tree so they could see the magic of Christmas in their children's eyes.

"What do you think we should do, Dad?"

"Do? We're going to do what we came here for."

"You think they'll let us through."

"Only one way to find out."

They had parked their rental down the block behind a red pickup where they hoped it would be safe. A light dusting of snow had melted and turned the road's dirt shoulder to mud sticking to the heels of Stan's leather loafers and turning the toes of Rachel's white boots brown. The police were off to their left facing off with the protestors. Stan took his daughter's hand and began treading his way behind the group, hoping to sneak by.

"Woah man, this lot is closed. Go get your tree somewhere else."

Three demonstrators peeled away from the group to block their entrance. Seeing a confrontation in the making a few officers started to respond but were repelled by a barrage of stones. They held their shields up to repel the assault and fell back.

Stan shook his head. The hypocrisy was daunting. There wasn't a facemask to be seen among the protestors. That could be justified because they were outdoors, though shouting the way they were was, by their own definition, a mega spreader. And the boldest of them would normally wear a facemask even outside just to set an example. But the group formed a chain locked arm-in-arm, the furthest thing from social distancing. To say Bill was evil for disparaging what he claimed was an overreaction to the virus, and then to so blatantly ignore the rules they themselves avowed, was ludicrous.

"I don't think so," Stan said. "They don't look closed. I see customers still inside, and the gates are open. I'm pretty sure they're still doing business."

"You miss my meaning. They're no longer open because we're shutting them down."

"Why would you do that? Money from the sale of these trees goes to charity."

"No, dude, you've been lied to. The whole thing's a scam. The man takes the people's money and lines his own pocket, then throws a few bones at a local foodbank and says he's doing God's work. He's being investigated by the IRS for fraud."

"Really? That's awful. I guess I'll have to go see what the man has to say for himself." Stan took a step forward but was pushed back.

3

"I suggest you turn around and go. Like I said, the place is closed."

Stan glanced at the police who seemed powerless to intervene.

"Forget about it. They're not going to help."

Rachel brought her phone up to record the conversation. Stan nodded at her. "Touch me again, and your problem won't be whether the police arrest you. It will be having your paycheck garnished after I sue you for assault."

Then all eyes went to Santa who came to the gate holding a growling wirehaired dog by the collar. "Sic 'em, Willie," he said as he released the dog who rushed into the crowd snapping at the heels of the protestors, corralling them like a herd of sheep. Pandemonium broke out as the chain of people broke apart and scattered trying to stay out of reach of the crazed animal.

Seizing the opportunity, the police rushed in and began making arrests. Rachel and Stan used the distraction to slip inside followed by several of the onlookers who had been waiting for the situation to be resolved.

"Thanks, Santa," Stan said, as they passed through the gate.

TWO

BILL TURNED HIS BACK to the melee and stood stroking his white Santa beard, marveling at the number of people still foraging through the rows of trees inside. The pandemic had caused the closure of many businesses but it hadn't hurt the sale of Christmas trees. You just couldn't get a freshly cut Christmas tree online.

In fact, the Christmas season had come with fervor. They were closed Thanksgiving Thursday, but made their holiday opening Friday morning with the parking lot full and families walking as much as a quarter mile down the snow-dampened street to stand in line for free hayrides and a visit with Santa. The barn was decorated with lights strung across the beams. Bales of hay were stacked along the walls with hundreds of Christmas trees on display. Families strolled about enjoying the holiday spirit while sipping hot chocolate from paper cups. It appeared most of them hadn't even noticed the confrontation outside. Christmas music played nonstop from speakers mounted throughout the property. Santa Bill smiled as he made his way over to greet the children.

"Have you got your Christmas tree yet, Dad?" Rachel said, as they made their way into a barn with an American flag draped over the entry doors.

"You mean for the shelter? No, not yet. It's on my list of things to do as soon as I get back."

Stan looked over at the line of children waiting to see Santa who sat on the leaf spring seat of an antique sled painted red. He was dressed in full regalia, white fluffy cuffs and collar on a red velveteen coat with brass buttons, black boots and a belt with a huge gold buckle. He had a full white beard and granny glasses, and on his head was the red elfin hat trimmed with a furry white ball. Beside the sleigh was a sign that read: "This barn is considered an open air environment. Please feel free to have your child's picture taken with Santa. Masks optional." Santa handed a small boy over to his mother and took another child onto his lap.

"Looks like we're going to be here awhile. You want a hot chocolate while we wait?"

"Sure, why not?"

They went to the tables draped in red and green. A young woman sat in a wheelchair watching as people dropped money into the donation box. It was strictly voluntary. Kids frequently dropped in dimes and quarters. The man reached into the inside pocket of his tan trench coat to retrieve his wallet and pulled out a ten, folding it before slipping it into the slot.

The girl giggled, her shoulders twisting involuntarily. Her hand jerked erratically as her head tipped back, but her mouth exploded with a smile as bright as the Christmas star. "Thaaaaaaak youuuuuuu," she said.

The man returned her smile and turned back to his daughter. "Name your poison. Looks like hot chocolate or hot apple cider, your choice."

"Hot chocolate, definitely. And one of those cookies."

Bill's wife, Mary, was manning the table while caring for their daughter, but unless you knew her well, you probably wouldn't recognize her. Her cheeks were rouged, as was the tip of her nose, and in a green and white stripped dress with furry white cuffs and collar, a black vest embroidered with sprigs of green and red holly, a green Santa hat, and pointed ears, she looked like a giant elf. She turned around and pushed the spigot on the five-gallon decanter, filling the cup. "You want marshmallows on that?"

"Oh, absolutely,"

Mary slipped a candy cane into the melting miniature marshmallows. "And what kind of cookie? We have double-double chocolate and Macadamia Nut."

"I'll take the Macadamia Nut."

The cookie was handed back wrapped in a napkin. The young woman brought it to her nose enjoying the fresh-baked smell as she took a bite. It was still soft and gooey. "Oh, that's good," she said, wiping a crumb off her lip with a thumb.

"I'll have a cider, no cookie," the man said.

Across the barn, a woman surrounded by three young girls was holding a tree up for inspection. Their coats were rubbed shiny with the pockets frayed. One girl had pants that rode above her ankles. Another had a wool mitten with a finger poking through.

The mother appeared to be pleased with the tree, but one of the girls crossed her arms and with a pout shook her head defiantly. "Too small!" she said. "Daddy always wanted a big tree." She went back a few feet to another pile and pointed. "I like that one."

Her mother walked over and tried to lift the tree, but it was too heavy and the boughs too long. They wrapped around her legs preventing her from getting the tree off the ground.

A young volunteer rushed over to help. "Let me get that." He held the tree up so they could stand back and look at it from a distance. The girl's mother was already shaking her head. "We'll never get that in our living room. It's too tall."

But her daughter was adamant. "We should get one like that," she said, pointing to the ten foot tree in the center of the barn. It was the house tree, fully decorated with strings of multi-colored lights, ropes of garland and dozens of sparkling glass bulbs. The old gray war dog had wandered inside and now lay under the boughs absorbing heat from the lights.

"Honey, we couldn't fit that tree in our living room. You know that."

"But we can this one," the girl responded. She went over and took the tree sweeping her hand across one of the branches. "Look Mommy, it's so beautiful. And it smells so nice. I know this one will fit. I know it.

7

And we have so many decorations left from before… We couldn't even fit them on the tree last year. Daddy would want us to have this one. You know he would. Please, Mommy, please."

Her mother bit her lip and then looked at the yellow price tag tied to one of the branches. "I'm sorry, honey. We just can't. We'll take that one over there," she said, speaking to the boy holding the tree. "You think you could tie it on my car while I pay?" She went over and removed the tag from the branch. "It's the blue Buick parked by your sign on the street."

The boy nodded, and the woman turned and walked off in the direction of the cash register, leaving the little girl with her arms crossed, her bottom lip protruding. She tucked in her chin and kicked the straw with her rubber rainboot.

"Come on girls. I don't want you getting separated." The trio turned and traipsed after their mother, though the stubborn girl lagged behind.

A few feet away another couple, a well-dressed man and his wife, were haggling over the price of the tree they had picked.

"Seventy bucks, are you kidding? That's highway robbery. Where's the spirit of giving?"

"It's for charity, sir."

Stan had watched the scene unfold. He reached for his wallet and approached the boy who was cutting string to wrap the lady's tree before carrying it out.

"Wait a minute," he said. "What's that tree cost?" he nodded toward the one the woman couldn't afford.

"Seventy bucks. This one's only fifty."

"Here," Stan said, handing the boy three twenty's and a ten. "Leave me out of it. Just go tell her the tree's already paid for, and then go put the bigger one on her car."

"That was nice, Dad," his daughter said as he walked back over.

He nodded. "I was just thinking about how many Christmases you went without a tree. It just didn't seem right."

The line for Santa was still too long. They dropped their empty cups into a trashcan and with their arms locked together, headed outside.

A tractor sat puffing clouds from its exhaust. It was hitched to a wagon with stake fencing and bales of hay along both inside walls. A dozen people sat on the bales waiting to be taken into the farm's interior to learn about the growing of Christmas trees.

"All aboard," a man in a train conductor's hat and bib overalls said as he helped a toddler up into his mother's arms. "This is a forty-five minute ride, so if you have someplace you have to be, please keep that in mind."

"Looks like fun. We have time to kill, don't we?"

They climbed into the back and found seats on bales of hay as the driver placed a stake gate into the slots to prevent anyone from falling out.

"My name is Charlie, and I'll be your guide for our tour of the farm."

Charlie climbed onto the tractor seat and shifted into drive. The tractor lurched forward causing the passengers to sway for a moment. "For those of you who want a little history, this farm began as a charity back in the year 2000 when the owner was approached by a group wanting to know if they could cut trees on his land to sell in support of kids with muscular dystrophy. They were hoping to be able to cut trees in those mountains," he said, pointing, "but it didn't happen. Oregon law prohibits cutting trees without special permits, but it turned out the man had his own child with special needs, so it set him to thinking, and the result is the farm you see today. This farm now grows fifteen thousand trees on ten acres of land, comprised mostly of Douglas fir, Nobel fir and Grand fir. The trees are grown in six to eight year cycles, so the trees you purchase today were planted many years ago."

The wagon hit a bump, jostling its passengers so that they rubbed shoulders, but they were huddled into family groups. A few wore face-masks just to be safe, though they'd probably been vaccinated, and were outside. Charlie turned to look back and make sure everyone was okay. "They say being a farmer takes patience, and it does. The typical farmer has to till the soil, plant his seeds, and then wait three or four months until the crop is ready for harvest. Not so with us. We have to till the land, plant our crop and then wait eight years for the harvest.

Now that takes patience. And of course, every year we plant new trees to replace the ones we've harvested the year before and start all over.

"By the way, as many of you already know, this is a nonprofit enterprise. The farm is a registered charity, which means no one makes any money from the sale of these trees. All the profits go to helping disadvantaged and underprivileged children, and yes, for those of you who are business minded, you can use your receipt as a tax write off.

"We're coming up on our drop off point. Those of you who are wanting to cut your own, this is where you get off. Make sure you get your saws from the bin right behind me."

Charlie climbed down from the tractor and came around to remove the gate and put a box down for people to step on. "Remember, any tree under four foot is thirty dollars. Four to six foot trees are fifty dollars, and the six to ten foot trees are seventy dollars. You're free to walk the property and choose any tree you like. I'll be back around in about an hour. But the last ride out is at 4:30. Please remember that. We don't want anybody wandering around out here after dark. Alright, go have fun."

"You want to get off and walk around, or stay?"

"Let's just stay."

About half the people on the wagon disembarked. Adults headed over to where Charlie stood with both men and women taking saws from the metal container. Families formed into groups and, with their little ones disappearing like rabbits into a bush, headed out to play pioneer, mucking through the melting snow and mud to find the perfect Christmas tree.

The afternoon was growing cool. The sun disappeared behind a layer of clouds with backlit edges of gold. The smell of pine saturated the air. Stan turned up the collar of his coat and folded the lapels over his chest crossing his arms to hold them in place. Rachel snuggled into her scarf. "I could think of worse places to live," she said.

"Don't jump the gun. I haven't said anything to Bill about your staying here."

Charlie hit the gas and they continued their bumpy journey over the ruts and rills of the dirt road. He turned around looking back over his shoulder and said, "The rest of us are gonna get into the spirit of the season by singing Christmas carols. And I expect you to sing loud. And that goes for you adults too, not just you kids. Here we go, follow me. Oh Christmas tree, oh Christmas tree, thy leaves are so unchanging…"

They were singing a chorus of, *We wish you a Merry Christmas*, when they arrived back at the barn just in time to see a squadron of Canadian geese flying in perfect chevron formation across the rows of trees, heading south for the winter. Stan and Rachel watched until the birds became an arrow shaped silhouette on the golden clouds.

"Look at that. Beautiful. Those geese were once on the verge of extinction, but now there are so many the Canucks are calling them a nuisance. Mana from heaven, I guess. One minute we're complaining about not having enough, and the next we're saying there's too much." Stan hopped down but grimaced when his foot hit the ground.

"You okay?"

"Fine. Leg's a bit stiff, that's all." He raised his hand to help his daughter. She stepped onto the box Charlie had put down and then onto the ground.

"What do you want to do next?"

Stan looked around. It was about four in the afternoon. The police had moved the protestors off the property, and the crowds were beginning to thin. The light in the sky was turning from gold to red. He shivered, pulling in the lapels of his coat. *"Burrrrr.* I should have worn something warmer." He cupped his hands and brought them to his mouth, heating them with his breath as he rubbed them together. "Let's go back inside and see how Santa's doing with those kids."

"You want to get another cider?"

"Actually, a hot cup of coffee sounds good right now."

They walked arm-in-arm, father and daughter, fearing their time together might be short. The smell of cinnamon greeted them as they entered the heated barn. "Hark The Herald Angels Sing," resounded from the speakers.

Santa had two children on his lap, the little one crying and trying to break free while the older one patiently held a piece of paper waiting for a chance to give Santa her list. Their mother stood in the sawdust trying to take a picture but her baby was refusing to cooperate.

Rachel loosened her scarf and went to help. "Why don't you hold your baby and let me take a picture of all of you?"

"Oh, thank you? That would be great." The woman handed off her phone and went to take her child from the red velvet arms of Santa. The baby stopped crying and snuggled into his mother's breast, letting her know that no one could replace her scent and touch. The woman stood beside the sleigh with her heels on the runners, leaning in to be as close to Santa and her daughter as possible.

They all smiled, and then blinked at the flash.

"I'll take one more, just in case."

The woman came around to view her phone's digital display, "Oh, that's perfect," she said. "Thank you so much." She went to help her daughter down, and Santa handed each child a candy cane along with a small book of colorful pictures. It was the story of a child born in a Bethlehem stable, a child destined to become a king. The last picture showed Santa on his knees before the manger, a fourth wise man honoring his Lord. The young family thanked him and made their way outside.

Stan approached, extending his hand, placing it in Santa's white glove. "Hello, Bill, I've been anticipating this moment for some time. Let me introduce you to my daughter. This is Rachel." Then he turned to his daughter, and said, "Rachel, this is Bill Best, the man I told you about. Santa stepped down from the carriage, his large black boots picking up sawdust like a magnet. He kept up his smiling Kris Kringle facade but his eyes were wrinkled at the corners. "And you are…?"

"Oh, sorry, Santa, I forgot. We've emailed and spoken over the phone so many times I feel like we know each other, even though we've never met." The man extended his hand again. "Stan Powers, Senator from the great state of Illinois, at your service."

THREE

THE LOGS BURNING in the fireplace snapped and crackled, licking up sparks and sending them up the stone chimney. Those stones had come from the Watalong River, carried by Bill up the levee to his truck, one gunny sack full at a time. It was all part of knowing he had built the cabin himself, the way his forefathers would have done. Mary thought he was crazy. He could have bought river rocks from any landscaping business in Portland, and had them delivered. But that wasn't Bill, never would be, so he'd suffered the injury of her words and pressed on. Now when she sat by the fire and called it beautiful, he took satisfaction in knowing it was of his design and making.

In the center of the room, a lamp made of a wagon wheel laid on its side was suspended from four chains attached to a single chain that hung from the vaulted ceiling. Six kerosene lanterns, now fueled by LEDs, were mounted around the wheel's circumference. The room was filled with warmth and light.

"I wish you would have let us know you were coming, I could have had steaks on the grill. Now you have to put up with my chili, but I do make a mean chili, if I say so myself." Bill stirred the meat sizzling in a frying pan on his gas grill and went back to chopping onions. "Some people like their chili without beans but I like the extra protein," he said, opening cans of pinto and kidney beans and dumping them into a blend of diced tomatoes, chili peppers, jalapenos and onions. "And of course I always toss in a clove of garlic and some chili powder for good measure." He mixed the ingredients together with a wooden spoon and placed the large pot over an open flame, stirring in the meat.

A young woman sat in a wheelchair over by the dining room table. Her arms moved erratically when she tried to adjust her position. Bill introduced her as his daughter, Angie, but avoided mentioning her obvious affliction. Stan surmised it was cerebral palsy. He recalled seeing her at the tree farm collecting donations for the hot chocolate.

"I can leave this to simmer for a few minutes," Bill said, reaching for a towel draped over the handle of the stove to wipe his hands. "Sorry about all the confusion earlier. You kind of took me by surprise. And thanks for being patient while we closed up, but now I'm all ears. Tell me why you're here and what I can do for you."

Across the island stove, Stan was seated in the living room on one of the two thickly upholstered chairs that faced a leather couch. His cashmere coat was hanging on an antler rack by the door, but his dress slacks, polished black leather shoes, and shirt and tie, felt pretentious in an atmosphere that might better have suited Daniel Boon. A rug woven by Navajo Indians featuring triangular geometric patterns was at his feet, with a glass-topped circular coffee table made of twisted pieces of driftwood in the center. He had to look around the two foot tall Paiute basket filled with dried reeds and cattails to see Rachel, who occupied the other chair. He felt unsettled, like a visitor in a museum. On the other side of the stove, Bill was wearing faded denims, scuffed steel toed boots, and a red-and-black plaid mackinaw. He glanced over at the bedroom door. Mary had rushed off to change out of her elf costume. Stan half imagined her coming out wearing a deerskin dress and strings of beads with an eagle feather knotted in her hair.

He sighed, measuring his thoughts before giving an answer. "Well, I'll tell you sir, it's like I said, we've had enough telephone conversations to make me feel I know you, Bill, even though, officially, we just met. As to why I'm here, I suppose there's any number of reasons, my daughter chief among them." He leaned forward to look around the basket of cattails at Rachel, and nodded. "It appears we've run into a little problem we're hoping you can help us with, but if you don't mind, I'd like to save that until after we eat. I've been following your podcasts and I know you think the government's reaction to the whole

Covid thing was overreach. But aside from that, I'm curious to know where you think this is all headed."

Bill tossed the towel on the stove, his eyebrows furrowing in. "Now that's a loaded question."

"Why?"

"Because I'm a political commentator, and my observations about the virus delve into the spiritual realm..." Mary drifted out of the bedroom, heading straight for the kitchen to help Bill set the table... "Let's pick this up later, Bill said. It's a big subject, and like you said, we need to eat."

"Sorry I took so long," Mary said. "I had to remove all that costume makeup and, well, you know how that goes," she glanced over at Stan's daughter, "right Rachel?"

To Stan's relief, Mary wasn't dressed in buckskins. She was wearing form-fitting denims that flattered her slim waist, a green flannel shirt, and fleece lined leather moccasins. Her brunette hair fell long on her shoulders. A handsome woman, by Stan's estimation. Bill was a lucky man. She bent over and kissed the cheek of the young lady sitting in the wheelchair. "How are you doing, honey, you okay?"

"*Yassssssss,*" Angie responded. Her lips were twisted and her head was writhing around on her neck, but her smile was genuine.

Mary went to the counter and placed a cookie sheet filled with pieces of thickly sliced French bread smothered in garlic butter, into the pre-heated oven.

Rachel hopped out of her chair, her long blond ponytail swinging back and forth with the sudden excitement. "Can I help with anything?" she said, bouncing over to lend a hand.

"Sure," Mary pointed to a drawer, "cutlery's in there, napkins are on the sink, you can leave the bowls until Bill fills them. I'll pour the drinks. We have milk, but it's skim so you may not like it. Not everyone does. There's water of course, some diet sodas in the refrigerator, and even some eggnog if you're into Christmas cheer."

"I love skim milk, so that will be fine. Dad, what about you?" Rachel opened the drawer, looking back over the stove that separated the kitchen from the living room.

"I'll just have water," he said. Gripping the arms of the chair he pulled himself up with a grimace and balanced with his weight on one leg.

"You okay?"

"Fine, honey."

"I notice you walk with a limp," Bill said.

"It's nothing."

"He got his leg blown apart on one of his secret missions," Rachel rejoined.

"Classified, not secret."

"Same thing."

"Thank you for your service," Bill said.

"I only wish I could do more. The world's gone crazy. Like those protestors you had today. It's getting so you can't speak your mind without paying a price, and I can't seem to keep my mouth shut. It's bad enough we've got everyone worried about dying of Covid, but now the administration is back on fixing climate change and I'm on a senate subcommittee looking at the ramifications. Opinions run the gamut from those who think we have to act now, regardless of the cost, to those who think the data is flawed and that we would end up spending huge amounts of money to fix a problem that doesn't exist. Which is particularly worrisome when you consider what Covid has done to our economy."

Bill took a spoon, filled it with chili and brought it to his lips. *Hummmm*, "Perfect. You're gonna love it." He took a ladle and began filling the bowls. "Yep, I suppose I could help with that. I've got a boatload of information arguing both sides."

"I appreciate that, but I can't say it will do much good. The government only listens to what it wants to hear. Anything else is like whistling in the wind."

The bread was golden brown. Mary slid the tray from the oven, the smell of garlic wafting through the air. She took a wicker bowl made by a local Paiute Indian, and lined it with a checkered hand-towel before laying the slices of garlic toast inside. "Bread's ready," she said, picking the bowl up in both hands and heading for the table

Rachel had just finished setting.

Bill brought two bowls filled with chili and set them down. "Stan, Rachel, take a seat." He rolled Angie up to the table and drew back a chair for Rachel, and then went back for the remaining bowls, bringing them over for himself, Angie and Mary. He took Mary's hand on his right and reached out for Angie on his left. Rachel followed suit and connected with her father who in turn took the other hand of Mary, completing the circle of grace.

Bill bowed his head. "Father, we thank You for sending Senator Powers and his daughter here to join us in breaking bread. We recognize that this is a meal You have provided, and for that we also give You thanks. Please bless the food as we eat it. In Jesus' name, Amen. Alright everyone, dig in."

The warm smell of the chili and garlic bread receded with the washing of the dishes as the two men settled into a conversation over cups of hot coffee. Mary and Rachel took to clearing away the mess, not because Bill and Stan were unwilling or unable, but because both women sensed the importance of the discussion that was about to take place and allowed the men the freedom to continue without interruption. The fire was waning on the hearth. Bill got up and placed another log on the embers and used a poker to excite the flames. "You asked where all this was going," he said. "I'm no prophet, but I can say I believe we're entering the end times spoken of in the Bible."

"Agreed," Stan responded. "That's why I'm curious as to why you haven't mentioned it in any of your podcasts."

Bill nodded, knowing the truth would likely diminish him in the eyes of his friend. He wasn't a coward, but there was a practical side to not always sharing everything you know, especially when it came to the safety of his family.

"Sadly, the things I believe tend to make me look like a conspiracy theorist at best, and a total nut job at worst, and I can't afford to lose my audience. I used to have a syndicated column followed by over a million readers. But it's like you said about not being able to speak your mind anymore, a bunch of my critics got together and convinced advertisers my words were bigoted and racist and demanded they pull their spots from any paper that printed my column. Racist! What a bunch of hogwash. I just call it as I see it. Anyway, my revenue stream dried up to where I could no longer afford to keep publishing. Now, as you know, I'm resigned to doing podcasts. There's a strong base that still supports my work, I get most of my revenue from them and I actually earn more now than I did before, but they want information on the world's political landscape, not my Judeo-Christian beliefs." Bill got up and poked at the log once more, sending sparks swirling up the flue. The fire licked up and embraced the wood again, causing it to brust into flames. "I've also received a number of death threats, and references to the wellbeing of my wife and family," he said, turning around.

Stan set his cup down, careful to use the coaster provided by Mary. Apparently the rough interior of the log cabin was subject to a woman's touch. "I hear you. We've experienced that ourselves, which we'll get into in a minute. So, what is your view then? Are we headed for the rapture? I mean, I know Christ said no one would know the day or the hour, but He also said when you see certain things happen, you'll know the end is near."

"If by, 'certain things,' you mean the direction in which the world is heading, you're bang on." Bill was still standing. He was a big man, his hands broad and thick, and callused from cutting trees. In his heavy wool mackinaw and work boots, and with his white Santa beard puffed up on his chest, he looked like a lumberjack just down from the mountain. He put a boot into the fire and kicked a log to turn it and give it more air. "Look," he said, "the Bible has never been wrong in predicting future events. What it says will happen, always does. And it clearly says a day will come when a persuasive and charismatic leader will assume control of the world. And frankly, I fear that day isn't far off."

Stan looked up at the giant before him and felt like a pigeon waiting to be tossed a crumb of bread. He nodded so Bill would know he agreed.

"I mean," Bill continued, "we have Nano technologies, developed at MIT, ready to be injected into the forearm of consumers. They want to call it a travel pass, or health passport, or something innocuous like that, and say it's necessary to make sure no one spreads the disease. I'm not saying that's going to happen. I'm just saying it could, and I know it's being talked about.

"Then we have crypto currencies starting to be accepted by central banks around the world. As the acceptance of the digital dollar escalates, and men become comfortable with the health passport, they'll likely be merged so that your financial transactions can be kept in your body with your health information and made available with a quick scan of your wrist. At the same time we have 5G technologies bolstering the communications infrastructure, and technologies like the new Frontier supercomputer able to process quintillions of calculations per second. Just a few of these could give us the ability to track every human on earth in real time along with every purchase they make." Bill brought a hand up and placed it on the mantle, stooping over to make sure the fire was now fully engaged.

"Technologically, we're ready," he said, straightening himself. "What's missing is a common enemy the nations are willing to give up their sovereignty to fight. Wait here a second, there's something I want to show you."

Bill turned and went to his office, his boots clomping on the plank wood floor. He returned a few moments later holding a book entitled, *The First Global Revolution*, by Alexander King and Bertrand Schneider. He held it up for Stan to see. "This book was sanctioned by the Club of Rome in their bid to create a global government. I'm just going to read one short quote. Listen to this.

> "'In searching for a common enemy against whom we can unite, we came up with the idea that pollution, the threat of global warming, water shortages, famine and the like, would fit the bill. In their totality and their interactions these phenomena do constitute a common threat, which must be confronted by everyone together.'"

19

Bill closed the book but kept a thick finger marking his place. "See, they admit they were looking for a common enemy, one that the whole world needed to fight. They chose climate change because they felt people would put aside their national differences if it meant saving the planet." He opened the book and continued reading.

> "'All these dangers are caused by human intervention in natural processes, and it is only through changed attitudes and behavior that they can be overcome. The real enemy then is humanity itself.'"

Bill folded the book under his arm. "They're saying we need an attitude adjustment. Well, they've done a pretty good job of doing that, only now they've been given a better invisible enemy, the Covid virus, so you don't hear much about climate change anymore. All the urgency about how we must act now seems to have disappeared, though I suspect it will be back as soon as they get everyone vaccinated and the Covid issue is resolved, if that ever happens.

"The point is, they need the world united around a common enemy, like climate change, or another virus, or some other boogeyman yet to be invented, so they can step in and form a world government to keep us safe. With that in place, and the technology ready to go, the stage will be set and the curtain drawn back to reveal the son of perdition spoken of throughout scripture. He'll demand total allegiance in exchange for keeping the world prosperous and healthy, and the world will worship him as a god, except those who don't, who quickly find they no longer have access to their money.

"But that's just my view. There are probably a dozen other scenarios that could play out. The important thing to know is, one way or another, many of the technologies we see being developed today, along with our move to globalization, will ultimately usher in an era the Bible calls the Great Tribulation."

"That's exactly what I've been saying," Stan said, "but it doesn't explain why you're not letting people know about it."

Bill shook his head. "I can't talk about that kind of stuff publicly.

To most people, it sounds crazy. I can only make a case based on what's happening in the world today; how climate change and the pandemic and a plethora of other world catastrophes are being used to scare everyone into accepting the coming world government. I just hope those familiar with Bible prophecy are able to infer the rest."

"They might," Stan said, taking another sip of his now lukewarm coffee, "but what if they don't? Might be good to get the word out and provide people with a warning, don't you think?"

Bill leaned over to set the book he was holding on the coffee table. He sighed. "You make a good point, one I've given a lot of thought to lately, but I also have my family to think about. This place is secluded, and we've done our best to make sure no one knows where we live, but I'm pretty sure if anyone wanted to make a concerted effort, they could find me. I don't take the threats we've received lightly."

"I'm glad to hear it." Stan used the arms of his chair to push himself to his feet, but swallowed the pain that shot through his leg. "I also have something I want you to see." He marched off, his limp barely visible as he made his way over to the cashmere coat that was hanging on the rack of antlers by the front door. Bending the lapel back, he retrieved a letter and ambled back over to the fire, handing it to Bill.

"What's this?"

"Read it."

Bill shook the letter open and scanned the page. "So, you too."

"That's third one I've received."

"What about Rachel, has she seen it?" Bill's eyes went to the kitchen but the girls had wheeled Angie out of the room and were now occupied with helping her get ready for bed.

"Of course. It's her life they're threatening. It wouldn't be right to keep it from her."

"So, you gonna change your vote?"

"You mean, am I giving in to their threats. No."

"So what are you going to do?"

"Like you said, no one knows where you live. I was hoping I could impose upon you to let Rachel stay here for a while. Just till things blow over."

FOUR

BILL COULDN'T SLEEP. He lay on his back, his fingers interlaced behind his head, staring through the darkness at the overhead fan. The drone of the ventilator, the sound of bubbles gurgling in the humidifier, the hot water heater turning off and on, whirred in his ears, but it was his thoughts, not the noise, that kept him awake. Mary was curled up beside him, her soft breathing making him envious of the rest he wanted for himself.

He couldn't blame Senator Powers. The man didn't know about the promise he'd made to his wife. He couldn't please them both, and they both had compelling reasons for their requests.

He tossed the covers aside and planted his bare feet on the floor. The heat pump was sufficient to keep the room from freezing, but pulling heat from the ground in the middle of winter didn't really make the house warm. He curled his toes against the cold and stood, replacing the blankets and tucking them against Mary's back so she'd be less likely to notice his absence.

It was almost five. He wanted to be at the farm by seven, but this was something he had to do even if it made him late. He pulled his jeans up and tucked in his wool shirt, buckling his belt to cinch everything tight. He would get the fire going for Mary and his guests, in case they woke early.

The coals from last night's fire glowed red, a dim light, but enough to tread his way through the darkness without bumping into furniture. He fanned the embers with a newspaper until they burst into flame and stacked small sticks of wood in a teepee to get them burning, adding thicker pieces on top until the fire was going strong. If Mary awoke, she would know he was looking after her. Hopefully, his guests were late risers, but even if not, he'd only be gone an hour—hour and a half, tops.

His boots were in the mudroom. He went over and pulled them on, doing up the laces, and taking his heavy down jacket from the peg, slipped it on, zipping it all the way up.

Bill stood on the porch with his arms wrapped around his chest. He could barely see the shed that housed his truck. He clapped his gloves together, frost puffing from his mouth, and clomped down the steps. The path winding through the trees to the lake was invisible, but he knew the way well enough to walk it blind. There was a light dusting of snow on the ground, but it would be gone by late morning.

He didn't expect the lake to be frozen, it was too early in the season, but he found it covered with a light skin of ice. Bill picked up a branch and poked the surface. It broke through with ease—just a thin crust, nothing that would prevent him from making his journey. He found the old canoe overturned on the shore where he'd left it. It was an ancient dugout carved by Chinook Indians in the late eighteen-hundreds. Bill rolled it over and pushed it into the lake, the keel breaking through the ice as it entered the water. He waited until the stern was about to float free and stepped inside, seating himself in the back where it would be easier to steer. Reaching down into the hull, he found his paddle and used it to push off the bank sending the canoe out into the water. One long powerful stroke sent him off on his quest to find God.

The fringe of ice disappeared as he moved away from the shore alternating strokes left and right to pick up speed because the hour was growing late. Just hearing the flow beneath the hull eased his tension. He took a deep breath, imbibing the smell of the pines surrounding the lake. The water was black as ink and the shoreline hidden from view. A Snowy Owl hooted somewhere off in the distance. There were probably a hundred animals watching him, deer and raccoons, beaver and mice, all questioning why a human would be out on the water before dawn. He couldn't see them, but he knew they were there. He plotted his course by memory.

Bill pulled his paddle back and stopped stroking, letting the canoe glide ahead unbridled. Water trickling from his paddle broke the silence, leaving small rings spreading on the lake's surface. He paused to look at the stars, a billion orbs of light pinned to the black curtain of space—*the heavens declare the glory of God*—then relaxed and took another deep breath. This was how God meant it to be, peaceful, quiet, without man's lust for wealth and power. If everyone could experience this, they would beat their swords into plowshares. It's hard to hate your enemies when you're sitting at the feet of God.

The senator, Stan Powers, got it right when he quoted John Adams, the nation's second president, in saying: "Our Constitution was made only for a moral and religious people. It is wholly inadequate to the government of any other," because only when people understood that they answered to God, could they have the moral veracity to govern themselves.

Bill began to paddle again, dripping water into the canoe with each pass over the hull from left to right. A faint light was beginning to appear on the eastern horizon. If he didn't hurry, he'd miss it.

It had been a good discussion, but not enough to keep him awake when he needed sleep. He didn't want the children receiving only a half-hearted rendition of Santa. Maybe they shouldn't have stayed up so late, but he rarely had opportunity to share his thoughts with someone of like mind, and couldn't resist taking advantage of the opportunity. Climate change, racial unrest, the pandemic, social justice, a whole myriad of things, were coming together in the spiritual realm to prepare the way for the coming antichrist. Not so much climate change itself, or the pandemic, or anything else. These were just forces of nature. But Satan was aligning these forces to unite the nations and further his goal of establishing a world government, the leader of which would be his proxy, the son of perdition.

The coming of the antichrist was inevitable. It was foretold in scripture and the Bible was never wrong. In laying out his premise, Bill suggested that the rise of socialism fit right into this scenario because socialism was based on the premise that all men should work together for the common good, again reinforcing the need for a centralized world government. He was pleased to find Senator Powers agreeing with everything he said. His final caveat was in suggesting that many of the judgments of God, which were foretold to come during the Great Tribulation, might be explained away by pointing to man's failed efforts to reduce greenhouse gasses. The Great Tribulation, then, would be seen as the judgment of nature, not God, eliminating man's need for repentance.

Bill shook it off. He needed to focus his thoughts on his current situation. He was nearing his destination. The waterfall could be heard pounding in the distance, though it was still a quarter of a mile away. Pulling harder on the left, he did a J stroke turning the craft toward the shore. The whitewater of the cascading falls came into view illuminated by the approaching dawn. He would have to hurry. He gave an extra hard stroke, let the canoe slide up on the shore, and stepped out pulling the canoe up further so it wouldn't drift away.

He hiked in, quickly covering the last hundred yards down the misty trail. The wind channeling off the falls felt icy on his exposed skin and for a moment he was glad to still have his beard. Defrocked plants surrounding the fall's basin were covered in a vail of frost. It was still dark enough to make the path hard to read. He began his climb, making sure his footing was secure. Until he got above the fall's spray, the rocks would be icy.

It took him fifteen minutes to reach the top. By then the sun was already beginning to crest the mountain. He placed his hands on his knees, out of breath, but glad to have made it. He tipped his head back and watched the wonder of the sun as it broke over the edge of the planet. It was a fabulous sight, like the dawn of creation. Glorious beams of red fanned out across the curve of the earth shining down on the forest below. The waters of the lake took on a crimson glow which as the minutes passed turned violet and then yellow, the sky fading from purple to blue. Bill sat on a rock he liked to think had been there since the beginning of time, taking it all in.

He'd been fishing when he discovered the place. An eagle had stolen the granddaddy trout he'd been trolling for, much to his chagrin, but he'd forgiven her when she circled over the face of the cliff and landed on her nest. Couldn't hold it against a mom for taking care of her young.

On subsequent fishing excursions he'd found himself watching the nest to observe the eaglets as they grew. Until one day the mother didn't return. He'd waited, watching the nest day by day, but the eagle was gone, probably shot by poachers. He'd climbed to the top of those falls to rescue the fledging birds and was rewarded with the discovery of the place where he now sat, an outpost on the edge of eternity where he could sit and commune with God.

He had brought both his boys here as infants, wrapped in their baby blankets, held in his arms as he waited for the sunrise to dedicate them to the Lord. It was his special place, a respite where he could come when he found himself grappling with questions he couldn't answer. Such a time as this.

Senator Powers had skirted the issue for most of the evening, but before turning in for the night, dropped the weight on Bill's shoulders, challenging him to use his platform to share with the public what they had discussed. Coming against the global agenda could put his family in danger. All it took was Satan putting it into the head of some off-balance individual that his death, or that of his family, would serve the greater good.

Bill had never been intimidated or deterred by idle threats, but it was different for Mary. He had a duty to protect his wife. She never asked him to stop writing completely, just to avoid writing about things that endangered their lives.

Senator Powers jammed a stick into his spokes by suggesting every effort should be made to block the rise of the antichrist. Since the Great Reset was, in his opinion, helping pave the way for the antichrist's rise to power, every effort should be made to impede its coming.

As Bill sat looking out over the Cascade Mountains, with unending miles of evergreen trees and vaulted blue skies, he recalled a passage of scripture. It was a verse from the book of Genesis where God promised Noah:

"While Earth remains,
Seedtime and harvest,
Cold and heat,
Winter and summer,
And day and night,
Shall not cease."

That was the undeniable truth. Man didn't have to worry about climate change or planet sustainability. He didn't need a global government to control the world's population or manage its resources. God wasn't going to let the world be destroyed until He was ready. Then He would create a new heaven and a new Earth, and it would be all-inclusive because the saints who inherited it would be from every tribe and tongue and nation, and it would be sustainable—forever!

The question was, should he talk about it, and what danger might that pose to his family? He raised his eyes looking toward Heaven.

"Lord, You know why I'm here, and You know I'm toying with the idea of doing what Senator Powers said, but I want to know if it's what You want, so I'm asking for a favor. Please, Lord, when I bring this up to Mary, have her receive the idea with grace, because if I sense even the slightest hesitation, I'm going to take it as a sign from You that I shouldn't do it. Is that fair enough? All I ask is that You let me know what You want by having Mary prod me one way or the other."

The sun was up, its early morning rays dappling the face of the water. Bill swung his dugout canoe onto the beach in front of his cabin. Smoke was coiling from the chimney. He figured Mary and their guests were up by now, probably enjoying a breakfast of pancakes and eggs.

Mary had hit it off with Rachel. She relished having someone other than a man to talk to. Living isolated in the woods had its benefits, but didn't allow her much chance to be around other women, except Angie, who could only speak a few muddled words. With their son Josh deciding to remain in the city, even after the university closed its doors to prevent the spread of Covid, she was ready to welcome

27

some lively conversation. It made the decision to let Rachel stay with them that much easier.

Bill stepped out and grabbed the raised helm of his Chinook and drug it up onto the shore. He hadn't yet turned around when he heard the sound of feet pounding the turf behind him.

"Bill, hey, let that go, you have to come right now, *ah huh*. There's been a fire."

Bill swung around to see Stan grinding to a halt so suddenly he nearly tripped over his shiny black loafers. He looked sallow, obviously out of breath.

"There's been a fire, *ah huh, ah huh*, at the tree farm and the police needed a property owner, *ah huh*, so Mary had to rush off to meet them, *whew*, and she took Rachel. You've got to get down there as fast as possible."

Bill sucked in the frigid air as he threw his chainsaw into the back of his pickup and climbed into the cab. A fire at the tree farm, no other information. The door creaked as it slammed shut—*bang*—and the engine groaned to a start. Over a hundred thousand miles on the old truck, but its only purpose was to get him up and down the mountain so it served him well. His wheels spun up gravel as he swung out of the shed and onto the ruts of the old logging road.

First morning light brushed the tops of the trees. Bill held tight to the curves as ice melted on the windshield, his tailpipe wheezing steam. He'd had to leave Stan back at the cabin because Rachel had rushed off with Mary and someone needed to stay behind to take care of Angie. He wished he knew what this was all about but Mary had run off without her phone, leaving him in suspense.

Bill caught a sudden movement and hit the brakes—hard. The truck spun on the ice, turning into the inside wall of the mountain. *Crunch.* He felt his driver's side fender crumple as he was thrown forward into his seatbelt. *Ouuuufff!* Two deer leapt in front of him, bounding across the road, their upturned tails waving goodbye as they disappeared into the bush. *What the…*Bill slammed his fist against the steering wheel. "Son-of-a-buck!" He pounded it again. His head fell back against his headrest as he closed his eyes.

He tried to open his door but he was jammed up against the mountain wall and couldn't squeeze out. He threw the truck into reverse, the wheels spinning. "Oh, come on!" Bill put the vehicle in park, unhitched his seatbelt and slid to the right to climb out on the other side.

He'd paid too much for those steel-belted, all-season, good for nothing radial tires. All they did was dig trenches. Useless! Trying again would only make the ruts deeper. He went back to his cab, got a shovel from behind the seat, and went to inspect the fender. It was caved in, but not so much as to interfere with the wheel's ability to turn. At least he wouldn't need a tow. He just had to get the wheels out of the ditch. But it would take time.

Bill worked quickly, using the blade of the shovel to scrape snow and ice off the road behind his tires. Then he dug into the mountain and replaced the ice with shovels-full of fresh earth, and covered that with gravel from the side of the road. *That outta do it. Scheech*, a fire and an accident in one day, talk about Job, he caught himself and added, *No, don't you do it Lord, don't You let Satan touch my family. Please God.* He climbed in behind the wheel and started the engine, easing the transmission into reverse. The accident wasn't bad, and he didn't yet know the extent of the fire. It might be nothing. *Yes!* He found traction. *Thank You, Lord!*

Bill backed up to where his truck faced the road again and continued his trek, slower now, but still too fast for the icy conditions. It would take a good half hour to reach the lot.

They had originally considered farming a valley only a few miles from his cabin, one that had been stripped bare to satisfy Ma Bell's need for telephone poles. That made sense right now because it would have been closer, but it was obvious the forest had begun to rejuvenate and he didn't want to upset the new growth. He'd decided it would be better to cultivate their crop in the lowlands where the product would be more accessible to his customers.

He pulled up to the security gate, surprised to find it hanging open. The barrier was needed to keep unwanted visitors from reaching the house, but Mary, in her rush to get to the farm, had apparently left it unlocked. He pulled through and got out to close it, gritting his teeth at the delay but knowing the threat to his family was not to be taken lightly.

Coming down off the mountain the road was elevated allowing him to get partial glimpses of what was going on below. He saw the smoke rising into the air, a specific column contained by the borders of his property. *What the heck?* The rest of the forest wasn't on fire, just the acreage that comprised his farm.

He rolled up and parked the truck beside what used to be his barn. The structure that only yesterday had served to excite customers with the prospect of owning a fresh cut Christmas tree now stood in a pile of smoke charred rubble. Two fire trucks were on site, one with ladders extended. They were still hosing down the saturated piles of steaming wood, though, as far as Bill could tell, the flames had been extinguished. In the distance he could see row upon row of barren trees standing like blackened bottle brushes. Mary stumbled over and grabbed him, her head tucked against his chest, her tears wetting his beard. "Oh Bill. What are we going to do? This is awful. We're ruined."

Bill put his hands on her waist gently pushing her back. She stared up at him through eyes glossy and red.

"No, we're not ruined, not by a longshot. I know how it looks but this didn't happen without God knowing about it. There's a plan in all this; has to be."

"But the charities, how will we help them?" Mary wiped her cheeks with the palm of her hand and sniffed.

"Mary, the first two weeks after Thanksgiving are always our best. We did really good this year. We'll still have something to give."

"But next year...and the next." She was breathing hard, the air fluttering in her breast.

"We'll replant and start over. In the meantime we can buy our trees from a wholesaler and sell them at a markup. The charities will get less, but at least they'll get something. God is good, we must never forget that." He looked over Mary's shoulder at the ruins; the sky was like grey cellophane, the remains of the barn like the shell of a bombed out city. Only the brick foundation remained, a charred rectangle on a plot of blackened earth. He smiled, halfheartedly. "You know how much money I put into fixing the roof of that old barn every year, and it still leaked. Now, with the insurance, we'll be able to get us a new one. Blessing in disguise. Now, come on, I need to talk to the fire chief." Bill took his wife by the waist guiding her over to where Rachel was speaking with someone in a hazmat suit.

The lingering smoke rose from the ground like a fog that smelled of burning tires. Soot was clinging to the soles of his boots. He held his hand out as they approached. "Bill Best," he said. "Got any idea what caused this?"

The man removed his glove and took Bill's hand, shaking it firmly. "Ideas? Plenty. You the owner?"

"In a manner of speaking. We consider it to be God's, but my name's on the paperwork. So what happened?"

"Arson."

"Arson?"

"No doubt about it. They cut the lock on that fuel tank over there," the man pointed to the twelve-hundred gallon tank on a raised metal frame Bill used for filling his backhoe and tractor, "and doused the place. You can see where they walked around the perimeter of the barn pouring gas on the ground, then whatever was left in your tank, they used on the trees, at least that's my take. Fire marshal will be out to investigate. But there's also this." The man held out a piece of cardboard, pushing it at Bill. It was painted in large red letters. "We found that nailed to a telephone pole down the street."

KILL GREENHOUSE GASSES
OR THE WHOLE PLANET IS
GOING TO LOOK LIKE THIS!

FIVE

H E AWOKE WITH a bell ringing in his head, sweating and itchy and lying on his bed wearing his ski pants and sweater. Josh didn't like skiing. He'd only gone because it offered him a chance to get to know Marie, a girl he'd been after since, at the urging of his roommate, he'd attended a meeting of Students for a Just Society. Afterwards, the group had gone out for coffee and talked until midnight, though he hadn't said much because he wasn't sure where he stood on many of the issues. And when it was suggested they all spend Sunday on the slopes, he'd jumped at the chance to go. Big mistake. He'd wiped out on the first run, making a complete fool of himself.

Ted had always been the skier in the family. Put a pair of barrel staves on that boy's feet and he could fly. They would start out together but by the time he got to the bottom, Ted and his father were always there waiting. "Good run, Ted," his father would say, patting Ted on the shoulder. Then he'd turn to Josh and say, "You should try to keep up, son. Maybe your skis need more wax."

Josh swung his feet around and tried to stand but his six-foot frame felt wobbly and he had to sit back down. *Never ever again*, he vowed, bringing his palm up to cusp his forehead. A clapper was striking the brass bell of his head, echoing in his brain, his throat felt rusty, and he itched like he'd slept in a bed of poison sumac.

His roommate, Ron, stepped out of the bathroom with a towel wrapped around his waist. He was using a washcloth to dry his hair. They shared a small studio apartment which offered them about as

32

much room as two mice in a shoebox. When the room was clean, they could at least see the floor and wave at each other across the five foot distance between their beds, but when the room was strewn with blankets and towels and clothing, as it usually was, there wasn't space to turn around.

Josh and Ron weren't close. They had found each other on the school's interactive bulletin board where students posted their wants and needs. The school had announced that, in the wake of Covid 19, it would be closing its physical property and conducting all future classes online. Neither boy wanted to move back home with their parents, so both boys posted that they were looking for someone to share an apartment with off campus. Thus their alliance was formed. They didn't spend much time together, particularly since Ron was forever occupied with attending one meeting or another. Josh found this to his liking. He kept mostly to himself, keeping his social excursions to a minimum. The thought that someone might find out who he was never left his mind. PSU was the most liberal university in one of the most liberal states in the nation. Josh's dad was an ultraconservative online political commentator. You either loved him or hated him. There was no in-between. Those who loved him considered him an intellectual giant with insight and wisdom few men of his generation possessed, but those who hated him regarded him a blight on the evolution of society.

Josh wanted no part of his father's politics. He hated confrontation. He believed in live and let live, but if they knew he was Bill Best's son, he would be called to defend his father's views. So, with his mother's understanding, and father's chagrin, Josh had gone to the provost and asked if he could change his name, not legally, but for the purpose of his academic life. Surprisingly, at least to him, the provost had agreed. All of Josh's paperwork was subsequently processed using only his initials, JCB, which only the provost knew stood for Joshua Christian Best. And Josh became known to his teachers and friends as Josh Bradly, a nom-de-plume of Josh's own design.

But today Josh and Ron found themselves in the room together biding time because the semester was winding down and students we're gearing up for finals.

Ron, with his long hair and full beard, looked more like a sixties hippy than an enterprising scholar. He wore comfortable clothes: faded jeans, flannel shirts, and tennis shoes. His sandy blond hair and blue eyes gave him a look of quiet composure, but he had a sharp wit, and Josh had learned not to engage him in debate.

Ron finished drying his hair, the static electricity causing it to frizz. He dropped the towel he'd held around his waist, retrieved a pair of underwear from the floor, and turned to address Josh directly. "Man, that must have been one heck of an après-ski party. You smell like puke. Go take a shower. And make sure to brush your teeth."

Josh nodded, but didn't get up. He was trying to figure out how he'd gotten home. Had he brought his skis in with him, or were they still strapped to Donnie's car? He didn't remember getting there, didn't remember finding his way to his room, didn't remember crawling into bed. He didn't remember anything. "You see my skis anywhere?"

"They're in the closet; boots too. The guys who brought you in said you owe them for gas."

"Guys?"

"The ones you went skiing with."

Josh nodded and made another attempt at standing but had to use the bedside table to support himself. *Okay, I'm up, now what?* He let go of the table. The room had its usual look of disarray, like it rested in the path of a twister. Ron's pants were draped over the back of his chair, and his shirt was on the floor next to a pizza box with a few leftover slices. The desk was buried under papers, yellow sticky notes, books and journals. The washcloth he'd been using to dry his hair had been flung onto an unmade bed with blankets that looked like they'd been dropped by a cyclone passing through the room.

Josh suffered his way to the bathroom to find the Tylenol. His final paper for his sci-fi class had to be in by two o'clock, Professor Mertz's artificial deadline for the start of his Christmas break. He had vowed to delete any papers delivered to his inbox after that. Josh wasn't going to make it. And the paper was worth twenty percent of his grade, but he couldn't write a paper with his head ringing like a bell. He popped the cap off the bottle, poured three extra strength tabs into the palm of his hand, and tossed them into his mouth. The water coming from the tap was warm. He'd hoped it would be hot, but his roommate had just used the shower, and the studio apartment they shared had a water heater that should have been replaced before the turn of the century. He moved the handle to the cold side and stooped over with his lips around the spigot, swilling the painkillers down. *Bummer.* He hated taking lukewarm showers.

"I don't know how those guys do it," he said, as he stepped back into the shoebox he called home.

"Do what?"

"Drink like that. I mean, I don't normally drink, you know that, and I'm glad because the side effects aren't worth it." Josh cleared his throat and brought a hand up to scratch the itch under his sweater. "Man, those guys were tipping back one after another, and they were still skiing after I puked my guts out out. I think I passed out in the car and then they drove me home. Go figure. Those guys should have been toast."

Ron puckered his lips, his eyes popping. His towel dried hair stuck out like his fingers were in a socket receiving two hundred joules of electricity. He went to his dresser and rifled through the drawer, looking for something. Then he turned and held out his hand. Resting in his palm was a small white pill.

"What's that?" Josh asked.

"It's an amphetamine, an upper. It'll get you going."

"No thanks, I'll pass."

"Look bro, I don't do drugs either, poisons the brain, but it's not like you're smoking dope or anything. This is more like taking No Doz, like a pep pill, that's all. It's how those guys stay awake. Believe me, you're going to need these. We're heading into finals. It's the only way to fly when you're up all night cracking the books."

Josh shook his head. "*Ahhhh*, no man, I'm not into drugs."

"Guaranteed, not going to get you high, just awake."

Ron held out his hand, the little white pill like bait on a hook.

Josh hesitated. He had a paper to do. An important paper. Maybe

35

just once. "You sure?"

"They're righteous, man. Promise."

Josh picked the pill up and tossed it into his mouth, thinking to swallow it without water, but his throat was too dry. He stumbled back into the bathroom to use the faucet.

Josh sat at a small desk, his fingers flying across the keys of his laptop as fast as he could get them to go without making mistakes. He couldn't believe how good that wonderful little pill made him feel. *Thank you Ron.* It was like his thoughts came a hundred times faster than they normally did.

He'd gone online and found summaries of the assigned novel. He'd condensed his thoughts into a two-page document, more than enough to dazzle Mr. Mertz, his professor, who only required a one-page precis to be written.

Josh went back to his typing, his fingers feeling light as they thumped the keyboard, his mind sharp and focused. This could only be written one way. The professor was using his tenure to promote his politics, the obligation to teach Science Fiction notwithstanding.

Josh paused to corral his thoughts. They were flying at warp speed, faster than he could put them down. He shouldn't have to cater to someone else's opinions. The man was a droid hiding behind a facade of academia. He was tall and thin and bald, but had a well-trimmed goatee and small black reading glasses perched on the end of his nose. Josh had been in his class before the pandemic broke out. The man had worn the same outfit every day: a faded blue corduroy jacket with a white shirt, blue jeans and brown leather loafers with no socks. He had a small rhinestone embedded in the lobe of one ear.

Josh remembered his first lecture. The professor had begun by tapping the blackboard with a piece of chalk, hard and fast like a woodpecker digging bugs out of a tree, *tap, tap, tap, tap, tap,* and once he had everyone's attention, scrawled four huge letters on the board that spelled out a crude synonym for sex.

"Does this word offend you?" he'd said. "Because if it does, and you can't get over it, I invite you to drop this class right now." He'd put the challenge out there, but no one moved.

"In this class we will learn to set our minds free from the oppression of societal norms. Before we begin I want you to ask yourselves why this word seems offensive. It's just four random letters. The only meaning they have is what we ascribe to them. If I told you the word meant, baseball, it would no doubt become part of your regular vocabulary, but because someone applied a rude meaning to it, we feel we should bite our tongues and refuse to use it, especially around children because it could hurt their sweet little ears.

"We're here to free our minds from the evil of unwarranted expectations. Wait a minute; did I just say the word evil? What does evil mean? Frankly, it means different things to different people. If I said the mass murder of millions of Jews by Hitler was evil, I'm sure you would all agree. But from Hitler's perspective, the Jews were polluting the Arian race so getting rid of them, was a good thing. So to him it was good." He spun around, placing his hands on his lectern to make eye contact with his students. "Please don't misunderstand, I'm not advocating the Holocaust, so please don't go out there and say I'm promoting Nazism. I'm simply trying to point out that what one man sees as evil, another can see as good." He let go and resumed his pacing. "It's not up to us to accuse someone else of being evil, because good and evil are subjective terms. In fact, there really is no good or evil, there's only our own biased interpretation of it. Are you with me? I see a few of you nodding. Good. Perhaps the rest of you slower, more closed-minded, individuals will catch up later." The comment caused a light, somewhat uncertain, chuckle to flitter through the room.

"The point is, we want to free our minds of everything we've been taught by our parents, our mentors, our pastors, and yes, even our teachers. The world out there is rapidly changing and to survive we have to throw out the old, and welcome the new."

Josh remembered wondering what all that had to do with Science Fiction, which was the subject of the course he'd signed up for, but he'd refrained from asking.

He went back to his reading. Professor Mertz was firm about not accepting papers timestamped after they were due, which in this case,

Josh looked at his watch, was in twenty minutes. He could see how his professor's politics were wrapped up in the assignment. The class was told to read the novel, *Dune,* by Frank Herbert, and write a paper about the influence of capitalism in the year 10,191. After reading several online synopses, Josh concluded that his instructor wanted his students to assail the greed and lust for power that led to the conflict for control of the planet Arrakis, and its coveted spice industry. Since it was in his best interest to satisfy his professor, he wrote accordingly, even though he didn't necessarily agree. As Mr. Mertz had pointed out, there were two sides to every coin.

He'd noticed the absence of George Orwell's classic, *1984,* on the professor's reading list. He'd looked for it because he'd read it as a senior in high school and figured it would be one less book he'd have to worry about. Its absence confirmed what he already knew about Mr. Mertz. He wouldn't want his students studying a novel about a society that repressed individuality and demanded adherence to party dogma. It was too close to the way socialism limited individual freedoms for the good of the state. *Big brother is watching.*

Now that he thought about it, another omission was Huxley's, "Brave New World," where the government programed emotions and individual thoughts out of children to prevent them from thinking for themselves, and discouraged permanent relationships because citizens were seen as objects whose only purpose was to serve the state. Josh shook his head. He hadn't thought about that book in years. Where were all these ideas coming from? One tiny little pill and it was like his neural network was clocking at the speed of light.

He heard a chime and realized his phone was ringing. The tone identified the caller as his mother. He didn't have time for a call from her right now. The paper was due in a few minutes. He thought to ignore it but she'd been calling for several days and he couldn't put her off forever. It was probably about his coming home for Christmas. She'd be hurt if he wasn't there. The phone continued to ring. He slid it from his pocket.

"Hello, Mom," he said, as he brought it to his ear. "Listen, I can't talk right now; I'm on a deadline with one of my assignments."

"Josh? Where have you been, Honey, I've been trying to reach you all week."

"Yeah, I know, Mom. I've been really busy. It's the end of the fall semester and we're into finals, so I mean it when I say I can't talk."

"You didn't see it on the news?"

"See what?"

"About the fire. It's been several days now, but it was in all the papers and on TV. You couldn't have missed it."

"What fire?"

"The Christmas tree farm Josh, someone tried to burn it down."

"What? What are you talking about?"

"Josh, you really need to pay attention to what's going on. We had a fire at the Christmas tree farm, and it wasn't an accident. Someone, or maybe more than one, poured gas all around our barn. It was completely destroyed, and most of our trees…"

"No way. Was anyone hurt?"

"It was horrible, but lucky for us, we were closed, so no, no one was hurt, except, well, you remember Dad's old dog Willie, he didn't make it. Police think he was probably put down before the fire because he would have tried to stop whoever did it. Poor thing. And the damage set us back ten years. We're going to have to start all over."

"That's awful. Who'd do such a thing?" Josh was rubbing the back of his neck. The itch was still there, even after his shower.

"That's what the police want to know. Oh, but Josh, we've had such a wonderful response from the community. People we don't even know came from all over to help, and a few churches too, everyone pitching in to clean up the mess."

"That's good, Mom," Josh paused for a second, and then said, "You think it was dad?"

"Josh! Why on earth would you say a thing like that? Your father would never…"

"No, no, not him personally, it's just, you know, he's made a lot of enemies." Josh glanced up to see if Ron was listening, but remembered he'd left for another meeting. Still, he lowered his voice. "You know what I mean. Dad's not the most popular guy around. It's possible one

39

of dad's enemies was trying to teach him a lesson."

"Yes, and that's one of the things the police are looking into. But that's not why I called, though I did wonder why you hadn't tried to find out if we were alright. It's been nearly a week. Anyway, I want to make sure you're going to be home for Christmas."

Josh smiled sardonically. He could read his mother like a book. "That's the plan, Mom."

"Because we haven't seen you since before the semester started. You really do need to keep in touch. You don't even know we have a guest staying with us, do you? A young lady. Her father is Senator Powers, a friend of your father's from Illinois, and he asked if we could let his daughter, Rachel, stay with us for a while to keep her safe. I guess some people aren't happy with the way he's been voting. See, your father's not the only one who gets threats. Seems like you can't say what you believe without putting a target on your back. Isn't that crazy? Whatever happened to freedom of speech? So we, of course, said yes, but with the fire and everything the poor girl has taken to watching your sister while I help your father organize the cleanup. She says she doesn't mind because it gives her time to study. She's taking her courses online too, only at Northwestern, but I think she'd like having someone her own age to talk to for a few days. Your dad's going to be busy with this right up to Christmas, and I have to be there to let customers know why we're closed and explain what happened so we can keep up the goodwill and make sure they come back next year..."

"Aw, Mom, don't"

"Don't what, hon?"

"Please don't try to set me up with a friend of a friend. You know that never goes well. I'll be there for Christmas, but please leave me alone, okay?"

"But she's a lovey girl, Josh…"

"Mom…"

"And a Christian."

"Mom!"

"Okay, got it. I'll let your dad know you're coming. He'll be thrilled."

"I'll bet."

"He will, Josh, he loves you, but you know how he is. Oh, he's waving at me. I need to go see what he wants. Love you. Bye."

The phone went silent. Josh's lips formed a smile, though it was abject in nature. Perhaps there was justice in the universe after all. *Dad's pet project burned to the ground. Project, phooey, his hiding place. Go help all the kids you want, dad, just leave me alone…*

Josh looked at his watch. He had just enough time to get the document finished and sent in. *Thank God for that little white pill.*

SIX

THE UPROOTED TREES were being stacked and set ablaze, the twelve foot high flames sending black smoke and ash roiling into the air. Bill had spent the past week seated on his backhoe, the clanking machine digging the trees charred skeletal remains out of the ground, just so the bulldozer could scrape them into piles for burning. Bill did a quick estimate. It looked like they still had about eight-hundred to go. They were small trees, to be sure, ten foot tall at most, but with twenty to a pile, the bonfires were raging. It was Dante's inferno, without the disinterred souls. And hot? Boy was it ever. The last time Bill could remember being this hot was when he'd chased into a burning house to save Angie's cat. That was the time he'd met Mary, a reminder that good things could come from bad. *My brethren, count it all joy when you fall into various trials. Uh huh.* Bill rubbed his arms. He couldn't walk between the pyres without feeling the heat blistering his skin. Two fire trucks from the Tantamoa volunteer firefighter's brigade were standing by to ensure the fires remained controlled.

The base of each fire was an intense conflagration, roaring like the blast from a furnace. *Hot as hell*, Bill thought, while trying to imagine what it would be like to have those red hot flames peeling away his skin as he stood in the midst of the blaze. Why would anyone want to risk spending eternity in such a place, especially when all it took to avoid it was submission to God? But then, men didn't believe in God anymore, or if they did, they believed He would forgive their every trespass as long as they did more good than evil. Fools. In God's economy, you commit one sin, you're guilty of all. Everyone held to the same standard. Receive Christ for the forgiveness of sin—be they few or many—and you're heaven bound. Reject Christ and, well, *kuff, kuff,* you only get what you deserve. Bill wiped the water in his eyes with the back of his hand, leaving a streak of black soot on his cheek. His lungs felt the pressure of the heat, *kuff, kuff,* and the hair of his arms curled as if blown by a hair dryer. He took a step back.

A breeze agitated the flame sending it after Bill again. He turned away, wanting to avoid his beard getting singed. But deep in his chest, it was his heart that burned the most. What a waste. Ten years of labor, of planting, watering, pruning and harvesting, gone up in smoke. They'd probably never catch those who did it, but it didn't take the local police, the FBI, or Homeland Security, to know what happened. It was an act of domestic terrorism. Of those miscreants that tried to shut him down, several had raised their fists and screamed they'd be back.

He turned around and saw a few volunteers waving to Mary as they left the lot. Fewer were showing up every day. That was to be expected. Most of the work was being done by the backhoe and dozer, so they weren't really needed, but he did appreciate their willingness to help. He headed toward the barn. One large rectangle of brick was all that remained of the century old building, though over the years it had survived winds and floods and the erosion of time. Finding a piece of property with a barn already on it had been a Godsend. With its hewn beams and plank board walls, it was perfect for the selling of trees. It had that kind of romantic charm that got people into the mood for Christmas. The insurance company had already alluded to the idea of putting up one of those modern steel structures but Bill was having none of it. It would be wood or nothing. And even then, clean unweathered wood would never feel the same.

He stared at the brick foundation, hesitating before going inside. So far, he'd kept busy, avoiding the barn's interior, afraid of what he might find, but it was time. He wandered about, kicking the remnants of wasted pitchforks and plows, implements he'd left around the stalls to create the feeling of yesteryear, a time when things were less hectic, when people didn't lock their doors and still took time to smile and say hello when you met them on the street. And, *oh no*, was that his sleigh? A few chunks of carved wood with blistered red paint were all that was left of a once bright emblem of days gone by. Only the steel bands of the runners were intact, and the leaf springs of the seat where he'd held gleeful children on his lap. *Merry Christmas.* Who would do such a thing? They were a charity, for Pete's sake. Using violence on people with whom you disagree was a totalitarianism reminiscent of the Khmer Rouge. Even democratic socialists, which Bill suspected these kids were, should be appalled by that.

Something smooth and gray, reflecting the light, caught Bill's eye. He walked over to see what it was, his boots scuffing up soot and ash, making him, *kuff, kuff,* cough. He brought a hand to his mouth as he reached down to uncover the hidden treasure. It was their office computer, the one Mary did all their books on, only now it was melted down to a flat puddle, like a piece of modern art. He lifted it up, amazed at the way it held its basic shape while molded into something new. The monitor had melted and folded over on itself looking like a ballerina taking a bow. He could still make out the keys, though the numbers and letters were indiscernible, and the computer housing was nothing but a lump of shiny smooth plastic. And that melted blue stripe, that had to be Mary's flash drive. *Woah*—that was their backup!

JOSH LAY ON HIS BED, his covers looking like a whirlpool of blankets. He scratched his itch and pulled his book in front of him again. With winter approaching, the building's AC unit had been turned off. The sun streaming through the window left water droplets on the glass, the warm moisture making the room smell more like a gym locker than ever.

He needed to focus but his mind kept wandering. He had to keep pulling himself back into the story. He glanced at his watch for the hundredth time. *Where's Ron?* He turned the page and realized he couldn't remember what he'd just read. How was he ever going to pass the final? And if he didn't pass his dad would stop paying his tuition and make him move home, and he couldn't handle that. Ron always wore a headset and listened to music while he studied. Josh couldn't concentrate as it was. Music would only provide greater distraction.

There was a sound at the door. Josh's head snapped up as Ron entered with a baseball cap on his head and a laptop under his arm. His beard looked like it grew out of his hat and wrapped around his face to become part of a disguise. He nodded at Josh and closed the door.

"Ron, there you are. Boy am I glad to see you."

Ron went to the desk and cleared an empty ice cream carton and half eaten bag of red licorice out of the way to make room for his computer. "What's up?" he asked, lifting his head to address Josh.

Josh rolled off the bed and set his book on the table, but lost his balance and bumped the book off again. He reached over to pick it up and tossed it on the bed.

"Hey Ron, I uh, hey, thanks for helping out with my little problem the other day. I gotta tell you, I aced it, got the paper done and turned in on time and, what's it been, two days, and I still don't feel tired. But here's the thing. I've got one more final to take and I think I'll be up all night reading and there's no way I can do this unless I stay awake. I'm wondering, do you know where I can get some more of whatever it was you gave me?"

Ron nodded, his mouth behind his beard remained flat but his eyes creased with a smile. "I can make a call," he said. "But listen, you're new to this so I want to be straight with you. Be careful. I don't want you getting strung out."

Josh's eyes went to the window, watching a bead of water roll down the glass until it reached the sill. He knew he had to ask, but he was afraid he wouldn't like the answer. He turned back to Ron. "Are they addictive? I mean I don't want to get hooked on some kind of narcotic."

Ron's face tightened. "No man, nothing like that. Narcotics are class A drugs, these are class B, but they can be habit forming, so as long as you take them only when you need them, no problem, you won't feel bad if your source dries up. But if you start needing them all the time, I suggest you pull back because just like with cigarettes, or booze, or any other habit, it's hard to quit cold turkey. Capeesh?"

Josh caught a lucky break when Ron's supplier said he was open for business.

They meandered through the campus, now nearly deserted, but they'd agreed to meet at the school because it was a place they were both familiar with. A car on the street roared by, flexing its muscle, the stereo so loud, the words of the song got tangled in the music to where the whole thing sounded like mush.

They entered the parking garage, heading into a section that was darker than the rest. Several of the lights were out, but whether by design or accident Josh couldn't say. He just knew it was dark enough to facilitate criminal activity, and it made him nervous. He rubbed the goosebumps on his arms and held his breath. He hadn't thought to bring a facemask, the transaction was supposed to be outdoors, which the garage, for the most part, was, but he needed something to mop the sweat from his brow. His imagination drew a picture of a two hundred and forty pound linebacker waiting with a gun to take his money.

"Hey, Ron, good to see you man." A figure in a hoodie stepped out of the shadows bumping fists with Ron. He was about five-ten, and extremely thin, like he never ate. Josh recalled Ron telling him that girls took the pill to lose weight. A diet pill for them, a pep pill for him, *cool*. If this guy was an example of their proficiency, the pills must work. Beneath the shadow of his hood Josh could see the man was white. He had a mask covering his mouth, which he probably used to hide his face as much as repel disease.

"You too," Ron said. "You got the speed?"

"Of course, bro. This the customer?" he said, tilting his head toward Josh.

"Yep. Tried the product, wants more."

"You vouch for him?"

"He's cool. Just naïve, that's all."

Josh didn't like what he was hearing, but he said nothing. The dealer was wearing a black sweatshirt with a tubular pocket that allowed his hands to slide in from both sides and meet in the middle. He reached in and removed a baggie, about a quarter full of small white pills.

"Got your bennies, man. Pony up the cash."

Josh reached for his wallet. The price was enough to let him know he didn't want this to become a habit. He handed the money over.

The man passed the baggie to Josh and raised his fist. Josh responded, doing the bump the way he had seen Ron do.

"Good doing business, man. Ron, catch you later." The supplier turned and disappeared into the shadows the way he'd come.

Josh followed Ron out of the garage into the light. He still felt anxious. His heart rate was accelerated and his goosebumps refused to recede. "Thanks, uh, Ron. I really appreciate it."

Ron doffed his baseball cap like a gentleman addressing a proper lady. "At your service," he said.

They walked without talking for a while. They were roommates, but they hadn't lived together long enough to get personal. Ron finally broke the silence. "So what are you doing over the Christmas break?" he asked. "Got any plans?"

"No, I'll probably just spend Christmas with my folks. Why?"

"No reason. A bunch of us are going out to Portland Heights. A friend's parents are vacationing in Hawaii for the holidays and he's throwing a party. It's BYOB, but lots of snacks. Thought you might want to join."

"Are you kidding? After last time, I don't think I ever want to drink again. Besides, my mom would be hurt if I wasn't there for Christmas."

"Whatever. I'm going, so you'll have the apartment to yourself."

"I thought you weren't into parties."

"I didn't say I don't drink, I said I don't like getting drunk. Too much of anything can get you into trouble. Besides, I'm not there for that. The party won't happen until later. I'm going up early to meet with a few friends. There's this girl, Marie, you know her, she was with those who took you skiing, she has a draft of how the government plans to implement the Great Reset and I'd like to hear what she has to say. I may not even stay for the party. We'll be finished long before people show up and get crazy."

"Cool, but how are you getting there?"

"I have a car."

"You have a car? Really?"

"I don't use it much. I keep parked in a low rent lot downtown."

"Seriously?" *The guy who says carbon fumes are killing the planet has a car. Cool. Marie will be there.* Josh thought of the pills. *Perfect timing.* "I guess if you're coming home early it won't be a problem. That is, if you don't mind giving me a ride?"

SEVEN

RON CLIMBED IN behind the wheel of his Toyota Camry Hybrid with metallic burgundy paint and tan interior, a car befitting a doctor, or lawyer, but not a second year student. He reached over to program the address into the GPS while Josh melted into the snugness of the soft leather seat. When Ron said he had a car he kept in storage at a discount parking garage, Josh envisioned something with oxidized paint and a dusty interior. Ron had explained that the car wasn't really his; it was a loan from his parents, a favor he didn't seem to appreciate. Instead of bragging about the low emission use of electric power, he complained about the nuisance of having to take it in once a week to get it charged. With a purr rather than a roar, they pulled into traffic heading for an onramp off the 405 to Portland Heights.

They drove about twenty minutes before veering off onto a winding street that climbed ever upward to the lofty heights where the homes had magnificent views of the city below. The car blended well with the upscale flagstone and shake-shingle neighborhood, though the vehicles of some of the other students might not go so unnoticed.

Josh fidgeted with the bag he held in his lap, a black wrapper for a seventy-proof bottle of rum. He'd gone into the liquor store with the timidity of a mouse, his head on a swivel turning every which way to make sure he wasn't recognized. The store was in a public mall filled with shops where people bought shoes, electric drills, and rattan furniture. Anyone could be there, and he didn't want to be seen by someone from his parent's church. What would they think? He'd ducked into the store keeping his face turned to the wall, wondering why he should he care. He wasn't attending services anyway.

Inside was no better. He didn't know a bottle of Jim Beam from East India Tea. His mom and dad were teetotalers whose lives mirrored the adage, "lips that touch wine shall never touch mine." Alcohol was forbidden and nary had there been a drop in the house. Should he buy wine, or beer, or whiskey? Ron headed straight for the shelf where all the bottles were amber, the hard stuff, and reached for a bottle of rum so Josh, not wanting to embarrass himself, did the same.

"Good choice," Ron said. "Don't worry about the mix; I'm told they have an icebox full of Coke." Josh kept the bag tucked under his coat until they were safely back in the car.

They were meandering up a street where the homes had cobblestone walkways, gabled roofs and manicured lawns with automatic sprinklers. The sky was a mix of sun and clouds. One moment it was warm and bright and the next, dark, dreary, and threatening rain. The air smelled heavy, like a storm was heading in. A digital voice from the GPS announced they had arrived at their destination. Ron rolled into a driveway that curved off to the left where three other cars were already parked.

Josh got out and followed Ron into the house, holding his bottle of Captain Morgan like it was a shady cousin he didn't want his friends to meet. It would still be on the shelf in the liquor store if Ron hadn't insisted this was a no freeloader soiree, hence the price of admission. Josh felt edgy. The cost of the ski trip and the pep pills had already exceeded his monthly budget.

Ron led as they went into the kitchen and set their bottles on the sink with the others. They removed the bags, stuffed them into the trash, and placed the bottles face out. The artwork on the labels showed a blue caped man in a pirate's hat and red cloak leaning on his sword with his booted foot on a barrel. *Captain Morgan I presume. Yo, ho, ho and a bottle of rum,* Josh grinned as he turned around—and stopped.

There she was, her dark sultry eyes drilling holes into his chest. Her brunette hair was pulled front to back across the top of her head and held in place with a gold clip, while the sides cascaded down along the line of her jaw, curling in an inch below her chin. She wore a red dress, cinched around her waist with a wide red belt that matched the color of her lipstick. Around her neck was a thin gold cross. *Maybe she's a Christia…*

Ron put his arms around Marie's waist and leaned to kiss her cheek. "Good to see you girl," he said.

Smooth skin, abrasive beard, a scouring pad on fine china. Josh put his heart in quick retreat, though he still felt a thudding in his chest.

Marie smiled, dimples forming in her cheeks, her eyes focused on Josh. He turned away, unable to find his tongue. About a dozen people were already in the living room reclining on lazy boy style chairs with their feet raised, or sitting on the fake leather sofa. The furniture wasn't as plush as he thought it would be. He'd expected high end silk and satin pillows, this was more blue-collar, laid back and comfortable. A table was set in the middle of the room with chairs positioned around its circumference and an erasable white board at one end. For once the girls outnumbered the men, but they weren't like Marie. Most had on jeans, and sweatshirts, with their hair either hanging loose or twisted on top of their heads. It appeared most everyone was holding a beer, or some other kind of drink. One of the girls passed a hand-rolled cigarette to the guy beside her, the smoke trailing behind.

Marie stepped into the room and handed Josh a fat short glass of clear brown liquid topped with cubes of ice. "Ron said you liked rum and coke. I took the liberty." She held her own glass up and winked.

Josh smiled benignly and nodded. The glass felt cool and wet in his hand.

"Alright, now that Ron's here I think we can get started." People rose from their seats and made their way to the table. Josh set his glass down and pulled out a chair for himself.

"Before we get going, how many of you saw this load of crap put out by our friend, Bill Best, this week?"

Josh cringed as Marie held up a newspaper clipping and glanced around the table. A few raised their hands, but most looked on blankly waiting for further explanation. "This is unbelievable. We got this guy who overcharges for his trees, at Christmas no less, and then says he gives the money to charity while keeping the lion's share for himself. Listen to this," she said, as she started to read.

"A word of thanks. As was reported, the Christmas tree lot owned and operated by William Best Holdings, a registered nonprofit dedicated to helping children with special needs, was destroyed by fire last week. While this will result in cutbacks to the charities we support, there are a few things to be thankful for. First, I want to thank God that the fire was set (yes, the authorities have ruled that it was arson) during the hours when we were closed so no one was hurt. Second, I want to thank the many people who showed up to help us clean up the mess. Your support of our ministry was most gratifying and demonstrates true Christian love. Also, your generous gifts will enable us to give almost as much as we would have, had we been able to remain open. Third, to those who, regardless of their motivation, started the fire, I extend my thanks to you as well. Our barn was in bad shape and in constant need of repair, but our insurance company assures us that we are covered and that our new barn will soon be under construction, so thank you as well. Sincerely, William Best. William Best Holdings, Ltd."

"Did you get that?"
"Unbelievable! People actually gave him more money?"
"Insanity reigns."
Josh sank back in his chair hoping no one looked his direction, but he kept his expression flat just in case. He'd made the right decision in changing his name, *true*, but this was over the top. Had they started the fire? Should he turn them in? His father's opinions tended to rub people the wrong way, but this was more like hate. Why? His dad had a lot of bad qualities, but cheating wasn't one of them. *Keeping the money for himself? Not a chance.* Right or wrong, his dad believed in God. He

wouldn't do anything to make God mad.

"I thought you might enjoy hearing that," Marie said, "but let's move on. As you know, we're here to discuss a proposed rollout of the Great Reset. The counsel, or at least several of its members, see the Covid opportunity slipping away, so they're ramping up political support in case they have to implement sooner than planned. That doesn't mean they're giving up on climate change, but that's a longer process. Even bringing everything together with Covid takes time, and if the vaccines get rid of the virus altogether the window of opportunity will close."

"Yes, but new strains of the virus are starting to appear, and they'll probably be resistant to the vaccines, so that will help."

Marie looked over at the man who had raised his hand to speak but hadn't waited for her nod of consent. His hand dropped at her glare. "Yes, Jim, that could happen, and if it does, great, but that won't change anything. Whether we wait until the world becomes aware of its need to restructure as the result of climate change, or finds itself forced to do so because of a worldwide pandemic, we still need a plan to assist people after the world goes into economic collapse. And that's what we're here to discuss."

"What do you mean?" a girl at the opposite end of the table raised her hand, causing the boy beside her to cringe. He took her arm, pulling it down. "Jeanine, you said you'd just come and listen."

Aside from Marie, Jeanine was the only other girl dressed in reasonably nice clothes. She had on dark blue jeans that looked new, a turquoise blouse, and wore her blond hair long and straight like a surfer girl. With green eyes, a small nose, and pink lips, Josh thought she was cute, not beautiful like Marie, but definitely cute. She frowned at the boy next to her. "She said something I don't understand. Why do you think the world's going into economic collapse? And the other thing I want to know is, what's the Great Reset about? I mean, a lot of kids are talking about it, but I don't really know what it is. That's what I came to find out."

The boy shook his head. "Not now Jeanine. Sorry guys, I brought my girlfriend because I wanted her to hear what you have to say. She's from a religious family and they've got her all screwed up. They think all this stuff's a joke. I just want her to listen, not turn this into a debate."

The charm left Marie's face, replaced by a look of stern rebuke. "First of all, *Chuck*"—the emphasis on his name made it sound unsavory, like she was about to *chuck* him out—"you have no right to tell your girlfriend what she can and cannot say. You don't control her, and you certainly have no right to say she's screwed up just because she has a legitimate question."

The joint making its way around the table was about to be passed to Jeanine but Chuck intercepted it, took a hit for himself, and passed it on. He exhaled the smoke into the air and coughed, *kuff, kuff.*

A young man on the other side of the table chimed in. "I'm more interested what her religion's got to do with it. You can be spiritual and still know our planet's about to die."

"Yes, but that's not..." Jeanine started to respond, but Marie cut her off.

"Alright, Ed, we're not here to discuss religion. We're here to see how we can facilitate the plan I'm about to present. Now let's see if we can't get Jeanine on board, because in order for this to work we need as many people on our side as possible." She looked at Josh and smiled, but the smile felt like an accusation pointing out how he wasn't in total agreement with everything he was hearing either.

Josh slid down in his chair, hoping to disappear under the table.

Marie opened her notebook and went to the whiteboard.

"Alright Jeanine, here's the thing. Our planet, as Ed mentioned, is in a bad place. First off, the world's population is growing faster than our capacity for food production. If we don't do something to increase production, or decrease the population, sooner or later, half the planet will starve. Then we have climate change. If we don't stop releasing greenhouse gasses into the air, life as we know it will soon come to an end. Third, there's an inadequate distribution of food, consumer goods, and medical supplies around the world, which could be eliminated with better management of the world's resources, and sadly, there are also racial and social injustices to be dealt with, but I needn't belabor the point. The thing is, most of these problems can be solved using the proper mix of science and technology, with oversight by leaders who have the world's best interest at heart. But it can't be done at the local level, or even at the national, because they're global in scope. One country alone can't fix climate change, or slow the growth of the earth's population. It will take the entire world working together to do this. We want a world where, when we go outside, the air is clean and the water pure, where the production of food and consumer goods are controlled so that everyone can enjoy them equally. But to achieve this will take a change of people's attitudes. That's where climate change, or, as we'll be discussing today, the Corona virus, come in, because these are global problems that require global solutions. But they also bear the prospect of crippling the world's economy which will require, for lack of a better word, a Great Reset, to get things back on track. Now, does that answer your question?"

Jeanine nodded, but it seemed to Josh she looked a little more confused than she did a few minutes before. He watched the marijuana cigarette being passed to Ron, but Ron simply passed it on. *Good. I can do that.*

"Okay, now let's look at one proposed strategy. I'm sure some around this table will say they've seen this before with respect to climate change, and it could still be used for that if Covid disappears, but this version does contain significant variations that have been included to make the plan more amenable to the virus." Marie turned to the white board. "Now remember, everything I'm giving you here is based on the assumption, as Jim said, that the virus takes a turn for the worse. If it gets better, we'll change our strategy, okay?" Marie leaned in to write on her board:

"Number 1. Establish Isolation Facilities."

She looked up, her eyes darting around the table. "We need to establish places to house people all across the United States. What we plan to do here is purchase and recommission defunct hotels, apartment buildings, and warehouses so they can be used to isolate those who refuse to take the vaccine. It's not our job to do this physically. The federal government already has real-estate brokers around the country securing properties for this purpose. We just have to be ready to provide boots on the ground assistance when called upon.

"Number 2. Total Lockdown.

"Now this won't happen until we see a second, and possibly a third, breakout of more serious strains of the virus with increasing resistance to the vaccines. The rules will be stricter, and stringently enforced, allowing no one to leave their homes unless authorized to do so, all for sake of saving humanity, of course.

Marie looked at her notes and then at Jeanine but Jeanine looked away. The marker squeaked as she wrote her third caption.

"Number 3. Expand Unemployment Benefits.

"Of course we can't let people starve. We will have to provide for those who can no longer go to work. This program may later be phased into the universal basic income program that will hopefully be introduced by congress later this year. Everyone, whether working or unemployed, is entitled to receive a basic living allowance. It's the decent thing to do. But no matter how much we allocate to this, it won't do anything more than put food on the table. People still have to pay their bills."

Marie began writing another new headline:

"Number 4. Deploy the Military."

She paused to look at Jeanine making sure she had her attention, but Jeanine was staring at her fingers, occupied with picking at a cuticle. "Are you getting any of this, Jeanine? You said you wanted to know what this is all about."

Jeanine kept her head down, but her eyes rolled up to her forehead to acknowledge Marie. To Josh, she appeared to be getting smaller by the minute.

"Okay," Marie went on, "with hospitals overcrowded and people being turned away, and with people out of work and production down, the food supply will decrease and we'll start to see inventory shortages and further economic instability, and with that we can expect a certain amount of unrest. The National Guard will already have been called in to manage checkpoints and restrict travel, but now we'll need to rely on the full assistance of our military to putdown any potential insurrection."

The joint reached Josh. He passed it along as he'd seen Ron do, but a piece of ash broke loose and fell on the table next to his drink. He had yet to take a sip and now realized the ice cubes were melting and if he didn't soon it would overflow. He placed his fingers around the wet glass and picked it up, sipping to make sure his drink didn't spill.

"Now, mind you," Marie continued, "this won't be happening in the U.S. alone; this plan will be rolled out on an international scale. Every country in the world will be experiencing similar difficulties. That's the beauty of using this pandemic for the reset. It affects everybody. It's a worldwide thing. The prime ministers of England, Canada, Australia, Israel, and of course our President, have already been briefed on this plan."

Josh puckered his lips. *Not half bad, a heck of a lot better than chasing whiskey with beer.*

Marie turned back to her board, writing as she said:

"Number 5. International Monetary Fund Bailout.

"By now, of course, people will be defaulting on their loans, mortgages and credit card bills. This is the really great part because the banks may foreclose, but they can't collect so their own financial positions will be in jeopardy. Stock markets will fail and the world will be in economic turmoil. That's when the IMF steps in to save the day. Using the fund, governments will offer to pay off the debts of their citizens, and the people will let them because they have no other recourse. The banks already own their homes and cars and any other assets they have, due to their inability to pay their loans. But here's the catch, they'll have to sign over all property and assets to the state. They won't own their homes anymore, but then, they don't anyway due to foreclosure by the banks. They will, at the time, also be required to take whatever version of the vaccine is available, which will now include methods for location tracking, medical data, and in all likelihood, a global crypto-currency for the tracing of future transactions. The government, after forgiving their debt, is going to want an accounting of all personal dollars being spent…"

"You really think people are going to buy into this?" The question came from one of the other ladies at the table. "I think my parents would opt out. They own their home outright and pay off their credit cards bills monthly. I'm pretty sure they're debt free."

"First off, most people aren't like your parents, Cheri. Most people are up to their eyeballs in debt, and for them, there won't be a choice. The banks who hold their paper will sell it to the government to save themselves. But you're right, there are always those financially secure enough to refuse the program, but they still have to eat and by this time the world will have converted to using digital dollars so they're money won't be any good. And they still have to travel, so unless they want to live in the self-imposed prison of their own homes, they'll take the vaccine. They'll also be social pressure because they'll be viewed as a health risk by their neighbors and friends. Besides, those who refuse will likely have their property confiscated and be relocated to one those isolation facilities we mentioned at the start of this discussion.

"But, like I said, it may not be the pandemic that leads to the Great Reset, it could end up being climate change after all, or, who knows, maybe they'll be a worldwide EMT knocking out power around the globe sending us back into the dark ages. Doesn't matter. The Great Reset is coming. It's fait-accompli. Those who have spent years laying the groundwork for this, will step in and assume control of the planet. Mankind will at last have a benevolent overseer who can manage the world's resources, and its people to the benefit of everyone. One world, one people, one mind—united!"

"I'm not convinced this is such a great idea," Jeanine finally said.

"I'm not saying it isn't noble, I mean who wouldn't want to live in a perfect world, but one thing I see over and over again, especially when I read the Bible, is that man is hopelessly corrupt. So as long as men are in charge of the process, there's bound to be corruption and if corrupt men are running things, how can we assume it will ever be fair? Someone's bound to take advantage. Personally, I believe the world you're asking for won't come until Christ returns to set up his kingdom on Earth."

"See, that's why I'm an atheist," Ed rejoined. "We've got people who believe in a mythical God who think He's going to somehow take care of everything, so we shouldn't do anything except sit back and watch the planet be destroyed, and then we can say it was God's will."

Josh sat in one of the two reclining chairs sucking down his third drink. He was feeling mellow, but not tired because this time he had taken one of his pills, and there were still two more in his pocket if needed. But he was feeling hot. He peeled off his coat and wondered why he hadn't done it sooner.

His thoughts kept going back to Marie. She had made some good points. That other girl, Cheri, didn't think people would give up their property so easily, but Josh knew different. It had already happened, back in the day of Pharaoh King of Egypt after he made Joseph governor of the land. Seven years of famine had destroyed the Egyptian economy and the people were willing to sell everything, houses, land and livestock, to the king, just for grain to eat. It was a pretty sure bet they would do it again, if it ever came to that. And that other girl, Jeanine, was right, too. His dad was always saying the true New World Order wouldn't happen until Christ ruled the planet. An interesting discussion, for sure, but Josh felt it was best to keep his options open and his opinions to himself. His dad had been wrong before, plenty of times. He was wrong about Ted. Ted wasn't trying to save him, he was trying to save Ted, but that was a dispute he couldn't possibly win.

Josh could hear laughter and screams coming from the game room where a cue ball was being smacked around a pool table. He could hear the balls clacking as they were driven into their pockets. He'd gone in to watch, but he'd had to leave before the game ended. They weren't going to get him poking one of those stupid balls around.

Ed was a putz. Religion had nothing to do with the Great Reset. It was either something to be involved in, or it wasn't. Except his father, who on any scale would be measured high in his regard for the planet, was also one who believed God was in control of everything. Josh was still trying to figure that one out. He couldn't argue creation or the flood, feeding a million people with misty wafers that arrived at night and disappeared in the day, or feeding five thousand with a few fish and loaves of bread. He leaned toward scenarios that explained these events using reason and logic. He could still believe in God without believing everything written in the Bible.

Marie didn't seem hostile to religion; she did after all, wear a gold cross. Josh admired her self-assured confidence. She had a commanding presence that made everyone go along with what she said whether they agreed or not. But that only meant she'd never be interested in a milquetoast man like him.

Josh was pulled from his thoughts by the game of Mexican Railroad going on at the table. Two girls and a guy were positioned around a plastic docking station, each trying to be first to get rid of their dominos. "Ah, you motha," the guy screamed, "I was about to play that one."

The party's attendance had shrunk by two. Jeanine had left with her boyfriend, Chuck, after complaining of a headache. Chuck said he'd be back but Jeanine gave him a look that said he probably wouldn't, not if she had anything to say about it.

Someone had put music on. One of the girls pulled a guy off the couch and was undulating like a dancing lizard.

Marie came up behind Josh and threw her arms around his neck, leaning over the chair to rub his chest, her cheek caressing his. "What's the matter? You don't look like you're having a good time." Her lips were brushing his ear. He could feel the warmth of her breath.

Josh brought his head back, looking over his shoulder, her skin now pressing against his nose was soft, her hair tickling his face. "No, I'm fine. Having a great time." He lifted his drink for her to see.

"Ah, I get it. The strong silent type. I like that in a man."

"Hardly. I'm just shy, that's all."

"No need to be. We're all friends here." She stepped around the chair and reached for his hand, pulling him from his seat. "Come on, this is my favorite song, dance with me," she said.

The music had changed from heavy rap to slow rock. *Lady in red, dancing with me*, the singer crooned. Marie pulled him in and laid her head on his shoulder. They held each other, swaying in time with the music. "You're not a bad dancer."

"Really? That's surprising since this is the first time I've tried it. Dancing, I mean."

Marie pulled her head back, looking at him curiously. "Josh, you are one surprise after another." She laid her head on his shoulder again.

Josh could feel the heat of her body as they swayed with the music. It was a moment he wished could last forever—but it wasn't to be. The doorbell rang and a carload of people came through the door. "Someone say there was a party happening here?" one of the boys yelled holding a bottle up by the neck as he entered. He was followed by several others all waving their bottles as they crammed into the kitchen.

Marie let go of Josh and went to welcome the newcomers.

"*Whooeeeee,* let's get this party started."

Marie raised her arms in the air snapping her fingers and stomping her feet like a mariachi dancer. The guy she was with twisted the cap off his bottle and tilted his head back, taking several long swallows before stopping to take a breath. He held the bottle out for Marie and she did the same. Another carload of people came through the door, and suddenly the party was on.

Josh remained in his seat most of the night hoping Marie would see him sitting alone and have pity on him, but she was too busy dancing and cavorting with the rest of the revelers to notice his isolation.

It was two in the morning and the party was in high gear. Josh wasn't tired but he did feel rejected. He was ready to go. The dancing continued, the euphoria looking like the frenzied gyrations of primitive aboriginals. The stereo's volume had steadily increased over time. Someone spilled their drink on the fabric of the pool table interrupting the trajectory of the balls so the games had ceased, but they were using the table to stack their empty beer cans. Josh had inadvertently stepped into the bathroom at a time when several people were using a razor blade to cut lines of coke on a mirror. And pills were everywhere, being passed out like candy, but Josh refused those. He wasn't dumb enough to get himself hooked on some stupid opioid. A latecomer arrived on a motorcycle and rode it into the living room where he sat revving his engine. It had begun raining outside and the bike left wet tire tracks on the carpet. Josh got up and went looking for Ron hoping he might be ready to leave, but he found him in bed with one of the girls from the meeting, *Cheri*, he thought. He had to duck to miss getting hit by a shoe. *If they want privacy, they should lock the door.*

When the doorbell rang the party's host went to answer expecting to admit more merrymakers. He didn't expect it to be the police.

EIGHT

CLOUDS OVER THE Pacific blew into Portland pummeling the ground with rain that bounced off the sidewalks, washed into the curbs and plunged down the streets in torrents. Josh couldn't see the tempest outside, though he could hear it slamming against the police station's roof, but it wasn't anything compared to the storm brewing in his cell.

Bill clomped back and forth with the tail of his red plaid mackinaw hanging out and his heavy cork boots unlaced. It was enough to put the fear of God into any man, let alone a boy who grew up thinking his dad was a lot bigger than he actually was. He turned on his heel as he reached the end of the lockup. Josh could see the thunder rumbling in his dark face, and the lightning flashing in his eyes.

"I don't know what's got into you, son," he fumed. "We let you get your own place and what do you do? You go on a drunken orgy and get arrested for drug possession. What am I supposed to think? I should leave you here to rot. That's what I should do. I thought you could be trusted."

Josh fought the temptation to mount a defense. A real man would have hung himself, but he was a coward so he'd called his dad to bail him out instead. He didn't need a lecture; he needed help. He sat on the metal bench gripping the edge, knuckles white, praying he'd be able to hold his tongue.

Bill rubbed his chin. "Did you stop to think about what this will do to your mother if she finds out? No, I haven't told her. I just said you'd called and that I was going to get you. She's thrilled you're coming home and I'm not going to burst her bubble by saying I had to haul your butt out of jail. When are you going to start acting like a man with a little self-control? Huh? Well?"

Suicide would be better. Josh rubbed his face with his hands. His hair was disheveled and oily, his eyes bloodshot. The coat he wore looked like it had been dragged behind a truck. He raised his head to answer. "I…I don't know what to say," he stammered. "I shouldn't have been there, okay? It's like I told you. I don't do drugs. I only had two Benzedrine tablets. Truck drivers use them to stay awake. Students use them to study…"

"They're a controlled substance, which means they're illegal without a prescription."

"But they're practically harmless, and there were lots of other drugs floating around I could have taken, but I didn't."

"No, you just got yourself good and drunk."

"I know, I…I guess I just blew it, that's all."

Bill pinched the bridge of his nose, closing his eyes. He seemed to be debating whether he should lighten up, or continue his tirade of righteous indignation. He sat down on the bench clasping his hands with his elbows on his knees. He lowered his voice. "I know, but you've got to understand, a man has to be in control at all times. You're a Christian, Josh. You have to set an example. If you can't handle temptation, you'll never amount to anything. I need you to promise me this won't happen again because it cost me a big favor to undo this mess. I might do it once, but I'm sure as heck not going to make it a habit. Are we clear?"

Josh reached around his back to scratch an itch. The nylon of his jacket still felt moist. He'd been forced to stand in the rain while they brought the police cars around. He wanted out of this cell. He didn't like getting drunk, and he didn't like being in jail. "No, I mean yes, I mean this won't happen ever again. I swear."

"Alright," Bill said. He slapped his legs and stood, towering over his son. "I'll see what I can do about getting you released. You're lucky I've got friends in the department, and that's only because of the articles I wrote defending the police during the riots. I called the Chief on my way in. He's taking time from his family to look into the charges. Believe me, that's a big ask on Christmas Eve, but he said without any priors they shouldn't have a problem kicking you loose. I expect the officer that made the arrest has heard from him by now."

Bill pulled a red handkerchief from his hip pocket and blew his nose. "Now here's the deal, we're not saying anything to your mother about this," he said, folding the handkerchief and putting it away. "We're not going to spoil her Christmas. We're also having a guest, so I want you to get yourself cleaned up and be ready to entertain. I don't want you sitting in your room playing video games. You will join in the family celebration and act like you're enjoying every minute of it. Understand?"

Josh's head came up slowly, his eyes lowered to half-mast. "No problem. Just get me out of here."

"You're a Christian, Josh. You should act like one. Don't do this again; there won't be any second chances."

Bill beckoned the jailer to let him out, but the door slammed closed on Josh. The clanging of the steel bars echoed as his father clomped down the hall.

Stupid, stupid, stupid. He couldn't believe they'd let the party get so out of hand. They should have known the neighbors would complain. At least Marie was safe. They'd marched everyone into the living room and had them empty their purses and pockets, but she was clean, as were most of the others, including Ron. Those caught holding were lined up against the wall and handcuffed. If he thought being in a liquor store was embarrassing, it didn't compare to being paraded out into the rain and stuffed into the back of a police cruiser with a bunch of tattooed crack-heads and junkies. What would she think of him now? He stood and rubbed the lower part of his back where it ached. He'd been awake all day, all night, and all day again. He wasn't sure how much entertaining he'd be able to do, but so what? If he let his father down, it would just be another disappointment in a long line of disappointments. He'd been one big disappointment since the day he was born. *Whew,* he lifted his underarm. The first thing on his list was a hot shower. He scratched his head. It seemed like he itched all over.

CHRISTMAS DAY. The smell of turkey basting in hot butter, cinnamon floating on hot apple cider, pumpkin pie fresh from the oven and evergreen boughs from the lavishly decorated tree, wafted through the house. Rachel sat in a thickly padded chair in the living-room of the Best's mountain cabin. Her short-sleeved, black dress flattered her blond hair, her black shoes with flat soles worn because she thought heels made her look too tall. Her feet were resting on a plank floor covered with a woven Navajo rug. Warmth and the smell of hickory smoke emanated from the rock fireplace at her back. It reminded her of a time in her youth when another family had taken her in and showed her the true meaning of Christmas.

Mrs. Best sat at the helm of their upright piano, her fingers tickling the keys rolling off a slow romantic version of, Chestnuts Roasting on an Open Fire. Beside the piano, Angie sat in her wheelchair, her body moving erratically with the music. Both had smiles on their faces, enjoying the holiday cheer.

Around the tree were piles of gifts and loose wads of discarded wrapping paper with curls of ribbon still attached. There were more gifts than Rachel had seen since she'd stayed with the Robinsons as a foster child, even several for herself. The room looked like the set of a television show filled with scripted laughter. It was like being invited to spend the holidays with Santa and Mrs. Claus.

Her only regret was that her own father couldn't be there. Bishop Samuel, the mission's chief administrator, had tested positive for Covid, though he assured everyone he felt fine and that the test was a misread, but they couldn't take a chance, so he'd had to quarantine himself leaving Stan to manage the food bank alone. You couldn't leave a hundred homeless men and women without Christmas dinner.

Rachel liked the way the Best's dressed up for Christmas day. Mrs. Best looked serene as her hands lightly stroked the keys of the piano. She was wearing one of the new outfits her husband had bought her, a long slinky blue dress that he'd said was his personal favorite. She glanced over at Josh, easily the height of his father. No, he was taller, but thinner. He was wearing charcoal grey wool slacks and a dark blue pullover sweater with light burgundy threads woven throughout. The collar of his white shirt crept out and circled his neck like the vestment of a priest. On his feet were black leather loafers with little tassels dangling in front. His hair was medium length on the sides and long on top combed back in thick dark waves, and his deep brown eyes were set back beneath heavy brows.

She'd been there when Mr. Best and Josh arrived the day before. She had been getting to know Mrs. Best, sitting around a table with Angie as they talked for hours while putting together a puzzle. Angie joined in the conversation with an occasional mumble or groan, but it didn't interfere with their discussing everything from how Rachel had lived, before she met her father, as a homeless waif on the streets of Chicago, to Mrs. Best's love of music, and her concern for her son.

The skies had turned charcoal by the time Mr. Best and Josh found their way home. Mr. Best, in his mackinaw, looked like he'd been lumbering trees since dawn, and Josh like a homeless person who'd spent the last few nights sleeping on a park bench. She wasn't impressed. His hair was oily and dangling in his face and his clothes looked like they'd been rolled in a puddle and left to dry in the sun. He didn't stay and talk. He'd acknowledged her by saying hi when they were introduced, and then had gone off to his room to change.

An hour later Mr. Best found him asleep on his bed fully clothed. Bill had come back out making excuses about how Josh had spent the past week staying up all night to study for finals, and had sat down to help them finish the puzzle.

Bill had told her it was a Best tradition to dress up on Christmas day. She admired the practice. He'd worn a full white beard Christmas Eve, but he'd gone from calloused lumberjack to suave business executive overnight. He was wearing a dark blue suit with a crisp white shirt and red silk tie, and his face was cleanly shaved. He said they dressed up to honor the Lord, whose advent they were celebrating.

Josh's lanky six-foot frame was slouched on the couch across from her but he hadn't said a word and appeared to be fighting to keep from falling asleep. He wasn't talking to his parents either. In fact, he seemed to be brooding, not that Mrs. Best had noticed. As far as Rachel could tell, with her son home Mrs. Best thought the day was perfect, though

Rachel sensed Josh was purposely avoiding his father.

Mrs. Best turned toward Rachel. "Come sing with me. What's your favorite?"

Rachel shook her head. "I never learned any Christmas carols when I was a child." It saddened her to think about it. She did remember Mrs. Robinson singing at Christmas, but that was before she was taken from their home to live with a man who claimed to be her father, but wasn't. Then it hit her. There was one song she knew. The one from a cassette recording she had received as part of a school gift exchange. She was living with the Purveys at the time and they'd allowed her to play it over and over again. "How about Rudolph the Red Nosed Reindeer," she said? "I think I can get through that one."

Mrs. Best changed keys, rolling through the intro. "Rudolph it is," she said.

Rachel got up to join Mrs. Best and Angie at the piano, and turned to see Mr. Best standing there as well. His face looked cloudy, like he was more sedate than happy.

The trio began singing together with Rachel faking it most of the way because she didn't really remember the words. Mary paused at the end of the song, lifting her fingers from the keyboard. "Josh, come on over and sing with us," she said, looking over her shoulder, but Josh had his head tilted back on the couch, snoring.

Some of the joy left Mary's face. She closed the piano lid and slid off the seat. "I'd better go check on dinner," she said.

Rachel went back to her place in the living room, followed by Mr. Best who wheeled Angie in front of him. He pushed the wheelchair up beside the couch and leaned over with his hand on Josh's shoulder, shaking him briskly.

"Wake up, son. You're being rude."

Josh's eyes opened half-lidded. He brushed his father's hand away. "Don't! What? Is dinner ready?"

"Not yet. Come on, sit up straight and talk to our guest."

"No, please," Rachel insisted, "I'm fine."

"Sit up, Josh. I want you to watch Angie while I help your mother set the table."

Josh struggled to pull himself from his slump. He reached over the arm of the couch and grabbed the wheelchair, pulling it in close. "Hi, sweet girl," he said.

Angie's arm came up and accidentally swiped his face. He had to pull back to keep from taking one on the nose. "Irrrruvvvuuuuu," she said.

"I love you too. And I do love that outfit you're wearing. Is that the one you got for Christmas?"

"Yhhaaaeeeessss. Fffrrouuumdaaaad."

"I thought so. You look great in it." Josh swept Angie's hair out of her eyes. "I guess I'll have to get old Rusty out of Dad's cabinet to fend off all those boys who are going to come chasing you when they see you dressed like that."

Rachel took something from the exchange. Perhaps Josh wasn't as self-absorbed as she'd thought. His sister brought out a tenderness in him. It made her rethink her image of who he was. And it made her wonder if there was a way to make the new image permanent. Her major at Northwestern was psychology. She understood the complexities of man were infinite. Trying to encapsulate personalities into little boxes the way the Myers–Briggs Type Indicator did, was futile, though it was part of the school's curriculum. What personality type would they ascribe to Dr. Jekyll or Mr. Hyde? Which was the real Joshua Best? Maybe in time she could figure it out. "You and your sister get along well. I can see how much you love each other."

"What's not to love?" Josh said.

"No, I didn't mean…"

"It's okay. She's my bestie. I can tell her anything. She never judges me."

There it is. Judgement, probably his father's. Rachel could relate. She'd felt that way around Satchel, the man she'd thought was her father until Stan came along. It helped her better understand Josh's insolence. All she had to do was find a way of pushing his impertinence to the bottom while bringing his compassion to the top. Josh needed to take advantage of her counseling. "Your folks seem like really nice people," she said.

He nodded. "My mother's a saint."

"Yes, I got to know her a bit while we were waiting for you yesterday. Your dad too, he seems like a decent guy."

Josh held Angie's hand to keep it calm but looked at Rachel, squinting like there was smoke in his eyes. "He puts up a good front," he said, turning back to Angie. One of her feet had slipped onto the floor and was bent sideways. He reached down and gently took hold of her ankle, placing it back on the wheelchair's footplate. "There, that's better, eh girl?"

Right! The problem's dad. Rachel had thought it strange that while his parents lavished presents on Josh: the new tablet, several items of clothing, a gift card to a Christian book store, he had bought nothing for them. At least he'd gone over and placed his arms around his mother to say thank you and give her a kiss. His dad he ignored. "You're right, I don't know much about him, but I know he went to pick you up yesterday and I presume he had to drive a long way because he was gone a long time. I think that's pretty nice, don't you?"

Josh shook his head, frowning. "Is there a point to this conversation?"

Mrs. Best stepped into the living room wearing a Christmas apron with a stitched design of holly and berries.

"If any of you kids are hungry, I have dinner on the table," she said, wiping her hands on her apron.

"That's me!" Mr. Best called from the kitchen. "And if no one wants to join me, it's a pretty sure bet I can eat it all myself."

Mrs. Best rose to the challenge. "Not a chance, my love. I made sure that turkey had Angie's name on it. If you're lucky, she might leave a few bones on her plate for you."

Angie giggled at the mention of her name.

Josh pushed himself up from the couch and grabbed the handgrips of the wheelchair, spinning it around. He leaned over to where his face was close to Angie's. "You heard what Mom said. That turkey's got your name on it. But I hope you'll remember your poor old brother and save the drumstick for me." He started rolling Angie toward the dining room leaving Rachel to make her way in by herself.

The room held the warm pleasant aroma of the oven. It had been a long time since Rachel had been in a house with so many sweet fragrances. She'd helped her father feed long lines of homeless people in the Chicago slums, but the smell of the kitchen was usually over-powered by the odors that clung to the clothes of vagrants who had no place to shower.

"Take a seat anywhere," Mrs. Best said, but Mr. Best had already taken a place at the head of the table, and Mrs. Best sat down beside him. Josh rolled Angie up beside his mother, and took a seat on Angie's right. That only left two places to choose from. Rachel took the one closest to Mr. Best leaving a space between herself and Josh.

It was a sumptuous feast, with a golden brown turkey sitting on a silver platter like the centerpiece of a king's banquet. The table was set with fine bone china that clinked when touched by the silver cutlery. Bowls of stuffing and cranberries and mashed potatoes and gravy and green beans and hot buttered rolls, were positioned around the golden bird. Rachel wondered how Mrs. Best managed to fit everything in be-tween the place settings. And a pumpkin pie sat on the counter in case anyone had room for dessert.

Bill stretched his hands out to Rachel and his wife, and everyone joined in completing the circle, though Rachel and Josh had to reach out across the vacant seat to take each other's hand.

Bill bowed his head. "Father, first we want to thank You for your Son, whose birth we celebrate today, so thank You, Lord. But we also want to thank You for this wonderful meal, and for the hands that pre-pared it. Please bless it all, in the name of Jesus. Amen."

Rachel glanced at Josh. He was staring at his father. His face was expressionless but there was no mistaking the resentment in his eyes.

Bill stood and took the carving knife, and began to slice off big chunks of white meat. He served a slab to his wife and turned to Ra-chel. "White or dark meat," he asked.

"Definitely white," she answered.

He cut another big slice and put it on Rachel's plate. "Come on everyone, start passing the bowls around."

The rolls were in front of Rachel in a basket covered by a checkered

71

cloth. She took one, *ouch, hot,* waved her burnt fingers and passed the basket on and took the bowl of stuffing handed to her by Josh. She had to admit he was good-looking, in fact handsome, if she were completely honest. She was surprised he hadn't tried to flirt with her, which she found refreshing, if not somewhat ego-deflating.

Mary was cutting up small pieces for Angie to chew, which she smothered with gravy. Josh held up his plate to receive the large leg his father had pulled from the turkey without bothering to ask if that's what he wanted. It was clearly the part he liked best.

Mary looked up. "We haven't seen you in church lately, Josh. Are you still going?"

Josh took a bite of his turkey leg, feigning he hadn't heard.

"Josh, your mother asked you a question." Mr. Best said.

He set the drumstick down and wiped his fingers on a napkin. "See this is why I don't like coming home. All you do is grill me with questions. No, I haven't been to church, Mother. I've been busy with my schoolwork, and one weekend we went skiing, but don't worry. I'm not losing my faith. I'm sure you'll see me there sooner or later."

"Watch your tone, Josh!" Mr. Best stopped carving, his knife suspended midair.

"You wanted an answer."

Bill continued glaring, his lips pursed, his cheeks slightly red.

"Josh, can I ask you a question?" Rachel said, hoping to turn the conversation away from what apparently was a sensitive subject. "I wanted to look you up because, well because we're both Christians and both our schools seem a bit hostile to Christianity. I thought maybe we could get together and encourage each other, I mean if you want to, but the funny thing is, when I went to your school's website I couldn't find anything about you."

Josh stared at her, his eyes narrow, his teeth wrapped around the largest part of the drumstick about to take a bite. He backed the leg away from his mouth. "What do you mean?"

But Mary jumped in to answer. "That's easy," she said. "And it's kind of the same reason you're here. Josh's father is a high profile target and while a lot of people like him, there are also those who don't, so we get our fair share of hate mail, too. That's why we go out of our way to keep anyone from finding out where we live. Josh didn't want to draw any special attention to himself, so we decided in the interest of all concerned, to enroll him as someone else. He's still Josh, but to those at his school he's Josh Bradly."

"That wasn't it," Bill said, putting the carving knife down. "It was because Josh is ashamed of me. He thinks I'm an embarrassment. He doesn't want anyone knowing we're related."

"Bill!" Mary said disapprovingly. Then she looked at Josh. "Josh just wants to make friends. Isn't that right, Josh?"

"*Sheeesh*, what is this, the inquisition? Would everyone just get off my case?" The leg of turkey Josh was holding trembled in his hands.

And the mystery deepens, Rachel thought. *God if you're raising me up to help people, show me what I can do for Josh.*

NINE

DING, DING, DING, the old-world clock chimed, ticking off the hours. It was a beautiful piece made of walnut that curved over a round face with raised brass numbers. Seven chimes, seven hours since midnight, and he'd been up since five. He'd already been out to the woodshed and brought in the day's fuel to feed the fire. The clouds resting against the mountain had dissipated, leaving a red sun dawning on the crest of the Cascades. A corresponding drop in temperature had turned the lingering rain into snow, not especially heavy, but enough to cover the ground and cling to the boughs of the trees. He'd had to remove his boots to keep from tracking it inside.

He sat at his desk in an old slat-back teacher's chair with arms curled at the ends for a good grip. He wore his red and black plaid mackinaw, a deep color that wouldn't frizzle in the camera lights. His jeans were still wet where they'd absorbed the snow that fell from the firewood. His legs were crossed at the ankles and his feet smothered in thick wool socks.

He drummed his fingers on his desk, biting his bottom lip. Much to his surprise, and partial regret, Mary had agreed with Senator Powers. Bill thought the fire, which they both believed was an act of political terrorism, would have sent her into hiding, but her kinship with Rachel, whose life was being threatened but showed little fear, seemed to give her strength. *God's will be done.* Thus, at the urging of Senator Powers, and with his prayer answered, he was now committed to sharing a few of the things God had revealed about what was to come.

Bill looked straight into the camera. If he were a preacher of righteousness, then this was his pulpit. This was where he did the work of correcting the world's errant behavior. He pulled out a drawer, rifling through the pens and paperclips, stalling for time to collect his thoughts.

His office was a combination of work space and man cave. One side was all business. On the floor, blinking like a Christmas tree with red, green, and yellow lights, stood a five-rack server built on Intel Xeon processors and ECC RAM. It was his communications hub. You couldn't find his podcasts on YouTube or Amazon. His was a private network, accessed only by those who subscribed directly through him. The entire system was backed up every five minutes, and fully redundant.

Bill didn't believe in storing things on the cloud. With the way the world was heading, some future government might use what he said to prosecute him as an enemy of the state. He wasn't anxious to have his own words convict him, so he stored everything on local hard drives where they could be destroyed if necessary. Which reminded him of that little blue line on the melted housing of their business computer. Mary's flash drive was blue. He needed to ask her about that. She was supposed to back up the day's transactions and carry her flash drive home for downloading to the server. But over the years they had become lax. He couldn't actually say he had seen her transferring data for some time. Yes, he definitely needed to ask her about that.

He sat at a vintage light-oak teacher's desk harvested, along with his chair, from a condemned school. A brass banker's lamp with a green shade, and his walnut antique clock, provided an historic atmosphere broken only by his high tech camera, the vanity light he needed for smoothing his wrinkles, and the mike he used for recording.

The rest of the room was pure outdoor lore. On the wall behind him were five fishing poles of various lengths and colors resting on pegs, and two mounted fish, one a Largemouth Bass and the other an enormous Rainbow Trout. The wall provided a backdrop for his recordings and, with Bill in his mackinaw, gave the overall feeling that he was just a good ol' country boy full of wisdom and common sense.

75

A rack from an elk, sent to him by a fan in Canada, was mounted on the side wall. Several of his best pork-pie hats were hung on the points, pinned with dozens of his favorite lures. The wall opposite had a bookcase full of rare first editions, a collection that included *The Call of the Wild,* by Jack London, and *The Old Man and the Sea,* by Ernest Hemmingway. Over the bookcase was a montage of framed photographs of Bill and Ted trolling for fish on the lake, and showy pictures of them holding their prize catches.

He spoke into the mike and watched the needle on his sound board jump as he checked his audio level. Satisfied it was good, he snapped the switch on the ring-light, and hit the record button. A red LED blossomed on the camera.

"Welcome. This is Wild Bill Best coming at-cha from our secret location here in the snowy Cascade Mountains where the air is clean, but the politics dirty. God bless you for joining me once again, my friends.

"Today, I'm going to do a little something different. Most of you know I'm a Bible thumpin,' Bible believing Christian; I've never hidden that fact. I believe in God, and believe He created this great nation, and that we exist by His Devine providence. But I rarely use this pulpit to preach. Today I'm changing all that. Some of you will, at this point, be ready to turn off your computers. I urge you not to do so. We live in perilous times my friends, times I believe were spoken about in the Bible long before America was called to be a nation. I can't prove this to you; I can only show you what scripture says. If you want to say I've lost my mind, go ahead, that's on you. But if you listen, you may find I speak words of truth.

"There are forces of good and evil in this world. There is Satan and there is God. You may count this as myth, but I assure you it's fact. Satan is a fallen angel, created beautiful, intelligent, powerful, and given high purpose in the kingdom of God. But Satan chose to rebel against the Most High, his Creator, just as men do today. Someday I'm going to ask God why he gave men free will, because given a choice, men usually choose wrong.

"According to scripture, our entire universe, and everything in it, including the angels and other beings that inhabit the spiritual realm, were made by God, and God saw that it was good, but Satan, along with a third of the angelic host, chose not to honor God, and in quelling their rebellion, God banished Satan and his followers to Earth.

"And the lines were drawn. The forces of good and evil were set at war. Satan struck the first blow when he said to the woman, 'Hath God said,' causing her to question the veracity of God's word and—*boom*— score one for the opposition. And, friends, it hasn't changed since. So when the Bible says, 'In the beginning God created the heavens and the earth,' Satan says, 'Come on guys, there is no God. You're just a cosmic accident.' Or if God says, 'from the beginning of the creation God made them male and female.' Satan says, 'Wait a minute, there are twenty-seven gender classifications. What about that boy who thinks he's a girl? I'ts cruel not to have something for him.' And when God says, 'You shall not lie with a man as one lies with a woman; it is an abomination.' Satan says, 'Really? It's not hurting anyone; what's the big deal? Instead of calling it sin, let's call it love.' And when God says, 'Before I formed you in the womb I knew you, before you were born I set you apart.' Satan says, 'That's just a blob of tissue. You can't *know* a blob of tissue. You should get rid of that thing.'

"The point I'm making is that Satan always opposes God, and those who follow him become like him.

"But to what end? What is Satan's purpose? Frankly, he wants revenge. He wants to despoil God's creation, and take the worship we owe God unto himself. He knows how much God loves the people of Earth, so at his ousting Satan threw down the gauntlet and swore to take as many of us with him as possible. And we, like him, constantly rebel against God by turning our back on what God has to say, and listening to Satan instead.

"Now here's where it hits home. Satan's long term goal has always been to establish a kingdom for himself, right here on Earth. He wants to set up a world government run by his proxy, the antichrist, where he will be worshiped. Even you nonreligious types have heard of the antichrist, or at least you should have; he's the subject of so many Hollywood films I've lost count. This is something Satan's been working toward since the fall of man. He first tried to bring it together at Babel, but God wouldn't let it happen. Instead the peoples of Earth were scattered across the face of the globe to form the various tribes, and tongues, and nations we have today.

"He's tried to establish his throne in every ruling empire since: Babylon, Greece, Rome, Germany, but failed, and not because the kingdoms weren't evil enough for him. They were known for their mass murder, genocide, and moral depravity. No, my friends, Satan has failed because God always held him back. But now he's at it again, only this time, because we're living in what many, including myself, believe to be the last days, he'll probably succeed.

"Bringing the entire population of the world together isn't easy, but Satan has been working overtime to get it done. He's been using things like climate change and the global pandemic to test us and see if we're ready for such a change, and he's proven that we are. He's tested the power of the media to manipulate people into reacting to a series of disasters that while serious, were never as bad as what they were hyped to be. Look at what he did with the pandemic. He was able to establish martial law without having to involve the military. People stayed off the streets willingly. Over and again we were told we had to give up our freedoms, or risk the prospect of dying. And over and again we capitulated.

"We were told this was a global problem, opening us to the need for world governance. He tested the strength of the world's economies so we watched as we lost twenty-two million American jobs, which we're still trying to recover from, and maybe never will. Most important, he tested the will of the people to trust God. We didn't. Instead we looked to the government for a solution and closed our churches in direct violation of our first amendment right to freedom of religion without government interference. And we didn't fight it. We folded without a whimper.

"Today's college kids want to be citizens of a world without borders; our politicians say we have to join the rest of the world in fighting crises like Covid and climate change, and our scientists say they can provide the technology to make it happen. Satan now knows he has everything ready. Just throw out a few more eve-of-destruction scenarios and the world will fall in line.

"Satan is right on target. He'll soon have the means to centralize his power around a world leader who will assume control of the world's assets ensuring that no one is able buy or sell without first vowing their allegiance to him. Then he'll demand our worship.

"These are scenarios clearly laid out in the Bible and they're coming fast, which I'll talk more about…" Bill's head swung around at the sound of someone tapping on his door. "…the next time we get together," he continued as he looked back into the camera. "Until then, this is Wild Bill Best signing off. And don't forget to send your comments and questions in so I can answer them in our next Q and A. Adiós, mi amigos."

Bill hit the fade to black button and swiveled his chair around to see Rachel standing there looking flustered. She was wearing jeans and a flannel shirt, with her hair pulled back in a ponytail.

"Oh, I'm so sorry, Mr. Best, I didn't know you were busy."

Bill shook his head, "Nothing to be sorry about. I was wrapping up anyway. You're up bright and early. Did you sleep well? I'm sorry we had to put you up in the loft but with Josh here, it's all we had."

"I slept beautifully, and I loved being in the loft. It was fun, kind of like being in a treehouse." Rachel stepped into the room, seeing Bill's man cave for the first time. "You must like to fish."

Bill's face puckered. "Used to," he said.

"Not anymore?"

"I used to fish with Josh's older brother, Ted, but he died. I gave it up after that. I guess it lost its appeal."

Rachel glanced at the wall of photos. "But…what about Josh?"

Bill paused and took a breath, exhaling before he answered. "Josh never liked to fish. It was kind of a Dad and Ted thing. Anyway, that's not why you're here. What can I do for you?"

"I see. Sorry, I didn't mean to overstep. My father called and asked me to ask you what you'd decided. About what you discussed, I mean."

"Ah." Bill turned back to his desk. "I was just now working on that. You can tell your father I'll do my best, but it won't be easy, not because there isn't much to talk about, but because there's too much. I can only dedicate a few podcasts to this, and I probably won't change anybody's mind, but I hope to give those who are uninformed something to think about."

"I'm sure you will." Rachel turned toward the wall, her hand raised to feel the cork handle of one of his fishing poles. "Why do you keep them? I mean if you no longer use them, why keep them here?"

Bill had a sudden urge to tell her not to touch his gear, but he crossed his arms and swallowed his Adam's apple instead. He shrugged. "They fill the wall space, I guess. I haven't got anything else to put there. Besides, I might take it up again someday. Who knows? I can't brood about Ted's death forever. But I've been telling myself that for the past ten years."

There was noise coming from the kitchen, the sound of water running and plates scraping the counter. "Sounds like your wife's up. I suppose I should go say hi, and maybe mooch a cup of coffee." Rachel turned to go, but stopped with her hand on the door looking back. "You know, there's no time like the present," she said. "The sun's out this morning. I think I'll take a walk down by the lake, if that's alright with you."

"Of course, feel free, mi casa su casa." Bill watched as she disappeared around the corner. He hadn't thought about that day in a long time. She had no business messing with his memory like that. Some things were better off forgotten.

JOSH KICKED THE CANOE, leaving a mud streak across the side of a carved eagle, but the canoe didn't budge. It weighed a ton. He hated the beast. It was a Chinook, a dugout created by primitive Indians hollowing out a tree with fire and tools made of stone. The sides were decorated with carvings of deer, beaver and elk in a totem that spanned the hull. His dad had bought it at an auction and paid far too much because the auctioneer claimed it was the same vintage used by Lewis and Clark to map the great northwest. Josh kicked it again. If he didn't know it would cause friction, he'd set it on fire and burn it to the ground.

He turned away, zipping up his parka. He didn't want to be out in the cold, but he didn't like being inside where his father was, so it was the lesser of two evils. He pulled on his fleece-lined leather gloves. The sky was ice blue and the day frigid as frost. His breath met the air in a steamy plume. He brought a hand up, rubbing his nose to stop it from running, then pulled his skull cap down to cover his ears. He stepped up on a rock and down into the snow on the other side, sauntering along the lakeshore trail hoping to kill time until his mother was ready to take him back to Portland. There were tracks in the snow ahead of him. Someone had already been out. The lake lapping against the shore sounded like a paddle entering the water, but he despised that canoe and the lake was never his friend, so he let the thought pass.

He stopped to wipe mud from his tennis shoe. The sun was melting the snow causing it to drip from the trees, turning drifts into puddles that made the forest floor a bed of muck. He should have worn boots. He brought his foot up over a fallen tree and used it to scrape the glop from the bottom of his shoe.

Out over the water an eagle was making lazy circles on a breeze. It was a beautiful bird, maybe even one of the original two his father had rescued when he and Ted were kids. It was possible; eagles were known to live twenty or thirty years. The bird circled and then pulled in its wings dropping headlong toward the water, and at the last second, with its talons outstretched, splashed down and came away with a fish writhing in its claws. *Would you look at that,* Josh thought. *Beautiful.*

The water sparkled with flecks of gold. His eyes scanned the valley: the lake, the trees and the never-ending sky. A squirrel shimmied down the side of a tree to dig a pinecone out of the snow. He dug into the scale chattering like he'd just discovered the last seed on Earth. Josh hopped from rock to rock, climbed across bridges made of fallen trees, and left his footprints in the wet sand along the shore. It was a familiar route, though he hadn't taken it in years. A tree off to his right had his initials carved into its trunk but moss and growth rendered them practically invisible.

He wasn't planning on taking the trail all the way around the lake, though it went that far, but that would take most of the day and he didn't want to keep his mother waiting. A white-headed woodpecker began hammering the trunk of a ponderosa pine in search of hibernating bugs. Looking up he saw the eagle disappear behind the trees on the opposite shore. It was close to the falls where his dad had found the nest.

The rock standing out in the water called to him like an old friend. It was a safe harbor, an isle of refuge, and within easy reach, only a few stepping stones offshore. *Yes, I'm coming.* The rock was where he'd sat while his dad and Ted were fishing. He could watch with envy as they shared a camaraderie he would never know, and sit there knowing his feelings were hidden from view. It was the size of a bus with a natural ledge that provided good seating. He crossed the water, the stones acting as a bridge leading out to his berth. He climbed up just as he had as a child, but upon reaching the crest found he wasn't alone.

"Oh, it's you, Josh. Good morning," Rachel said. She held her hand over her eyes like a shade.

She was sitting where he'd always sat. *My rock. My spot.* He didn't know whether to chase her off, or turn and run.

"Come on over. There's room for two," she said, patting the surface of the rock with a bare hand. She was wearing the same jeans and blue long-sleeved flannel shirt she'd worn Christmas Eve. Her hair was back in a ponytail. *Cute.* "What are you doing here? Aren't you cold?"

"A little perhaps, but the sun's warm, and I'm from Chicago so I guess I'm used to it. Come and sit down."

Josh resigned himself. He stepped onto the ledge and slid down beside her. The shelf extended out over the water allowing their feet to dangle.

"I was just thinking about you," Rachel said. "It must have been hard growing up here surrounded by all this beauty and then have to leave it to live in Portland." She was looking out over the lake admiring the blue water and the frosting of snow decorating the trees on the opposite shore. "It's like a Christmas card. Did you see that bird a few minutes ago? I think it was an eagle."

Josh balked, not sure about how much of his childhood he should confide. Talking about the eagle was probably safe, and it was his dad at his best so... "Yeah, I did, and there's a story there. You can't see it from here but around that bend," he brought his finger up to point at a place where the water disappeared behind the trees, "there's a cove. We lease most of the land surrounding the lake and it includes all the forest beyond that inlet. If you take a canoe up there you'll come to the river that feeds into the lake, and if you hike upstream you'll come to a sixty-foot waterfall. Those eagles have a nest on the side of that formation and when I was a boy, my dad, and some missionary he knew from Mexico, scaled that cliff to rescue two baby eagles that were abandoned when their mother was shot by poachers. It's funny, because my dad ended up tripping and busting up his leg, and that missionary had to haul his butt all the way down the mountain and then put him in the canoe and bring him home. And the guy had never been in a canoe before and didn't know how to paddle." Josh tried to stifle a grin. "Anyway, We took the birds to a wildlife rescue center and they were later released back into the wild. I think that's one of the eagles my dad saved."

"Really? Wow, that's amazing. I'd love to see those falls. Maybe you can take me there sometime."

"Maybe, we'll see. It's kind of a private place my dad likes to keep to himself. He's got 'No Trespassing' signs all around it to keep tourists away. So why are you out here all by yourself? And without a coat. You must be freezing."

It was chilly, Rachel rubbed her arms, the flannel sliding up and down providing warmth, but nothing compared to being homeless during winter on the streets of Chicago. "I wasn't planning on staying out long. I just wanted a little time to sit and talk with God. You know how it is."

Josh didn't. Not really. "You ever get the feeling..."

"What?" Rachel said.

But Josh was staring out across the water at a canoe that had just pulled around a bend in the distance. The shape was familiar but it was too far away to be sure. The public had access to the lake from a landing maintained by the forest service at the lake's northern end, so it wasn't unusual to see other boats on the water, but as the canoe drew nearer, its size and shape took on definition. It was their Chinook... and his dad was in it—*fishing!*

TEN

THE APARTMENT was generally a catch-all for everything worn, carried, or eaten. Josh kicked up a pair of jeans, stepped on an empty pizza box, and grabbed a shirt off the back of a chair, stuffing them along with a pair of socks from his desk, and two pair of his skivvies, into a dirty pillowcase.

He was wearing the same clothes he'd worn the night of the bust, had subsequently slept in, and then put on again this morning before leaving the cabin. *Pewww!* He had no need for the slacks and sweater outfit he'd worn Christmas day, so he'd left them behind, but now he had nothing clean to wear. He grabbed a sweatshirt that at least didn't look slept in and pulled it over his head. He needed to do his laundry—*but later*. Rachel was waiting. He shoved another pair of pants into the pillowcase and tossed it onto his bed. He had to leave now.

The door opened and Ron plowed through with his arm around the same girl Josh had seen him with at the party. She was thin and not particularly fetching. Her hair was piled on her head like a coil of rope and her face, au naturel, disdained the use of makeup. They were laughing like someone had just told a sidesplitting joke, but with their masks covering their mouths, their glee was muted. When they saw him standing there, they froze.

"Josh, man, good to see you," Ron said, letting go of his squeeze. "I thought you'd still be in jail." Ron peeled his mask from his face and stuffed it in his pocket. Cheri drew hers down and tucked it under her chin.

"Why would you think that?"

"You know, because…hey man, you didn't say anything, did you? I mean about me. I've been laying low in case the man comes knocking. You didn't cut a deal or anything did you?"

Josh took a breath and crossed his arms, surprised at his roommate's paranoia. "Relax. I only had two bennies so they cut me loose with a warning. I was wondering where you've been."

"I've been staying at Cheri's. We spent Christmas together." Ron tilted his head toward the girl beside him. His laptop was under his arm. He walked over and cleared a place for it on the desk. Cheri went over and pushed the covers aside to sit on Ron's bed. She began picking at her cuticle with a fingernail.

Josh reached for his wallet to make sure he had enough money to pay for his coffee. He counted several bills and placed it back in his pocket.

Ron took his laptop and opened the case, turning it on. "I'm glad you're here, I've got something to show you."

"What's that?"

"It's something I've been working on. I know we've still got the virus to deal with, but people are starting to get concerned about our planet's temperature again." He began clicking keys as the machine warmed up. "I've done a beautiful model to show how we can lower our emissions without throwing the world into economic chaos. It'll mean making some sacrifices, like people choosing to drive a lot less, but I'm not advocating a complete end to the use of fossil fuels." He turned the computer toward Josh. It was a graph showing a decline in carbon dioxide corresponding to an increase in the use of alternative forms of energy. "Our problem is we're jamming space with carbon dioxide molecules. Same thing as drinking too much, we're drunk on our use of gasoline. We need to sober up and consume less and make the determination not to drink so much in the future."

"Sounds good, but hey, I can't do it now. I'm supposed to be meeting someone."

"Oh, okay, no problem, but you can still see it. I'll be giving a presentation at the Tortoise today around three o'clock. Stop by and check it out."

Perfect. Josh hadn't seen Marie since the party. She was bound to be there. "I'm just heading out, but," Josh looked at his watch, "I should be done by then. Sure, I'll try to make it."

LIKE MOST BUILDINGS contracted to the lowest bidder, the Washington D.C. office of the Internal Revenue Service was drab. Computer terminals, linked by a local area network, sat on laminate topped counters in fabric cubicles where people worked day-in and day-out tabulating data. The walls were boring beige with only a few framed pictures of the kind found at local poster stores, hung here and there to break the monotony. There were three private offices, two for departmental supervisors, and one for Calvin Moody, head of the Internal Revenue Service's Criminal Investigation Division.

Cal was fifty-seven years old and had been with the IRS since graduating from university back in the nineties. He was five foot seven, fifty pounds overweight, and wore rumpled suites that always looked like they'd just come out of the washer. With his round face, thinning hair, and thick brown glasses, he looked like an owl, an image bolstered by the fact that he was asthmatic and often wheezed when he spoke.

Cal was one of the few people on the floor to have a dedicated printer, which was now spewing out reams of paper. The paper tray held five hundred sheets, and he'd filled it twice already, and he was just in the C's. This was too much. If he didn't shut it down, he might be accused of misappropriating company supplies. He reached over and switched the printer off.

He was just trying to get ahead of the game. Word had come down that Congress was considering a bill to remove the tax exemption from places of worship, so he thought printing a list of all the churches in America would show initiative. It would be his group, after all, that would be called upon to ferret out those churches that refused to comply with the new code, so why not be ready with a list? He'd counted approximately fifty line items per page, which meant he would have twenty-five thousand names per ream. One ream of paper should have done it. But it hadn't.

Cal sat down at his computer and did a google search on the number of churches in America. *No freaking way.* Over three-hundred-and-fifty-thousand! No wonder the government wanted them taxed. They were losing huge revenues. He looked up.

"Hey, Cal." Nancy Pilsner, one of the girls from the secretarial pool, was standing at his door. "There's a man here to see you. He gave me his card," she leaned in to pass the small white business card to Cal who had to suck in his stomach to reach across his desk and take it. "I seated him in the meeting room. He's waiting for you now."

The card had a logo with an eagle whose breastplate was the American flag in the shape of a shield. The image was printed on a blue circular background with the words, "National Security Agency," around its circumference. "What the heck would the NSA want with me?" he said, starting to rise from his chair. "Whoever it is didn't make an appointment. I'll go see what he wants, but give me about five minutes and then pop in and say I'm late for my next meeting. I don't have time for any interagency crap right now."

Cal walked down the hall to a room not much bigger than his office. Six folding metal chairs surrounded a blond colored Formica table, and in one of the chairs sat a man in a dark blue suit. He stood as Cal came in.

"Victor Damshie," the man said, holding out his hand, "with the NSA."

"Yes, I see that," Cal responded, looking at the card as he shook the man's hand. "To what do I owe the pleasure?"

"Well, I tell you," Vic said, sitting down again. Cal pulled back a chair for himself and followed suit. "You probably heard that climate change has become a national security threat, which of course means the President has executive power to make decisions about it without congressional approval. He's calling the shots, and he considers this thing to be a direct threat to America's survival. That's where we come in. The NSA has been tasked with making sure people understand the seriousness of this problem and ensure that detractors and conspiracy theorists are contained."

"Contained as in…?"

"Silenced."

"Yeah, I thought that's what you meant. Like curbing their freedom of speech."

"No, like saving America from those who would subvert and destroy our nation."

"No, I get it. So why are you here?"

"Okay, then. There are certain people we've identified who pose a threat that must be dealt with. One of them is a character known as, Wild Bill. His real name is Bill Best, but that's what he calls himself. He used to be a syndicated columnist, a real nut job who wrote the most ridiculous stuff about climate change." Vic reached down for his briefcase and set it on the table, popping the lid open. He reached in to remove a short stack of newspaper articles. "Here, I brought you a few samples," he said, laying them on the table, "never hurts to know your enemy. Several years ago our undercover agents infiltrated a few subversive groups and got them to pressure the newspapers into dropping him. We thought he'd disappeared. But we were wrong. He just went underground and started doing podcasts. Now he's built up his audience again, and is doing as much damage as before.

"We need to get this guy off the boards. Not that he's the only one. There's a whole cesspool of voices we've got to stop. Freedom of speech is a constitutional right, but we draw the line when the rantings of one individual put the whole country at risk. That's what national security means."

Vic paused, making sure he had Cal's attention. His eyes were a light shade of green, and his jaw firm, his upper lip covered by a blond mustache. When he smiled, one side of his mouth rose higher than the other. "But you're probably wondering why I'm bringing this to your attention," he said. "You may not be aware of it but you already have a complaint against Bill Best on file in this office. He has a side business that's supposedly a non-profit 501c3, but certain people are saying he's skimming, keeping the profits for himself and tossing the charities a few crumbs." He reached back into his briefcase and withdrew another document. "Here's a copy of the complaint for your reference. We need you to dig up everything you have on this guy, tax filings going back three years, profit and loss statements, all of it, and we want you to do it quickly. The President won't abide any threats to our national security."

Cal rocked back in his chair, his hands folded over his protuberant belly. "Sorry, Vic, but with all due respect, I'm afraid that's impossible. We have a whole backlog of cases that need our attention, and too few agents to handle the load, and even if I assigned this to one of them, they'd still have to obtain evidence, and that means conducting surveillance, doing interviews, executing search warrants, subpoenaing bank records, reviewing financial data, and all that takes time, the president will probably be out of office before we get around to prosecuting."

"Cal…"

"You have to work with Criminal Tax Attorneys to ensure the legal aspects of the investigation are addressed. And after all the evidence is gathered and analyzed, the special agent has to file his report for review…"

"Cal…"

"Then you have to get the Justice Department involved to carry it forward to prosecution…"

"Cal, stop. None of that is going to be necessary. The reason I'm coming to you directly is that we want you to cut through all the red tape. This is a sanctioned investigation. Normal rules don't apply. Just get the goods on the guy and hand it off to the Justice department. They'll do the rest." Vic stood, signaling the meeting was over. "The President will be monitoring your progress, personally. He expects nothing less than your full cooperation."

Cal pushed himself up, struggling to his feet, feeling slighted. *That's it, no ifs, ands or buts?*

Vic reached out to shake Cal's hand. "You've enjoyed a good career so far, Cal, I suggest you don't blow it."

"But…but what if we investigate and don't find anything?"

"Then the President will be very disappointed. But I'm sure that won't happen. Remember Al Capone? They couldn't nail him for murder, so they put him away for tax evasion. We're counting on you to do the same."

THE SKY LOOKED like a giant grey sponge wrung by the hands of God. It hadn't been raining when Rachel and his mother dropped him off, but it sure was now. Rain pelted the ground forming puddles Josh had to dodge to avoid getting his tennis shoes wet. He pulled the hood of his sweatshirt over his head and hurried down the Park Blocks, damp leaves sticking to the soles of his feet. He was late.

His mother had asked him if he would mind entertaining Rachel for a few hours while she did her weekly grocery shopping and ran a few errands. Part of Josh wanted to decline. His mother was playing Cupid, and he resented it—*almost*—but Rachel was attractive, *no*, not so much attractive as stunning, but not like Marie, only he found that he enjoyed talking to Rachel, so maybe they could be friends. He'd agreed, somewhat reluctantly, on the provision that they would drop him at his house first so he could change. Rachel would be waiting in a coffee shop a few blocks down the street.

Most of the people he passed were smart enough to use umbrellas. He had one in his closet but in his rush to get out the door, hadn't thought to bring it. A guy riding a twenty-seven speed racing bike sped by, spinning water onto his pants. Josh had to stop to sweep it off. *Idiot!* He loathed the silly teardrop helmets worn by racers. And the lime green spandex. They looked like harlequins dressed to make people laugh.

Water poured off the eves of buildings and ran into the streets to be swept back onto the sidewalks by passing cars. Soppy leaves, mushed into clumps, were beginning to decay. The air smelled of compost, not an acrid odor, more like a yearning for the coming spring. Josh slapped his wet pant leg one more time. He kept hoping the rain would let up, but instead, it seemed to be falling harder. He picked up his pace.

He'd been to the coffee shop before. He was familiar with its layout, which was why he'd suggested it as a place to meet. He stepped into the building and immediately saw Rachel smiling at him. He nodded, acknowledging her, and negotiated a path through the tables, making his way over. She wore her hair loose. Her long blond tresses picked up light from the windows like a hint of sun on a cloudy day. He pulled a chair back and settled in.

"Looks like it's still wet outside." Rachel said. She had her fingers on the table with her thumbs hooked over its rim. Her nails were pink, matching her lips.

Josh slid his hood back to get it off his head and wiped the water off his sleeves. "Yeah, it's nasty out there. I wish I'd thought to bring an umbrella."

Rachel reached for the one beside her. It was wet but she was dry. "Your mom loaned me this one." She thought for a moment and then said, "If we take a walk later, we can share it."

"Really? Because I was thinking maybe we should take a streetcar. I guess it depends on how wet it is when we go. So, you've been here a few weeks. What have you been up to?"

"The usual. Loads of study. I thought taking courses online might be easier, but you still have the same amount of work to do." She picked up a spoon, turning it in her hand puzzling over something.

"What's the matter?"

"Sorry, it's nothing. I was just thinking about your father."

Josh's face slackened. He nodded. "Did you order anything yet?"

"No, I was waiting for you."

"Shall we, then?" Josh slid his chair back, the sound of wood scraping the floor as he stood. Rachel fell in behind as they moved to the coffee bar.

The menu posted overhead had a list of coffees, expressos, teas and hot chocolates. "What are you having?" Josh said, reading through the choices. He turned to look at Rachel. She was tall, perhaps only a few inches shorter than he was, and he topped six feet. Her eyes were blue as Caribbean water, her cheeks the color of a tropical Hibiscus. She pulled her hair to the front letting it fall over her shoulders in long rolling waves.

"I'm having a latte," she said. "I like the little pictures they paint on the coffee's surface but I've never ordered one before. I thought I'd give one a try."

The girl taking orders looked at Josh expectantly. "Two lattes please." Josh said, reaching for his wallet.

"I can pay for my own."

"I'm sure you can, but I've got it."

"Thanks."

"No problem."

They stood off to the side waiting for the barista to fill their orders. He was a chunky man in a black apron and a white shirt with rolled up sleeves. Individual letters were tattooed on his knuckles but he moved too fast for Josh to catch what they said. He poured milk into two small pitchers and inserted them under a stainless steel steam-wand to aerate the liquid with heat. Then he drizzled just the right amount of foamy milk over the espresso and drew his pitcher back in such a way as to leave a perfect flower on the skin of the coffee, an artist not just in design, but in process as well. Josh glanced at his watch. It had taken nearly five minutes. He hoped it was worth the wait.

When his name was called, Josh stepped up to the counter and picked up both cups. He nodded at Rachel, indicating she should lead the way back to their table, and placed a cup in front of her as they sat down.

"Look at that. Isn't it beautiful? I got a heart. I wonder how they do that."

"Yeah, I think mine's some kind of tulip."

Rachel fanned the steam from her latte. "I kind of hate to break up the picture, it's so pretty, but I do want my coffee." She picked it up with both hands and brought it to her lips where she held it for a moment, thinking. "Can I ask you a question?" she said. "It's about something I've had on my mind ever since we left the cabin."

Josh raised his eyes over the rim of his cup, studying Rachel. People who ask if they can ask a question usually have something serious in mind. "I suppose," he said, "but I won't guarantee an answer." He blew across his coffee and took a sip, leaving a vein of white foam on his lips.

Rachel wiped her mouth with a napkin. "Good, but a bit strong."

"What did you want to ask?"

Rachel set her cup down and folded her hands in her lap. "It's about your father. I noticed when we were on the lake and you saw him fishing, you seemed surprised. He told me he had stopped too, so

93

I was happy to see him out there, but I wondered what made him stop in the first place. I was in his office and it was obvious he enjoyed the sport. What made him quit?"

Josh set his cup down and sat back in his chair, his lips knotted. Rachel was becoming a friend, but a new one. He'd never shared his story before, let alone with someone he hardly knew...

It was the kind of morning where the sun comes pouring in through the windows with cosmic dust dancing on its beams and you stretch and push the covers off knowing that every breath you breathe is a gift from God and that all creation is awaiting your good pleasure—but Josh knew such thoughts were transient. Especially now with the sun overhead radiating like a furnace, and his nerves making him twitch. He and Ted were in that shell of a once living tree, floating on the cold purple water. Josh could almost hear the tree crying out for revenge.

"Come on, Josh. You have to paddle too."

"You haven't said where we're going."

"It's a surprise."

Josh didn't like surprises, nor did he like being in a canoe that looked like a coffin. A canoe should be sleek and glide effortlessly through the water. Piloting the Chinook was like pulling a boxcar through mud.

Josh glanced around. "Did you bring the lifejackets?"

"We don't need them. You can't sink this old barge. It's like the ark, made to stay afloat."

"I told you to bring them. I said I'd only go if you brought them."

"Quit whining. I threw one in for you. Check under your seat."

Josh reached down and pulled out the vest. He slipped his arms through the shoulder harness and battened down the Velcro fasteners. It was too big, but it was better than nothing. He hadn't wanted to come. He didn't like being on the lake. When he was a toddler his mother had signed him up for swimming lessons but, as the story went, he'd cried so loud she'd had to take him home before his toe even touched the water. Ted, on the other hand, was said to have been the best swimmer in the class.

"So where are we going? Come on, you have to tell me." Josh could feel the sun soaking into the orange material of the vest, warming his back. At least that felt good.

Ted raised his finger, pointing to the end of the lake. "There," he said.

"That's the roller coaster. We're not going there. Dad forbids it."

"Dad's not here. He's in Washington at a convention."

"I'll tell."

"You little dweeb, you won't say a thing because if you do, you'll get in as much trouble as me, and you know how Dad gets when he's mad."

The lake flowed toward the mouth of the Watalong River. Ted didn't really need Josh's help. The current pulled them along. Josh looked up and saw the silhouette of a large bird circling the sun overhead, its backlit feathers looking as orange as a phoenix. It was the same bird he always saw over this part of the lake. He liked to think it was watching over him.

They were getting close now; close enough to hear the sound of the water pouring through the rocks as the lake narrowed and became a river again. "Okay, we're close enough," Josh said. "We need to turn around and go back."

But Ted just kept paddling. His shoulders were red where his sleeveless cutoff exposed his skin.

"What are you doing? We have to turn back."

"Nonsense. We're going to run the rapids. Whitewater rafters do it all the time."

"Not in a canoe."

"Some of them do. Besides, Dad says a Chinook can handle any kind of turbulence."

"But you can't leave it down there. How are you going to get it back? He'll be so mad."

Ted took another stroke with his paddle. "Don't plan to. I know where Dad keeps the keys to his truck. We're going to park it on a sandy beach and then you and I are going to drive Dad's truck down and throw it in the back and bring it home. He'll be none the wiser. Here we go!" *Wheeeeeeee.* And with that they slipped into the rapids, the choppy water now translucent green splashing up over the sides of the canoe. They rode out a series of short falls and then the river dipped and fell into an eddy that spun the canoe around, leaving them going backwards. Ted lost control. All he could do was push off the rocks with his paddle to avoid a collision. They passed through a narrow channel of water and entered a riffle where the water became calm enough for Ted to get the canoe turned back around, but it was short lived. A few seconds later they were thrust between two rocks and slid down into a vortex that had them spinning again.

"Teddddddddd!" Josh cried. All he could do was hang on as they bounced over one fall after another banging the side of the canoe against the rocks. Then they glided over a seemingly innocuous rock and fell into a hole where the hydraulics turned the river back on itself and flipped the canoe, sending both Josh and Ted into the air. Josh came down on his back, the surging water sweeping him downstream, his arms flailing as he tried to take purchase of a limb, or tree, or find someplace where it was shallow enough to crawl out on land. The river rushing into his eyes made it hard to see but he caught the blurry image of a tree growing by the shore with a branch extending out over the water. He reached out and grabbed it, hanging on. The water was surging through his clothes pinning him down but he managed to roll over and cast a glimpse upstream only to see Ted about to pass him.

"Great fun, eh, Josh!" his brother cried, waving as he went by.

Josh clung to his branch, turning so he could see behind him again. It looked like Ted was trying to stop his plunge by pushing off a rock, but the current spun him around leaving him coursing down the river head first. He was plummeting toward a gap where the water sluiced between two huge boulders. Then the unthinkable happened. As Ted slipped though the channel he attempted to right himself by pushing off the rock but his shoe slipped into a fissure and became wedged, holding him in place with his head downstream. The force of the current was pushing him under. All Josh could see of him were his hands splashing the water like two starfish looking for a rock to suction to.

Josh let go. The surging water swept him downstream but his lifejacket kept him bobbing on the surface until he reached the rock where Ted was caught. There was nothing to grab but the toe of Ted's tennis shoe. He seized it and held on, bringing his knees up to push against the rock in an attempt to yank Ted's foot free but the surge was too powerful. Ted's head was deep underwater. He let go and clung to Ted's clothes, the river forcing him on until he reached Ted's torso. He felt Ted's arms frantically wrapping around his legs, pulling him down.

Josh was kicking his feet trying to find ground but it was too deep. One of Ted's arms shot up, a hand breaking the surface and then fell back, the other still wrapped around Josh's waist went limp. Josh was hanging on to Ted's clothes to keep from being swept away but realized he was only holding his brother down. He let go. The last thing he saw was Ted's face, his eyes wide open staring up at him through the crystal clear water, but by then, Ted was gone.

"My dad thinks I'm responsible. Either I was too weak, or too inept to save my brother, or I was jealous and wanted him to die. Take your pick, it doesn't matter. He didn't like me before and it's only gotten worse since. And that's why he doesn't fish. Ted was his fishing partner; I was just bait on the shore. I was surprised to see him out there, too. I didn't think he'd ever fish again." Josh looked down at his cup. He picked it up and brought it to his lips. "It's cold," he said, setting it down again. "Sorry, I don't mean to be so melancholy, but you asked. Maybe we should take a walk down the Park Blocks. It's not that pretty this time of year, but there are a lot of nice shops along the way. You might see something you like. You about ready to go?"

ELEVEN

CAL STORMED DOWN the hall wheezing like an old tin lizzie. *What the heck. Who is this guy, thinks he can barge in here and order me around? Ahh wheeeeze, ah wheeeeze. I suggest you make it a priority,* like I've got nothing better to do. *The President will be monitoring your progress.* Right. I won't be intimidated—the President? *Ahh wheeeeze.* Cal stopped, his breath catching in his throat. He reached for his inhaler, but it was back on his desk. His name would be on the report. Had to be because he would be running the investigation. *The President? Might mean a commendation. Ahh wheeeeze.* He stared at the folder in his hand, a few newspaper articles and a grievance. Not much to go on, but they had the guy's tax filings. That was a start. *Ahh wheeeeze, ahh wheeeeze.* He skimmed to the back to see who had signed the complaint. It was anonymous. His mouth twisted into a knot. So what? That wasn't unusual in these situations. *Ahh wheeeeze.*

Nancy was coming down the hall, ready to bail him out of an unscheduled meeting.

Cal spun around and headed back. "Nancy, grab Steve DeMarko and send him to my office. I've got a special assignment for him to start working on."

THE RAIN POUNDED the earth, refusing to let Rachel and Josh take a leisurely stroll in dry clothes. Josh wanted to take a streetcar, but Rachel argued that standing outside waiting for one to come would get them as wet as walking. They ran for a yellow awning over the door of a shoe repair shop giving Rachel time to snap open her umbrella.

Other pedestrians scurried by avoiding puddles that shone with the reflection of the lights in the store windows. They headed out with Rachel holding her umbrella overhead but it wasn't large enough to cover them both. The first time she held it at an angle Josh felt the runoff flow down his collar. *Burrrrr.*

They stepped off the curb at Salmon Street, and crossing the road, entered the Park Blocks. A car zoomed through a slough whisking water from its tires but Josh pulled Rachel back in time to avoid the deluge.

"Thanks," she said.

They weren't conversing. The despair of Josh's story only deepened as they engaged the storm. Birds flittered in the branches, but they weren't singing. The only music in the air was the sound of cars whooshing by on both sides of the road.

"I'm sorry about your brother," Rachel finally said. "I can understand why your dad wouldn't talk to me about it. It must have been horrible for you."

"If I wanted to be calloused, I'd say my brother got what he deserved. I told him not to go, and I told him to wear a lifejacket. *Stupid.* Just plain stupid. A lifejacket would have kept his head above water and saved his life, but he never listened. He always pulled stunts like that. I don't think it ever occurred to him that he might get hurt, let alone die."

"I guess you can take consolation in the fact that he didn't. I mean, he was a Christian, right?"

"Right, well, at least that's how my mother sees it."

"What about your dad?"

Josh looked over, amused by the statement. "Dad, oh sure, he says he'll see Ted in Heaven, but I know he feels cheated. He wanted him here on Earth. Instead he got me."

"I'm sure your father loves you, Josh."

"Right." Josh didn't know whether his dad loved him or not, and truth be told, didn't care. All he felt was a sense of abandonment, like papa lion had taken his eldest and gone out hunting leaving momma lion to raise their youngest cub alone. "My father would have felt better if I were the one who died."

"Josh!"

"No, really. I heard him say it."

"Seriously? Come on."

"He did. It was at the funeral. He didn't know I was listening but I heard him say, 'Why did it have to be Ted?' He was crying on Mom's shoulder, I mean literally sobbing, and she was stroking his back like he was a baby that needed burping."

"He didn't say he'd rather it was you; just, why Ted?"

Pigeons pecking at discarded peanut husks took flight, their wings beating the air with the sound of helicopter blades. The rain tapping on the umbrella rolled off its rim. Josh squeezed his shoulders in to keep from getting wet. Rachel adjusted the umbrella to cover more of his side and slipped her arm through his to bring him closer, but Josh stiffened at her touch. "Your dad's a good man, but he's not perfect. You can't let him define who you are," she said, releasing his arm.

"Say again?"

"You're hurt because your dad seemed to favor your brother, and your dad's hurt because your brother was taken away, so you're both hurt. And it's like the old cliché, 'hurt people, hurt people,' so you're both still hurting each other. You're a Christian, Josh. You've got to look beyond that. Your hurt comes from letting your father define who you are when the only thing that matters is how God sees you. He's your real father."

"Tell it to my dad."

They stepped off the curb at Clay Street. Rachel saw the rain washing down the gutter and hopped over the flow, but Josh inadvertently stepped into it. The water overran his ankle, soaking into his tennis shoe. *Great!* Now every other step he took squished like a wet sponge. Why were people always telling him to act different because he was a Christian? He liked who he was. *Squish*, step, *squish*. That's what he got for entertaining drivel. "Okay counselor, but save the psychobabble for someone who cares."

"It's scripture Josh. We're here to please God, not just our earthly fathers. And one more thing. We're supposed to forgive, so even when your father hurts you, you have to forgive him. Only then will you be free enough to forgive yourself. Think about it."

I think I'd rather die; that's what I think. I didn't put Ted into that canoe. I just got blamed for it.

Josh washed up on a sandy shoal another hundred yards downriver. Three hundred feet, that's all Ted needed and they both could have climbed out on dry land. Three hundred feet, or a centillion lightyears to Heaven, that was Ted's choice. *You always took the hard way, didn't you,* Ted? Josh lay on his back looking up into the void of space *See you, brother, if that's where you are.* He was panting, hardly able to catch his breath. He sat up. He had to get help. They needed to get Ted's body out of that stream. How would he explain this to his mother? He closed his eyes and inhaled deeply, thankful that he wouldn't be the one telling his dad.

Josh rolled over and pushed himself up. The road was at the top of the gorge. He started to climb, forcing one foot after the other, his wet clothes sucking up dirt like tape in a sandbox. The ground broke loose, sending him back a few feet, his tennis shoes filling with gravel. He went down on one knee, breaking the skin, and sending loose rocks sliding down the steep slope. He wiped the blood away smearing dirt on the wound, then continued up, one foot after the other, sliding and slipping and pulling on loose roots and clumps of ferns until he reached the old logging road and stood on level ground. He didn't have time to think. They had to get Ted.

Josh half-limped and half-ran the next two miles, not stopping until he saw the cabin rising out of the clearing in the pines. He broke through the front door panting, expecting to find his mother, but instead saw his dad standing there, a mountain of stone, frowning. He leaned over with both hands on his knees, trying to catch his breath.

Ah huh, ah huh, ah huh. "You have to come now, *ah huh, ah huh,* There's, been an accident," *ah huh.*

"What? Slow down. What accident? Where?"

Ah huh, "you gotta come. Ted's been in an accident." *Ah huh.*

Bill stared at his son. The tea kettle on the stove began to whistle.

He went to extinguish the flame, his boots thudding across the plank floor. His keys were in his pocket but he felt the bulge in his jeans to make sure they were there as he headed for the door. "Well, don't just stand there, let's go."

Josh had to half skip, half run to keep up with his father's strides. His knee hurt. He cupped it with his hand as he climbed into the truck. "You're gonna need a rope to get him out. He's stuck."

Bill slammed the door, *bang*, and started the engine. "There's one in back. Take me to Ted."

Josh sat in silence as his father sped down the road, gravel crunching under the tires. The trees whisked by. Wind coming through the open window blew Josh's hair, the road dust filtering into the truck's cab. He had to tell his father that Ted was already dead. He just didn't know how.

Bill had both hands on the steering wheel, his knuckles turning white. He glanced to the side at Josh. "Okay, where is he?"

Suddenly it occurred to Josh that he didn't know. He'd come up out of the ravine and headed for the house without stopping to get a fix on his position. "I'm not sure," he said. "We were down by the river and Ted slipped and his foot got stuck so I went for help."

"You don't know where you were? Good golly, boy, you're smarter than that." Bill slowed the truck. "Okay, look around. You see anything that looks familiar? Anything you might have passed on your way up to the house?"

Josh stared out the window. "Shouldn't we have told Mom where we're going?"

"I got home two days early. She wasn't expecting me. She took the car into town for groceries."

Then it occurred to Josh. "Wait a minute. I was wearing a lifejacket, but I took it off when I reached the road. Look for an orange lifejacket. That's where I came up. I'm sure of it."

"Lifejacket? Why were you wearing a lifejacket?"

Josh looked down, realizing his mistake, but it was too late. He pushed hard on his knee as though the pain would make the truth easier to deliver. "Ted wanted to shoot the rapids. We were in the canoe and…"

"WHAT?"

"I told him not to, but he wouldn't listen…there it is. I see it. Over there." Through the dusty windshield Josh pointed at a lump of orange cloth by the side of the road.

Bill slammed on the brakes, dust flying past the truck as it slid to a stop. He pulled the brake handle. "You two are in big trouble." He opened the door and jumped out, going around back for the rope.

Josh collected the vest and threw it in the truck.

"Forget that. Take me to your brother."

Josh went to where the shoulder of the road fell off the side of the mountain, and stepped down. Bill followed with the coiled rope over his shoulder, both of them hanging onto trees and limbs to keep from slipping while sending loose bits of stone down the hill in small landslides. They reached the bottom. "Which way," Bill demanded.

"Upstream. I was wearing the vest so the river carried me further down, but not far. It's that way," Josh said pointing.

Bill stepped over a skinned log and started up the river, climbing over rocks and fallen trees. The river bellowed like thunder.

Josh was trying to keep up but it was useless. He raised his hands and cupped his mouth, shouting to be heard above the roar. "Dad, hold up! You need to know something."

"What?" Bill said, not looking back.

Beside a pounding waterfall, with the spray wetting his face, Josh let out what he'd been trying to say since they got into the truck. "I think Ted's gone, Dad! I think he's dead!"

Bill stopped, looking back over his shoulder. "What?" Then he smiled. "Ted put you up to this? Okay, big joke, but you're still in trouble, both of you."

Josh stood in the spray, his hair damp from the mist. He didn't move or say anything else.

Bill was still smiling as he grabbed an outcrop and pulled himself over the next boulder. *Stupid kids.* Standing atop its crown, he looked down at a place where two huge rocks pinched the water into a powerful flume. A shoe was sticking up out of the stream. The grin fell from his face. There, between those rocks, with the river cloaking him like a shroud, was the sodden body of Ted. Bill tried to understand what he was seeing. It didn't look real, more like a doll caught in the force of a firehose. He gazed at the sight for over a minute. Then he turned back to Josh. "How could you..." He cried.

The rain had stopped but it continued to drip from the trees forming tiny rings in the pools of water at their feet. Rachel kept the umbrella over their heads. A squirrel ran across the lawn leaving tracks in the wet dew. Josh turned to look at Rachel to get her reaction but her face was as blank as it was white. Her lip began to quiver. "Josh, your dad was in shock, maybe even in denial. He didn't know what he was saying."

"Right, I know, I've been over it a million times. The question is, why was that the first thing out of his mouth? He could have said anything, but his first thought was that I was somehow responsible for my brother's death." He shivered, folding his arms over his chest to keep warm.

"I think you're being too hard on him. He's still your father, and you still have to forgive him. That's not an option, at least not for us."

But Josh didn't want to forgive, and he certainly couldn't forget. He was done being backhanded by his father. And he didn't need pop-psychology to tell him how to behave.

Josh looked at Rachel. Her eyes were moist, the dripping of her umbrella like a second rain. Maybe she meant well, but it wasn't any of her business.

CAL TWISTED IN his seat, breathing deeply to relieve the burning sensation in his chest. Must have been the jalapeno laced chilidog he'd had for lunch. *Ahh wheeeeze.* They always gave him heartburn, but they tasted so good—*but never again*—though he'd said that a few times before. He brought a hand to his mouth and burped, then pressed his sternum to ease his discomfort. Doubly bad when combined with his asthma. He wanted to take an antacid but couldn't. His cardiologist said his aortic valve was becoming calcified. *Oooooh.*

Another flow of stomach acid surged into his esophagus.

He took a deep breath *Ahh wheeeeze,* and brought his inhaler to his mouth sucking the relief into his lungs. His wheezing subsided. He waited expecting more, but the air passage had cleared. The folder was lying on his desk. He had to read the articles. He flipped it open. Several newspaper clippings slid into his hand. "Know thy enemy." That hadn't come from the NSA; that came from the ancient Chinese general Sun Tzu. He placed the articles on his desk, arranging them in order by date. *Oooooooh,* his chest constricted, burning like molten lead. The heartburn was back. He needed those antacids. He didn't relish the idea of reading a bunch of nonsense. If the man was so foolish as to think climate change wasn't real, then he was certifiably nuts, so why bother? *Know thy enemy. Right.* He might as well get to it. He drew the first of the articles in and read the headline.

"Why I'm Not A Climate Change Denier."

Okay, maybe the guy's not as nuts as they say. His eyes continued to scan the page.

"It may surprise some of my readers to find that I'm not a climate change denier, though it's a hat I'm often accused of wearing. Allow me to set the record straight. I am an environmentalist. I love this planet. I love the mountains, the skies and seas, and every creature that flies swims or runs. I love everything God has created. When we look at the changes taking place in our environment I seek to find a rational explanation and wholly support every effort made, within reason, to protect nature against capital destruction.

"It's the within reason part where I differ from many of my colleagues. I want to be given an unbiased look at the situation and be offered a sensible pathway to its solution. Unfortunately, it seems today's scientists, and their political puppeteers, would rather scare me into submission than win me over with facts. Science, I am told, says the earth is overheating. To question this makes me either ignorant or naive.

"But therein lies the rub.

"An often cited justification for spending a proposed fifty trillion dollars to alter the effects of climate change, is that an overwhelming number of scientists believe this is necessary. This idea comes from a 2013 Cook review where it was found that out of nearly twelve-thousand studies on climate change, only seventy-eight explicitly rejected the notion that humans are responsible for global warming. (Note that word 'explicitly,' because it's important, but we'll come back to that in a minute.) Thus it was concluded that the vast majority of scientists believe climate change is wrought by man, case closed, argument over.

"Well, not so fast.

"When you take a close look at the Cook review, you find that sixty-six percent of the studies voiced no opinion as to whether or not global warming was caused or produced by humans. In fact it turns out only sixty-five of the roughly twelve-thousand papers 'explicitly' stated that man contributed to climate change, a smaller number than those that explicitly said man didn't. But that's not what you've heard, is it?

"Another study conducted by Purdue University revealed that forty-seven percent of climatologists challenge the idea that humans are the primary reason for climate change. So the idea that the argument is over is nonsense. It's misinformation, and it leads me to question everything, especially since most of what I hear is alarmism designed to scare people into accepting facts not in evidence.

"I was a young man when Stanford University Professor, Paul Ehrlich, wrote, *The Population Bomb*. His book opened with the following statement: 'The battle to feed all of humanity is over. In the 1970s hundreds of millions of people will starve to death in spite of any crash programs embarked upon now. At this late date nothing can prevent a substantial increase in the world death rate...'

"Ehrlich went on to propose we add 'temporary sterilants' to the water supply, that men receive compensation for agreeing to permanent sterilization, and that legislation be passed to guarantee every woman an abortion. 'The mother of the year,' he wrote, 'should be a sterilized woman with two adopted children.'

"Ehrlich's book sold over two million copies, all based on alarmism. He manipulated data and inflated numbers to scare people into believing an inordinate part of the world's population would die of hunger in the 1970's. But the starvation he predicted never occurred. Instead, over the years the percentage of undernourished people in the world has been reduced by more than half, from thirty-three percent to about sixteen percent.

"That was the opening salvo of a long list of doomsayers predicting an end to life as we know it. Fortunately, their prophecies have never come true.

"Remember the ozone hole? If you do, you remember being told that the ozone layer in our atmosphere, the layer that protects life from harmful ultraviolet radiation, was being depleted. 'Everyone should be alarmed about this,' Michael Kurylo, manager of upper-atmosphere research at NASA said. 'It's far worse than we thought.'

"We heard doctors were being inundated with patients experiencing sun related skin rashes, farmers described heat damage to their crops, and ranchers claimed their livestock were being blinded by radiation. Scientists around the world came together to analyze the problem and find a solution.

"In 1974, a paper was published claiming that chlorofluorocarbons used in spray bottles were destroying the ozone. The discovery earned Paul Crutzen, Mario Molina, and F. Sherwood Rowland, the Nobel Peace Prize.

"The world panicked and banned the use of sprays containing chlorofluorocarbons. The 'Beacon Journal' wrote that the discovery was so alarming it changed U.S. policy.

"Those who are as old as I am will remember all the hoopla and hyperbole that surrounded this perceived threat, but ask your kids if they've ever heard of the ozone hole and you'll find them shaking their heads. So where did the ozone hole go? Well, some say regulations against the use of chlorofluorocarbons in cans of hairspray saved the day, others claim that changes in our climate filled the hole back in. The point is that the whole world panicked at the shrinking of this invisible layer surrounding our planet, but eventually the scare went away and nothing more was said.

"Skip forward to Al Gore, the face of Global Warming. Al traveled around the world warning anyone who would listen, of the dangers presented by the increasing temperature of our planet. His claims were so well received, in 2007 he also received a Nobel Peace Prize. In his acceptance speech he said there was a seventy-five percent chance that the entire polar ice cap would melt within the next five to seven years, (which should have happened between 2012 and 2014). Instead, according to a report by the Danish Meteorological Institute, during those same years the Arctic ice cap expanded two years in a row, a trend confirmed by the U.S. National Snow and Ice Data Center. Al's prophecies included exaggerated numbers about the extinction of polar bears, and the swamping of coastal cities after melting ice caused the oceans to rise; all delivered to us with a specter of alarmism.

"It is in similar fashion that we're now being told we must spend fifty trillion dollars to eliminate the use of fossil fuels, and that not doing so will bring our planet to a catastrophic end. Having heard such arguments before, I feel like a character in, 'The Boy Who Cried Wolf,' one of Aesop's Fables. The moral of the story is that when your calls for alarm prove to be false you stop being taken seriously.

"We've been warned about the dangers of Global Cooling, the China Syndrome, the Ozone Hole, Y2K, Global Warming, and Climate Change. We just keep going from one world crisis to the next, without ever seeing any of the doomsday prophesies fulfilled. Personally, I thank God for that.

"Climate change is a natural force of nature, and it is real. How much man contributes to it is still up for debate. We're not being given all the facts. We're just urged to get on board or risk global annihilation. It's at this point that I step off the climate change bus. No, I'm not a climate change denier, but I have become a climate change skeptic."

Okay, the guy is nuts. Cal slipped the article back into the folder. His team was auditing Mr. Best, but they needed more information.

Ohhhaaa. More acid tried to escape his stomach. The pain was excruciating. He could hardly breathe. *Awwwww. It'll clear in a minute. But no more chilidogs, I swear!* He closed his eyes, waiting for the attack to pass. His hands were flat on his desk, his fingers splayed. As he felt the pressure ease he began taking long slow breaths until he could breathe normally again. *No more chilidogs, ever!*

He leaned into his computer, clicked his mouse to open his word program, and began typing a letter to Mr. William Best.

JOSH MADE HIS way to the back of the pub. He was late. After saying goodbye to Rachel, he'd attempted to do a load of laundry but it had taken longer than planned. Ron was already halfway through his presentation. His computer was open and plugged into a projection system which displayed the same graph he had shown Josh earlier that day.

Marie jumped out of her chair. "Oh Josh, thank God," she squealed, throwing her hands into the air. "Ron told us you'd be here." She ran over and hugged him, holding him tightly with her face buried in his chest. "I was worried. I thought you were in jail." He could smell her hair and feel the pounding of her heart through her shirt. The heat was so intense he thought he might melt.

"Hey guys, okay if I finish my presentation?"

"Sorry, Ron, you're right. Go ahead. Josh come sit with me." Marie took Josh by the hand and led him to the table where her chair was waiting. They were using the back half of the Cheerful Tortoise bar and grill, an official college hangout, but there weren't more than a half dozen people in the room. Only one or two were wearing masks. Covid was out and climate change in, Josh surmised.

"As I was saying, it's not that we have to completely do away with fossil fuels," Ron continued. "We can heat our cities with solar and wind power, and use a combination of gas and batteries for transportation. Now if you look at the cost implications…"

The door burst open again and Molly, one of the girls Josh had met at the Christmas party, rushed in with several leter-size boxes wrapped in her arms. "I got 'em. This is awesome. They look great," she announced.

"Let me see," Marie said, jumping up once more to inspect what Molly was holding.

Molly lay the four boxes on the table in front of Ron's laptop. Each held a ream of paper. From where he was sitting, Josh couldn't see what they were looking at.

"Does anyone want to listen to the rest of my presentation?" Ron quipped.

"Just a second, Ron, this is important. Look at this." Marie took the top sheets from each box and held them up side by side. Josh read the headline before looking at the picture. One read, "Wanted: Dead or Alive," the other, "Public Enemy Number One," and both had a photo—*of his dad!*

TWELVE

BILL CAME THROUGH the mudroom kicking off his boots and hanging his coat on a peg. Two smells greeted his nose: the wood-smoke from the fireplace, and the aroma of the garlic tomato sauce Mary had simmering on the stove. He felt the warmth of each, and would have normally begun to relax, but this time neither could ease the unsettled feeling in his gut. He'd gone to the post office for their mail and inside his box found a note saying they were holding a registered letter for him at the front desk. He had signed for the letter but had yet to see what it was about. Bill walked to the kitchen in his stocking feet, his hand holding the bundle of mail which he deposited on the counter. Raking tree stumps out of the ground and dragging them into piles to be burned was feudal labor. He was a walking ball of soot in desperate need of a shower.

Mary was at the stove with her apron tied around her waist, stirring a large pot that had steam rising up to the hooded vent. He had to put on a good face, as though nothing were wrong. He went over and placed his hands on her shoulders, turning her around.

She used the back of her hand to push the hair off her forehead, hooking it behind her ear.

"Hi doll," he said, leaning in to give her a kiss.

She reciprocated but kept her hands between them, then pushed him back. "Go take a shower; dinner's almost ready."

Bill grunted but didn't leave. Instead he went to the wheelchair where his daughter sat reading a book. Angie's aptitude was never in question. On every intelligence quota she scored well above average.

111

Her muscular coordination was spasmodic, her arms flinging out when excited, her legs curling reflexively, but she read more books each year than most people did in a lifetime.

"Hey, sweet girl, how you doing?" he said bending down to kiss the top of her head. "Looks like you're about ready for another trip to the library."

Angie's head twisted back, her jaw tweaked to the side, her smile big as the sunrise. "Yaaaaeeessssss," she squealed.

"Well then, how 'bout early next week?" He tossed her hair playfully and went to the counter to go through the mail he'd brought home, separating out those addressed to him.

"Where's Rachel?" he asked, as he sorted through the envelopes and shopping flyers.

Mary looked over her shoulder, wiping steam from her brow with the back of her hand. "She's in her room. The new semester just started and she's already waist deep in work to do."

"Yeah, I remember the good old college days. Seemed every teacher piled on the work like theirs was the only class you were taking. Alright, I'm off to the showers," he said. He gathered up his mail and went to his study, tossing the envelopes onto his desk, perhaps a little too hard as they slid up against the base of the old-world clock. Bill reached under the green convex glass and pulled the chain of his lamp, snapping it on. His curiosity was killing him, but he'd waited this long, he could wait a moment longer. He reached over to close the door.

Turning around, he stared at his computer's black screen and considered whether or not to check his emails to see if there were any more comments about his latest podcast. He decided against. Most of his followers were dyed in the wool patriots with strongly held Christian beliefs. His views would have come as no surprise to them. Some questioned his timing, saying the apostles believed they would live to see Christ's return, and since men have always believed the return of Jesus was eminent, there was no reason to get excited about it now. He would deal with those in future podcasts. A few however thought, as one man expressed, he must have fallen from a tree and hit his head on a rock.

He fished in his drawer for his letter opener. There were only five pieces of mail and three were bills which he opened and set aside for payment later. He sat down, pushing his chair back on its casters giving him room to put his feet up on his desk so he could read the other two. The return address of one was that of his insurance company, probably something to do with his claim. He set it aside. The other was the letter he had signed for. The envelope bore the logo of the Internal Revenue Service. *What's this about?* He hadn't paid his taxes yet, but they weren't due until April. He leaned back and shook the letter open.

William Best Holdings
P.O. Box 225
Tantamoa, OR 27298

Mr. William Best

Pursuant to complaints filed against William Best Holdings received by this department, we are hereby advising you of an external audit currently being conducted by the Internal Revenue Service. To facilitate this audit we are authorized to demand all documents pertaining to:

Financial and Income Statements
Charitable Donations
Investments and Annuities
Loans and Debentures
Claims and Settlements
Business Asset Sales and Purchases

Please provide records as per the above for the past three years. And note that time is of the essence. The requested documents must be received by this office within thirty days of receipt of this letter. Failure to comply may result in the seizure and/or forfeiture of all personal and company assets.

Regards,

Calvin B. Moody

Criminal Investigation Division
Internal Revenue Service

"What the Heck!" Bill stood, gripping the letter so hard it furled at the corners. He didn't have time to assemble three years of financial history. Did they know what they were asking? *Complaints?* Has to be a mistake. Should he tell Mary? No, best to keep her out of the loop. She was already stressed-out about the fire. He'd bring her in once he knew what this was about. He slipped the letter into his drawer. Arching his back he pushed his knuckles into his lumbar to ease the ache. His cheeks felt like sandpaper and his hair like soot and grease. He left his office, unbuttoning his shirt, and headed for the shower. Mary didn't like it when she had to serve the food cold.

IT HAD BEEN raining all week so on Friday, when the sun finally made an appearance, it provided welcome relief. Josh scratched his scalp and felt his hair warm his fingers. He was wearing his hoodie with the top down, allowing the sun to toast his head. But even though the rains had been blown out to sea and the sun now dominated the sky, walking about town was still unsettling.

From every angle, Josh saw his father staring at him, his face nailed to trees in the park, taped to lampposts along the curb, and front and center in the windows of stores along the street. He had helped put those posters up, working late into the evening with Marie and half a dozen other students to blanket the Park Blocks area of Portland, always anticipating that at any moment someone might say, "hey, this guy looks like you," but they didn't. While he shared his father's DNA, he looked much more like his mom. But it could still happen and it made him nervous. What would he say? My dad's Hitler, so what? He didn't think either Ted Bundy or Charles Manson had children, but if they did he knew how those kids felt. They couldn't tell their friends their dads were serial killers, any more than he could say his believed the devil was ready to take over the world.

And he didn't need to see his dad's face everywhere reminding him of their failed relationship. For once, he was glad it was Portland's rainy season. Half the posters had become soggy and blurred and some had fallen from their anchors. He could see several stuck to the ground ahead of him. With any luck they'd soon all disappear.

The wind came up tossing his hair but he smoothed it with his fingers as he stepped into Cascades Coffee. He hadn't seen Marie all week. He should have asked for her phone number but he'd wimped out, though they'd come here for coffee after the poster hanging event. He was hoping to bump into her at random and, if the mood was right, and the opportunity presented itself, perhaps he would ask her on a date. Maybe it was wishful thinking, but wishes could come true.

He looked into the darkness, his eyes adjusting to the dim interior.

"Josh?"

He twisted around and saw Rachel sitting at a table behind him, the only person he didn't want to see. She knew him by his real name. She might slip and use it around one of his friends.

"Josh, I'm glad I bumped into you," she said, indicating she wanted him to join her by reaching for a chair and pulling it back.

Josh felt trapped, but maybe if Marie came in, she'd see him with a pretty girl and get the wrong idea. Jealousy could work in his favor. He sat down.

"Have you seen those awful posters? I wanted to tell you how bad I feel about what they're doing to your father's reputation. It must be hard on you."

My father? See. What if she says that around someone else? Josh felt his tongue catch in his throat. He stared into her eyes, keeping his face void of expression.

"Does your dad know about this?"

There, she did it again. Her sweatshirt was dark blue similar to the one he was wearing. Was she imitating him? Now he was being silly.

"Doubt it. I just saw those things myself. I've been really busy. What are you doing here?"

"Oh, your mom thought I might be getting bored so she loaned me her car and said I should do some shopping. I remembered this place so I came here, but I was shocked to see all those horrible pictures of your dad. They're everywhere."

And again! He started to get up. "Sorry, you caught me at a bad time, I have to go." Josh turned to leave, but Rachel rose up like his shadow.

"I'll walk with you," she said. "It'll give us a chance to catch up."

Josh didn't want to catch up. His dad's face was everywhere. He couldn't have her pointing to one of those posters and making the connection public. She followed him outside into the sun. *Now what?* How do you scold someone's who's only trying to be nice? He needed to explain the ramifications of what she was doing. She was easy to talk to, she'd understand, and the faint smell of her perfume was catching. But she could also blow his cover. He stopped, turning to face her. Those doll blue eyes and baby's-breath skin shattered his resolve.

A guy wearing shorts and a lime green Seahawks basketball jersey pumped by in tennis shoes white as the clouds. His hair looked like brown grass dancing in the wind. He glanced to the side as he passed, did a double-take, and backed up. "Rachel?" he said.

She turned at the sound of her name, her eyes brightening with recognition. "Oh, hi Jim."

Their faces were animated, amiable and familiar, but Josh couldn't tell if they were just being sociable or whether something else was going on.

"Hey, I wanted to tell you, that comment you made about Israel's ultimate reconciliation was bang on." The man was a few inches taller than Josh, maybe six-foot-three, and willowy. Probably a basketball player.

"Thank you. I appreciate that. Oh, sorry, I'm being rude." She turned to Josh and placed her hand on his shoulder. "Josh, this is Jim. He's new around here and he just started attending the same church as your parents, which, of course, is where I'm going now. We attend the young adult Bible study together."

Clouds had been building on the horizon. The first to make it inland slipped in front of the sun, turning it five degrees cooler and several shades deeper gray.

Jim smiled at Josh and chuckled. "Rachel's the teacher's pet. She makes comments about things even he doesn't know."

"Do not."

"Yes you do, and that's no joke, it's a compliment. Listen, I'm glad I caught you. Some of us have formed an interdenominational Bible study group, not a social thing, for serious Bible students only. We'd love to have you join us. I think you'd have a lot to contribute."

Rachel tossed her head back looking at the cloud for a moment, her hair falling long and yellow over her shoulders. The cloud moved off, blinding her with sun and making her squint. She nodded and looked at Jim. "You know, I think I'd like that. When do you meet?"

"Right now. I was just on my way over. You should come."

"Now?" She glanced at her watch. "Alright, I guess I can do that." Rachel looked at Josh, her eyes soft and apologetic. "Josh, why don't you come too. It'll be fun."

He shook his head. Fun wasn't a word he'd use to describe a Bible study. "Some other time," he said. "I have to go."

"You sure? Alright then," she flicked him a wave as they moved away.

Josh watched her go, but he couldn't help wondering how a girl he hardly knew could get him to confide so many things he'd never told anyone else, and how someone he'd wanted to get rid of only a few moments before, could leave him feeling so all alone.

BEHIND THE BEST'S cabin was a screened-in porch. The room itself was a simple frame construction with windows on runners that let in light and slid to the side to provide air on warm summer nights. Bill had installed baseboard heaters to keep the room comfortable in winter. The floor was a slab of cement covered with an outdoor carpet that resembled a green plastic lawn. Mary had asked Bill to paint the interior walls a coral pink.

This was primarily her room. Bill had built it at her request because she wanted a place where she could sit and relax in the cool of the evening. And she had insisted on being given full reign of the décor. She had no issue with the rest of the house, the fact that it was all Cowboys and Indians, but she wanted one room, besides their bed and bathroom, that had a more feminine touch. She had decided on a tropical theme, even though it was incongruous with the rest of the house. She'd gone out and purchased two white wicker chairs with cushions that had a green palm-frond pattern. A white wicker table with a glass top was positioned in front of the chairs with several travel magazines and a large conch shell. Potted palms stood in each of the corners, and the beams that supported the corrugated roof had hooks with macramé hangings of ferns and grape ivy. Overhead, Bill had installed a Casablanca style fan with four fluted lights.

Bill sat in one of the wicker chairs listening to the rain tapping on the corrugated steel roof. He had his Bible open on his lap considering how Isaac had loved Esau because he was a hunter, but his wife, Rebekah, had loved Jacob, and Jacob was God's choice. That's how it worked with him and Mary. He had loved Ted while Mary favored Josh. Was Josh God's choice, too?

Earlier that morning he had gone out fishing for the second time. The sun was yellow and the water blue. It was a perfect day until a storm front moved in and ended the excursion, but the experience had been cathartic. He'd realized that his fear was unwarranted. He'd always presumed being on the water with a fishing pole in his hand would elicit heartbreak. Instead he'd found himself fishing for the joy of fishing. He had Rachel to thank for that.

He'd even let the canoe drift to the end of the lake, right up to where the waters began their thunderous roar, breaking through the rocks on their way to the Pacific. He'd thought of it many times but was never able to fully accept his part in the death of his son, until now. Ted knew those engaged in white-water rafting used rubber rafts or kayaks but he had chosen the Chinook because his dad had said the Chinook was unsinkable. Bill had to take ownership of that. Ted was just doing what Ted always did, seeking a thrill without counting the cost.

Mary was sitting in the second wicker chair with her feet curled up beneath her and a light throw covering her lap. She took a sip of her coffee and set the cup back on the table, the ceramic mug chinking on the glass top. "Penny for your thoughts," she said, pulling the throw up to cover her shoulders.

Bill closed his Bible and brought his hands together in his lap, his mouth puckering. He nodded. "I can't explain it," he said, "but ever since I went fishing this morning, I've been thinking about Josh." He looked over at his wife. "I think I've lost him, Mary. Not like Ted, but he's gone just the same."

"What brought that on?"

"Like I said, fishing. I was just thinking how nice it would be to have Josh out there with me."

"Don't get confused. Ted was your fisherboy, not Josh. I hope you're not planning some scheme to get Josh out on the water, because I can assure you, it'll backfire."

"No, nothing like that."

Mary leaned into the table to retrieve her mug. She took a sip of her tea and set it down, pulling the blanket up again as she relaxed into the cushion of the chair. "You can't mold Josh into your own image. He's not like you. You want him to be Ted, but he isn't. He's sensitive. You want a man's man, but he's a momma's boy and you need to accept that."

Bill let out his breath, nodding. "I was hoping for a little sympathy, but I guess I deserve the rebuke."

Mary brought her arm out from under her blanket to push the hair off her forehead. She smiled. "No you don't deserve rebuke, and I'm sorry if it sounded that way. It's just, I wish you could accept Josh for who he is. Oh, look."

Three deer had entered the yard, their noses touching the ground as they sniffed the grass. It wasn't unusual, but always welcome. A couple of times a month Bill put out salt licks and corn husks, and sometimes even a basket of rotten apples, to help the deer get through winter. They passed by the windows of the screened-in porch taking no notice of the occupants inside. They were heading for the garage where Bill left the treats.

"Where's Rachel? I bet she'd like to see this," Bill said.

"In her room. I've never seen anyone so in love with schoolwork."

"That's probably for the best, and Angie?"

"Down for a nap, why?"

The rain had stopped, but Bill could see residual beads of water clinging to the backs of the deer. It looked like crystalline jewelry. The doe was older than the two young males. Mature bucks rarely came down into the yard. They chose to remain out of sight behind the trees and tangles of blackberry. But younger males were often seen. These were probably in their first year, not yet fully grown but no longer wearing the spots of a fawn. The deer wandered off out of sight.

"We need to talk, and it's probably better if we're alone."

Mary glanced over at Bill. His appearance had grown sullen and apprehensive. "Bill? What's wrong?"

"I've been waiting for the right moment to tell you about this, but with Rachel staying here and Angie always underfoot, it's hard to find a moment to talk privately."

"Now you're making me nervous."

Bill smiled warmly and reached out, taking her hand. "It's probably nothing, but the other day I received a letter from the IRS. They're subpoenaing our financial records. They want to do an audit. It seems someone's complained that we aren't managing out charitable donations properly."

Mary dropped Bill's hand and sat up, letting her throw slide down from her shoulders. "Complaint? Who would complain about us? We do everything by the book, including not taking salaries. Everything we make goes to charity…"

"I called and tried to find out who filed the complaint, in case there was some kind of misunderstanding we could work out, but I ran into a brick wall. They say they have to keep their sources confidential. It doesn't matter, the fact is we're being audited and we have to give them our financial records for the past three years."

Mary sunk back into her chair. "That's ridiculous. Who would want to complain about us? All we do is help people. First the fire, and now this…" She paused as the thought grew. "Oh Bill, you don't think they're connected, do you?" She looked at her husband for reassurance.

"Bill's face furrowed, but he shook his head. "You mean, do I think the group responsible for the fire also filed a complaint with the IRS? I can't say I haven't thought about it, but no, I don't think so. It doesn't matter anyway. We're not battling men. You know the verse, 'we wrestle not against flesh and blood…' When things happen in rapid sequence, you start to feel like Job, and we know Satan was behind that. But my concern is not for myself; it's for my family. I'm willing to take the heat, because I know God's going to win in the end, but I am sorry it has to involve you and Angie, and probably Rachel too, if she stays with us for any length of time, but in her case that's already happening, because that's why she's here…"

"Bill."

"What?"

Mary closed her eyes and sipped in a breath, letting it out slowly and audibly. "I can't support you in this. I don't have the strength…"

"I know, Mary, I…"

"Wait. Let me finish. I can't, but I know God can. You're a good man, Bill Best. You just keep on fighting the good fight and let God take care of me and Angie, and Rachel too, of course, as long as she's here."

"Honey, I don't want this to touch any of you, and I'm pretty sure it won't. Once they see our books, this will all go away. Which reminds me. I was able to retrieve the data from our backup files on the server, all except this year's transactions. You have those still on your flash drive, don't you?" Bill saw the expression on his wife's face and knew the answer.

"On no, Bill, please don't hate me. I mean, yes they were on my flash drive, but no, I don't have them. My flash drive was lost in the fire."

THIRTEEN

CAL STARED AT the cartons on his desk—five file-size boxes containing reams of paper—and sighed, *wheezing,* glad he wasn't the one going through them. *A least the man's prompt,* he thought. He reached for his phone and punched in the extension of Steve DeMarko.

"Steve, stop what you're doing and get down here; I have a present for you," he said, hanging up before Steve had a chance to respond. An envelope was taped to the top box. He reached for his scissors and cut it loose. Steve could handle all the grunt work. He was more interested in what the man had to say.

Cal had interrupted Steve in the middle of dictating a letter to one of several witnesses he wanted to interview. He had developed a list based on the known associates of William Best, which included companies he purchased supplies from, directors of charities he was supposed to give money to, and the pastor of the church where Bill attended services. Steve was hoping one of them might know something about Mr. Best that a strict crunch of the numbers couldn't reveal. It was possible. Many men had secret lives—*gambling addictions, expensive mistresses, cocaine habits*—things that might lead them to embezzle money. It wouldn't be hard to figure out if someone thought Bill was showing signs of guilt, or of displaying inappropriate or clandestine behavior.

So far, his forensic analysis had yielded zilch. When it came to paying his taxes, Mr. Best crossed every T and dotted every I. If it were up to him, they'd close the investigation now. He couldn't understand why

Cal was so anxious to move forward with this. They had dozens of cases where the tax fraud was obvious, why single out this guy? Steve held his miniature voice activated recorder to his lips as he hustled down the hall. "I'll call next week to set a time and date and look forward to meeting with you then."

He stepped into Cal's office, saw the boxes and instantly knew what they were. "So you got them. That's gonna put my interviews off a week. You really think we're going to find something we missed? I mean, far as I can tell, this guy is squeaky clean."

"No he's not. You're just not digging deep enough." *Wheeze, ah wheeze.* Cal pressed a hand to his chest and reached into his drawer for his inhaler.

"Nuts. If I dig any deeper I'll be in China. What's with you on this? We haven't found anything worth investigating. Any other case would have been dropped by now. Instead you have me flying out to do interviews, which we never do unless there's evidence of maleficence. With all due respect, I think we're wasting our time."

Wheeze, ah, wheeze. Cal pinched his nose, bumping his glasses off-kilter, his eyes watering. He took another hit on his inhaler and felt the air flow into his lungs. "Look, Steve, this doesn't leave this office, right? It's not me calling the shots here. This comes from the top, and I mean all the way to the Whitehouse. They want us to find something on this guy, even if we have to make it up. But we won't because this Bill Best guy is hiding something. I can feel it. That's why I've got you on it. You're ruthless, and tenacious. You get hold of something, you don't let go. Just do your job. And get these boxes off my desk; I've got work to do."

Cal dabbed his watery eyes with a tissue and realigned his glasses, waiting while Steve removed the last box from his office, then reached for the envelope to see what Mr. Best had to say. The letter slid into his hand. He shook it open.

Calvin Moody
Criminal Investigation Division
Internal Revenue Service

123

Dear Mr. Moody,

In compliance with your request, we have assembled all financial records going back three years. I expect you will find all is in order. There is however, one omission. From April of last year to the present, the files are missing. This is due to a fire we suffered last November which destroyed our computer. We usually do regular backups of our data, but during this period we failed to do so, and thus had not backed up the data since last April when we prepared our taxes.

Our business remains closed from January to November so there were no sales to report during this period. We did incur expenses, like the trees we purchased for planting, fertilizer, machine maintenance, etc., but I have hard copy receipts for these items which you will find enclosed. Our selling season is limited to the months of November and December. We were in fact only open a few days before the fire struck and hence, you are missing only the few days of sales we had right after Thanksgiving. For this, we have supplied the bank deposit slip and hope this will suffice.

I trust you will find this sufficient.

Be Blessed,

Bill Best
William Best Holdings, Inc.

Be blessed? Oh yeah, I'll be blessed when I see you in jail. Cal clapped his hands together. No information from April till now. *I knew it. He's hiding something.* He picked up his phone and called Steve DeMarko's extension.

"Steve, get down here. There's something you need to see!"

TWO WEEKS CAME and went before Josh saw Marie again. He tried querying his roommate as to her whereabouts, but Ron was so taken with his new girlfriend, Cheri, he'd lost touch with Marie. "Out saving the planet somewhere," was all he said.

He was on his way back from having coffee with Rachel, something they'd done several times because she was good at conversation and because it made his mom happy, when he spotted Marie in front of the Millar Library standing on the brown grass of the Park Blocks, passing out flyers. Josh had seen several others up and down the Blocks doing the same, but he'd passed them by. He didn't need another piece of paper to carry around, but now he had to know what this was about. He stayed under the branches of the leafless trees, avoiding puddles, with his eyes fixed on Marie. He was hoping at any moment she would see him and rush to give him a hug, but she was preoccupied and didn't look his direction. In her red blouse and matching slacks she looked like a cardinal feeding her chicks. Some refused her offer, but those that accepted generally nodded in approval and shared a few words of encouragement before moving on.

Josh looked at his watch. If he stopped to talk he would be late for his Zoom meeting with other students taking a class on Culture, Imperialism, and Globalization, which as far as he could tell had little to do with literature, but was nonetheless on the schedule of courses for English majors.

Marie spun to the right, and then to the left, trying to get her document into as many hands as possible. Josh felt his heart palpitating, a deep burn welling in his chest. Ron had been right; she was out trying to save the planet. It hurt that she hadn't tried to solicit his help. Of course she didn't have his number, but she could have asked his roommate.

The sun shone down through the trees creating puzzle patterns on the grass. Sparrows hopped along the sidewalks looking for tidbits to eat. A young man dove to catch a Frisbee. Most of the days in February were overcast, so it was special that today should be full of sun. Marie's dark brunette hair glistened in the light, her bright red lipstick shimmering with every smile. He would marry this girl if she gave him the chance.

Josh came up behind her and was handed a flyer, but Marie quickly turned to give another flyer to someone else.

"Hi Marie," he said, in a woeful attempt to announce himself.

She spun around. "Josh, oh, I didn't see you; I'm glad you're here. Here, take a stack of these and start passing them out." She peeled off a stack of leaflets and thrust them in his direction.

Josh backed up. "Woah, I can't," he said raising his hands, palms out as if to push her away. "I've got a class. I just saw you and wanted to say hi."

Marie reached out to shove another pamphlet into the hand of a girl with a Miniature Schnauzer on a leash. The dog sniffed her leg while the girl opened the flyer, and then handed it back. "Sorry, not interested," she said.

"I thought you came to help." Marie said, addressing Josh again.

Josh put his thumbs under the straps of his backpack to ease it off his shoulders. "I would have, if you'd called. I didn't know anything about it."

Marie continued reaching around him to pass out flyers, making him feel like he was in the way. He backed up another step, giving her room.

"Maybe we could exchange numbers and keep in touch."

Marie swirled around and handed a flyer to someone trying to squeeze between them. "Good idea," she said, "but I'm kinda busy right now and this is really important. We have to make sure everyone knows. How about I see you at the demonstration? We'll do it then."

Josh glanced at his flyer, trying to grasp her meaning. "Right, okay good, I'll see you then." He moved away, underwhelmed by her enthusiasm. If she regretted not seeing him, she masked it well. *Saturday? That's tomorrow.* At least he knew where she'd be, and she'd said they could exchange numbers, so it was a win.

He picked up his pace pulling his backpack up on his shoulder, the saturated grass feeling spongy under his feet. He started to jog while trying to read the flyer but it was no use, "Stop Jack Palco from speaking in Portland," was all he saw before it folded across his hand. He'd have to read the rest later.

The lecture had started by the time he got his computer turned on and was seated at his desk. The small apartment smelled like sweaty

socks, the warm sun streaming through the window creating a tropical humidity. Josh got up and went to the kitchen for a glass of water.
When he returned, his professor's talking head filled the screen of his
laptop. It looked like she was waving the same flyer he'd received from
Marie but it was mostly out of view. Her blond hair was parted in the
center so that it hung down to her ears on both sides where it was
cropped short. It looked like someone had placed a bowl on her head
and cut the hair beneath it all the way around. The lenses of her glasses
were two large circles over small dark eyes.

"This is what I'm talking about," she said, apparently continuing a
rant she'd already begun. "This germ, this malignant piece of trash, is
coming to Portland. Now I don't know about you, but when someone
comes to my town preaching that gays should be kept in the closet, and
blacks should still be picking cotton, and women should be kept barefoot and pregnant in the kitchen, I have to scream, NO! I want them
tarred and feathered and run out of town. Portland is an enlightened
city, we are blessed, so it's up to us to draw a line in the sand. We're
compelled to say no to bigotry, no to racism, no to misogyny, no, no,
no, not here, not now, not ever! If you learn nothing else in this class
this semester, learn this: oppression is a thing of the past. We're not
cave dwellers dragging our women around by the hair. This has to stop.
We don't want Mr. Palco bringing his draconian ideas to Portland, or
anywhere else for that matter.

"I expect to see each and every one of you at this rally. And since
we're here to learn about culture, imperialism, and globalization, I'm
going to give those who attend five points extra-credit. We're going to
close the door on this capitalist clown. Remember it's at the Downtown Bigtree this Saturday. And you might want to bring a sleeping
bag, because no matter how long it takes, we're going to shut this place
down."

Professor Goodall went back to her lectern and clicked her computer mouse. A PowerPoint slide appeared on the screen. "Now, let's
look at what happens to societies who fall prey to Imperialism."

Josh slouched in his chair, extending his legs with his feet crossed at
the ankles and his arms folded over his chest. The name Jack Palco was

familiar. He was a conservative talk show host, one his dad listened to, and though Josh hadn't actually paid close attention, what he'd heard from time-to-time seemed benign. But Marie would be there, and his professor was giving extra credit for going, so why not?

THE SOUND OF water gushing from the bathroom tap woke Josh. He pulled his pillow over his head. It was Saturday, why couldn't they let him sleep? A belt of sun was pouring through the window, un-usual for February in Portland, especially two days in a row. He kicked off his blankets and stood, stooping to look out the window to see if there were clouds on the horizon, but the day looked clear. Down in the plaza he saw trees bending in the wind, an indication that it might be cool outside. Sheets of yellow paper scuffed up and swirled around, dancing on the breeze. Probably photos of his dad, or maybe their new antagonist, Palco.

He grabbed his jeans off the floor and slipped them on, buckling his belt. He'd lost a few pounds. His stomach was flat, his loss of ap-petite the result of the bennies he was taking. He didn't need them, but the only time he had to study was at night, and they did help him stay awake.

Ron came out of the bathroom in his boxers with his bellybutton on display. He had a toothbrush in his mouth, pumping it up and down. "Mornif," he said, with toothpaste dribbling onto his beard. He turned and went back to his morning routine. Josh heard voices and knew Cheri was with him.

Josh scratched his head and slipped his hand up under his T-shirt to rub his stomach. His sweatshirt was on the back of a chair. He slid it over his shoulders, popping his head through the hole and twisting his arms through the sleeves as he brought it down around his waist. His tennis shoes were loose enough to put on like slippers. He stooped to catch his reflection in the window. The image was transparent and faint, but enough to let him know he looked fine. He brushed his hair with his fingers, the natural wave snapping back into place. He'd show-ered the night before but lifted his arm to make sure the sweatshirt didn't have an odor, then turned and went through the room picking up articles of clothing. "How long you going to be, Ron? I need to take a leak."

Ron stepped out of the bathroom, holding Cheri's hand. "All yours, bro." Cheri clutched his arm and tucked her head behind his shoulder. She kept her face turned away like she was trying to hide, but Ron broke free so he could get dressed. "We're going to head on over, and maybe grab a coffee and muffin on the way," he said, buttoning his shirt.

Cheri turned toward the door. It wasn't like her to be shy. She'd slept over before, so it wasn't modesty, and she didn't wear makeup or fix her hair with any real purpose, so it wasn't her lack of grooming. Josh nodded. "Okay, catch you later."

"Hey, remember to wear your mask. I know it's outdoors, but we may end up storming the hotel and if things get dicey, you'll need something to cover your face."

"Thanks, man."

Ron yanked a coat from a hanger and slipped it on, slid his feet into tennis shoes, and left, dragging Cheri with him.

Josh went to the bathroom to finish getting ready. Residual steam from Ron's shower coated the mirror. Josh took a washcloth from the sink to wipe it away. Cheri was upset about something. He'd caught a glimpse of her as Ron pulled her out the door. Her eyes were moist and red, like she'd been crying. He ran the tap to brush his teeth. It was none of his business.

MARIE WAS STANDING over by the courtyard fountain talking with Ms. Goodall, the professor with the bowl shaped haircut who'd insisted her students be there. A gust of wind sent the plume of water off course, causing them to duck to avoid getting wet. They put their heads together again, hunching over a stack of paper like they were putting the finishing touches on a strategic plan.

Perfect. Josh could make sure his teacher saw him, and connect with Marie at the same time. The wind sweeping down the lane felt like the slipstream of a jet. With the sun out he'd thought he wouldn't need a warmer coat, but now saw he was wrong. His hoodie flopped up against the back of his head, temporarily warming his neck. Marie looked up, nailing him with those dark sensuous eyes as she waved him over.

"Hi Josh. You think you could pass these out to people as they arrive?" she said, handing him a stack of yellow flyers.

She was wearing her red ski coat with a red wool cap that framed her face, accenting her eyes, her petite nose, and the red gloss of her smile. Her tight jeans revealed her slim figure, which was good because her puffy coat made her look a little like the Pillsbury doughboy.

Josh smiled and nodded, making sure his teacher saw him taking the stack of yellow paper. He had to hold them tight to keep the sheets from blowing away. But the crispness of Marie's words and the brevity of her greeting squelched the excitement he felt over seeing her again. If she was as attracted to him as he was to her, she had a funny way of showing it. He walked over and began handing out the leaflets to people, pressing them tightly into their hands, but a few still escaped and went spiraling away.

The wind came in gusts. Cars were unloaded and baggage stacked at the curb, awaiting bellhops who collected it on brass carts for delivery to the guest's rooms. By Josh's estimation, only about twenty-five protestors had shown up so far, not enough for the hotel's staff to even notice.

A few of the demonstrators brought signs, but the wind caught them like sails making them almost impossible to hold. Each flyer Josh handed out furled as he passed it on. The recipients had to grip them in both hands to read what they said. He was starting to feel cold, and sorry he'd come.

"Hey Josh," Molly said, taking a flyer from his hand, her red frizzy hair tossed by the wind. It made him feel better to be recognized.

"Hey, girl, you gonna give 'em hell?"

"You betcha, big guy. Ain't no Cracker Jack gonna pollute my town." She walked away, melding into a crowd that was growing by the minute.

Josh didn't know most of the people he handed flyers to, but all treated him with deference like he was one of them. Just his simple presence made him part of the group.

"Thank you, my man, keep up the good work," said one, patting him on the shoulder.

"We're going to bag this guy, eh bro," said another.

Ron came by and took some of his handouts. "There are people in the parking lot we're missing," he said. "I'm going to cover the other side." Josh nodded, noticing Cheri wasn't with him.

"No problem, I've got plenty. Hey, where's your girlfriend?"

Ron rubbed the side of his face and scratched his beard, then said, "She wasn't feeling well so I took her home." He hustled off toward a line of cars parked along a hedge of boxwoods.

Josh returned to his assignment, connecting the dots between Cheri's illness and her tears. He went back to passing out flyers and a few handouts later saw Donnie.

"Hey, dude, a bunch of us are going around to the south side of the building. There's an exit over there a lot of people use. We want to make sure Jack doesn't sneak in that way. We plan to stand locked arm in arm to block the doors. You want to come help?"

Josh hefted the pile of flyers. Several slipped out of his hand and scattered, tumbling across the courtyard. He placed his other hand on top to hold them down. "Sorry man, I can't, I've been recruited to hand these out."

Donnie punched his shoulder. "Do what you gotta do, man. Catch you later." He disappeared around the corner with a half dozen other protestors, his super-fine hair spinning on top his head like an orange tornado. The crowd had grown to about fifty, now assembled behind the fountain in the hotel's courtyard.

Two police vans pulled onto the street and parked at the curb. Squads of officers in dark SWAT uniforms piled out. Hotel management had finally clued into the fact that they were under siege. The officers marched to the hotel's entrance and staged themselves in a line across the building's façade, holding shields in front of them, making sure hotel guests could come and go without being harassed.

Three media vans with satellite dishes on their roofs pulled in. Camera crews assembled their equipment, anxious to record any trouble that might break out. Josh saw a camera panning the crowd and turned his back.

A man took to the podium and held a portable megaphone to his mouth. He wore a black sweatshirt with the hood pulled over his head and a mask covering his mouth. "Alright, thank you for coming. It's good to know so many people are concerned about what's happening and are willing to step up and do what's right. You know why we're here?" he screamed. His voice through his mask was muffled, yet still tinny in the plastic cone of the loudspeaker. "We're here because a virus is coming to our city and this one's worse than the coronavirus, and we can't afford to let it spread."

A few cheers erupted from the crowd.

"We're here to prevent this new virus, we call it the Palco virus, from infecting our town. Palco is a germ of hate and intolerance. That's not who we are. Portland is better than that."

The shouts grew louder. *At least it isn't about dad,* Josh thought, taking comfort as he looked around to be sure the cameras weren't recording him, but they seemed focused on the man speaking. Suddenly Marie was at his side. "Josh, I just want to thank you again for helping out." She grabbed his arm, squeezing it affectionately, her warm body nuzzling close to his.

The crowd broke into loud chants of:

"FASCIST, RACIST, ANTI-GAY,
CAPITALIST BIGOT, GO AWAY."

The cameras spun around to pan the crowd. Josh saw several students pulling on facemasks. Marie let go of his arm and turned her coat collar up zipping it to where it covered her mouth, then pulled the wool cap down over her ears leaving just the window where her eyes could be seen. Josh felt his face to make sure his mask was in place. With new-found courage he raised his fist and joined the other voices yelling,

"FASCIST, RACIST, ANTI-GAY,
CAPITALIST BIGOT, GO AWAY."

BILL WAS SITTING at the counter enjoying brunch. If he had his druthers he'd be out fishing, a beautiful day like today was a sad thing to waste, but Saturday was the one day of the week he and Mary and Angie got to eat breakfast together. The fish would still be biting when the red evening sun was shimmering on the lake.

The telephone rang. He set his fork down and pushed his plate of steak and eggs aside.

"Now who would dare to interrupt our quiet Saturday morning repast?" he said as he went to answer. "Better not be a robo-call."

Mary was helping Angie, who after many years of practice could just about feed herself. All Mary had to do was be there to help guide the fork into Angie's mouth if it happened to go astray, but Angie had learned to chew and swallow on her own.

"Paaaaacaaks myyyyfavvvooorite." Angie intoned.

"Mine too," Mary said, taking a napkin to wipe syrup from Angie's lips.

Bill picked up the receiver and put it to his ear.

"You got Bill," he said.

"Bill, this is Jack."

"Hey Jack, what's up?"

"Sorry, but I'm going to have to cancel our dinner plans."

Bill was watching Mary fill a fork with pancakes for Angie. "Why? What's the problem?" he said, turning back to the phone.

"Turns out I won't be coming to Portland after all."

"What? I thought you were en-route."

"We were, but the hotel cancelled our reservation. Apparently, a few opposition types showed up and started harassing the hotel's guests and of course the police came and the press. Next thing you know I get a call saying they've closed the convention center. A lot of people are going to be disappointed when they show up and I'm not there."

"Sounds like you've got a lawsuit on your hands."

"Maybe, but I'm not anxious to sue. We've emailed everyone who planned to attend. I'm sure most will get the message. And I'm not faulting the hotel, they have their interests to protect. But it's a shame how a few twisted people can prevent three hundred citizens from meeting just because they share a different point of view. Seems like those who claim they're for tolerance aren't very tolerant at all, at least not of me."

"Say no more, I get it."

"I'll bet you do. I got a call from a professor at PSU saying how sorry she was about the cancellation. She's a closet conservative who seldom gets to share her political views, but she let me know it wasn't personal and went on to describe the attack on you. I guess you've been hit pretty hard, too."

Bill reached for his fork and shoveled another bite of eggs into his mouth. "Say what?"

"You know, the posters and all."

"Speak plain, Jack. I haven't a clue what you're talking about."

"Seriously? You haven't seen it. She texted me a few pictures. Hang on, I'll forward them to you."

MARIE AND JOSH stood with their fists raised, chanting deliriously. Silencing men like Palco was compulsory if they wanted to save America.

"FASCIST, RACIST, ANTI-GAY,
CAPITALIST BIGOT, GO AWAY."

The brass doors of the hotel's lobby opened and a man in a gray suit with a shiny gold name badge came out waving his hands. "Please, please, I have news. Quiet please." But he couldn't be heard above the boiling mantra.

"FASCIST, RACIST, ANTI-GAY,
CAPITALIST BIGOT, GO AWAY."

He went over to the man with the megaphone and shouted in his ear and the man stepped onto the podium holding the megaphone to his mouth. "Quiet down for a second, Quiet down," his words sounding like someone speaking through a comb wrapped in wax paper.

"The hotel manager has an announcement."

"He's the problem, not the solution!" came a cry from the back of the crowd.

"Capitalist pig!" Someone else yelled with their fist raised.

A water balloon sailed out of the throng striking the hotel manager squarely on his bald head, only it wasn't filled with water, it was filled with paint.

The man spread his arms out and stood there with red paint dripping down his collar and onto the lapels of his suit. "I…I was going to say you'd won."

Several more water balloons were thrown hitting the hotel's front windows painting them blue and red and yellow and green. *Splat, splat, splat.*

The police rushed in to quell the protestors with tear gas and flash bangs and were immediately pelted with more balloons, but their shields took most of it. They looked like psychedelic art. *BANG! BANG!* the power charges went off. The mob broke into a panic with people scattering in every direction. Josh took Marie's hand as they ran past the fountain, off the curb and into the street heading for the nearest streetcar stop, giggling all the way.

FOURTEEN

RISING BEFORE DAWN, Bill had pulled the Chinook out of the woods and dropped it in the lake while there was barely enough light to see. He couldn't resist. It was forecast to be another fine day without rain. And yes, it was Sunday, but church didn't start until eleven. He could easily get in a few hours of fishing before they had to go.

He'd thought to come yesterday when the late day feeders were snapping at flies in the crimson sun, but he'd become lost in doing the prep work for his podcast. Usually, the material he required could be assembled in less than an hour, but this time it ended up being a research project that took most of the day.

His treble hook caught against the last loop of his pole. Bill secured it there. He laid the pole on the seat of the canoe and reached for his thermos, twisting the cap off to pour his coffee. Any attempt to lure a fish now would be futile. The waters were too dark. Steam broke around his nose as he raised the cup to his mouth. He smiled and winked at a moon that was still bright on the horizon. The best darn coffee in the world was the coffee served in a canoe with the chill of the morning fresh in your lungs and the sound of songbirds warbling in your ears. He sighed, feeling relaxed for the first time in weeks. Nothing like a moonlit lake for washing trials and tribulations away.

The minutes passed in a peaceful calm, *thank you, Lord.* It was such a privilege to be back out on the lake with the water gently lapping against the sides of the canoe, and his mind stayed on God rather than the foolishness of men. It was something he should have started doing many years ago. The encroaching light began painting the landscape in subtle shades of dawn, the sun spilling on the water like liquid gold, the outline of Mount Hood becoming more distinct as the moon faded and the sky changed from navy to violet. *For purple mountain's majesty,* Bill thought. America was beautiful, with its oceans and forests and mountains and rivers, probably the most beautiful nation on Earth, and truly blessed of God.

America, America,
God shed His grace on thee,
And crown Thy good, with brotherhood,
From sea to shining sea.

But where had it gone? There was a time when America the Beautiful was a land of brotherhood, when the people were Americans first, when they cheered for one another, and fought beside each other, and grieved one another's losses. Political ideologies may have differed, but the citizens listened to one another, respected diverse opinions and agreed to disagree to the point of saying: "I may not agree with what you have to say, but I'll defend to the death your right to say it."

Bill took a sip of his coffee, the light of day spreading to the opposite shore where the trees were taking on an emerald glow. *Crown thy good with brotherhood,* indeed. Forcing Jack to cancel his trip was akin to Nazis burning books they didn't want others to read. And those posters, "Wanted Dead or Alive," come on. In a sane world, that would be considered a death threat. He'd deleted the photos from his phone to make sure Mary never saw them.

The water became dappled with petals of yellow as the sun crossed the horizon. Bill finished his coffee and screwed the cap back on his thermos. Taking his pole from the canoe's seat he slackened the line enough to free the hook.

He swung his pole over the side, letting out the line until the sinker hit the water with a *plunk,* sending out a series of concentric circles. He'd completed his second podcast for Senator Powers, relieved that it was now behind him. The lack of tension on the line let him know his

137

weight had found bottom. He began jigging the lure up and down to imitate the feathery spines of an insect. Hopefully some granddaddy bass would think it was breakfast.

Doing this piece had kept him on edge all afternoon. There was too much to say and too little time in which to say it. *You fish better wake up and get hungry pretty soon, 'cause I can't stay out all day.* He slipped his cell from his pocket and logged onto his server just to see if anything he'd said made sense. His image appeared on the screen dressed in the same red mackinaw he was wearing now with his fishing gear providing a backdrop on the wall behind him, his face shadowed by the topic he was about to present. He turned the volume up and found himself already into his presentation, his voice breaking through the morning quiet.

"…is an element in our world that seeks to create a centralized world government, not a political party, but an overreaching body that desires control of everything from banking, to food production, to medicine.

"I know what you're thinking; Bill's become a conspiracy theorist—but have I? Did you know every year three thousand of the world's richest and most influential people meet at the World Economic Forum in Davos Switzerland to figure out how to run the world's economy, not as separate nations, but as a global community? Their agenda's not hidden. It's a public event scrutinized by the media.

Many of those who attend are also members of the Club of Rome, an organization founded in 1968 by Italian industrialist Aurelio Peccei. Wikipedia defines the club like this: 'The Club of Rome consists of current and former heads of state, UN bureaucrats, high-level politicians and government officials, diplomats, scientists, economists, and business leaders from around the globe.'

"For the most part, their work isn't secretive. If you want to know their stated ideologies look no further than the books sanctioned by the organization. The first titled: *The Limits to Growth—A Report by the Council of the Club of Rome,* sold thirty million copies. You can still buy it on Amazon today.

"The Club's second release, *The First Global Revolution*, also still available, contains the following statements:"

> "'Sacrilegious though this may sound, democracy is no longer well suited for the tasks ahead. The complexity and the technical nature of many of today's problems do not always allow elected representatives to make competent decisions at the right time.'

"Don't let that slip. It's important. This group of highly placed world leaders does not believe in democracy, but rather that they, the elite, should be in charge of making critical decisions that affect the world. They aspire to a Marxist Socialist type of government where decisions from the top are made on behalf of the lower castes like you and me. Now the second quote:"

> "'In searching for a new enemy to unite us, we came up with the idea that pollution, the threat of global warming, water shortages, famine and the like would fit the bill.'

"Read that, and think about it. Nearly all the so called doomsday crises we've been warned about over the last fifty years fit those criteria. They admit they were looking for an 'enemy' like global warming to rally people around the idea of needing global solutions. Then Covid 19 unexpectedly fell into their laps. What could be more perfect? A killer virus. All they had to do was make people think they were going to die and allow countries to go bankrupt trying to solve the problem and The Reset would become inevitable. Klaus Schwab, founder of the World Economic Forum, wrote a book about it called, *Covid 19: The Great Reset,* in which he describes the Covid virus as a window of opportunity to be seized upon. And let me just say this, friends, it's not a conspiracy when they tell you what they're doing. We're not talking about a pandemic, this is a plan-demic, a purposeful attempt to use Covid 19 to restructure our world.

I'll speak more about the Great Reset in an upcoming podcast but know this, whether they use Covid, or climate change, or something else, we are on the verge of the Great Reset happening.

"You have to understand that Satan wants to be your God. He wants you to worship him. He knows God has already promised those who love Him a perfect world, which will be established under the authority of His Son, Jesus, so Satan wants to get the jump on God and do it now. And mankind will be so enamored by the illusion of a better system, they'll follow on like sheep to the slaughter.

"Now in order for Satan to set up his kingdom, which he'll rule through his proxy, the antichrist, two things must happen. First, we must have the technology in place that allows him to monitor and control every person on earth. These technologies are being developed as we speak and in many cases are already in place to make it possible. This will be the topic of my next podcast so you don't want to miss that.

"The second is our topic for today, and that is how the economies of the world must soon collapse. Because as long as the nations of the world are independent and prosperous, there's no need for the antichrist to do anything. If things are going smoothly, we don't need him.

"But they aren't going smoothly, and there are three reasons why:" Bill counted them off on his fingers, "climate change, the Covid virus, and hyperinflation. We're already feeling the devastating effects of the virus. It's estimated that the US government will spend more on Covid than it did on all of World War II.

At the same time the IPCC is pushing the world to spend fifty trillion to solve the climate change problem, a course of action that will saddle us with even more debt. The money the world is being asked to invest has to come from somewhere. Governments either have to print it, or get it through taxation. With printing money comes hyperinflation and with increased taxation, less money for people to spend. Either way, the people will come to the point where they can no longer pay. Governments that depend on taxes to survive will collapse, giving globalists the opportunity to step in and assume control.

"Satan has been at this a long time. Truth be told, he doesn't really need a virus, or some manmade fear of the planet's supernova, to move his agenda forward. He's already got just about every nation on earth so hyper-inflated their economies are about to implode. Let me use America for an example.

"The United States debt today stands at about twenty-eight trillion dollars. I doubt anyone in my listening audience has a real grasp of how much that is, so let me break it down for you. Let's say you have about a million seconds. That's about eleven days. If you had a billion seconds, you'd have about thirty-one years. But if you have a trillion seconds, the number jumps to a whopping three-hundred and seventeen centuries. You want to guess how long twenty-eight trillion seconds is?

How long do you think it's going to take for us to pay off our national debt? Well, if you had a billion dollar debt and you paid one dollar per second, you could pay it off in twenty-two years, but one trillion would take us more than thirty–two thousand years, which would put us somewhere around the year of 34,000 and that's just one trillion, but we owe twenty-eight trillion, which brings us to the year 952,000, or nine-hundred and fifty-two thousand years from now. And that's only if we pay off our debt without adding any more to it. But we can't do that because we still have to borrow to pay for our safety-net programs like Social Security and Welfare, not to mention the cost of health care and education, or the costs of Covid and climate change. Guys, I'm telling you, we're heading for a major economic collapse.

"And that's just what the globalists want because it will give them the opportunity to change all the currencies in the world to crypto dollars, not notes made of paper and coin, but digital ones and zeros stored on the cloud in blockchain cyberspace where the use of it will one day be monitored and controlled, so, as the Bible says, 'no man might buy or sell except that he has the mark or the name of the beast or the number of his name.' And for you non-religious types, that's from the Bible so you can bet it will happen." Bill looked at his watch.

"I've got more to say, but I'm out of time so I'm gonna have to sign off. But thanks for hanging in there. I'll try and talk less next time when we look at some of the technologies being developed to make all this possible. Until then, this is Wild Bill Best riding off into the sunset, saying, adios amigos." The screen faded to black.

Bill slipped the phone back into his pocket and jigged his line up and down, hoping the spinning spoon would attract a Largemouth to the lure. *Dang I look old. I'll have to change that lighting. It's just not erasing the wrinkles like it used to. Come on, fish. Not even a nibble, but the essence of fishing is patience.* It's just that Bill didn't have time for patience because Mary would be anxiously pacing the floor thinking they were going to be late for church. *Come on, bite!* If there was one down there, it should see the bait and come running. In the meantime, he needed to relax and enjoy his surroundings: tall ponderosas mixed with noble fir and western hemlock interspersed with blackberry bramble, trillium, foxglove and purple lupine. The indigo blue sky was so rich it looked like a photo from a calendar. If the planet was dying, you sure couldn't tell.

He felt the line tremble, his first nibble. He jerked the pole back to set the hook prematurely and the fish slipped away. He swung his line slowly back and forth to make the lure look like an insect swimming, but whatever fish he'd attracted had either lost interest or been frightened off. He let the lure sink back into a straight line and began jigging again.

He felt his line quiver, *hold it, hold it,* there! His line began to run, and for a second he saw a dorsal fin and the fish's glistening green body as it swam to the surface, rolled and headed for the bottom. *Dang! It's a big one.*

FIFTEEN

HE TRIED TO establish his balance but his internal compass was on the fritz. He wasn't going to make it, but he had to, he'd promised. Josh propped himself against the door, his eyes half-mast and red after a night of doing shots with his fellow agitators celebrating their victory over the forces of darkness. Or at least over Palco and his attempt to sway the minds of gullible Americans. It was a scene reminiscent of the ski lodge, only this time he had taken two bennies to help him stay alert. Marie had sat beside him sharing an unspoken intimacy almost to the end, but around one in the morning, had begged off saying her roommate would be wondering where she was, and she didn't want her to worry. She kissed Josh's cheek and squeezed his hand, melting him like butter in the sun.

Now his head was in a vice. He wished he hadn't had coffee with Rachel on Friday. He would still be in bed, and she wouldn't be on her way over to escort him to church. He'd wanted to say no, but there were too many reasons why he couldn't. Rachel could validate that he had been to church and get his mother off his back, but he also held Rachel as a confidant and friend and wanted to stay on her good side.

But, boy, he did not feel that way getting out of bed. She'd awakened him to a migraine with the walls closing in. He'd wanted to smash the phone with a shoe, but he'd put on a bright and cheery façade, and far as he could tell, had pulled it off. Now he just needed to keep it up the entire morning. He was resolved to keep his commitment in spite of his obvious impairment, two doses of Tylenol notwithstanding.

He pressed his hand to his gut and stumbled out into the bright sun, closing the door behind him. *Sheesh, turn down the lights.* Most of the stores were still closed, Sunday being a day when few were up and about before ten.

Rachel had said she would meet him at nine. It was a quarter till and he needed coffee. The plan was to hook up either outside his apartment or sitting at a nearby sidewalk cafe. There was movement behind the glass front of a bagel shop. He staggered over. Surely they had a pot on the burner. His stomach released a burp. He put his hand over his mouth and realized his breath smelled like whiskey. Brushing his teeth hadn't worked; this came from down deep in his gut where last night's booze was still fermenting. Coffee was the cure for everything. He paid the Chinese man baking the Jewish pastry an extra three bucks because the store wasn't open yet and the cash register was locked and Josh didn't have change. It was worth every penny. Josh took a seat in front of the shop to await Rachel's arrival.

He hadn't been their five minutes when he saw her approaching, looking like an angel with her white dress backlit by the sun, her hair glowing like a halo. "Morning Josh, glad to see you're on time," she said as she sat down.

Josh nodded. He took another sip of coffee. "You too, but I guess my mom had to let you off early to get back in time for their service. So, where are we going? I thought you said it was casual." His eyes fell on her white dress and string of pearls and then at his own outfit, black denims, black sweatshirt and dirty tennis shoes. They were perfect together, black and white, good and bad, right and wrong. He ran his fingers through his hair hoping to neaten himself.

"That's what they said, but remember, I've never been to this church before. It was recommended by a girl in that Bible study class I went to. She said a lot of students go there so it's very relaxed. I just dressed a little nicer because I remembered how your dad dressed nice at Christmas to honor the Lord and I thought, why not do that all the time. But don't worry, I'm pretty sure you'll fit right in, and I'll be considered overdressed. Are you ready?"

Josh yawned, using the back of his hand to cover his mouth as he let out a sigh. He stood, brushing the lint from his pants.

Rachel got up, took her Bible from the table and headed off with Josh fumbling along behind, at least that's how he felt. He raised a hand like a visor to block the sun.

She looked back over her shoulder, her eyes implying that he should catch up. "Would you be interested in taking up jogging with me?" she said.

The clouds were rolling in, getting thicker and blacker by the minute. Josh's stomach rumbled. Not the right question. Not the right time. If they started jogging now, he'd probably puke. "What brought that on? I've never been jogging before. I doubt I'd last very long."

"I know, me either. That's why I'm asking. Jim wants me to go jogging with him, and I thought maybe I should try to get in shape before I say yes and embarrass myself."

Josh glanced at her profile, the imprint of a goddess on a Roman coin. If she weren't such a goody-two-shoes he might even be interested. But no, he was not going to end up like his dad. Still, there was that twinge of jealousy. "Uh, yeah, I guess so. How hard can it be?"

They walked down Broadway from Jackson to Market Street before Rachel turned and began a zigzag course through a number of city blocks. Josh was trying to keep up, but the vigor in her stride made it impossible.

"You sure you know where you're going?" The wind picked up, sending scattered bits of paper looping around in a cyclone. "*Whew*, I'm out of shape."

"That's why we have to start running."

"But not now."

The sky grew ominously dark. A few fat drops spattered against the sidewalk. "Looks like we're in for some rain." He had no more said it than the heavens opened and they found themselves standing on the bow of Noah's ark with the wind raging and the tide starting to swell. Lightning broke across the sky, followed by an ear-busting peal of thunder. Josh scrambled, looking around to find shelter, but there was none. They would be drenched in minutes. "What do you want to do?"

"Run!" Rachel said.

Josh and Rachel got their first chance to go jogging as they raced back down Broadway, splashing through puddles till they looked like two long haired cats thrown into a river. Of the two, Josh looked worse, with his hair clinging to his face like the strings of a wet mop. He had pulled his hoodie over his head as they ran and passed it to Rachel to save her hair from the deluge. It did little good, but scored points for gallantry. They stood dripping under the awning of a local hotel, because it was the first building they came to with an external shelter. Josh was stooped over with his hands on his knees catching his breath, but when he placed his hands on his waist and straightened himself, he found Rachel laughing.

"What? Told you I wasn't so good at jogging."

She covered her mouth and shook her head, trying to stop, but her laugher was infectious and soon they were both busting a gut at the hilarity of their situation. Street cars were running in and out of the Urban Center tunnel, the sound of rain drumming the sidewalk accompanying their mirth.

"Sorry we missed church," Josh said, trying to sound sincere.

"Maybe next week. And we'll bring umbrellas in case. Here," Rachel took hold of the hem of the borrowed hoodie raising it around her waist.

"No, keep it," Josh said, waving her off. "I've got others and you have to wait until my mom picks you up." Josh used both hands to fold his hair back on his head and noticed the pounding of his temples was gone. Considering his head had started out like Hemingway's, *For Whom the Bell Tolls*, he was feeling good.

The rain was coming down in sheets, sluicing off the building's roof and flooding the downspout. Rachel still needed the hoodie to keep her Bible dry. She acquiesced and released her grip on the shirt. "I think we should do this again sometime. You up for tomorrow?"

"How 'bout we play it by ear. It wasn't supposed to rain today, and look." He lifted his chin indicating the torrents moving through the parking lot in waves. "I'd much rather do this when it's dry. Come here." He was still breathing hard but he curled his fingers in toward himself, coaxing her in.

"What? Why?"

"My phone. It's in my sweatshirt."

"Oh, right." Rachel reached into the pocket and withdrew the phone, leaving her Bible in place as she handed it to him.

Josh slipped it into his pocket, wondering what there was left to say. "Well, I guess we could go get coffee. It looks like it's letting up a bit."

The smell of her hair mixed with the light fragrance of her perfume was stimulating, but that was a road he wasn't prepared to travel. The pounding rain settled into a mild drizzle.

"Right," she said, "but we should jog. We won't get as wet that way."

"How bout we walk. I doubt we could get any wetter than this," he said, raising his arms to show his sagging shirt.

Rachel smiled as they moved away with their steps synchronizing like musicians in a parade.

CAL STOOD IN FRONT of his favorite hotdog cart shivering. It was a sunny day in Washington, the yellow light bleeding through leafless trees, but clear skies always let in cold air. *Burrrrrrrr*. It had dropped ten degrees overnight. At least the snow was gone—for now. He wrapped his arms around himself, his thick faux fur-lined coat stretched over his bloated stomach refusing to keep his legs warm. He stepped up to place his order. He didn't need a mask, they were outside, but he wore one anyway. His asthma made him more susceptible to disease than other people. He couldn't be too careful.

"Leave off the chili this time, Earl."

"But you like chili, Mista Moody," the cart operator's eyes widened, the white orbs big as golf balls against his black skin. He wore an apron and a hat with the front snapped down over the bill. His faded red cotton long-sleeve shirt his only protection against the cold.

"Yeah, but man it gives me heartburn," Cal said bringing his fist up to pound his chest. "I'd just as soon avoid it if I can."

"Okay, you da boss." Earl lifted the lid on the deck of his stainless steel cart and used his tongs to remove a bun from the steamer. He held it open and reached for a hotdog from the rotisserie grill and placed it in the bun. It used to be that the grill was the only thing shielded by plastic, but now Earl stood behind a sheet that covered his entire cart, though he wasn't wearing a mask. "You want anything on that? I got mustard, relish and onions."

"Mustard and onions will do, thanks."

Earl squeezed a bead of mustard down the line of the hotdog and then sprinkled it with a coat of chopped onions and wrapped it in a brown paper towel. "Dare you go suh," he said, handing it around the plastic wall to Cal.

Cal took his lunch and handed Earl a ten dollar bill. He looked around and found his favorite park bench empty and went over to sit down. While standing in line the sun had begun to warm his back. The seat was cold, but in full sun. He would be warm in minutes. He dropped his mask and unfurled his dog, the steam rising from the bun as he brought it too his mouth. He chomped down and began to chew. It was tasteless and boring. Maybe he should have tried the sausage.

He paid no attention to the other man that sat down—until he heard his name.

"I got to tell you, Mr. Moody, we're not at all happy with your progress. Looks like you're not taking this seriously." The man crossed an ankle over his knee and stretched his arm across the back of the bench. He swatted his thigh with a newspaper.

Cal's head jerked to the side. It was Victor something-or-other, the guy from the NSA. "What do you mean? I have my best man on it. These things take time." Cal shoved a huge bite of his hotdog into his mouth, his cheeks bulging.

"We don't have time, Mr. Moody. Intel suggests Mr. Best may be planning a series on government corruption, naming names and all that."

"Corruption?" he said, still chewing. The bread tasted like paste. He should have bought a drink to wash it down.

"Okay, right. Corruption is systemic. It's how the game is played. But it's an old boy network, something you're brought into as you move up in the ranks. It's nothing for ma and pa to worry about."

Cal shook his head, his glasses so smudged he could barely see through the lens. He gulped the bite down. "Not what I meant. I thought you said this was about climate change." He took another bite, but smaller this time.

Victor smiled, but it was a crooked smile that lifted one side of his blond mustache higher than the other. "That too. Look, it's not for you to questions our reasons or motives. All you have to know is, Mr. Best is standing in the way of progress, and as such, is an enemy of the state. Your job is to give us something we can use to put him away. And I suggest you do it quickly. People at the top are getting impatient, and right now it's not looking good on you." Victor let go of his ankle and stood looking down on Cal. "Have a nice day, Mr. Moody," he said, and walked away, disappearing into the pedestrian traffic as quickly as he'd come.

Cal sat for a moment, looking at his half eaten hotdog. Then, no longer hungry, got up and went to the nearest trashcan to throw it away.

A WEEK PASSED without Rachel and Josh getting together. Either they had conflicts with their schedules, or Mary was out with the car, or it was pouring rain. Friday came, and while they had talked every night that week, the run they were hoping to do was forever put on hold. Finally, out of pure frustration, Rachel called and said, "Josh, I'm going out today whether you come with me or not."

"They're calling for more rain."

"We can use the indoor track at your school's rec center."

"The rec center? Yeah, right, they do have a track. Why didn't you say something sooner?"

"Because it's where Jim works out when it rains and I'm not ready to bump into him yet. The whole idea is to build up stamina before we go out jogging together."

"Okay, your call."

"I say yes. I need to get in shape, and from what I saw last Sunday, so do you."

Josh hung up and tossed the phone on his bed.

Ron turned away from his computer and popped the earbuds from his ears. He stood, arching his back. "You finally get a date with that chick?" He was barefoot, wearing pajama bottoms and a neon green T-shirt that read: "Forward to a Fossil Fuel Free Future."

"Just a friend. Did you see where I put my shorts?"

"On the floor over by the chair. But you like her, right?"

"Like I said, the only thing we've done is attempt to go to church."

"Yeah, too bad. I saw you with her once, looks sweet but you're best not going there. Chick like that will spin your head around, all that religious mumbo-jumbo. You going to the meeting tonight?"

Josh placed his hand on the back of the chair and leaned over to scoop up his shorts. "Plan to. Speaking of girls, where's Cheri? I haven't seen her all week."

Ron pursed his lips and then scratched his beard. "Naw, that's history. We broke it off."

"You broke up, why? You seemed to be getting along."

"Chick went and got herself pregnant. Wanted me to do the daddy thing and I'm not ready for that."

Josh sat on the bed, pulling on his shorts. "Seriously? I doubt she got *herself* pregnant."

"No, she really did. Found out she wasn't using protection. Said she liked it natural, but she knew we were just having fun. I told her I'd help get rid of the thing, but that's it for me. She wants to keep it. That's on her."

Josh stood. He pulled his cut-off T-shirt over his head, slipped into his tennis shoes, and headed for the door. "Too bad. She seemed nice. Catch you later," he said, as he skated outside.

Suck egg, Ron supports feminism. Not. You can't have a girl, and toss her aside like a used Kleenex. Nope, takes two to tango, my friend.

Josh trotted down the sidewalk, but stopped and knelt to adjust the tongue of his tennis shoe for more comfort. He wasn't proud of being a virgin. It was a topic he shied away from around his college buds. If they ever discovered his secret, they'd get him drunk and bring some skank in to amend his sad condition.

He wasn't holding to some altruistic dogma fed to him by his parents. He was his own man. He would decide when the time was right,

150

but he didn't see any point in waiting until he was married. You don't buy a car until you've gone for a test drive. But it would be nice if the first person he shared himself with was someone like Rachel—*what? no, wait*—where had that come from? No, someone like Marie. He liked Rachel, but not like that. He just missed seeing her, that's all—but as a friend. And she was on his mind because they were about to meet. Her name slipped out in a stream of subconscious thought. But the nice thing about Rachel was, she was probably a virgin like him, and that meant they could learn together. He might even wait until they were married. That's what God wanted, the biblical way, so she would want it too. Whereas Marie was probably an old pro and would have to show him what to do. *Stop it! Get your mind out of the gutter.* He had to focus on the walk. He began pumping his arms as he picked up his pace. He was seeing Rachel, but as a friend. *Just a friend.* It was only a few blocks down Sixth Street to Harrison. *Focus, focus, focus.*

The sidewalks were wet and the sky gray, and there was a chill in the air, especially since he'd opted to wear his shorts and cutoff shirt without a jacket. But at least it wasn't raining.

The building that housed the student recreation center was largely brick and glass. He had passed it many times, but had never gone inside. He could see people walking around the interior with sculpted bodies like poster boys for the master race, only they wore masks, so it kind of defeated the image. Outside a dozen people stood in a circle batting a giant pink ball back and forth.

He stepped into the building, noting it hadn't rained on his way over, though rain was in the forecast. He slipped his mask up over his nose, looking through the window at the sun breaking through the clouds. Maybe he should find Rachel and take it outside where they could really pump. The thought of running didn't particularly move him but power walking was a great way to build up one's stamina. Maybe she'd go for that.

A sign said the track was on the fourth floor. He started up the stairs and was about half way to the top when he stopped and looked around to see if Rachel was already there. She was. She was down on the main floor standing just to the side of a column talking to someone he

151

couldn't see. She did look good in shorts, he'd give her that. He reached the second floor and walked around to where he could see who she was talking to. It was Jim. He was about six inches taller than Rachel, a decent height for a girl as tall as she was. They made a good couple. Jim slipped his hand behind her ponytail, pressing against her back as he guided her toward the elevator. Josh waited until they were inside and the doors had closed. He turned and started back down the stairs. He had not come to run around the track with Jim.

SIXTEEN

VICTOR DAMSHIE FUMBLED, trying to get his phone out before the caller disconnected, *three rings, four,* because it was in the inside pocket of his suitcoat, which was under the folds of his overcoat and buried behind his wallet and miscellaneous other items, *five rings, six,* and because the Chicago temperature was in the thirties and he was wearing gloves which made it impossible to know what he was feeling. He finally resorted to pulling everything out, leaving him to shuffle through the collection until the phone was on top. He brought his finger up and bit the tip of his glove pulling it off so he could tap the answer button.

"Victor," he said, as he brought the phone to his ear.

"Victor, it's Mark Wessler."

"Senator Wessler? Everything okay?"

"I'd be fine if we weren't having problems with Mr. Powers again. He's on several of the committees I chair…"

Victor slid the phone under his cheek and held it in place with his shoulder trying to get his glove back on before his fingers froze, but it was difficult because he still had his wallet and other paraphernalia in his hand.

"…A real naysayer. Can't see we're on the side of the people. I fear we won't get anything done until we apply a little pressure. What's the status of the girl?"

Victor began walking again, if for no other reason than to keep his body moving so he didn't freeze. "Nothing new. Far as I know, she's still in Portland."

"I asked you to keep an eye on her. You should have followed her out. I don't like not knowing where she is."

"With all due respect, Senator, We've been through this before. I'm not comfortable flying in this environment. You're the one pushing to have everyone take the vaccine before boarding a plane. You should know better than to ask."

"You could drive."

"And do what? There's got to be several hundred-thousand people living in Portland. How am I supposed to find her?" He rolled his collar up to block the wind. The sooner he got to his car and got the heater going, the better. He picked up the pace, walking briskly.

"You're still working on Bill Best, right?"

"Yes, met with our IRS guy last week. Had to set his pants on fire to get him moving."

"So now you got two reasons to be there."

"How's that?"

"Bill lives in Portland, and he and Senator Powers are friends. I'd be willing to bet that's where she's staying. Go watch Bill and I bet you find her. Kill two birds with one stone, so to speak."

"Maybe, but Mr. Moody will probably sit on his butt while I'm gone. And it's a long drive to Portland. You want me out there, fine, but it'll cost you double, and that's whether I find the girl or not."

"Understood. But while you're watching Bill, you'll be able to see whether or not the IRS is doing its job. As for Stan's daughter, just track her movements. I'll let you know what to do next. Are we clear?"

"We're clear." Vic hung up the phone, packaged it with the other stuff in his hand, and slipped it back into his pocket. *All the way to Portland, huh?* Most of his assignments were easy. This one, not so much.

STEVE DEMARKO PICKED UP his briefcase and headed for the door. It was the third interview he'd conducted since arriving in Portland, and he was batting zero. He prided himself on having an instinct for things like this. He could discern a tightening of the eyes or a sustained pause when people were asked uncomfortable questions about someone they knew. The clearing of the throat or a tremor in their voice always gave them away. But so far he'd seen none of that in the people he'd talked to.

He stepped outside into a day of mixed sun and clouds. That lady, Mrs. Brewster, wasn't lying. She honestly believed Bill Best was a saint. The eleven-thousand dollar check her group of runaway teenagers received last year had put food in their mouths for several months and helped pay the rent on the building. She hadn't received anything yet this year, but said she understood, what with the fire and all. "Bill Best is a fine young man," she'd warbled, which brought a smile to Steve's face because Mr. Best had to be at least sixty. Perhaps young was a matter of perspective, since Mrs. Brewster's crown of silver hair suggested she was probably in her eighties.

But that had been the case with the others he'd interviewed as well. The picture they painted was that of Saint Nicholas, bringing food and toys to starving children. Considering that Mr. Best played Santa at his tree farm, the image was appropriate.

Steve was having difficulty keeping his bias out of the equation. He didn't like Mr. Best. The man's politics did not align with his own. Back when Bill was doing radio, Steve cringed every time he caught one of Wild Bill's broadcasts. He had a nationalistic bent that bordered on fascism.

The world was getting smaller. Steve firmly believed it was time to start tearing down the walls that divided one country from another. People of the earth had to start getting along and pooling their resources to create a higher standard of living for everyone.

Having said that, he couldn't help but admire Bill's charity. He claimed no income from the tree farm, and apparently passed every cent earned from selling the trees through to people in need. It was a rare quality to be found in a capitalist. That was the problem. His Boss, Cal, wanted Mr. Best taken down, but everything he'd discovered about Bill was good. If he acted on his own prejudices, he'd side with his boss, but that would breach an ethical boundary. How could he accuse Bill Best of being dishonest, and then be that way himself?

Of course, he still had a few more interviews. It only took one person who knew something the others didn't. Bill might even turn out to be a closet pedophile with ulterior motives for helping kids. He certainly hoped so. He wasn't thrilled with the idea of putting an innocent man in jail.

THE ROOM WAS a maelstrom of activity. Around the conference table people were working at computers and manning the phones. The place had the aura of a sweatshop, each worker diligent in completing their assigned task, except Marie, who spent her time walking around the perimeter inspecting the work of others.

Josh was beginning to wonder if she ever wore a dominant color other than red. This time it was a sleeveless red pullover with a white belt, a string of white beads, and white fabric shoes. Her lips and nails were, of course—red! She needed a little variation to spice up her life, or at least her wardrobe, but he shouldn't complain. She at least tried to look nice, as opposed to other feminist types who made an effort to maximize their plainness. And who was he to talk. He'd adopted a faded blue-jean hoodie look for himself.

The central focus of the meeting was obviously his dad. Taped to a whiteboard on the wall was the same poster he had helped plaster across the city, "Public Enemy Number One."

"What's going on?" Josh said.

Marie spun about, her red lips breaking into a broad white-toothed smile. "Where have you been?" She came around the table and grabbed his arm. "I thought you'd be here sooner, but never mind, you're here now. I have something special for you to do." She began walking the perimeter of the table with Josh arm-in-arm. "We're gearing up for another assault on our friend here," she said, nodding at the poster. "His second podcast aired and it was worse than the first, if that's even possible. He's claiming we who want a peaceful, sustainable world are operating in concert with the devil. Now he says he's working on a third podcast, and we have to stop him."

Marie let go of Josh and turned to a young man at a computer.

"Jeff, how you coming with that program?"

Jeff leaned back in his chair and brought a pencil to his mouth, biting the eraser. "Shouldn't take long, maybe a couple of days. Mr. Best is about to get hit with so many emails his system will probably go into anaphylactic shock."

"And they won't just go to junk mail?"

"Got it covered. Our database has over a hundred-thousand email addresses. Every email is going out under a different name, all of them legit, and since the system can't determine whether any particular one is junk mail, it has to deliver them all."

"Well done, Jeffry."

"Ross, what about the robo-calls?"

Josh took a step back, glad for the first time to be apart from Marie. Her body was as ripe as the others, or maybe she was the one he smelled all along. But he did admire her strength. She was like a general commanding her troops.

"We've run into a bit of a snag there," Ross answered. "I can set up the calls with a prerecorded message and flood his phone lines, but we're going to need a bigger server to handle that many outgoing calls."

"So what's the solution? We've got to get those messages to him. They're what he needs to hear most."

"Working on it," he said.

Josh glanced around the conference table. His roommate, with his electric green fossil-fuel-free-future shirt looked up and gave him a nod. All these people were pouring their souls into denying his father's right to free speech. His father was a jerk, but this seemed a bit much.

"Are we sure all this is necessary? I mean the man's just giving his opinion. No one pays attention to him anyway."

Marie grabbed Josh's arm and pulled him around. "What did you just say?" Her voice was choked, her eyes narrowed with irritation. "Are you nuts? All it takes for evil to succeed is for good men to do nothing, and I won't be party to that." She shook her head like a mother reproving a child, then turned back to address the table. "Ron, could you come over here for a minute?"

157

Ron puckered his face and nodded. He got up and padded around the table in his stocking feet.

Marie leaned in toward Josh and in a more conciliatory tone said. "Josh, we have to stop Mr. Best. The world is in great peril and we're at war to save it. Yes, I suppose our tactics may seem extreme, but the alternative is to do nothing and watch our planet die, and I can't do that, and neither should you." She took her hand and placed it on Ron's shoulder. "Our plan calls for a three pronged approach. First, we're hoping to flood Mr. Best with emails and jam up his system. That will keep him from writing an explanation to his constituents who will think he's abandoned them, and hopefully crash his servers. Then, we'll inundate his phone line with so many robo calls it'll drive him mad. But what we really want to do is confront Mr. Best directly. Who knows, once he hears the voice of reason, maybe he'll change. This is where you come in. Ron, why don't you share with Josh what you told me?"

Ron sucked his cheeks in till he looked like a bearded guppy and then let his lips loose with a smack. "Okay, here's the deal. That girl you've been talking to, Rachel, you guys dating?"

Josh felt his stomach tighten. "No. We've had coffee a few times, and she invited me to church. That's about it."

"Good. We have connections with political types all across the country. You remember that race for the senate last year in Illinois? Made big news because a conservative nobody beat out the long-standing incumbent, Senator Weiss, a solid supporter of our movement. The guy's name is Stan Powers, he's the senator now, and this guy's bad, maybe even worse than Bill Best. So I got an email from one of our contacts in Illinois and he asked me to keep my eye out for this dude's daughter, and guess who that is." Ron held up a copy of the email displaying a large photo of Rachel front and center."

"So?" Josh said, his lips pursed, his chest starting to flutter over where this might be going.

"So it turns out that Senator Powers and Bill Best are friends. Bill writes articles applauding the senator's work, so they gotta be tight, right? We want to meet with Mr. Best but he won't meet with us. So we want to send a small delegation to his door to try to reason with him, but no one knows where he lives. We want you to try and get close to the senator's daughter and see if you can get her to ask her father for Bill Best's address. Not the post office box, we've got that, but the actual address where he lives."

Josh grimaced. They were asking the impossible. Their house didn't have a physical address. The property was owned by the forest service and granted to them under a sixty year lease his father acquired from a logging company that went bankrupt. The only thing that identified the property was a lot number in a map-book that showed where the parcel of land was situated with respect to Mt. Hood. Rachel was lucky to be staying there. It was about the safest place she could be. "I'm not sure what I can do," Josh said, "but I'll try."

"I knew it. I told you he'd do his part. Hey guys," Marie said, addressing the group, "Josh thinks he might have a way of getting Mr. Best's address."

"Cool!"

"Way to go, bro."

"Awesome, dude."

Thumbs up, big smiles, and fists raised in solidarity, welcoming him into the fold.

"Josh, I love you," Marie placed her hands on his shoulders, raised herself up on her toes, and kissed him full on the mouth.

And Josh nearly died.

SEVENTEEN

A CHIPMUNK BOUNDED up the porch steps and climbed onto the arm of the rocking chair where Mary sat. It was a small creature, brave in the face of a giant, but it stood chattering to get Mary's attention, determined to steal the remaining sunflower seeds from her hand. She unfolded her fingers, allowing it to see its reward.

Angie sat beside her, her chrome wheelchair reflecting the early afternoon light, but the critters were more cautious around her because she was prone to excited movement. Still, she laughed gleefully at the success of her mom.

The chipmunk took time to stuff its cheeks with the remaining seeds and jumped down, racing off to the safety of a nearby Ponderosa Pine. Others, jostling about in the branches of neighboring trees, cautiously waited, hoping for their turn.

It was a routine they'd worked on over the years, because it had taken that long to build up the tiny animal's trust. But on any given day, Mary knew she could sit in that rocking chair with sunflower seeds and before long one or more would be lured to her hand for a free meal.

Mary had rolled Angie out onto the porch right after their Saturday brunch. Bill had helped to clear the counter and get the dishes into the washer, but then he'd begged off saying he had another podcast to do, though he mentioned how he regretted not having time to take the canoe out on a morning like this. Working at the farm five days a week left only Saturday to get his podcast done.

Mary brought her feet up on a footstool and began rocking her chair in a peaceful swaying motion. The air smelled of pine, and of wood-smoke drifting in from campfires on the other side of the lake. Another chipmunk hopped up to a place just off the edge of the porch. It stood on its hind legs trying to see if there was any food left. Mary held her palms out showing they were empty. "Sorry, all gone," she said, wiping her hands together.

Angie twisted in her seat and moaned, the unexpected movement sending the chipmunk scurrying back into the woods.

Through the trees Mary saw several canoes on the water, their bright fiberglass red and blue and green standing off the deep blue like a Leonid Afremov painting.

When Bill had first suggested they build here, she was apprehensive. Being isolated and remote didn't line up with her perfect-life plans, but she had married an outdoorsman, and knew he wouldn't be happy living in the asphalt jungle under an umbrella of smog.

When the logging company folded and Bill seized the opportunity to acquire the lease, she'd envisioned being locked away like Rapunzel, only able to see the world from the window of her tower, but that hadn't happened. The constant company of Angie and the birth of their two sons more than compensated for any emptiness she might have felt. And the town of Tantamoa was just forty minutes away at the bottom of the mountain. She had quickly joined the congregation of Tantamoa Bible Chapel, where they'd worshipped ever since, giving her ample opportunity to mingle with others.

But if one thing stood out in her mind as the main reason she'd fallen in love with their mountain refuge, it was the animals. She loved watching the deer coming down to feed from the oil drum Bill had cut in half and plopped on its side over by the garage. She loved the chipmunks that fed from her hand and the goldfinch and chickadees and blue jays that pecked seeds from her feeders. She loved walks along the lake in the fall when the leaves were turning red and gold and pink and Canada Geese soared in V-formation over the placid blue waters. She had never regretted their decision to move here, not even when the river stole the life of their son.

Now more than ever she appreciated the sanctuary Bill had created. She viewed what was happening to her husband, the protests, the fire, the tax audit, as manifestations of an evil overspreading America like a cloud, though he always downplayed any such thoughts to keep her from worrying. He didn't need to. She was stronger than he knew. Perhaps she vocalized the, "what ifs," more than she should, but ultimately, she trusted God to see them through. And even if they eventually lost everything they would know it was God's to give and God's to take away. "Naked came I forth from my mother's womb, and naked I shall return." That's what Job had said during his time of trial.

She looked over at Angie. If anyone had a reason to complain about the hand they'd been dealt, it was her, but she was a rock. When Ted had died and Bill walled himself off and she wanted to crawl into bed and never come out, Angie had been there to pull her through. "Ittt's oooookay, Mommm. Taaaeeed's whhhiffff Jeeeeesus." And with her wheelchair bumped up next to the mattress, she'd reached out and fitfully stroked her mother's hair. "Ittt's hooooookay,"

Mary set her coffee down, wiping moisture from her eye. This was no time to be sad. She reached out and took Angie's hand and held it to keep it from pulling away. "I love you," she said, kissing her daughter's fingers.

"I...I...I luffffff yoooooo toaaaa."

Bill sat at his desk preparing the final notes for his podcast. He'd wrestled with this one. Heck, he'd wrestled with them all. That was the burden of being a commentator, you had to take a stand on an issue and know there was a good chance your viewers wouldn't agree with anything you said, though in this case he was preaching to the choir. For the most part, his audience was composed of God fearing people, many of whom were looking forward to Christ's return. So far, they had been overwhelming receptive. But there were also those who went to church each week, sent their kids to Sunday School, and believed in Jesus as their Savior, but weren't into deep Bible study. Many had pastors who preached the good stuff about Christ's redemption and love, while avoiding negative topics like judgment and hell. Controversial subjects weren't their forte, especially concerning the biblical account of creation, the flood, and especially prophecy. Their position was that much of scripture should be taken with a grain of salt. Bill also lumped into this group those Christmas and Easter Christians who seldom attended church or read their Bibles, but who claimed Christianity as their faith because they were, by God, Americans, and America was a Christian nation. He had the feeling they were listening, but holding back their opinions until he was finished. Lastly were those who had little or no background in biblical Christianity, thought Christ was only a curse word, or were downright atheistic. He worried about these more than the others, because they were most likely to reject what he had to say. Without a deep understanding of the validity of the Bible, and the intricacies of prophecy, it would be difficult not to think of his rantings as anything but science fiction.

The three-by-five cards that contained his notes were spread out on his desk in the order of his presentation. His stomach felt queasy. He really didn't like having to defend his beliefs. If Senator Powers hadn't challenged him to say something, he would have avoided the subject altogether. Raising his eyes to the ceiling, where rows of glazed yellow logs supported the roof, he petitioned God's help in presenting his monolog. Then he took a deep calming breath and switched the camera recorder on.

"Here we go, this is Wild Bill Best, back at-cha with another cautionary tale about the New World Order and the coming antichrist. Boy, that ought to get your attention right there. Sounds like a late night horror flick, don't it?

"But first my disclaimer. As I said before, this a bit of a juncture from my usual political commentary. I'll be taking much of what I say right from the Bible, and I make no bones about that. If you don't like it, I'm sorry, but I'm not making this stuff up. It comes from God's Word, written thousands of years before you or I were ever born. The rest will be my view of what's happening in the world around us, and

163

how it fits into Bible prophecy.

"I'm going to start by using a passage of scripture found in the book of Daniel, just a small innocuous verse that most would skip over without a second thought. It comes out of Daniel, chapter nine. God had just revealed to Daniel what to look for as we approach the last days, and then in closing dropped this little note." Bill's eyes went to the open Bible on his desk. "'But you, Daniel, shut up the words, and seal the book until the time of the end; many shall run to and fro, and knowledge shall increase.'"

"Okay, so what?" he said, looking back at the camera.

"Well, the thing is, in Daniel's day, which was approximately six-hundred years before Christ, not many traveled 'to and fro.' Back then the chief mode of transportation was your feet, or if you were financially well off, maybe a camel or donkey. And that's the way it remained right up until the late eighteen-hundreds. Today we circle the globe by plane, and drive thousands of miles each year by car. Travel is commonplace. So when Daniel is told to seal up the book until the end when many will travel to and fro, the reference can only be to a day like today.

"What about where it says, 'and knowledge shall increase?' When did that happen? From Daniel's time until a little over a hundred years ago, things had remained pretty much the same. People still walked or rode horses. They used kerosene lanterns to light their homes, and got their water from a well. For thousands of years knowledge didn't increase all that much. But boom! In little more than a century we've got cars, planes, computers and rockets to the moon. And within the last fifty years, knowledge has increased exponentially. So when Daniel was told to 'seal up the book' until the end, when knowledge will increase, what time period do think was being talked about? Answer, right now! We are living in the last days.

"While Daniel records information about the antichrist, how he will rise to power and demand our worship, it is the Apostle John who lets us know that the antichrist will be in total control of our economic system. He gets right down to the nitty-gritty when he says that no one will be able to buy or sell without taking this guy's number on their right hand or forehead.

"I explained last time how the world's economic collapse could facilitate the Great Reset, and about how this was playing out through exorbitant spending on things like social programs, climate change, and the Covid virus. Today I want to talk about recent advances in technology.

"This is the other side of the coin. Without an economic collapse, there is no reason to redo the world's monetary system, or hand it over to Satan's muse. But highly advanced technology will also be required if the antichrist wants to assume management of the world's capital and resources. So let's take a look at just a few of the things on the horizon that will enable the antichrist to control just about everything.

"In the not so distant future, your bank account, along with all your financial assets, will be stored on the microchip that's already embedded in your credit and debit cards. When you get paid, your earnings will be wirelessly loaded onto your card, and when you purchase something, money will be removed. But make no mistake, the ultimate plan is to carry your money on a microchip implanted in your wrist or, if you happen to be armless, your forehead. This technology was developed at MIT some time ago, and people in various parts of the world are already having it injected into their wrists for a number of different reasons. I bet you've heard of chips like these being inserted into animals to help reunite lost dogs with their owners.

"You probably won't see microchips being used for carrying money around for some time. More than likely the program will be introduced it as a health pass, with medical information stored on the chip so when you board a plane, you can validate that you've received all the latest vaccinations and aren't a threat to anyone. Loading money on the chip won't necessarily come until we start using cryptos as a standard form of currency.

"Having your financial information stored on your body is one thing, but you can't have your wrist in several places at the same time, so how do you make transactions remotely? No problem. You'll have a personal scanner that transmits the information taken from your chip and sends it out over the internet. And don't worry, you'll always have an internet connection. Right now thousands of very-low-earth orbit satellites, or VLEOs, are being sent into space via SpaceX rockets. When this project is complete, almost twelve-thousand satellites will blanket the planet with a persistent internet connection with speeds of up to one gigabit per second, connecting almost everyone on earth.

"But keeping track of every transaction worldwide will take an enormous amount of computing power. This couldn't have been done even a few years ago, but today we have supercomputers which are growing faster and more powerful every day. A good example is the Frontier which uses exascale computing, in which processing power is measured in exaflops, or quintillions of calculations per second. A quintillion is a one followed by eighteen zeros, that's one, zero zero zero, zero zero zero, zero zero zero, zero zero zero, zero zero zero, zero zero zero, calculations per second. Frontier is reckoned to have as much processing power as the next one-hundred and sixty fastest supercomputers combined. A few of these installed on every continent will, yes, give the antichrist just what he needs. He'll know everything you and I buy or sell, and when, and where. If we refuse to take his number, or try to opt out of the program, he'll just put a freeze on our account and you and I won't be able to buy or sell a thing. But friends, don't do it. The Bible says in taking that number you're aligning yourselves with Satan, and thereby incurring the wrath of God.

"So, here's what it boils down to. We are living in an age when those things foretold thousands of years ago are coming to pass. There are men, rich, powerful, highly educated men, who are actively trying to usher in a world government. Satan, through his proxy the antichrist, is prophesied to one day rule the world, so guess where that idea comes from? The world's monetary systems are, at some point in the future, destined to collapse, and when that happens it will make sense for everyone to adopt the new digital currency so all nations can trade freely using the same economic platform. Buying and selling by individuals will then be a matter of extending your wrist to a scanner to have digital dollars removed or added to your personal account. Those are two more ideas that, according to the Bible, line up with Satan's plan. And we'll welcome them, along with all the other technological advances on the horizon. It will seem like we're living in a perfect world run by a genuine mastermind, who according to scripture, is also called the son of perdition. But we call him the antichrist because he has come to set up Satan's kingdom, not God's.

"But rejoice! We're in the enviable position of seeing prophecy fulfilled right before our eyes. And whatever you do, don't get discouraged. We may lose a few battles, but we, through Christ our Lord, win the war. I've got more to say on this, but I've once again run out of time. So, happy trails to you. This is Wild Bill Best, signing off until we meet again. Adios Amigos.

Bill hit the fade to black button and rocked back in his chair, wondering if anything he said could penetrate the darkness. They were after him. They'd already burned his trees, and now were manufacturing a phony charge of tax evasion. And Rachel was having her life threatened for the way her father voted. And Palco was being driven out of cities where he'd been invited to come and speak. Dark days indeed—but like Luther said: 'And though this world with devils filled, should threaten to undo us, we will not fear for God hath willed, His truth to triumph through us.' Amen!" He leaned forward shut the system down. The sooner he got away from all this, the better.

Bill found Mary and Angie on the front porch enjoying the afternoon breeze. The day was beginning to grow dim as the sun fell into the western horizon leaving a pale yellow sky. He drew in a lungful of pine-scented air and felt a release of the tension in his shoulders, the natural result of finishing another podcast, especially one that dealt with exposing the devil's plans.

Perhaps he shouldn't try to spell it out so clearly. There was nothing to be gained by scaring people. If making his viewers aware of what was likely to come served any purpose at all, it should be to let them know Christ was coming soon, the time was at hand, and encourage them to watch and pray. Only God knew if it was too late for one more revival.

He pushed through the screen door wearing a beige denim vest

167

with his fishing pole in hand, and pork-pie hat on his head, the quintessential fisherman.

"Leaving us so soon?" Mary said, looking up from the book she was reading.

"Just going fishing, hon." Bill walked over and leaned in with his hand on her shoulder, kissing the top of her head.

Mary brought her hand up to cover his. "I know, and I'm glad fishing helps you relax, but I kind of miss you being here."

"What do you mean? I'm here." Bill scooted around until he was in front of Mary.

"No, you used to be. All those years you couldn't bear the thought of fishing without Ted, you were here for us, but now, when you're not at the farm, or doing one of your podcasts, you're out alone on the lake. We miss you, that's all."

Bill glanced over at Angie. She put her hands together twisting them in a knot, "Yeeeessssssss," she said. Her head tilted back, her jaw sliding to the side as she forced the word from her mouth.

"Wow, I didn't know. I guess I got so caught up with being able to enjoy fishing again, I didn't realize. But hey, I have a great idea. Why don't you and Angie join me? We haven't been out together in ages."

Mary's lips curved down, her eyes wide as she shook her head. "You know it upsets Angie to see you drag in a fish with a hook in its mouth. She feels the pain even when you release it."

"No, no, no, you got me wrong. I don't need another fish. Let's just go out and enjoy the sunset together. What do you say? I need to get away from all the junk I've been dealing with." Bill's eyes shifted to Angie. Her head tipped to the side shaking up and down. "Good it's settled. Let me go put my pole away and I'll be right back."

Bill came out the door wearing blue jeans and a brown flannel shirt, his fishing pole, vest, and pork-pie hat gone. He watched Mary, her blue polyester jacket shimmering in the light as she wheeled Angie down the trail to the lake, maneuvering the wheelchair over small roots and rocks till she was at the shallow beach. Bill trundled down the porch steps and chased after.

Angie was already getting her vest on by the time Bill reached the shore. He helped Mary cinch the fasteners, but left Angie in her chair as he handed Mary a second vest. The canoe was overturned to keep it from filling with rain. He rolled it over and slid it out into the water, allowing Mary to step in and get seated before the launch. Angie reached out. He took her in his arms and handed her to Mary, who settled her in the bottom of the canoe. They had long ago decided this was best. There was too much chance she might rotate excitedly and topple off-balance into the water, were she allowed to sit on one of the seats.

Bill straight-armed the canoe, sliding it back. It was heavy before, but with two extra people it felt like he was pushing a small car uphill. Maybe he was just getting old. When all but the stern was in the water he stepped in and used the paddle to shove off.

And suddenly they were free of the shore, gliding out onto the lake, the smell of sodden loam and pine filling him with serenity. He took a deep breath to clear his head and began stroking the water, taking them deeper and deeper into God's country. Nuts to all those who wanted to suppress individual thoughts and freedoms. If they ever got off their big city butts and got out here where God lived, they'd get a whole different view of what He intended.

"Isn't this great?" he said.

The sun was now just off the horizon looking like a giant yellow lollipop, it's beams splashing against the waves made by the canoe's wake. There were trails of smoke from the campfires on the opposite shore. It wasn't the best time of year for camping, but they were people like him who loved the outdoors rain or shine.

Then he heard it.

Eeeeeeeyyyyyy, eeeeeeeyyyyyy, eeeeeeeyyyyyy.

He looked up, the sun glinting off the band above the eagle's talon. It spread its wings, circling overhead.

"You see that honey? That's one of the birds I took from its nest when it was abandoned. Remember? Look at that."

They watched as the eagle circled farther and farther into the distance until it became a spot too small to see. "Dang, I wish Josh was here to see that." Bill flinched, blinking furtively. He drew his paddle out of the water and laid it across his lap. He'd surprised himself. It was the first time his thoughts had brought up Josh's name—*instead of Ted's.*

EIGHTEEN

PORTLAND WAS SOCKED in, the fog like a gray blanket covering the ground. Josh raised his foot. Decaying leaves were stuck to the bottom of his tennis shoe. *Stupid leaves.* He began picking them off. The nuisance would be around until the trees were in bloom again and the grass needed mowing. He thumbed the stack of papers in his hand and then looked up. The sky was dull, a fog so thick it shrouded the day's possibilities. Sometimes it felt like he was living in a wad of cotton. He rolled his shoulders, and rubbed the arms of his hoodie to lessen the chill.

From the height of their cabin, he had been able to look down on the flatlands. From there he could sit on the porch and watch the clouds back up against the mountains covering Portland while he was above it all in the sun. Didn't matter, it was early March. The daffodils were in bloom and soon the cherry trees would blossom.

Marie stood in front of the Millar Library where she always positioned herself. She was a full block away, but through the mist he could see her passing out flyers in her tight blue jeans and red sweater, almost forcing her leaflets into the hands of passersby.

Josh was less productive. He reached out, offering a flyer to anyone curious enough to take it, but pulled back when they waved him off.

They hadn't begun the assault on his father, they were still fine tuning the system, but the plan was to launch the program later that day. In the meantime, Josh was involved in another project. He glanced at the handout again, reading down the list of senators and house members who disparaged environmental initiatives like the

New Green Deal. Each name had a phone number beside it. The flyer implored people to call and voice their opposition to everyone listed.

A student on a skateboard flipped his wheels up and parked in front of Josh. He took a flyer and read it.

"Good stuff, man. I'm up with what you're doing, but I got no time to make calls. Sorry." He handed the flyer back and zoomed off down the sidewalk, weaving around a young lady walking her dog. The dog pulled against its leash, barking to let the skateboarder know the invasion of its space wasn't to be taken lightly.

A girl rolling a baby stroller took one and paused, looking at Josh for a moment. The infant was wrapped in a pink flannel blanket and had a matching knit beanie on its head. All you could see were its puffy rouge cheeks, and button nose, and two tightly shut eyes. The girl smiled and flipped the brochure over to write something. She slipped it to Josh and kept going. He held it up to see what it said. It was a phone number with the words, "Call me."

Marie seemed to be having better luck. Most of the people she approached walked away holding a pamphlet. She wouldn't like how he was doing. His stack of flyers was about as thick as when she'd given it to him, minus maybe a dozen he'd managed to give away. He glanced around the park and found what he was looking for, a trash can only a dozen feet away stationed behind an elm tree. He made his way over, looking around to make sure no one was watching, and dumped half his flyers into the bin.

His guilt was to be expected. He wasn't trying to be dishonest. It wasn't like he was stealing or lying or anything, he just wanted Marie to think he was doing his part. It wasn't his fault no one wanted what they were selling. He went back to passing out the yellow sheets in plain view, just in case Marie turned around to see his progress, but she was too busy to pay him notice. She was whirling this way and that, pushing her flyers into the hands of everyone she saw—a woman in control, confident and commanding.

The burn in his chest was back, the attraction of the male to female species that came every time he thought about her. He didn't know if it was a product of evolution, as just about everyone else believed, or something God planted in man to proliferate his creation. He leaned toward the latter, because the former couldn't answer the question of how male and female parts, evolving independently, somehow ended up perfectly fitted for procreation. At least that's the way his dad had explained it. But there was definitely something about love that brought a man to a place of weakness, and that's where Josh was now. And if it meant passing out a thousand flyers, then he'd pass out two-thousand. He started pushing the yellow sheets at everyone he saw. Anything to get her approval.

"Lighten up dude, I don't want it, okay?" said a man with his palms up, pushing back.

"Hey, get your hands off my girl," said another.

He wasn't trying to molest anyone. Why couldn't she just take it and read it later? Marie was passing out sheets like candy. Maybe it was harder to say no to a girl.

"Josh!"

He didn't see her bounding up, he just heard her say his name, and then: "You go on ahead, Jim, I know you're late for work. I'll catch up with you later."

Josh saw marathon Jim jogging by, his sneakers slapping the pavement, his bright green shorts and sleeveless T-shirt bearing the Viking's logo. "Alright, babe, see you," Jim said as he spun around trucking backwards for a few steps so he could wave.

"Babe?"

Rachel came to a stop, breathing hard, her ponytail resting over her shoulder, her pink tank-top slightly moist from her run. She raised one hand and placed it on her hip while using the other to mop her brow. "Josh, where were you?" she said, panting. "You stood me up."

Josh reached out and handed a flyer to someone who actually took it, but the next person clamped their arms tightly around their breast and said, "No thanks."

"What do you mean?"

"Friday. You were supposed to meet me at the rec center."

Josh held his flyers at arm's length, poking them every which direction but encountered rejection time and again. He dropped his arm with the yellow sheet still in his hand. "I was there, but you were already with Jim so I didn't stick around. I didn't want to run as a threesome. But I guess it worked out. Looks like you two have started running together."

Josh handed another flyer to a passerby who took it, but then veered off to toss it in the trash.

"Josh, the only reason I risked going was because I thought you could be a friend and act as a chaperone. I don't want Jim getting the wrong idea."

"Oh, is that why you're out running with him again today?"

"I'm out running with him because he asked me, and because your mom seems eager to loan me her car. And, surprisingly, I found out I can keep up with him, though I suspect he's holding back a little. What are you doing anyway?"

Josh handed Rachel a flyer without thinking, then realized what he'd done and made an attempt to retrieve it, but she spun around ignoring him as she read. "Are you kidding?" she said, handing it back. "You're seriously asking people to call my father and complain about how he votes? Good luck with that. Why do you think I'm staying with your folks?"

"I didn't make up the list, but if he's on it, it's because he's against reducing our CO_2 footprint and he needs to know that's dangerous. They're after my dad too, about a bunch of weird stuff he's been saying."

"Josh, this is insane. What's going on with you?"

"Just trying to be environmentally smart. We need to take care of this planet. It's the only one we've got." Josh reached out to a trio of kids, one of which grabbed the leaflet. They giggled amongst themselves pulling it out of each other's hands to see who got to read it first.

"What makes you think we're not? There's only so much you can do without getting ridiculous. Your father wrote a few articles about that. Have you even read what he had to say?"

"You bet, and let's just say I disagree, along with about a bazillion scientists, practically every teacher on this campus, and most of the student body. My dad's not a scientist or a college professor, and neither is yours, so what makes you think they're right and everyone else is wrong?"

Rachel waved the flyer at him. "Come on, Josh. You're better than this."

Josh saw Marie looking his direction. It caught him off guard. Rachel was his assignment. He didn't need Marie coming over and spoiling the plan. "You have to leave," he said.

"Why?"

"Because you're Senator Power's daughter, that's why. Look, we'll get together and I'll explain it, but right now I think you'd just better go."

Rachel followed Josh's eyes to a girl in a red sweater handing out flyers on the next block. She looked annoyed. "Whatever," she said.

Josh watched as she turned and took off running again, her ponytail rolling out like a gold flag furling in the breeze.

Rachel ran up the block till she was even with the girl who kept staring at her, but she didn't stop, or take a flyer. Instead she looped around under the ancient copper beech and kept going until she stood at the entrance to the library. Her eyes were burning. It was the Doctor Jekyll, Mr. Hyde syndrome, Josh the kind, sweet guy, or Josh the jerk. Josh was coming under the influence of some very wrong-minded people.

STEVE STOOD ON the porch of the Burke family residence, at least it was the address he'd been given by the pastor of the Tantamoa Bible Chapel. It was a nondescript bungalow, one of five similar bungalows that lined the curb, each as miserable as the others, all of them grey and dank. His mood was exacerbated by the low ceiling of clouds that hung down on him like a depressing spirit. He sneezed and raised his mask to wipe his nose, then quickly pulled it down so they wouldn't think he had Covid and refuse to let him in.

He'd gone to the church because he'd wanted to verify the accuracy of the charitable donation Bill Best had filed on his income tax return—and especially the anomaly. Bill, in years past, had given the church around three-thousand dollars a month, which seemed excessive until Steve realized that traditional church giving was around ten percent. Bill had listed his regular income, not counting his charitable organization, as just shy of three-hundred thousand, so it made sense. What Steve questioned, however, was the sudden increase. Over the past year his donation had jumped to ten-thousand a month. By any measure, that was excessive. Steve suspected Bill and his pastor were scheming to fraud the government. Rich people were always looking for tax shelters. What better shelter was there than a church?

Pastor Wilks had been polite, but wary. The sudden interest in Bill was, he said, a little disconcerting. Apparently someone else, a Victor Damshie, had been there the day before asking if the church could direct him to where Bill lived. Pastor Wilks cited the church's policy of not giving out personal information, and when the man took out a hundred dollar bill and tried to bribe him, was promptly shown the door.

Steve showed the pastor his I.D. confirming he was with the IRS and there on official business. Though still a bit stiff, Pastor Wilks had asked their accountant to open up the books and Steve was able to verify that the church had received the money and had deposited it into their bank account. Bill's increase in giving, the pastor explained, was in response to the Covid pandemic. The church had been forced to close for a few months and when allowed to reopen, mask regulations and social distancing stopped many from attending, which meant tithing was down. The church was in danger of shutting its doors, but Bill had stepped in to take up the slack.

Steve shivered. He hated wet cold weather. Winters in the northeast were cold, but they didn't sink into your bones the way wet weather did. He was having a hard time finding something to use against Bill. His boss was all over him, discretely implying that he either dig up something, or make something up, but Cal wasn't out here in the field talking to the people the way he was. If he had been, he might have come to the realization that they were trying to take down an elephant with a BB gun.

Steve looked back over his shoulder. A child, maybe six or seven, had come up behind him, his cuffs and tennis shoes wet from traipsing across the lawn.

"You wannn my mom, or myyyy d-d-dad?" he said, looking up through eyes as big as a Precious Moments figurine. His face was as flat and white as a porcelain plate, his nose upturned like someone had pushed it back and fixed it in place. His mouth hung open with a swollen tongue, a drool of saliva sliding down his jaw. *Down syndrome,* Steve thought.

"Hello, young man," Steve said, stooping over slightly to shake the boy's hand. The boy responded by extending a set of small pudgy fingers.

"Myyy name is Billy, w-w-what's yours?" he said.

"I'm Steve."

"Myyy brother's name's Steve. Do you know Steve? Hee's my friend."

Steve took his hand back and straightened himself. "No, I don't believe I've had the pleasure."

"You can. Yoooo want to meet him? This, this, is our house."

"That's nice, but I'd really like to meet your par..." he hadn't finished but the boy squeezed by and opened the door.

"Come on, I'll ta-ta-take you to him."

Steve didn't know whether to step into the house or not. It certainly wasn't etiquette to walk into a home unannounced, but he was invited. He wiped his feet on the mat before stepping inside hoping to dislodge any bits of wet gravel he might have picked up on the sidewalk.

"Billy, were you outside again? You know you're not supposed to go out unsupervised." The voice came from another room. A second later a woman appeared, looking startled as she tucked a strand of cranberry red hair behind her ear. If it weren't for the shadows under her eyes, Steve would have thought her attractive.

"I'm sorry, I don't mean to intrude. I was hoping to speak with someone, and Billy here, asked me in." Steve glanced around. The furniture was modest, mostly padded, without wood or other hard surfaces. He tried to recognize what he was smelling, and then realized it was soup with a heavy tomato base.

177

The woman, nodded, rubbing her arm. "It's okay. What can I do for you?"

Steve reached into his suitcoat and withdrew a business card, handing it to her.

"IRS?" she said, squinting.

"Don't worry," Steve held his hand up like a traffic cop. "I'm not here about your taxes. I'm sure they're fine."

Billy had raced off but was now back with another Down syndrome child, perhaps two or three years older than himself. He pulled him by the hand shuffling over to Steve. The boy kept his eyes to the ground refusing to look up.

"This is my b-b-brother," Billy said. "Heee's shy. Steve, this is Steve too, just like you. You, you, yooo need to shake his hand." The new boy stood there shuffling his feet, but after a few seconds, turned and walked away. "Steve-eve, that's not nice," Billy said, taking off after him.

"I'm sorry." Steve reached out to shake hands with the woman. "My name is Steve, too. I guess it got Billy excited to meet someone with the same name as his brother."

"Beth," the woman said, extending her hand. "They're not really brothers, but everyone who lives here is part of our family, so in a way they are. We don't wear masks inside. Feel free to take yours off if you want, or leave it on, your choice."

"Thanks, it's hard enough to breathe, let alone talk through these things." Steve unfastened his mask and slipped it into his pocket. "I'm here because your pastor, Mr. Wilks, said I should talk to you. It's about Bill Best."

"Really? What about him?"

"Nothing serious. He makes a lot of donations to charity and claims them on his taxes, which, of course, gets our attention, not that he's done anything wrong, but it's our job to check everything out. Just to make sure things are above-board."

Beth tucked in the blouse that had apparently become undone while at the stove. "Well I don't know what you expect to find, but I doubt I can be of any help. Please, have a seat," she said sweeping her hand out toward the sofa. Another child ran into the room, grabbed a rubber ball off the floor, and ran out again, squealing. "We aren't a registered charity so I doubt he uses us as a tax deduction." The little girl ran back into the room and exited through the door at the opposite end, screaming in a shrill high-pitched voice all the way. "That's Marcie. She's ADHD. Bill does give us money, but we don't issue tax receipts. I wonder why Pastor Mark sent you here." The girl was back with a cotton stuffed rabbit, swinging it by the ears. "Marcie...Marcie, you're going to hurt that poor bunny. Try to play nice."

"Looks like you've got your hands full."

"You don't know the half of it. Come, I'll show you." Beth turned and walked down the hall toward the back of the house. Steve followed but she stopped when they came to a bedroom with an open door. Steve looked inside. In the middle of the room sat a girl in a wheelchair, her body twisted like a pretzel. *"Aaauuuuuaa,"* she exclaimed, as they entered. "Yes, honey, I know, it's past lunchtime. Just give me a few minutes and I'll get it for you."

"Aaaauuuuuuaaah." The girl was rocking back and forth, obviously agitated, like she wanted out of her chair but didn't know how. *"Aaaauuuuuuaaah."*

"I'll be back in a minute, sweetheart, don't worry." Beth stepped out of the room and continued down the hall. "That's Katie. She's our only child, I mean by blood. She has cerebral palsy, diagnosed when she was three months old, a terrible shock to my husband and I. There's no history of the disease in either of our families. Bill, the man you're looking into, has a daughter with cerebral palsy too. Did you know that?"

"Yes, I think so. He claims her as a dependent, along with her medical expenses."

"We met Bill at church and felt an immediate connection, soldiers fighting the same battle, so to speak. By then we had already adopted Steve and Billy. These are kids nobody wants. Kids that without love, would just be tossed aside like yesterday's garbage. Now we have seven special needs children to take care of, and it's Bill that makes it possible. When he saw what we were doing, he volunteered to finance it. He knew we couldn't. I tell you, that man is a real Godsend. You know he has a TV channel on the web. They say he has over a million viewers, but he doesn't charge anything to watch his program. He just asks people to give what they can to help cover his costs. And people do. But he never keeps the money. Gives practically everything away to others, especially those in need. And his wife, too. She's such a doll. You gotta love people like that..."

BILL COULDN'T HEAR his phone over the grinding of the old Ford tractor. It rang over and over again, but he remained clueless. The tractor was a beauty. It had oxidized Ford blue paint with a signature white stripe and blue lettering. He'd picked it up at a farm auction, a rust and dust classic from the 1980s. The tiller had even more rust than the tractor, but it did the job. He was watching the ground for rocks and upended roots while looking ahead to make sure his furrows were straight.

He was plowing under the soil that had been blackened by the fire. The morning fog had burned off, leaving an afternoon full of sun. After days of rain, mud stuck in glops to the tractor's tires, causing more dirt to be lifted out than furrowed in. He brought the tractor around, going wide, creating a keyhole at the top of the row and swinging back to line up with the row he'd just finished. The phone continued to ring.

A crow atop a power pole cawed and flew off in the direction of the Watalong River. Bill watched it disappear, subconsciously thinking about what they should do for Josh's birthday. He would be twenty-two this month, a man, at least in age, if not in character. Mary wanted to have a surprise party and invite a few of his church friends, but Bill disagreed. He didn't want to discourage his wife, but the idea made him apprehensive. Josh had quit hanging with his Christian friends long before he stopped going to church. Inviting them over might make him feel like they were pushing an agenda, causing him to further rebel.

Bill swung the tractor around at the bottom of the row and cut the throttle, switching the engine off. He stood bringing his leg over a blue-plastic seat mended with duct tape, and jumped down. He wasn't finished but he needed to refuel. The phone rang again. Bill removed his gloves and retrieved it from the pocket of his coveralls.

"You got, Bill," he said, in his familiar greeting.

"You are accused of crimes against humanity. Please desist or there will be consequences. You are accused of crimes against humanity. Please desist or there will be consequences. You are accused of crimes against humanity. Please desist or there will be consequences."

Bill pulled the phone away from his ear. "What the…" He pressed the disconnect button, but the phone immediately rang again. "You are accused of crimes against humanity. Please desist or there will be consequences." Bill shook his head and pressed the end-call button. *Some kind of sick joke.* The phone rang again. This time Bill refused to answer. He stormed off toward the construction site. Saws were rasping through wood sending plumes of sawdust into the air. Nail guns slammed two-by-sixes together, the frame being assembled before it was raised. He walked over to a man holding the architect's plan up for inspection. The phone in his pocket continued to ring.

The straw barrier gave way to his boots, his nose transitioning from the smell of the pine scented outdoors to the gasoline he'd accidently spilled when he'd filled the tractor that morning.

"You think I could use your phone for a minute. Mine seems to have a bug. It won't stop ringing and I can't call out." The man shrugged and handed over his phone. Bill took it, glad to hear a dial tone. He dialed 911.

"Public Safety, Sergeant Hanagraph. Is this an emergency?"

"No," Bill said. "Well yes, kinda."

"Which is it? You need 911?"

"No, not that. I um, it looks like I'm the victim of a cyber-attack."

"Yeah, we're getting a lot of those. What seems to be the problem?"

"Someone has hijacked my phone. It keeps ringing with a pre-recorded message, you know, one of those synthesized voices that sound like a computer talking. I can't make or receive any calls because they keep blocking the line."

"Ouch, sorry to hear it, but at least you weren't conned out of your pension like some of the folks around here. Unfortunately, there's not much we can do. I mean if you want to come down and file a report, that'll be fine, but this is Tantamoa, we don't have a cybercrimes division, and regular police aren't able to follow up on this kind of thing."

"So, what am I supposed to do?"

"You'll have to call Portland. In the meantime, try shutting off your phone and removing the battery."

Bill drove his pickup with its collapsed fender creaking, up the winding mountain road to the cabin. He'd left after trying to call home and getting only a busy signal. It was slow going. The rains had eroded the gravel, creating ruts where the water washed across the road. Every spring he had to drive his tractor up the damaged logging trail to fill the channels in again. *Oooffffff!* He bounced over another kidney-punching ditch.

He pulled up to the security gate. Whoever was doing this knew their stuff. He'd tried everything: turning the phone off and on again, removing the battery to see if a restart would delete whatever bug he'd acquired. It was no use. The gate swung back. He pulled through, and waited to lock it behind him. Aside from his tormentors calling it quits, or his getting a new number, there was nothing anyone could do. Tantamoa's police department wasn't big enough to fund a cybercrimes division, and when he tried Portland, which did have one, he was told their backlog would preclude looking into it for at least a month.

He parked his truck by the garage with his hand on top of the steering wheel, lost in thought. The lights were on, though it was barely dusk outside. He drummed his fingers on the wheel's rim. He had to be careful how he told Mary. It didn't take much to figure this was linked to his recent series of podcasts. He didn't want her to be afraid of a silly prank.

He felt his pocket to make sure he had his phone, and leaned his shoulder against the window, popping the door open. The hinges creaked as he stepped down. Early season crickets were chirping. The few warm days must have brought them out of hibernation. He heard it before he got to the porch. The house phone was chattering. "Son of a buck!" They had attacked his home too. He pounded up the steps and plowed through the door. Mary and Angie were there to greet him with balls of cotton stuffed in their ears.

"Thank God, you're home," Mary screamed. "This has been going on all afternoon. It's driving us nuts."

Bill walked to the phone on the kitchen counter and unplugged the jack.

"Oh," Mary said. "Why didn't I think of that? Sorry, Angie. I'm just so flustered I can't think anymore."

Bill went to the bedroom to disconnect their extension phone, and came back out. "You say this has been going on all afternoon?"

She nodded, her eyes becoming glassy. "I'm glad Rachel wasn't here; it's been driving us crazy. And that's not even the worst part. They're threatening us. Said there would be consequences..." A tear rolled down her cheek, then another as her face knotted.

"...if we don't desist, yeah, I know. They got my cell number too. I've been getting the same message all day."

Bill put his arms around his wife, pulling her in. "It's okay, hon. It's okay."

"I...I...I didn't know what to do. I thought they might be outside trying to break in. I know that's crazy but I couldn't help it. I kept thinking we might be killed," she sobbed.

Bill massaged her back. "I'm here now. Everything's fine. How you doing, sweet girl?" he said over his wife's shoulder to Angie.

"I...hokaaay."

Angie, ever the rock.

Mary turned and broke free of Bill's arms. She grabbed a tissue from the box on the sink and went to sit on one of their woven branch chairs with the tissue held in her lap. Her breath fluttered in her chest, her eyes red and veined. She stood again. "I...I think I need to go lay down. Just fix something to eat for yourself and Angie. There's plenty of leftovers in the refrigerator."

Bill found a container of beef stew and poured it into two bowls. He put the first in the microwave and set it to three minutes. "No worries. I got dinner covered," he said to Angie. "Give me a minute to go wash up."

But Bill didn't head for the bathroom. Instead he went into his office. He didn't like what he was thinking, and hoped he was wrong. He pulled his chair back and flopped into it, leaning back with his eyes rolled to the ceiling. "You mind lending a little help, Lord, 'cause I'm steamed up enough to blow. Please give me patience." He leaned forward, tilting the chair upright again and reached for the mouse to awaken his computer. For a moment he stared at the email icon, fearing what he might find, but then he placed the cursor over it and clicked. His fears were realized. His email program opened and said there were over four-thousand emails waiting to be read. Four-thousand and counting, and he just knew every one of them said: "You have been accused of Crimes against humanity. Please desist or there will be consequences."

His fist came down on the desk so hard the faceplate of his clock popped open. "Son of a buck!"

NINETEEN

THE ROOM WAS STUFFY. The longer warmer days of March, in conjunction with the building's heating system, made it feel like they were sitting under a dome of glass in the high desert. The group was sweltering.

Josh mopped his forehead, suffocating behind his mask. He had dressed too warm. It was getting time to retire the hoodie but until he found something else to wear, it was all he had. Marie was feeling it too, not that she'd said anything, but the same odor he'd smelled before was following her around again. It was like she'd tossed out her loofah and had instead scrubbed herself with soiled kitty litter. Someone should tell her deodorants weren't necessarily a bad thing.

A girl with pink hair had joined the group, apparently impressed with what they were doing. She had taken the sheet handed her and had called every name on it, screaming in the ear of whoever answered the phone about the evils they were committing, much to the approval of those seated around the table. As far as they knew, she was the only one to have done so.

Josh's roommate, Ron, was seated across from him, wearing a black mask with message that read: "Reduce CO2," which seemed ridiculous since he was taking in oxygen and exhaling carbon dioxide with every breath he took. If he wanted to reduce CO2, all he had to do was stop breathing. Marie was to his right, also wearing a mask, though hers was red. Donnie, with his red corn-silk hair, sat at the other end of the table. Ross and Jeff, the designers of his dad's communications meltdown, sat beside each other, their chests puckered with the

185

acknowledgement of their success. The chairs in between were occupied by people whose names he couldn't recall, especially since most of their faces were hidden behind masks.

Marie pushed her chair back and rose, taking her body fragrance with her. Josh inhaled deeply, knowing the reprieve wouldn't last. Her bouquet notwithstanding, he still loved her, though she hadn't yet responded in any meaningful way. He was drawn to her sensuality, her alluring eyes, and the commanding way she took charge of every situation. Still, something was missing, something he couldn't quite put his finger on, but that kept him feeling nervous and insecure.

Marie went to a whiteboard and popped the cap off a marker to write: "Cancel Bill Best!" which she underlined and emphasized with an exclamation point. Then she turned around to face the group again. "We need to thank Ross and Jeff," she said, pulling her mask down to give each of them a nod, "for the excellent assault on Mr. Best's phones and email system. I understand he's still crying about the 'lowlifes' that did this to him. Loved the article in the paper, by the way." She held up a newspaper clipping and read:

"Political Pundit Decries Hijacked Communications"

"Oregon resident Bill Best, known for his ultra-right-wing views, has drawn the ire of progressive activists in the Portland area. According to Tantamoa Public Safety Sergeant Henry Hanagraph, the incident took place on Monday March 11th when Mr. Best complained of having his telephone and email systems commandeered by local activists. The incident is said to have been in response to a series of podcasts authored by Mr. Best warning of a doomsday scenario involving the antichrist's takeover of the world.

"According to Mr. Best, the attack contained a veiled threat to his person and those of his family. No group has come forward to claim responsibility for the incident but sources say…"

"Anyway, you get the rest. Well done, gentlemen." Marie applauded lightly and was joined by those around the room. She let the article go. It rocked on a current of air, floating down as it slid to the center of the table.

"The problem is, we haven't stopped him. His third podcast aired last week, and in it he alluded to having more to say, though, thanks to your efforts, it will be a while before he gets that one out, but what an idiot. He's just showing his subscribers what a nut-bag he is. I doubt anyone pays attention anymore, except the wackos who agree with him. But unfortunately there are too many of those, and that's why he has to be stopped. Josh, how are you coming with getting his physical address?"

Josh kicked his chair back on its rollers, stretching out with his feet crossed at the ankles and his arms folded across his chest. "I'll be seeing Senator Powers' daughter again this afternoon. We have this regular thing now where we meet Mondays, Wednesdays and Fridays for coffee. I mentioned our request and she was open to helping. But she says congress is in session and her dad's kind of hard to reach, plus she has to catch him at just the right time when he doesn't have a lot on his mind, but she'll come through."

Marie wore tight fitting black denims and a red T-shirt. She popped the cap back on her marker and set it in the tray of the whiteboard, then turned back to Josh, smiling. "That's great, as long as we get it before his next podcast, but one word of caution. Be careful. I saw you talking to her when we were passing out flyers. That was her, wasn't it? She went right by me and I nearly got frostbite."

"Yeah, that was her. She's okay, a bit old-school but her heart's in the right place." It was Marie's smile that did it, those voluptuous lips and magnetic eyes, they disarmed him every time. Was she jealous?

"Just keep your guard up, that's all I'm saying, at least until you find out where her loyalties lie."

STEVE FOLDED HIS SUIT into his zippered travel bag and set his polished wingtips on the bottom to keep them from soiling his other clothes. Freshly showered, and dressed in jeans and a long sleeve blue cotton shirt, he was ready to travel. He wouldn't need his suit again until he got back home.

He glanced around the room, making sure he wasn't leaving anything behind. The hotel was comfortable. The wallpaper with wainscoting and the plush bathroom towels were upgrades compared to his apartment back in D.C. Thankfully, the government received a special discount from the hotel chain or he wouldn't be there. They were, after all, using taxpayer money.

He went over and drew back the window shade. It was a sunny day in Portland, a welcome relief from the two weeks he'd spent in the cold and rain. He was packed and ready to go. He looked at his watch, but it was only nine-thirty. His plane didn't leave until two. He turned and went to the coffee pot, filling the Styrofoam cup with another dose of morning caffeine.

He should probably start writing his report. He had time to kill. At least he could dictate something to be transcribed after he got back. His only hesitation was knowing Cal wasn't going to like what he had to say. He went to the writing desk and snapped his laptop open, glancing over his notes. There wasn't the slightest infraction, nothing he could point to that might incriminate Bill Best. If Cal wanted to manufacture something, that was on him. Steve had decided he wanted no part of it. His job involved bringing the guilty to justice, not framing the innocent.

His voice recorder lay beside his computer. He picked it up and switched it on.

"Case number 11247.

"Subject, William Best.

"Pursuant to a criminal investigation into the tax liability of Mr. Bill Best of William Best Holdings, LLC, initiated by the Internal Revenue Service on January 23rd, I have concluded a detailed forensic audit. Said audit took place in our Washington office using surrendered files from Mr. William Best, between the dates of February 4th and February 21st. This was subsequently followed on by a series of external interviews conducted between the dates of March 7th through March 22nd, with prejudice toward probable indictment. This investigation has now reached its conclusion, and my findings are listed below…" Steve heard his phone ring and reached over to pick it up.

"Steve DeMarko." Steve put his phone on speaker and set it down by his laptop.

"Steve, it's Cal. I hear you're coming back today."

"Yes sir. Got my bags packed. Just waiting for my flight."

"So what do you have for me? I don't want everything, just a quick summary."

Steve leaned back in his chair. He'd been dreading this moment, knowing the day would come, but hoping to forestall it as long as possible. Perhaps it would be easier over the phone than face to face. "Nothing," he said.

"Nothing?"

"I'm afraid that's what I have. Nothing. I've spoken to seven different charities, each of which was listed as having received donations, and every one produced documents showing Mr. Best's contribution, and their bank deposit validating the amount. I checked out that spike in his giving to his church, but found he'd increased his donation to help it stay open during the pandemic. The pastor there gave me the names of three other families he supports off the books. One takes in kids with special needs, seven in total, plus mom and dad, and he foots the bill for all of them, but they're not a charity so what he gives is over and above everything else he does, without tax credit. You'll get my full report soon as I get back, but you know me, I'm thorough. You're not going to bring this guy down for tax evasion. He's the epitome of honest."

Steve waited, the silence growing like balloon ready to pop. Then it did.

"Steve…"

"Yes?"

"You're fired!"

"Excuse me?"

Cal was wheezing again, his voice pinched and breathy. "You're protecting this guy, *husweeze*, I can tell. No one's that clean. I didn't say you had to find something big, just something we can use, *husweeze,* but no, you've been against me from the get, pushing back every time I say go, *husweeze*, even when I said it wasn't from me. This comes from the top. The President himself wants this guy out of the picture, and if we don't find something, both our jobs are on the line."

"Give me a break, Cal. You can't fire me, and they can't fire you. We'd both sue for wrongful dismissal."

"*Husweeze*, good luck with that. In the meantime, I'm going to handle this myself."

"Waste of time. If I couldn't find anything, believe me, it doesn't exist."

"You think so? Well let me tell you something, *husweeze, husweeze.*" Steve heard Cal take a hit off his inhaler, his voice clearing almost immediately. "If you'd been doing your job, as I've been doing for you, you would have questioned why we couldn't find Mr. Bill Best's web hosting service. You knew we were looking into it, remember, because we thought they might know something about the money flowing through their system? But we hit a dead end, right? Well I didn't give up, which is why I just received a subpoena for Bill Best's servers. That's right. Because Mr. Best keeps everything on servers right in his own freaking home. And I'll tell you what. I'm going to go get those servers and I'm going find what you missed."

Steve was staring out the window. The sun, for the first time in days, spread across his laptop, the glare preventing him from seeing what was on the screen, but it didn't cloud the facts. "That's a load of crap," he said. "We have copies of the disks already. We've been through them with a fine-tooth comb. You're not going to find anything we don't already have."

"You're forgetting about the cash. He may log the checks and credit card donations, but I'll bet there's a ton of cash he doesn't report, and I'm gonna find it. Anyway, it doesn't matter, once I have his servers, I can add files for donations that never existed, files he never reported, making him guilty of tax fraud. That's what you should have done."

"No. That's not what I should have done, and it's not what you should do either. You know, Cal, I always thought you were a pretty decent guy, even with all the wheezing, but a straight shooter. Guess I was wrong. We'll see you in court. And I will get my job back. You can take that to the bank."

JOSH HAD BEEN on trips to Portland all his life, but he'd never seen anything like this. Perhaps they had always come a week too early, or a week too late, when the trees weren't ready. Cherry blossoms had a short blooming cycle, but this time, owing to an early spring, they were bang on the money. It was like the city had set off a fireworks display over the river that burst from the sky and fell to the earth in dazzling pink sparkles that stuck to the limbs of the trees.

"Wow, this is awesome," he said.

"Pretty neat, huh? Jim turned me on to it. He suggested we come running here." Rachel reached for her phone but it was a robo-call. She slid it back into her hip pocket. She didn't notice the man over by the bicycle rack with his face turned toward the sun. There were hundreds of faces in the crowd, but if she had glanced his direction, she might have recognized him. He'd been tailing her for several days. He was about her height, a few inches shorter than Josh, but better built with muscular shoulders and a thick chest. His face was oval, his hair curly and blond, his eyes green. He wore his sideburns to the bottom of his ears where they flared out, and had a blond mustache covering his pink lip. He had his phone to his ear.

"...yes, you were right, she is staying with Mr. Best, but not in Portland. They live northeast of the city near a small town called Tantamoa...Yes, but there's not much there. They only have one church, and I talked to the pastor. He wouldn't say where Mr. Best lived, but he didn't deny that they went to his church so the next Sunday I sat out in the parking lot and, as expected, they showed up. You saw the photos. That was her, right? ...No, I can't get near the house. I followed them home, they live outside town on a dirt road, but I had to hang back so I wouldn't be seen and then had to turn around when I came to a security gate...No, it won't be hard. She has a car. Drives into town several times a week to see Mr. Best's son, fact she's with him now...I will. You just say when, and I'll pick her up..."

Josh and Rachel were strolling down the waterfront viewing the

191

one hundred Akebono cherry trees that grew beside a wide concrete walkway along the Willamette River. The traffic was thick with bike riders, joggers and pedestrians. The word always spread when the trees were in bloom, and Portlanders turned out by the thousands to enjoy the first sign of spring.

"I'm glad you called," Josh said.

"And I'm glad you agreed to meet. There's something important we need to discuss."

"Oh, what's that?"

They were approaching the Steel Bridge, the second oldest bridge of its kind in the United States. A double decker with blackened steel girders that looked like a structure right out of H. L. Mencken's, *The Libido for the Ugly.*

"You ever been over that bridge?" Rachel asked.

"Sure, plenty of times. You forget, I grew up here."

"Jim and I did it last week. It was loud. Pedestrians have to walk across on the lower deck with the trains. The cars and trucks above create such a racquet you have to almost cover your ears. You hungry?"

"I suppose, a little. I've been over the bridge, but never walking. You have something in mind?"

"The Pine Street Market. Jim and I went there. They have all kinds of places to eat."

Jim and I, Jim and I, Jim and I, Josh didn't want to hear it. It sounded like a horoscope—*Gemini, Gemini, Gemini.*

A jogger ran by, his head turned to eye Rachel as he passed.

Keep your eyes to yourself, friend, Josh thought, relieved to see it wasn't Jim.

"This way," Rachel said, steering them off the sidewalk onto the grass. They passed beneath the boughs of the cherry trees, causing Rachel to glance up and say, "It's like being under a pink parasol," and continued on across the lawn till they came to the street, where the pastel colors of the park were replaced by traffic and noise. They found the mall of restaurants converted from an old industrial complex now flaunting a hip postmodern facade.

The place was choked with people enjoying a late lunch. Having just come from outside, and knowing they were about to eat, they didn't reach for their masks. They squeezed through the crowd looking for something that sent their taste buds to salivating. Kim Jong Smokehouse, Teote Outpost, Bless Your Heart Burgers, and not a fast food chain in the bunch. *Cool.*

"Got any suggestions?" Josh asked.

"Well, Jim and I had Checkerboard Pizza and it was great. Four bucks a slice is hard to beat."

Gemini again. Josh shook his head. "I think I'd rather have tacos. You should try something different," but he only said it because he didn't want to follow Jim's lead.

"Sure, we have lots of pizza in Chicago, but not much Mexican. I'm game."

Josh started off, but turned around and took her hand, pulling her with him like a child he didn't want getting lost. Her fingers were soft and warm, and she didn't pull back so he didn't let go until they were standing in front of the Teote Outpost. There were two seats at the counter. Josh quickly sat down before they were taken. Rachel sat beside him and turned his direction. Their knees touched. He felt the warmth of her skin, a surprising intimacy, but she didn't flinch, and neither did he. "I really need to talk to you about something," she said.

"Just a second. Let's order first." He passed her a menu and began scanning the one in front of him.

"I don't know Josh, it all looks good to me, but I'm not really a connoisseur of Mexican food. Why don't you order?"

"You like tacos?"

"Sure, I guess."

"Okay then." He flagged the server who came over at his bidding. "We'll have the Taco Trio. Make one the El Diablo with the roasted poblano chiles, and one the Smokey Pallo with the chicken and cabbage salad, and one the PaBellon with the beef brisket, sweet peppers and onions." He passed the menus to the waitress and turned to Rachel. "I think this is going to be good, not your typical ground beef with lettuce and tomatoes, but the real thing. Now, what did you want to say?"

Rachel took a sip of the water the server brought and set it down, the sides of the glass sweating with condensation. She looked at Josh, her blue eyes fixed directly on his like a gas flame. "Josh, why haven't you returned your mother's calls?"

Josh looked affronted, his mouth skewed in apprehension. "Is that what this is about? Did she put you up to this?"

"No, Josh. I took this upon myself, but she did want me to ask you a question since she can't reach you."

"That's 'cause I know what she's going to ask. She wants to know if I've been to church, and I don't want her harping on me because, as you know, I haven't. Did you tell her that? Did she ask?"

"She did, and I told her you hadn't, but that's not what she wants to know."

Josh relaxed, releasing his breath. He picked up his own water, the ice cubes clinking in the glass. "Really, do tell."

"Apparently you have a birthday next week. She wants to have you over for dinner, that's all."

Josh swallowed and sucked his cheeks in, slowly shaking his head. He set his glass down, his fingers cold and wet. "No, I don't think so. I don't want to see my old man."

The waitress brought their meal and set it on the counter; three blackened corn tortillas piled high with meats and cheeses and onions and cilantro, and a sundry of sauces. Josh took his knife and cut each tortilla in half and handed a fork to Rachel. "Bon appetite," he said, digging into the one with the poblano chilies and glazed red maple sauce.

"Josh, you need to work at getting along with your father. Besides, I get bored having dinner with just your folks. I want you to be there. Please, do it for me."

Josh looked up, his eyebrows raised, his cheeks bulging as he chewed. "Go on, take a bite. This is really good," he said.

TWENTY

THE SAYING, MARCH comes in like a lion and goes out like a lamb, proved to be true in Portland that year. The last week of the month produced warm sunny weather right up to Josh's birthday on the thirty-first. Josh was standing in the park that bordered Market Street with the lawns just beginning to turn green and buds swelling on the nodes of the trees. He could smell the fresh cut grass and see the groundskeeper on his orange riding mower a block ahead, mulching the remaining dead leaves.

He folded his arms, his toe poking at the ground, already regretting his decision. Blue jays and juncos and grosbeaks flittered in the branches above, excited by the coming of spring, while robins hopped along the ground pecking for worms that had worked their way out of the newly thawed earth. At least he had negotiated his way out of dinner. He could not have handled that, cake and family time was bad enough. He heard the light *beep* of a car horn and turned to see his mother's white Ford Fusion sitting at the curb.

A gray squirrel ran up the side of a blooming dogwood to hide among the thousands of white flowers. Josh kicked a small rock out of his way. It dinged against the car's fender, thankfully, without leaving a mark. He leaned in to open the passenger side door. "Morning Rachel. I figured Mom would send you," he said, climbing in.

They drove through the center of town out into the suburbs and on into the low hills of Tantamoa, crossing over the Watalong River Bridge, on past the family Christmas tree farm, and on up the abandoned logging road into the evergreen forests of Mt. Hood.

195

Josh lay his head against the headrest, his eyes half closed. The sun streaming through the glass warmed his face. So far, the gin he'd used to bolster himself had gone undetected. Friends said gin was hard to smell on one's breath, but he'd chewed five Tic Tacs just to be sure.

They were passing the place where he had climbed up out of the gorge in a full blown panic, running to find someone he could tell of Ted's fate. The brush had grown thicker hiding the exact spot where he'd emerged, but not enough to keep him from recognizing it as the place where his father's favorite son had died. He brought his eyes back around and caught Rachel staring at him.

"That's where it happened, isn't it?"

He sighed before answering. "I tried, I really did, but he got pulled under. There was nothing I could do."

"Have you been back since?"

"Nope, never."

"You might try it. Confronting your demons can be therapeutic."

Josh waited till she looked away then rolled his eyes and sighed. "I'd prefer to leave the past in the past, if that's okay with you."

They pulled around the last bend leaving the crunching of the gravel road for the soft bed of pine needles in the yard. Rachel pulled to the front of the cabin and shut the car down. The raccoon that regularly raided the trash jumped down from the aluminum garbage can, knocking it over with a metallic clatter and waddled off into the woods.

Rachel got out. She was dressed for the party in a peach skirt and cream-colored turtleneck sweater. Her blond hair was neatly combed and hanging over her shoulders. She looked at Josh and smiled, and then headed for the door. He watched her walk away and then looked down on himself and cringed: soiled denims, dusty black jacket, and tennis shoes. He ran his fingers through his hair to smooth it out, ever the nonconformist.

Josh followed her up the steps and across the porch, her low pumps clapping on the wood boards. She stood aside inviting him to enter first. He reached for the door and pushed it open. His mom and dad were standing there arm in arm, like they'd been waiting years for his return.

196

"Happy Birthday," his mom cried, as she reached out, embracing him in a hug.

"Welcome home, son," his dad said, patting him on the shoulder.

He looked back, his eyes pleading for help from Rachel, but she just nodded with a smile.

Presents, neatly wrapped with ribbons and colored paper, were stacked on the dining room table and balloons filled with helium were tied to the backs of chairs.

Rachel handed the car keys to Mary who slipped them to her husband. He dropped them into a small velvet bag while she went to the kitchen to finish the cake.

Rachel followed behind. "What can I do to help?" she asked.

Mary went to a drawer, found a box of candles and a book of matches and handed them to Rachel. "You can do the honors," she said.

Rachel poked twenty-one candles into the chocolate frosting and held one back which she lit with a match. She smiled, humming the tune of happy birthday as she used the one candle to light the rest until the cake glowed like the cone of Mount Vesuvius.

Josh caught her eye, imploring her to come rescue him from his dad who was trying to engage him in conversation, but she ignored him.

"All ready," she called over to Mary.

Mary wiped her hands on a towel and laid it on the counter. "Come here, Josh. You have to blow out the candles."

Josh was sitting on the living room couch with his father, uncomfortable at being the only one not dressed in his Sunday best, an outsider in his own home. He burped and felt the alcohol rise to this throat, and reached into his pocket for his Tic Tacs. He popped another five into his mouth, chewing fast and hard.

"I guess they're calling us," he said, glad for the interruption.

He pulled himself up and went over to Angie, who'd been left by the door alone and forgotten. He spun her wheelchair around and rolled her to the table. "There you go, sweet girl. I wouldn't want you to miss the fun." He sighed, resigning himself to the attention he didn't want, or feel he deserved.

Rachel grabbed his arm and pulled him over to the cake.

Mary began singing, "Happy birthday to you. Happy birthday to you. Happy birthday dear, Jaaa—osh. Happy birthday to you." Josh heard his father singing in the background, his rich baritone the loudest voice of all. Angie joined in the fun squealing, *Haaaaaaaay Birrrrrrdaaay frrrr yoooooo.*

"Make a wish," his mother insisted. He closed his eyes like he was thinking, and then leaned in to blow out the candles.

"Alright, good job," Rachel applauded.

"Not so easy when you get to be my age," his dad joined in jovially. Josh felt his father's hand on his shoulder but he turned his back, refusing to acknowledge the gesture.

Mary pulled the candles from the cake and took up a knife to begin cutting. She set each piece on a plate and handed them to Rachel, who passed them around. "Here Josh, I saved the corner piece for you," she said, giving him the biggest slice she'd cut so far. "There's cola in the refrigerator, just help yourself."

What, no beer? Josh thought. He dug into his cake with a fork and looked at his mother with his mouth full and cheeks bulging. "Umm, that's good, Mom," he said. It was the double, double chocolate he loved best. He brought his eyes up and glanced around the room. "What about Angie, did she get a piece?" and then saw his sister with chocolate smeared on her mouth and fingers and a huge smile on her lips.

"*Yaaaaeeeeeesss,*" she howled.

Josh turned and headed back toward the living room, cake in hand. The cabin was aglow with a fire burning in the hearth, and the wagon-wheel chandelier fully lit.

"Wait, don't wander off," Mary said. "We want you to open your presents."

Josh came back, set his cake down, and took the package his mom was handing him. It was wrapped in paper with Happy Birthday spelled out in multicolored balloons. He pulled the ribbon from the corners of the box, tore into the paper, and lifted the lid, separating the tissue to reveal two Ivy League button-down shirts, one with a green and blue crosshatch pattern and the other with vertical blue and white stripes. "Thanks Mom," he said, setting the box aside.

"Do you like them?" she asked.

Josh puffed air from his nose, his expression flat. "It's not really my style, Mom, but I do need summer shirts so if you don't mind, maybe I can exchange them. It's the thought that counts, right?"

His mother's face registered disappointment. "Why don't you at least try them on? I think you'll look good in them."

"Mom, don't."

Rachel handed him another package, which he opened to find, *underwear?* "Mom, really?" Rachel brought a hand up to cover her grin. He didn't want her thinking he wore briefs. He liked boxer shorts. He used the tissue to cover the offensive garments, and received another present packaged in a box bigger than needed to disguise its contents. Inside were three CDs by contemporary Christian artists whose names he didn't recognize. At least it was music, not something he had to wear.

He knew from the shape, size, and weight, what the next gift was. He lifted the box away from the paper and saw he was right. A Bible. No disrespecting this one. "Thanks, Mom, I love it." He leaned in to give her a kiss on the cheek. In terms of buying him things he didn't want or need, his mom was batting a thousand.

"It's genuine leather. Look inside. I wrote you a note."

Josh hesitated for a moment, then drew in his breath and flipped the book open, its cover still stiff with newness. The message inside read:

Dearest Josh,

It is my fervent prayer that you once again give the Lord first place in your life. You love to read, why don't you start reading the Bible, just a little each day? The rewards will be great. The Lord is coming soon, are you ready to meet Him? Will he say, "Well done thou good and faithful servant?"

On your twenty-second birthday,
Love Always,
Mother.

Josh felt the burn in his eye and swallowed the lump in his throat. He put the Bible back in the box and set it on the table. It was just the emotion of the moment, and what was he supposed to do with a Bible anyway? Leaving it here would hurt his mother's feelings, but he couldn't have it lying around his apartment either.

"We have one more for you son," his father said, handing him a small velvet sack.

"What's this?"

"Open it."

Josh could feel what it was through the soft green material. He unlaced the top and dumped the keys into his hand. "Really?" he said.

"We're giving you mom's car. We thought about it and decided you needed something to get around Portland," his dad said.

"And we're hoping you'll use it to visit us more often, and maybe even go to church," his mom added.

"Unbelievable. That's...totally awesome." Josh rose and went to the front door anxious to see his mom's old car through the eyes of new ownership. Mary got up and began clearing the table. Rachel started gathering his presents to get them out of the way.

Josh was outside sitting behind the wheel of his new vehicle with the visor down pleased to see the registration already filled out in his name. *Sweet.* So what if it was a few years old. She'd only used it for trips into town, it was low mileage, and his dad always kept their cars in top mechanical shape. It was clean enough to look new, though he wished it was any color but white, but white without rust was okay, and those nice wire wheels were cool. And it was a hybrid, perfect for riding around with Marie and the gang. *Now that's a gift worth coming home for.*

"You like it, son?" His father had found him and was leaning in with his arm on the open door.

Josh turned his head away like he was still admiring the dash, just in case his breath carried the lingering smell of alcohol. "I guess so. Sure, but what about Mom, how's she going to get around?" He said it realizing he was actually more concerned about Rachel. He didn't want to stop seeing her for coffee. The deep woods crickets were warming up for the night's orchestration.

"Already covered. Your Mom's getting a new one. And I had my mechanic give the Fusion a thorough inspection. It's had an oil change, the brakes are good, everything safe and sound, and I filled the tank with gas."

Rachel was placing the rest of his presents on the back seat. "You ready to go back inside?" she said, looking at Josh's reflection in the rearview mirror.

Josh climbed out of the car, making his father step away. It was still twilight but the moon was bright enough to paint shadows on the ground. "Sure, why not?" he said. He turned and started toward the door. His father, already ahead of him, stepped onto the porch.

"You know what, I think I'd like to sit out here for a few minutes, it's such a nice evening. You forget what crickets sound like in the city," he said, dropping onto a patio sofa.

His dad nodded and went inside, the screen door slamming behind him.

Rachel stepped onto the porch and sat sown beside Josh. "Mind if I join you?" she asked.

Josh had hoped for a moment alone, but shook his head. "Suit yourself." He reached into his coat pocket and removed a slim stainless steel flask, unscrewing the top.

"What are you doing?"

"Reinforcement. You expect me to go in there and sit around talking with my dad like we're old friends. Sorry, I'm not up for that." He tilted his head back taking a long swallow, then smacked his lips, burped, and wiped his mouth with the back of his hand. "That kind of thing takes a little fortification."

"Does not. Your dad's not going to bite your head off. He's trying his best to show how much he loves you. Can't you see that? He gave you a car. That's a pretty nice gift, don't you think?"

Josh glanced over. The moon shining on the car's paint made it look like a white turtle. "That was nice," he said, "but it don't make up for years of abuse."

Rachel paused for a minute, leaning forward in her seat. Her hands were folded in front of her. "Josh, your father is going through a really hard time right now. He could probably use your support."

"Yeah, I heard they crashed his computer network," he said, taking another hit off his bottle.

"You don't know the half of it."

"Want some?" Josh said, holding the flask out, but Rachel back-handed it away.

"Don't be ridiculous," she said.

"Hey, I was just trying to be polite, that's all."

The porch light was glowing yellow, a single moth orbiting it like a planet around the sun. Bill stuck his head out the door. "You kids want to join us. Your mom's getting kind of lonely…Josh, what is that?"

"What's what?" Josh said pulling the steel container into his coat.

"Are you drinking?"

"No! Yes. What if I am?"

"You know we don't allow liquor in this house."

Josh clambered out of his seat, but moved too quickly, throwing him off balance. He stumbled forward.

"You're drunk."

Josh straightened himself. "I'm not drunk. I've had a few drinks, but I'm definitely not drunk."

"Look at you. You can't even stand up straight. Get in the house," Bill said holding the screen door open wide.

Josh stuffed his bottle back into his pocket. He narrowed his eyes, looking at his father challengingly. "No. No way. I'm not gonna go in there and have you lecture me. You know what? Forget it. I'm outta here." Josh jumped off the porch heading for the car.

Rachel glanced at Mr. Best, hesitating.

Josh opened the door, the interior light illuminating the inside as he climbed in.

Bill stepped down off the porch. "You can't drive like that. You'll kill yourself. Your drunk. Get back here, now!"

Josh slammed the door.

"Ted would never have acted like this. Get back here and apologize."

Josh fired up the car and popped it into reverse. "Fine, here's your apology, Dad," he thrust his arm out the window with his middle finger extended, throwing that universal and unmitigated sign of defiance in his father's face. Then he snapped on the lights, threw it in drive, and hit the gas, shooting up a wave of gravel and pine needles and small twigs from under his wheels as he roared down the road.

It felt like God had dialed down the oven of space and cycled in refrigerated air, the warm evening dropping ten degrees. Bill rubbed the goosebumps on his arms, watching the red taillights disappear around the corner into the woody darkness. His pulse raced, his temples throbbing against his skull. He clenched his teeth, pounding a fist into his palm. *Ingrate.* He had to breathe deep and focus on relaxing his jaw. *Not his fault, I did it—again! Crud, crud, crud!*

Rachel was staring at him, but he refused to look her direction. He sucked in his breath, *God, help me, I screwed up again.* He gazed at the moon for a moment then closed his eyes. *I don't think I'm ever going to learn.* He let his arms hang limp. He needed to regain his composure. He looked at Rachel. She stood there frozen, her eyes big and white as the moon. Then he reached for the screen-door and let himself in, trying to look relaxed and nonchalant.

Mary was still doing dishes, but he could see she was uncomfortable, like she knew something was wrong. "I'm Sorry, Hon. I guess Josh got so excited about his new car he decided to go for a drive. Sorry. I didn't expect him to run off like that."

Mary turned to the sink, grabbing a dish to rinse. She wiped her cheek on her shoulder before sliding the dish into the washer. "He's not coming back, is he?"

Rachel slid in behind Bill and skittered off to her room.

Bill backed up slipping his hands into his pockets to keep them from shaking. "Probably not. He said he had to get going."

Josh was trying to control the car. He wasn't new to driving, but the bends in the road could be hazardous, and though he wasn't drunk, he knew there was alcohol in his system. He passed through the security gate. *See, if I was drunk I wouldn't be able to work the combination.* The dark pines rushed by with the moon behind them cut in pieces. The only sound was the gravel crunching under his tires.

He kept his eyes on the road, determined not to take his new ride over the edge. He was leaning forward on the wheel, the blue glow of the dashboard revealing his intense concentration. It always ended up this way. Why they kept inviting him was beyond comprehension.

Josh felt his resentment building, his grip tightening on the wheel, his foot pressing against the pedal. They had no right to impose their holier-than-thou lives on him. He continued staring into the darkness, rounding a curve with his wheels sliding toward the ravine but the car held to the road. So what if he died. Serve them right.

The road was narrow, one way only, designed for logging trucks to drive up to the loading dock in the morning and drive out with a haul of cut trees at night. Traffic was controlled at both ends by men on two-way radios.

He rounded another bend entering a series of S-curves winding in and out at recklessly high speeds. Each outside bend threatened to send him over the edge into the Watalong River. Josh cranked the wheel around a broad curve and came to a short straightaway. He hit the gas, his wheels spinning in the dirt, spewing up clouds of dust as he swung the wheel to the left, barely keeping the car on the road. He slid through another turn, sending rocks and gravel over the side.

He was coming out onto the highway. He pulled the wheel hard to the left, skidding onto the asphalt in front of an eighteen wheeler glowing with amber lights that screamed by with a long blast of its air horn, *haaaaaaaaaannnnnnnnnnk* missing him by a mere two feet, and slid out onto the four lane heading toward Tantamoa. His heart was thudding in his chest.

Bill finished brushing his teeth and went to the closet to hang up his shirt, leaving his jeans to fall to the floor where he could find them in the morning. He had helped Mary clean up and get Angie to bed, but little had been said. Now she lay staring up at the ceiling. The glistening of her eyes let him know she was in a fragile state of mind. He sat on the edge of the mattress, contemplating what to say.

"I screwed up, Mary," was all he could think of.

Mary pulled the blanket up under her chin. "My son hates me," she answered.

Bill looked at her over his shoulder. "No, honey, he doesn't. He didn't leave to get away from you. He ran off because of me."

"He hated everything I bought him."

"Everything we bought him," Bill corrected.

"No, you got him a car. He loved that."

"It was your car, Mary, don't forget. I'm sure he won't either."

"He just hates me. Everything I say rubs him the wrong way. He won't return my calls. No matter what I do, it isn't enough." She rolled over away from Bill.

He lay down and stretched out, then scooted in behind her placing his arm over her shoulder. "No, Mary, he loves you. I'm the one he hates, and for good reason. We've talked about this before. He's going through those rebellious years. Besides, you weren't there. You don't know why he left. It was me. He took off because I started lecturing him again, just like I always do. I've got to learn to let the boy grow up on his own."

Bill stroked Mary's hair. The moon outside the window bathed the room in a pale light. He could see the picture of the four of them on her dresser, probably the last photo taken of them as a family, and the cedar chest where she stored the baby blankets of both Josh and Ted, and the shine of her cheeks wet from the washing of her tears. "Josh loves you," he said, pulling her in tight, "and so do I."

Josh was frazzled, the tension in his body stretched like a guitar string wound too tight. He flicked on the wipers letting a stream of water wash the dust away. When his dad handed him the keys, the car had looked shiny and clean. He wouldn't want anyone to see it now. His eyes scanned the road looking for a place to leave the car.

The apartment he shared with Ron offered street parking only and the spaces were always taken. He'd seen multilevel garages on his downtown walks, but right now he couldn't think of where one was.

He cruised down Market past the Park Blocks, searching for public parking. He turned right at Fourth, hoping to find a city lot. His head swiveled left and right peering into the darkness, his face looking blue in the light of the dash. Five blocks later his search was rewarded. The sign at the entrance said it was a thirteen dollar maximum, and pay upon exit. *Perfect*. He pulled in, surprised to discover the parking was underground. He headed into the dimly lit tunnel that led down to a cavernous lot where dozens of cars were already parked. The vacant spot he took was around back. He got out and started walking up the ramp, considering himself lucky. The parking garage was only a few blocks from The Cheerful Tortoise, and he needed a drink.

TWENTY-ONE

THE PHONE WAS SINGING, "Lady in Red," over and over again. Josh couldn't say how long the song had been playing, but it seemed like hours. He blinked and tried to open his eyes, his conscious mind grasping for a reason why that miserable piece of plastic was interrupting his sleep. *The alarm!* He grabbed the phone and fumbled with his thumbs to shut it off.

His heart was pumping like a horse at full gallop. He was supposed to be somewhere—*the demonstration!* The timer was set for ten-thirty, which gave him a half hour to get ready. He had to be on the promenade by eleven to help Marie set up the podium and run the microphone wires for the rally at noon. He tried to raise his head, but it was like lifting twenty pounds of hollow brass. Closing his eyes, he grit his teeth and forced his legs around so he could sit up. He waited a minute to catch his breath, and then pushed off the bed to stand. The blood rushed to his feet, his stomach following the flow down his leg. *Ugg, no way.*

He'd just wanted to find a table where he could sit and brood over his dustup with his father, but Donnie had been there with Janet and Mickey, two girls he'd just met that evening. and Josh craved companionship. These were his real friends, people he could relate to. One drink led to another and he didn't end up getting home until after two in the morning stumbling in after getting lost a few times while trying to find the apartment. And now he was suffering the consequences. He wasn't up for another protest. Why did they need to have so, many?

His flask was on the counter. He unscrewed the aluminum cap and brought the bottle up, taking three long swallows before smacking his lips and wiping his mouth with the back of his hand. The cure wasn't instant, it would take time, but he felt better about his prospects for the day. He kept the bottle in his hand and shuffled over to the bathroom medicine cabinet for the rest of the treatment.

He cranked the knobs of the shower to get the water warm, then popped the cap off a Tylenol bottle and upended it over his mouth until he felt three of the extra strength tabs fall onto his tongue. He brought the bottle of gin up to wash them down, smacking his lips, and screwed the cap down tight on the bottle. It wasn't his purpose to get drunk, but the gin would reverse the effects of his hangover and help him feel right again. He dropped his shorts to the floor and stepped into the shower.

Clouds of steam rose around him as he lathered himself, still too weak to bend over and wash his feet. Couldn't allow the blood to rush to his head, no way, no how. He stepped out and toweled off, considering the whereabouts of Ron. Probably already helping Marie set up the stage. Josh stepped into the living room in his skivvies. Sun spilled in through the uncovered window, radiating heat. It looked to be warm outside. He grabbed a sweatshirt and threw it over his head, climbed into his pants, and slipped into his tennis shoes without putting on socks.

The Park Blocks, the heart of Portland's cultural life, had been a part of the city's heritage since Daniel Lownsdale first drew up a plat for the blocks in 1848. Rose bushes flourished along the residential and mercantile streets, where the sights to be seen included the Portland Art Museum, the Oregon Historical Center, and the University.

But like everything that degrades over time, much of the beauty of the Blocks had been denigrated by a growing homeless population. Certain areas had been given over to tent cities. Needles in the grass, the stench of body odor and human waste, and the buildup of garbage, had led to a downgrade of the parks on several prominent websites. Public restrooms were designated use at your own risk for the chance of contracting Hepatitis-C from contaminated surfaces. It was not uncommon to find addicts hovered around a candle heating heroin in a spoon.

But as Josh tramped across the campus, he was oblivious to all of that. He saw only roses and blue skies. The rally would take place on the university end of the Blocks where, for the most part, the dignity of the parks had been preserved.

He slouched into the venue like a homeless drunk. He was too tired to stand straight and too braindead to care. The elm, oak and maple trees were decorated with posters of his father, and others like him, who spoke out against globalism, but he no longer felt defensive. His father was getting what he deserved. He stood under a giant elm with his temples pounding and his stomach roiling like hot tar. Slinging a hammer with his damaged head was out of the question. Josh paused to look around, hoping to see a dash of red; Marie in her rouge-du jour. He found her on the stage holding a microphone and, as expected, wearing red shorts and a halter top—*lady in red*…

"Testing, one two, three, test." She tapped the microphone with her finger, *pop, pop, pop.* "Am I being heard out there?"

The screeching feedback made Josh grimace. A man he had seen several times before in other places, waved a hand at Marie. "We read you loud and clear." Same black hoodie, same goatee with flames growing up the sides of his cheeks.

Josh meandered over, wilting. His hands were stuffed in his pockets. He managed a tepid smile as Marie looked down on him. "I made it," he said, squinting against the sun in his eyes.

Marie shook her head, her features buried in silhouette. "Gee, Josh, we might have used your help a little while ago, but we're pretty much finished now."

Josh shrugged, looking around. They had erected a portable stage with a podium and microphone, a white canopy tent was off to the side, and posters were stapled to trees throughout the arena. He looked at his watch. It was five to twelve. "Sorry," he said, shaking his head with the water on his brain sloshing around his cranium. *Ahhh.* "I… uh…I must have overslept. I thought it was only eleven."

"That's okay, we had plenty of help. See that tent over there? We'll have people handing out information sheets and answering questions all day. Why don't you go see if you can give them a hand, maybe fill in for those who need a break, or get them coffee? I have to get going. We're starting now."

Josh turned and watched the people filling in around the stage. The man with the goatee joined Marie. He leaned in to say something Josh couldn't hear. Josh stepped back and slipped through the crowds to see if he could be of help at the tent. He chastised himself for being late, but his head was too congested to feel rejection, and the way it was going with Marie, he wasn't sure how much he cared.

Marie tapped the mike again, *pop, pop, pop.* "Thank you for coming," she said. "This day is so important. This is the day when we recognize that we are one human family. We're not African, or Mexican, or Asian, or American, we're not gay or straight or questioning, we're not man or woman or gender neutral, or Christian, or Muslim, or Buddhist, we're human beings, evolved from the same DNA. No one here can say they're better than anyone else. We are brothers and sisters, co-equal. We are one."

A few fists went up in solidarity followed by a few murmurs of approval.

"We're here today to proclaim that we, the next generation, have a better way. We're here to stop oppression, to stop bigotry, to stop racism. America's greatest virtue is tolerance because only through tolerance can the people of this world live in peace. We must allow everyone the freedom to live as they choose, marry whom they choose, and worship whatever god they choose. Our common goal is to build a better world where everyone has respect for everyone else, and everyone works together side by side as equals so that we all get along..."

Josh glanced at one of the posters of his dad, and sniggered. *What she should say is they tolerate everyone except those with whom they disagree.* The cheers were getting louder, but the shouts always increased in volume the more the person talked.

Josh sidled up to the white canopy tent. They had a counter set up in front stacked with pamphlets and sheets of paper. Two girls, one with long straight blond hair and the other with her hair done in spikes, were handing out leaflets. Josh had to stare long and hard at the second girl to be absolutely sure she wasn't a man.

"Marie sent me over to see if I could get you guys a coffee or anything," he said.

"Hey, that would be great," the blond exuded. The other girl frowned and shook her head, continuing to pass out pamphlets as though Josh was an unwanted distraction.

"Okay then, I'll be right back." He started to walk away but turned and said, "If you think of anything else you need, just let me know." Josh took off in the direction of the city, disappearing into masses that now looked several hundred strong.

"This planet is rich in resources," Marie's voice boomed from the speakers as he walked away. "Believe me, there's plenty to be shared by everyone, if we only stop being greedy, and hoarding stuff for ourselves. I ask you this, why is it right for some to have two or three houses when there are thousands with no place to live? Why are people dying when by giving up what we don't need we can provide for everyone? We need to get rid of greedy capitalism that exploits workers and builds fortunes for the rich while keeping shackles on the poor. We need to do away with democracy because it panders to lobbyists who bribe government officials to make their rich corporate bosses even richer while leaving the poor in a quagmire of debt."

The crowd was excited now, fully awake and hanging on every word. Their fists were raised and their voices loud in assent.

Josh found his way back, pressed on all sides by a mass of bodies bumping his arms, making him hold the coffees high to avoid a spill. He handed one to the blond girl. "Here," he said, reaching into the pocket of his sweatshirt for a half dozen packets of cream and sugar which he plopped on the counter. "You didn't say how you liked it so I brought plenty of everything." He popped the plastic lid off the second coffee and brought it to his lips. "Ah, perfect. I probably needed this more than you," he said, tipping his head to the blond.

"We need one central government that looks after the needs of all the peoples of Earth and takes care of our planet so it will be here for millennia to come," Marie continued. "We no longer need borders, we're citizens of the world. We're not many nations, we're one global community and we need to start acting like…"

Josh stood in the shade of the tent, his head too clogged to absorb much of Marie's speech. It sounded good. Why should one race, or one culture, or one creed, lord it over another? But men do need to be governed, whether by fascist dictators, or socialist elites, or money-grubbing capitalists, someone's still got to make decisions and lay down the law. And absolute power corrupts absolutely, which was why in every political scenario there were always problems at the top, and why so often citizens were left to vote for the lesser of two evils. *The heart is deceitful and wicked above all things.* He recalled his dad saying that, though it was supposedly from the Bible. So there were no perfect governments. Never had been, nor would there ever be. Rebellions just led to takeovers that established new regimes that were as corrupt as the governments they'd replaced. Did Castro make Cuba a better place to live? Havana was nice, the seat of power, but everywhere else they were dying to get out, not dying to get in. What if the rebels in their camouflage clothes overthrew their suit wearing oppressors and turned out to be the same greedy corporate bosses, just dressed in gorilla gear? What about Russia? The peoples of the Soviet Socialist Republics couldn't wait to decentralize power, leading to the dissolution of the Soviet Union. For decades the peoples of East Germany had died trying to escape to the West. And when the wall came down, the world was able to see why. The depletion of enterprise, medicine and education was appalling. What about Venezuela? Maduro was described by the Wall Street Journal as the "most capable administrator and politician of Chávez's inner circle," but as soon as he assumed power he used his United Socialist Party of Venezuela to drive his country's economy into the ground. How could anyone ensure that the New World Order wouldn't be just as corrupt and inept as any other? At least with democracy they could vote corrupt politicians out of office, whereas with a worldwide centralized power that might not be so easy. Inside

Josh's sweaty shirt, his heart was pounding. His head hurt from all the strenuous thinking, and worse was the realization that his thoughts were like those of his father. He hated his father—which just gave him one more reason to hate himself.

"Are we gonna have a march?" A carrot-topped boy with long hair and arms like twigs pulled Josh from his thoughts. He was wearing a gray T-shirt that read, "Liberté, égalité, fraternité—liberty, equality, fraternity."

"No, I don't think so. If we do, it will have to be spontaneous because there's nothing planned, at least not that I'm aware of. But here's a list of our upcoming events," Josh said, handing the boy a flyer.

IT HAD TAKEN more than a week for Darn Good Computer, the technical wizards Bill had originally used to set up his studio, to clean his drives, but they had successfully managed to delete the thousands of invasive emails. Bill walked into the store not to pick the drives up, he didn't trust taking them home again lest those who had attacked his system be of a mind to do it again, but he did want to use them to send out the short podcast he'd just put together.

He was shown to a room piled high with the carcasses of dead machines bolted to racks like erector-sets left behind by children that had grown up and found them of no further use. His own server sat on a scratched wood desk surrounded by old hard drives and defunct microprocessors, but, *thank You Lord*, its lights were brightly glowing. He removed the flash drive from his pocket and inserted it into the port. The LED flat-screen monitor sprang to life with his image, the speakers resounding with his baritone voice.

"Hey, all you good folks out there, it's Wild Bill Best back at-cha with another look at what's to come. I hope you've been with me over the past few weeks because we've been talking about the institution of a world government. This is nothing new. The powers of darkness have been at this a long time. They've tried to implement it in every major regime from Nimrod's Tower of Babel to Hitler's Third Reich.

"We're probably most familiar with the phrase, the New World

Order, which was coined following the First World War at the establishing of the League of Nations. Mankind wanted to make sure we didn't allow such a devastating event to ever happen again. Of course it was followed by World War Two, so it wasn't very effective, except in terms of Satan seeding the idea of global governance into the minds of world leaders. And it's been carried forward since that time by the United Nations and more recently the World Economic Forum. Only now we don't talk about the New World Order much. Now there's a new buzzword for globalization. It's called The Great Reset, which is apropos because those who favor it want to reshape our world and make it into something you and I wouldn't recognize. It involves dismantling the American financial system and replacing it with something 'more inclusive,' wherein climate change, sustainability and equality are the chief priorities, not individual rights, and where people forfeit their property in return for a guaranteed income.

"The underlying platform for this new world is socialism, but it's not really that, nor is it capitalism, though it carries elements of both. It's really best described as authoritarianism. Those selling this concept don't believe man is capable of self-government, the way our country was founded. They believe we need an overreaching central authority monitoring and controlling everything we do.

"I've often been asked why today's most powerful business leaders seem to favor this kind of radical change. They built their fortunes on capitalism and the free market, why would they now want to employ totalitarianism? The answer, at least in part, is that while they built their success in a free economy, they actually prefer tight government control, at least as long as it can be used to their advantage, and they're the ones calling the shots. The powerbrokers of capitalism are really set on becoming the elitists that determine how the world works.

"And believe me, this involves every area of your life. Klaus Schwab, founder of the World Economic Forum said, 'To achieve a better outcome, the world must act jointly and swiftly to revamp all aspects of our societies and economies, from education to social contracts and working conditions. Every country, from the United States to China, must participate, and every industry, from oil and gas to tech, must be transformed.' It's all diagramed on the WEF's website under seven headings that read: 'Shaping Economic Recovery, Restoring the Health of the Environment, Developing Sustainable Business Models, Revitalizing Global Cooperation, Strengthening Regional Development and Harnessing the Fourth Industrial Revolution.'

"Sounds fantastic, at least until you drill down into the subsets. Then you find how they want to control everything from what you eat, to where you travel, and how you spend your money. Under the Great Reset, the freedoms you and I enjoy would be stripped away.

"Think I'm kidding? Let me assure you, I'm not. The long-term goal of this program is to have everyone implanted with chipsets, ostensibly for our health, but eventually so that even our thoughts can be controlled. In defining the Fourth Industrial Revolution, Mr. Schwab openly speaks of a day when we will have a, 'fusion of our physical, digital and biological identity.' He's talking about transhumanism wherein men and machine are blended, turning us into human robots similar to the Borg in the TV series Star Trek. Every movement you make would be tracked and every thought read by an implanted microchip. I don't know about you, but I couldn't live that way. But it is the perfect way for the antichrist to have absolute control.

"Let me give you a look at the future as portrayed by Ida Auken, a young leader in the WEF. This is what he had to say:

> "'Welcome to the year 2030. Welcome to my city—or should I say, our city. I don't own anything. I don't own a car. I don't own a house. I don't own any appliances or any clothes.
>
> 'It might seem odd to you, but it makes perfect sense for us in this city. Everything you considered a product, has now become a service. We have access to transportation, accommodation, food, and all the things we need in our daily lives. One by one all these things became free, so it ended up not making sense for us to own much.

215

'Shopping? I can't really remember what that is. For most of us, it has been turned into choosing things to use.

'Once in a while I get annoyed about the fact that I have no real privacy. Nowhere I can go and not be registered. I know that, somewhere, everything I do, think, and dream of, is recorded.'

"This is the view of humanity in the coming new world, and it's almost an exact replica of the vision painted by George Orwell in his novel, *1984*. When it was published, the book presented a terrifying look at a world wherein truth, individuality and freedom were obliterated. Men were constantly under the watchful eye of Big Brother who took care of them, but denied them liberty. That's what those who promote The Great Reset want to bring to us, and it's coming soon.

"The technology you hold in your hand today is ready to be adapted to this future. Most of you know that your smartphone already has tracking software. You may think that if you're not using a GPS mapping program you can't be traced, but you're wrong. This is a feature built into your phone's architecture that can't be deleted or erased. You didn't ask for it, it wasn't an option, but you gave permission to let Google and Apple use it when you accepted their user agreements. And now they know everywhere you go. And when you sign up for Apple Pay, or Google Pay, you give them permission to track every purchase you make.

"It won't be long before we go digital with our money. Did you know VISA has applied for a patent on a digital currency? Or that an article in the 'Economist' stated, 'Rich countries must start planning for a cashless future,' or that Sweden is testing the world's first central bank digital currency, and that China has created a digital yuan which their citizens are already using like regular money, or that our own Federal Reserve Chairman has said, 'We've been focused on digital currencies for a couple of decades...we owe it to the public not to wake up someday and realize that the U.S. dollar is not the world's reserve currency because we missed a technological change.'

216

"Folks, virtually everything I've been telling you about over the past few weeks will be brought to fruition at the Great Reset. Our world is about to change in ways you and I would not have dreamed possible, and trust me on this, there's no going back. Satan is moving, but so is our God. My advice is that you, 'Watch therefore, for you do not know what hour your Lord is coming. But know that if the master of the house had known what hour the thief would come, he would have watched and not allowed his house to be broken into. Therefore you also be ready, for the Son of Man is coming at an hour you do not expect.' —Matthew 24:42-44. Enough said.

"Friends I've been riding hard all day so I want to keep this one brief. It's time for me to climb down from the saddle, tether my pony to a tree, and say so-long my fellow Americans, and God be with you till we meet again."

THE SHADE KEPT the sun off his back but Josh still felt the trickle of perspiration on his chest. He needed a T-shirt. Hadn't his mom bought him shirts for his birthday? Where were they? *The car!* His hand went to his pants, feeling the key in his pocket. His parents had given him a car. Where was it? *Dang*, he didn't know. He was drinking with Donnie. He could ask him. No, Donnie was at the pub when he got there. Where had he parked the car? In a city lot? Probably, but where? He was at the pub? He must have parked nearby.

"Guys, I have to take off for a while. Can I get you anything before I go?"

The girls manning the booth, neither of which he'd been introduced to, shook their heads. "No, we're good. Thanks for the coffee, appreciate it," the blond with long straight hair lifted her Styrofoam cup in salute.

"All right, good. I shouldn't be more than a half hour. If Marie comes by and asks, tell her I'll be right back, okay? Thanks."

Josh stepped out from under the tent's shade into the warm sun and got the shivers. A few moments before he'd been sweltering, and now he felt a chill. He gulped his coffee but couldn't finish. His body ached, his head throbbed, and his stomach felt like a rag tied in a knot. He meandered across campus, loose as water, but holding a course down Hall Street to Parking Structure One. His car wouldn't be there, but it was on the way. Since he didn't know where exactly he had parked, he thought it best to make sure, even though he knew he couldn't have used campus parking without a pass.

He entered the garage which, much to his dismay, was nearly full. A fragment of memory sent him to the lower level first. Yes, he was sure of it. He had parked underground. Going down didn't feel right, but if he had parked on the lower level he would have walked up, so that made sense. He made a circle of the lot but the car wasn't there. He took the stairs up to the ground floor and stepped outside looking up, squinting in the light. There was no way he was going to hike around those seven levels of parking when he knew he had parked below ground.

Okay, so his car wasn't in Parking Structure One. The Cheerful Tortoise was around the corner. If he could get to the front of the pub something might jog his memory, and if not, it sure wouldn't hurt to grab a cold beer and find a dark corner where he could sit and think.

THE PLANE HIT an air pocket and bounced, causing Cal's drink to scoot across his tray and almost spill. He didn't like flying even before the pandemic, but he liked it a lot less now. Out the porthole he could see the plane's wings tottering up and down like they might come loose at any minute.

Cal rankled in his seat. His mask was in his lap. They'd served lunch, or at least the few packaged food items they called lunch, and he wanted to eat. There was no reason to worry. He'd had the vaccine, but who knew how effective it was? He didn't like being unprotected. His asthma made him a prime target for the virus. One of his fellow travelers might sneeze and without his mask he might become infected. And with his weakened immune system he'd be a goner. He should get hazard pay for doing this. *Curse you Steve, for not doing your job.* He starred at the pretzels on his tray, the biscuit cookies, and his coffee, about as appealing as eating dough. The turbulence was making him queasy. He doubted he'd be able to hold anything down.

He wiped the smudge from his glasses. What if this whole thing was a waste of time? Steve seemed to think so, but Steve didn't have what it took to make things happen. It was inconceivable that this Best guy didn't have an address, but every source he'd checked listed only a P.O. Box number, including his tax records. Was that even legal? The U.S. Forest Service, from whom he apparently leased his homestead, could only provide a topical map with a dotted white line that showed five-hundred acres somewhere in the Cascade Mountains. His weak link was the tree farm. They knew where that was, and Mr. Best was reported to be there supervising the construction of a new barn. That would make it easier. Once Cal had those servers in his hands, Bill's days were numbered.

There was one more angle he wanted to explore. It had occurred to him that the fire that made Bill's accounts disappear had taken place just after they started their investigation. It wasn't much to go on, but worth looking into.

VIC PARKED HIS Caddy XTS on a meter in front of the Très Bien Café. The noise was channeling down the Blocks. He could hear it from where he stood. He closed the door and dropped the keys into his pocket, pumping his hands open and closed before smacking them together. Rachel was seldom seen on weekends, so he considered this to be a day off. And what a fine day it was. The flowers were in bloom, the trees starting to bud. He started down the street, crossing over to the median between the bumpers of cars which honked as he ignored their right of way.

"What do we want?"
"Social Justice!"
"What do we need?"
"Equality for all."
"Who do we fight?"
"Capitalist Bigots"
"What do we do?"
"Take them down."

The chant was repeated over and over, swelling to a crescendo that grew louder with each refrain. He passed a maple with a trunk two foot in girth and stopped. *That's interesting.* He took the yellow poster from the tree and went over to what looked like an information booth.

"You looking for this guy?" he said, slipping a picture of Bill that said, Wanted Dead or Alive, to the first person he saw.

"Sure. That's Bill Best. He's wanted for everything but his bad taste in clothes," a girl with spiked hair and muscles that flexed like a man, said.

"Such as?"

"Come on sweetie, you know, crimes against humanity, his racism and bigotry, his capitalist agenda. Haven't you read his blogs?"

Vic couldn't say he had. "No, but if you really want him, he's not that hard to find. Lives up one of the canyons outside town."

A girl in red shorts and a halter top spun around to join the conversation. Her eyes were dark and intense. She leaned across the counter taking the poster and holding it up. "You know this man? You know where he lives?"

"Sure, I have an interest in Rachel Powers, and that's where she's staying."

"You know Rachel?"

"Yes. Do you?"

"Sure, the senator's daughter, she's a seeing a friend of mine, a guy named Josh."

"That's right. Josh is this guy's son."

TWENTY-TWO

THE DARKNESS PROVIDED seclusion, drawing Josh into deep introspection. He sat in the recesses of the bar, as far from the billiard table as possible, contemplating his life and the misery of it, though it was better now. An hour before his head had felt like those resin balls cracking against each other, but now he was safely ensconced in an ethereal mist and feeling mellow. Thank God they didn't crank the music up during the day. He set his third glass of beer down, everything now restored to its proper place.

He brought his wrist up to check the time. Just after one. The demonstration would be wrapping up. He should be heading back, but he needed to locate his car first. Standing in front of the Tortoise his brain had conjured up a map that backtracked from the pub all the way to the parking lot. *Easy peasy*, as his mom liked to say. But he had to be certain.

Josh stood reaching for his wallet to leave a few *greenbacks* for his server. Greenbacks? See, now, that was his father's word. He was ready to purge the evil from his life. He would tell Marie where they lived and be done with it. And may God be his judge.

He trucked to the front of the bar feeling better than he had all day. His father had dealt the play; he was the one who thought strict adherence to the rules was more important than connecting with his son. Choosing Marie and her idealism over his father was the perfect payback. It didn't matter whether Marie was right or wrong, only that her opinion differed from his father's. If there was one thing he'd learned from his three beer psychoanalysis, it was that only by opposing his father could he ever be truly free.

He stepped onto the sidewalk, checking the traffic. There was a streetlight down at the corner, but he couldn't be bothered. He crossed the road jaywalking, and turned down College Street heading to Forth. The sun was raining down heat. He brought his sweatshirt up to mop his forehead. Last night it hadn't seemed so far, only two blocks, but then he'd been sober. He wasn't drunk now, just tired. The beer just helped take the edge off his hangover. Maybe he was consuming too much, but he wasn't an alcoholic, just someone who liked to drink, but that was what they all said—*wasn't it?* He shouldn't feel so tired, especially since he'd taken a few of his study pills. Study pills? *Haw!* They were amphetamines, but like Ron said, everything in moderation. A few didn't hurt. It wasn't a problem until you got strung out, and he wasn't there—*yet*. Maybe he should ease back a little, both with the booze and the pills. He didn't like the thought of being dependent.

He crossed Forth Street and took a right. The garage was there, exactly where he knew it would be, only he couldn't see it because it was underground. The only thing visible was the sign he'd seen last night. He walked down the ramp just as a car was coming up, shining its lights in his face. *Knock off the brights, idiot.* The car swerved away leaving him in a dimly lit tunnel. His heart was palpitating, this time with uncertainty. Would the car be there—*or not?* He turned the corner and—*there it is*—his very own bright shiny white steed. He padded over, slowing his pace as though rushing might awaken him from his dream, but he couldn't contain his excitement as he drew near. So beautiful, but not so shiny. The car looked like it had been through a dust storm. The windshield had hoops where the wipers had cleared away the road film, and the paint was filthy. Josh breathed out a sigh. She needed a good bath.

He reached into his pocket for the key and used the fob to snap the car locks open. The interior lights came on. He opened the door and slipped inside. The seats were charcoal leather, with light grey side panels and beige trim. He let his hand slide along the console, surprised that he'd never noticed how nice the car was when it was his mother's, but now that it was his… He leaned back against the headrest and closed his eyes, so comfortable he feared he might fall asleep. He opened his eyes again. Last night he had moved the seat to give his legs more room, but now he discovered several other adjustments for height, tilt and recline. *Cruddy windshield*, he thought, staring through his reflection into the darkness. He slipped the key into the ignition and turned it just far enough for the dash lights to come on; a beautiful blue, cool and relaxing. Center console, full GPS—*Sweet!* His hands gripped the wheel. He wanted to show it to someone, and especially to Marie, but how could he? She was adamant about reducing fossil fuels. Dang if she didn't make him feel conflicted.

It didn't matter whether she saw the car or not, he still wanted it clean, even if only for himself. The après event celebration would be at the Tortoise later that evening so this was a good place to park. He wasn't sure about giving up his spot, but heck, there were plenty of empty spaces. He should be able to leave and come back and still find a place to park for another night. But not long term. Thirteen dollars a day would eventually break him. Ron used a discount parking garage downtown. He needed to find out where that was. He started the car, used his GPS to locate a nearby carwash, and followed the exit signs up the ramp into the light outside.

THE WIND OFF the water chilled Bill to the bone. It had been a warm day, but as evening set in and shadows stretched across the lake, the temperature dropped leaving him wishing he'd worn a jacket. He was out too far to turn around and go back. His long sleeve wool shirt would have to do. It fit his image better, anyway. He'd long ago reconciled his theatrics; he was an actor at heart. He liked putting on a show for his audience with him playing the part of a good ol' country boy full of common sense, rather than have them see him as the profound thinker he actually was. He tightened his cowboy hat on his head so it wouldn't sail off in the breeze. He'd only done a podcast outside his studio one other time, and that was when they were fumigating for termites. This time his reason was totally different. He was about to engage the devil head on, and he wanted to be surrounded by the presence of God.

A Pacific loon was warbling in the cattails along the shore, easing the tension he felt. It was an early appearance for a bird that didn't usually migrate until mid-April and sometimes not until May. When the time came, their striated wings and dappled plumage would fill the skies like wind-blown leaves as they flew in by the thousands. Bill recalled the crickets chirping yesterday, too. All signs of an early spring.

He pulled his paddle in and let the canoe drift, pausing to take one last look out across the lake. The sun was just beginning to dip behind the crest of the mountain. He had to start now or it would be too dark. His tripod was seated in the hull with his camera attached. He leaned over and pushed the record button, his face breaking into a smile as the red light came on.

"Howdy folks, Wild Bill comin' at-cha from the wilds of the great Cascade Mountains." Bill took his paddle and stroked the water, turning the canoe in a full circle. "See what you're missing? This is where I live, in God's country, and folks I gotta tell ya, with all that's going on, I don't think I could cope anywhere else, though I have to admit I've been giving that some thought lately.

"This is going to be a different kind of broadcast. As you can see, I'm not in my studio, I'm out on the lake, breathing in the wonder of God's creation, which, right now, I have to do if I want to preserve my sanity.

"Most of you, I'm sure, are familiar with what's being called the 'cancel culture,' that's where people try to cancel your message if they don't agree with what you have to say. Well, I've been officially cancelled. For those of you who don't know, in just the past three months I've had a charity I run burned to the ground, an attack made on my communications system, and now they're accusing me of tax evasion. If you've read about that, don't believe it. It never happened and I have the books to prove it. I think we'll beat them in court, but with the way things are going, I might not, so if I happen to disappear and you hear I'm in jail, just keep the faith. God is the righteous judge, what can man do to me?

"If you've tried to email me, I apologize for not getting back to you, but as I said, they crashed my email server. Just before they took it down, however, I did receive a number of emails about the topic of my latest series. The vast majority have been positive, thank you for that, but for those who are disgruntled by all this talk about the future, rest assured, today's podcast will be the last on this subject.

"So let's dive in and look at another indicator that suggests the time is at hand. I'm talking about the decline of morality. In my first presentation I showed how Satan has been opposing God from the beginning. If God said right, Satan said left, if God said up, Satan said down. Today, I'd wager you can't find a single precept of God that isn't being challenged. God's Word is either deemed irrelevant, or passé. And it's only getting worse.

"I won't spend much time selling this one. Anyone with eyes can see the moral decline of America. If you're anywhere near my age, you remember, 'The Adventures of Ozzie and Harriet,' a television show about the Nelson family. In that day television standards were so prudish they wouldn't even allow the married couple to sleep in the same bed. Ozzie had his own single bed, and Harriet had one for herself, and the beds were staged five feet apart. God forbid we titillate the audience with the slightest suggestion that they might make love. Laugh out loud. Today, with only a disclaimer that the content might not be appropriate for young children, you get to watch content that's darn near pornographic.

"The world is becoming a dark place where every kind of perversion is being celebrated, where our politicians, as the prophet Isaiah forewarned, 'call evil, good, and good, evil.' Sadly, even the Church is turning away from the clear teachings of scripture. We've faltered to the point where acts the Bible calls an abomination are not only accepted, but praised, particularly with respect to the use of our bodies, which scripture calls the temple of God. Have we forgotten that His own spirit dwells within us, and that we are to be holy, just as He is holy?

"Satan likes to tell us that God loves all men, even in their sin, and that we shouldn't fret over what others do in the privacy of their own homes, as long as we keep ourselves pure. He likes to keep us busy so we don't have pause to think. We're so occupied with our social networking we no longer have time for God. But Satan is there to assure us that we're doing okay, and that God understands our need for attention. He assures us that we really would read our Bibles more, if we only had time. And little by little he gets into our lives and pushes God out until Satan is in full control, though we don't see it, because, after all, we still go to church on Sunday.

"But friends, know this, it's not enough for Satan just to own us, he wants us to be like him. Bible says he was a murderer from the beginning, so he wants to make us killers, not just through murder, but killing ourselves through suicide, our elders through euthanasia, and our children through abortion. Why, because once he's got us dead, it's over. We've run out of options. Once the soul departs the body, we lose our ability to find redemption through the Savior.

And he wants to mess with us while we're still alive, too. I don't need to tell you about all the lying, cheating, mass murder, sex trafficking, pedophilia, pornography, sexual immorality, alcoholism and drug abuse that define this generation. If you read the papers or listen to the news, you know all this, and you know it's of Satan. The world, in following him, has become a twisted place where, as Isaiah forewarned, men 'call light, darkness, and darkness, light.'

Satan is pushing this agenda because he's evil through-and-through, and his chosen one will be evil incarnate. Just as Jesus embodied the nature and holiness of God, so the antichrist will possess all the attributes of Satan. If the secular world were still moral, and the church upholding God's Word, the antichrist would never succeed. We'd spot him in a minute and run his tail out of town. But as the world slips further and further into the darkness, and the church becomes blind to the things of God and more like the world around us, we become desensitized, no longer able to understand what God expects of us. We're like a frog in a beaker with the temperature rising, getting cooked without noticing the water getting hot.

"I know I'm on a soapbox and you're probably wondering what all this has to do with signs that the end is coming soon, but there is a point to be made, and it's this: When addressing the second coming of Christ, the Apostle Paul said: 'Let no one deceive you by any means; for that day will not come unless the falling away comes first, and the man of sin is revealed, the son of perdition.' In context he's saying there will be a great turning away from God before the antichrist is revealed, and, friends, that's just what we're seeing today. Most of you listening to me right now, know evil is on the rise but hang tough 'cause it's only going to get worse. It may even come to the point where our major cities are full blown effigies of Sodom and Gomorrah. God forbid.

"I needn't belabor the point. Let me just summarize by saying Satan is alive and well, but he knows his time is short. He's pulling out all the stops in trying to set up his kingdom. He has politicians, heads of state, technocrats, and the uber rich, all clamoring for a one world government. He's got our economy on stilts, ready to collapse, and he has the technology to monitor every person on earth. Worst of all, he has our morals topsy-turvy upside down to where men no longer know right from wrong.

"Friends, we are living in apocalyptic times, but there is hope, and that hope is in being on the right side. Like I said when I first started this series, Satan is doing his best to overthrow God. If you want to be on the devil's side, you don't have to do a thing. You're already there. But if you want to be on God's side you must choose to follow Him. You have to recognize that you've sinned. It doesn't have to be a big sin, any sin, however small, will keep you from God. It's why Christ came to die, to pay the price for the sins we commit. Nor is there a sin too great to keep you from God, as long as you're willing to ask His forgiveness. But that's all it takes. You say, God, I believe you exist, and I believe that your Son, Jesus, died to pay for the sins I've committed, so I repent and give those sins to You. I want to be on Your side, so please, God, let me be yours.

Then, after you make that decision, I suggest you get yourself a Bible and find yourself a church that preaches the whole word of God and start living for Him. It's pretty darn simple, really. But, ah, I caution you. If you choose not to do this, you will one day stand before God and He will say, sorry, I never knew you. Depart from me. And you'll spend eternity with the devil and his angels. Believe me, that's not somewhere you want to be. I suggest you do it now, before it's too late.

"Here's a verse many of you are familiar with. Take it to heart, because this is the truth. 'For we do not wrestle against flesh and blood, but against principalities, against powers, against the rulers of the darkness of this age, against spiritual hosts of wickedness in the heavenly places.' That's from the Bible, Ephesians 6:12. It couldn't be clearer. All that we see going on around us is from Satan. But God wins in the end, so Maranatha, even so come quickly Lord Jesus. That's something to hang your hat on.

"Woooeeee, would you look at that?" Bill picked up his tripod and turned the camera around to point at the western horizon. The sun was resting on the lip of the earth, shooting its rays out across the lake so that the water looked crimson in its light. "Boy that's a beauty, and just a reminder that God is still on the throne presiding over his creation. He's not through with this world yet." Bill swung the camera back around filling the frame with his face. "This is Wild Bill Best singing happy trails to you as I ride off into the sunset. Adios amigos." He removed his cowboy hat and looped it around his head screaming, *yahoooo*, as he reached in to switch the camera off.

TWENTY-THREE

CAL SAT NEAR the door in the front section of the bar where the sun blinded his eyes every time the door swung open, but it was the only way to be sure he didn't miss his guest. He had yet to order, though he wanted a drink badly, but he didn't want to be rude. He might be sitting there with bourbon on the rocks when the marshal ordered wine, or sucking down a beer when the man wanted a cocktail. Decorum demanded ordering beer for beer, wine for wine, and drink for drink.

Before leaving his room he had emptied his preventative inhaler, sucking the last bit of beclamethasone dipropionate into his lungs to make sure he didn't wheeze in front of his guest. Funny, he'd never considered how his wheezing might bother anyone until Steve brought it up. Another reason he would be getting rid of that toad as soon as he got back. He looked at his watch. The door swung open, the glare preventing him from seeing the numbers on the dial until it closed, and when it did, he realized he didn't need to know what time it was because the man he was waiting for had arrived.

Cal scooted his chair back and stood waving the man over. He was easy to recognize in his white shirt with the Portland Fire Department logo stitched on its sleeve, but he read the man's badge just to be sure. *Fire marshal—good.* The man was tall, with a receding hairline, though not bald, and wore thick black plastic glasses and had a broad mustache covering his lip.

"Calvin Moody," Cal said, holding out his hand. "Thank you for joining me."

229

"Bob Underwood," the man responded. "I don't get many calls from the IRS and when I do it's not usually to invite me out for a drink. So, what can I do for you?"

"Right to the point. I like that. Please, sit," Cal said.

The men settled into their chairs around a small square table. A bar maid scooted up, adhering to Cal's instructions to wait until his guest arrived. "What can I get you boys," she asked.

Cal waited for Bob to order. "Bud Light," he said, and Cal, wanting to be agreeable said, "I'll have the same."

"On tap, or in a bottle."

"Bottle's fine."

"Me too," Cal said, and waited for the bar hop to leave, though he did give her a sidelong glance to appreciate her tight pants. He leaned forward, his stomach nudging the table. "I mentioned this was about Bill Best," he went on. "We've found a few discrepancies in his tax filings so we're conducting an investigation. I made a visit to his tree farm yesterday, at least what's left of it. I was hoping to catch him there, but he was away. I did however speak to one of the crew putting up the new barn and I'm given to understand the fire was ruled an arson."

Bob nodded. "It was pretty obvious, but yes, that's the case."

"And I understand no one has been arrested for the crime."

"No, we're pretty sure it was one or more of a group of protestors that were there the day before. Apparently, Mr. Best unleashed a dog on them and they threatened they'd be back but we were never able to get any names, so for now, we're dead in the water. But the case is still open. Why?"

"I'm just wondering if you looked at Mr. Best himself."

"Of course, but he had guests staying with him who say he was with them the whole evening, which gives him a pretty tight alibi, plus we couldn't establish a motive."

"But he had means and opportunity, right?"

"Yes, of course. There was a twelve-hundred gallon gas tank on the property that the perpetrator used to fuel the fire, so there was means, and we know he could have snuck out while his wife and guests were asleep and still have been back before they knew he was gone, so he had opportunity. What are you driving at?"

"What if I give you motive?"

Bob crossed his arms and leaned back in his chair. "Okay, I'm listening," he said.

"We're investigating Mr. Best for tax fraud. We asked for his records, but find they were destroyed in the fire. What if he started that fire to keep us from finding out what was in those files? That would be a motive for arson, wouldn't it?"

The waitress was back with their drinks. She set two napkins on the table and set the bottles on the napkins. "Anything else?" she said.

Cal shook his head and watched her walk away, admiring her cute derrière.

Bob brought his beer up, squinting as he tipped his head back to take a drink. He set the beer on the table again. "Yes, I suppose, but it doesn't make sense for him to destroy a business that's taken him years to build. We checked him out pretty good. It wasn't a money issue…"

"You don't know that," Cal interjected. "The contractor I talked to said the barn they were replacing was falling apart. He said the wood was rotted and wouldn't have stood much longer anyway. We know this Best guy is guilty of tax fraud, but he may have been killing two birds with one stone. He could have seen a way to get us off his back while at the same time getting his insurance company to pay for a new barn. He might be guilty of tax evasion, and insurance fraud, and arson, all at the same time…"

EVENING CAME TO the Cheerful Tortoise with sounds of glasses clinking, billiard balls clacking, people chattering, and rock-star wannabes singing, but all of it without Josh's presence. He'd restored his car to its original shine—washed and waxed, with chrome polished and tires blackened—but it had been about five o'clock when he'd returned to the parking garage. The group didn't generally gather until around eight, and he was exhausted. He'd decided to go back to his apartment and take a nap.

He had fallen into a deep trance, drifting from one set of random images to another until he found himself in a virtual reality. His bed was surrounded by flames, his mom screaming, Angie crying, and Ted running around the house frantically trying to save everyone. His father was nowhere to be found. He awoke with a start, the room dark with the faint light coming through the window, painting shadows on the walls. He jerked upright. *What time is it?* His phone's message light was blinking. He picked it up—*nine-fifteen*—and went to his messages and saw one from Ron. He pressed play, and against a background of raucous singing, heard: "Hey, we're at the Tortoise. Tried to wake you but you were out cold. Can't say I didn't try. Later man."

Josh flew out the door and down the elevator and half-walked, half-ran until he was standing inside the pub looking for his crew, hoping Marie hadn't already left. They were there, in the center of the room, with several tables pulled together to increase their acreage. Bennie, Donnie, Ron, the girl with the long blond hair, and the one with a lip ring whose hair was pink. He also recognized Ross and Jeff, the two who had engineered the attack on his father's network, but no Marie. His chest deflated as he approached the table and collapsed into an empty chair.

"Hey, guys," he said, nodding to no one in particular.

"I think Marie's sitting there," the long blond piped up.

Marie? Josh twisted around and found her up front singing karaoke with the spike-haired, man-girl from the information booth. They were holding hands facing each other singing:

"Two birds of a feather,
We can fly away,
Reaching for the heavens,
At the dawn of a new day…"

He turned back to the others. "Oh sorry, I didn't see her when I came in." He stood. Ron hooked a chair from another table and drug it over with his foot. He patted the seat with his hand. "Sit bro," he said.

"I see you tried to wake me earlier," Josh said.

"Right, that. You were out like a rock." Ron picked up his drink, which Josh surmised was a cola of some kind, and brought the straw to his mouth inserting it between his bearded lips.

Josh looked at Donnie, "Yeah, kinda did a number on me last night," he said, smiling.

"It's Microbrew Monday, three and a quarter a beer. Drink up," Donnie said. He swept his fine red hair off his forehead, but it fell back the minute he let go.

"I think I'll hold off for a minute. I had a few earlier and they put me out. I need to get my head above water before I start again." He brought a hand up to stifle a yawn, and the girls kept singing...

"No one can separate us
We'll build a nest for two,
Making love with each other
Beneath a sky of blue."

...while holding their karaoke mikes as they crooned words from a teleprompter. They were staring into each other's eyes swaying in time with the music.

"Those two sound good together."

"Barba ain't no Kenny Rogers, but her voice is husky enough to pull it off."

"Barba?"

"The spiked-hair chick. Barbara, but nobody calls her that."

The waitress came by and plopped a beer in front of Josh, the foam riding up over the rim spilling onto the table. "I didn't order that," he said.

"I did," Donnie said. "For hanging in there and helping me out last night. Worked out great for me."

Josh hefted the glass toward Donnie. "Well, if you insist, here's to you," he said. He took a deep swallow and set the glass down. Ron was the only one at the table without a beer. At least he stuck by his convictions. "You see Cheri lately?" Josh asked.

"Nope. Hasn't been around. Her parents are Catholic. I think they got her in a convent or something. I heard she dropped out of school."

Josh shook his head. *Morals of a demon, abstinence of a saint.*

233

Marie and Barba finished their number and took their bows, thanking the bar's customers for the applause. For a moment the bar fell quiet as they made their way to the table and sat down. Marie had changed into black slacks with a red blouse and sweater. Barba, with her muscles bulging under the sleeves of her T-shirt, looked the same as before.

Marie sat beside Josh switching drinks with her friend like she'd been previously seated in the other chair. "Hi Josh. When did you get here?"

"Few minutes ago." He looked back at Ron. "Hey, you know that car you keep parked off campus?"

"What about it?"

"You said you found cheap parking. I was wondering where that was."

Ron leaned back with his legs out straight and his arms folded over his chest with one hand stroking his beard. "Why?"

"I got a car."

"What?"

"A car. My folks got it for my birthday, and before you say anything, it's a hybrid so low fuel consumption."

"Cool."

Marie shook her head, her dark eyebrows furled questioningly. "Josh, I thought you were from the Midwest. How'd your parents get you a car?"

"I uh…no wait, no, uh…they ordered it on-line from some company that has distribution centers all across the states. I just had to go pick it up, see…"

Marie's expression changed, her curiosity becoming a pout of amusement. "Well at least they got you something eco-friendly."

"You want to see it?"

"Cool, dude, yeah." Donnie slid his chair back and Ron leaned on the table starting to get up.

"You know what, guys. I'd like to be alone with Josh for a few minutes, would that be all right?" Marie's eyes drifted around the table making sure no one objected.

Donnie settled back into his chair and Ron relaxed. "Sure, whatever."

Josh felt a surge of electricity run through his chest. *Alone—with me? Okay, that's got to mean something. Alone with me in the back of my car. Maybe this is it. Maybe this is where we express our feelings for each other.* He was on his feet, threading through tables piled with nachos and beer, following the red curve of Marie's knit sweater, out onto the street.

"Where to?" Marie said, as they stepped outside into the cool of the evening.

Josh took the same route he had used that afternoon, only earlier it seemed like the two block walk had taken forever. Now it felt like time was passing too fast. Neither spoke, like words weren't necessary to communicate what they were feeling. The moon was full and pale yellow, like a slice of potato. Marie slipped her arm through his as they strolled down the sidewalk. The burn in his chest was causing his internal organs to liquefy.

"Josh, we're friends, right?" she said.

"Absolutely, yes." He looked over, surprised at how short she was. In her role as commander-and-chief she always seemed tall, but in reality the top of her head was under his chin. The shine of her dark hair was reflecting the moon's light. He could smell the scent of her shampoo.

"You wouldn't hold anything back from me, would you?" Marie squeezed his arm, laying her head against his shoulder.

Josh gulped. His heart, already flopping in his chest, increased its rhythm. "What do you mean?"

"I just want you to know you can trust me, that's all. If you have anything to say, anything at all, go ahead and say it. I don't want there to be any secrets between us, okay?"

Inside, Josh was panicking. He wanted to tell her how he felt, he really did, but then again, he wasn't sure. What if he laid it all out and she didn't feel the same? He was taking her to his car, a place of seclusion where anything might happen. What if their passion exploded and they lost control and went all the way; was he ready for that? What if she wasn't the one?

"No, I get it, totally, I'm cool. The car's just down here." He turned in at the driveway leading down to the parking garage. "I'm keeping it here for the moment, but it costs thirteen bucks a day. That's why I was asking Ron about finding cheaper parking. That's it, right over there." Josh was pleased to see how his wax job mirrored the low light of the garage. The car shone like a model on a showroom floor.

Marie had let him go as they descended the tunnel, but she slipped her arm back through his as they approached the car. "It's beautiful, Josh."

"Really, 'cause I thought you might be upset."

"Why?"

"I don't know, don't use gas, save the planet, right?"

"Josh, I'm not suggesting we walk everywhere. We still have to get around. I just want everyone to do what they can to minimize their CO_2 consumption. Go electric, right? Your roomie Ron drives a hybrid, but he only uses it when he has to, and that's fine by me."

"Right. I never could figure that one out, the way he goes on about the evils of carbon dioxide." Joshed pointed his key-fob at the car and pushed the unlock button. The car's horn chirped and the interior lights came on. He released Marie and she opened the door, slipping inside. "This is nice," she said. "Nice seats, nice console, oh, look at me, I'm a mess." She was looking at the distorted reflection of herself in the windshield. "Does this thing have a mirror?" She reached for the visor and pulled it down. Josh caught her staring at his registration. Best, Joshua Christian. The address was his folk's post office box number. "Maybe under the other one," she said, flipping the visor back up.

TWENTY-FOUR

APRIL SHOWERS bring May flowers, but what did the Mayflower bring? Bill grunted. It was a stab at humor but his face held more of a pout than a smile. His windshield wipers cranked back and forth, *wafump, wafump, wafump.* His hand gripped the steering wheel, holding it tight. The rain was ruining his day. Clouds out over the Pacific were nestled against the mountains like a grey blanket. Lightning sparked, followed by a roll of thunder that echoed through the canyon.

The Weyerhaeuser seedling plant down in Aurora was just thirty minutes south of Portland, but longer when your starting point was Tantamoa. He'd crossed the Willamette River twice, just outside Wilsonville and again in Oregon City. From the bridge, the river's surface looked silver, like a saw blade stippled with rain. He'd been driving up the 205, but now was on 26 heading east toward Mount Hood in the direction of his Christmas tree farm.

His pickup shuddered in a gust of wind, rain sluicing from the gutters over the doors. Terrible weather for planting. He had two weeks to get the seedlings into the ground, and mud would only slow him down. He wouldn't be able to use his trailer to distribute the trees. The deep treads of the tractor's tires would pull the wet dirt out of the ground destroying the furrows he'd made. He would have to truck them in by hand using a garden cart. It wasn't hard physically, but it was a fair distance to the back of the property, too far to go with mud clinging to the soles of his boots. And too much rain might drown the fledging plants. No, by all counts, planting was better in dry weather.

He always looked forward to his annual trip out to the seedling farm. There was nothing like the smell of new growth pine. The change of scenery, the open road, and time alone with his thoughts, made it worth the drive. God was still in control, even though right now it didn't much feel like it. He checked his rearview mirror, but the back window was streaked with rain, too blurry to see how the cardboard boxes were doing. They were covered with a tarp anyway, to keep them from getting soaked. Two-thousand trees, ten boxes, two-hundred trees to a box, and they all needed to be in the ground by the first of May.

Bill toggled the wipers to a faster speed. "It never rains but it pours, eh, Lord?" he muttered to himself. Second only to the holiday season, this was his most demanding time of year, though he normally had to plant only a few hundred trees to replace the inventory he'd sold, not two-thousand. He had to dig two-thousand holes with a shovel, easy in the soft loam dug up by his tractor, but then he had to plant the trees, fill in the soil, and cover the base of each tree with a protective mat. Two-thousand trees in two weeks. About a hundred and fifty trees a day give-or-take, with time off for Sunday. He smirked. And he used to call this a hobby farm.

Bill leaned forward and looked up at the sky, hoping to see a break in the clouds. *Nada.* He actually didn't mind cloudy days. They were cooler. Toiling under a sweltering sun was unbearable. He just didn't like working in the rain. But having something to keep his mind occupied was good. He had spent the last two weeks moping around the house ruminating over the bout he'd had with his son. And it was causing division between him and Mary. He'd pulled back, kicking himself daily for the things he'd said, and she'd shied away to hide her emotions behind the pages of a novel. Poor Angie was left to arbitrate, but her words only sounded like tears.

You can't put the toothpaste back in the tube. Bill's gloved hand thumped the wheel. He knew he would end up having to apologize, but he wasn't sure it would do any good. Every bridge he tried to build crumbled before it was complete. He just didn't understand Josh, that was the problem. He didn't understand weakness. Ted would hear a criticism and come back with a challenge. He wasn't always right, but he was ready to defend what he believed. Josh just went to his room, closed the door, and sulked. He was too much like his mother, which didn't help because Bill didn't understand Mary either, though God knew he tried. And he'd tried with Josh, too. He tried to be accepting and complimentary and coddling, but dang it all, that was Mary's job. He just wasn't cut out for it. Josh saw through the ruse every time. It always ended up with Josh pushing his buttons, leading to more confrontation and he'd blow it again. He just couldn't keep his mouth shut. It was the curse Paul spoke of when he said: "For the good that I want to do, I do not do; but the evil I don't want to do, that I practice." It was the old sin nature reaching out to poke him in the eye over and over again. "Oh wretched man that I am," Paul said. Bill knew exactly what the apostle meant.

Bill's rain slicker rustled as he cranked the steering wheel, pulling into the driveway of the farm. Two-thousand trees to plant, each a foot tall with a six-inch root ball that would have to grow seven to nine years before being ready to harvest. He would plant another two-thousand each year for the next eight years, adding until the farm was filled again with trees of different sizes, determined by their annual growth. No one ever said growing Christmas trees was easy money. He swung the truck around and backed up to the tent he'd erected to help him stay dry. It appeared the construction crew was taking a rain day. The site was quiet, nary a hammer or saw to be heard. He flicked off the windshield wipers, killed the engine and stared at his reflection in the streaked glass—hair disheveled, cheeks creased, gray shadows—old and getting older. He balled his fists and pounded the steering wheel. If he didn't do something to get his son back soon, he'd lose him for good.

RACHEL WALKED ACROSS the Park Block heading for Cascades Coffee. She was supposed to meet Josh, but she didn't see his car. His mother had dropped her off in his dad's old truck which she said she hated to drive, but sometimes found necessary. Rachel sidestepped a puddle on the lawn, tipping her umbrella back as she stepped onto the curb. The man behind her, running with a newspaper over his head, ignored her detour and ended up splashing through the water, drenching his shoes. The rain continued to pummel her umbrella with the sound of children's feet pattering across a gymnasium floor.

She was supposed to be developing ideas for her psych 101 paper. They were nearing the end of another semester and it seemed every teacher she had was loading her with extra work. Somewhere along the line, she'd gotten the idea that taking courses online would be easier, but it wasn't, especially since lately her mind was preoccupied with Josh. She just couldn't stop thinking about him. They'd seen each other only twice since his birthday and both times had been a disaster. The first was when he'd called to ask if she'd told anyone his real name. He seemed to think his secret had somehow been leaked because his roommate was pumping him for information about his family and where he lived. Having to invent stuff about a fictitious high school, and summer odd jobs was making him anxious. "Oh what a tangled web we weave, when first we practice to deceive," thank you, Sir Walter Scott.

They'd gone to a restaurant, at least that's what he'd called it, but it was really a bar known as the Cheerful Tortoise. He'd sat there and downed one beer after another claiming he was stressed to the max. Someone was trying to out him, he said, and he feared exposure. Then he'd spent an hour berating his father over their little tête-à-tête. She had ended up leaving him there saying if he wanted to see her again, it would have to be in a fast food restaurant where they didn't serve alcohol.

The second time was worse. He'd called and asked to see her but when she'd arrived he was stone drunk, stumbling around the coffee shop bumping into tables. She'd brought him outside, more to keep him from embarrassing himself than to have a conversation, where he'd broken down and bemoaned his miserable life. He kept saying he wanted to die, though she didn't believe it, all the while bawling like a little child wanting attention. She had taken him to his car so they could sit and talk without being overheard, but she'd kept his keys and refused to let him drive.

But even after all that, she still wanted to see him—but only if he was sober. She couldn't help believing there was a good man in there somewhere, and it was her job to find him.

She stepped into the coffee shop and looked around, hoping to see Josh already there. The tracks of a dozen wet tennis shoes crisscrossed the floor. Her umbrella was folded but dripping on the tiles. She pulled the door back and reached out, popping it open to shake it off.

"Hey, I recognize you."

Rachel jerked back, struggling to collapse her umbrella. She twisted around to see a pink haired girl standing behind her.

"What have you been up to?" The girl brought a finger up and bit her nail then pinched the ring that was piercing her lip.

Rachel tilted her head, questioning the girl's familiarity. She was sure they'd never met.

"Not much. How about you?" Rachel snapped the band around her umbrella, her hair damp in spite of the protection it provided.

The girl was chewing gum, her lip ring bouncing up and down. "Yeah, well, I saw you and I wanted say how much we appreciate what you tried to do for us."

"Pardon?"

"You're Senator Powers' daughter, right?"

Rachel nodded, hesitantly. "I am, yes." So?

"So you've got your dad's ear. Josh said you promised to ask your father for that creepy writer's address so we can go stick it to him in his front yard. We're gonna do that, too. Hey, maybe you should come." The girl reached over and squeezed the tattoo of a butterfly she had inked on her left shoulder.

"What?"

"That Bill Best guy. Writes all that stuff about not needing to do anything to keep the planet safe. Speaks for a bunch of capitalist pigs who wouldn't lift a finger to help, but who'd blow up the whole freakin' planet if they thought there was a buck to be made. You know him, right?"

"I do, but..."

"Because Josh says your dad and Bill freaking Best are tight, and that you're trying to find out where he lives so we can go do a shout down in his front yard. Only the good news is, we don't need your help anymore because we found someone else who knows where he lives, so you're off the hook. By the way, my name's Dandy, well actually it's Dandelion. My mom named me after a weed, but Dandelion's too hard to say, so everyone just calls me Dandy." The girl offered her hand to seal their friendship. She had rings on every finger some stacked two or three high. Rachel didn't see how the fingers could close.

Rachel took the hand. "Nice to meet you," she said, "and thanks for letting me know. I'll have to speak to Josh about that."

Rachel had her phone up to her ear ten seconds after the girl dropped out of sight.

"This is Josh," he answered.

"What did you tell your friends about me?" Rachel challenged, her unchecked emotions loud through the tiny speaker.

"Rachel? I'm almost there, be about five minutes. I had to walk, 'cause my car's in a lot downtown..."

"What did you tell your stupid friends about me?"

"What are you talking about?"

"I just got broadsided by little Daisy Mae, no wait, no, Dandy, who said you told your friends I was going to help them get your father's address."

She waited for Josh to respond, but the phone was silent.

"You asked me to keep your secret and not tell anyone your real name, and then you go use my name to sell out your dad? What's wrong with you? Are you completely insane? You're not just damaged goods, Josh, you're completely broken. I...no, I've had it. I can't help you. Please don't call. I don't want to hear from you again. Goodbye, Josh."

"No, Rachel, you don't understand. I was stalling. They knew who you were, and that I knew you, and they asked me to see if I could get you to give up my dad, and I said I would, but I didn't mean it. But that was then. Look, the last time I saw you, that was bad. But I haven't had a drink since. Okay? I'm trying to get my act together. Just give me a chance, Rachel...Rachel?"

BILL PLACED THE boxes of Douglas fir, Nobel fir, and Grand fir on separate tables. He had to be careful. The first box he'd tried to pull from the bottom of the truck had become wet and tore apart in his hands. He needed to keep the boxes intact to load them onto his cart. He turned around, surprised to see two men standing at the tent door. That never would have happened if someone hadn't killed his dog. Willie would have notified him of their coming.

"Hello, Ed. What brings you out here?" Bill said. He removed his work gloves and tossed them on the table.

"You and this guy are on a first name basis?" the second person quipped.

The man Bill addressed was tall and wearing a dark blue suit. He was law enforcement, but he didn't wear a uniform. He was the Chief of Police. "I'm afraid I'm here on official business," he said.

"How so?" Bill said, untying his apron and lifting it over his head.

"I have a warrant for your arrest."

"And a search warrant." The second man jumped in. He was short with too much weight around the middle, and glasses that made him look owlish. Bill had an instant dislike of the man, though he didn't know why.

"A what?"

"You heard him, a warrant. And don't pretend you don't know what for. *Awheeze.* Cal put the back of his hand to his mouth and tried to cough, *kuff, kuff.* You've been cheating the government for years but it stops now. Officer, put Mr. Best in cuffs."

Ed spun around. "Mr. Moody, I said you could ride along but this is a police matter now, so I would appreciate your butting out."

"It wouldn't be if the Justice Department had arrived on time."

"Ed, what's going on?"

"This is Mr. Calvin Moody. He's with the IRS and they're formally charging you with tax evasion. I have to take you into custody."

"And I have a search warrant for your house. I need your servers."

"Ed, come on, this is ridiculous."

"Maybe, but it's out of my hands. I'm extending you a courtesy by coming out here alone and not sending a patrol unit. I wanted to bring you in myself and save you the embarrassment of having your photo taken in the back of a squad car, but that's the best I can do. A grand jury has already indicted you. You're going to have to stand trial. I'm just doing my job, Bill, that's all I can say."

"This is nuts. Tax evasion, really? Alright, no problem. I'll come along and see if we can't get this straightened out."

"You're forgetting my search warrant. I want access to your computers, not the copies you sent me; I want the servers with all your tax data. *Awheeze.* And since no one seems to know where you live, *awheeze,* we're going out there right now and you're going to hand them over to me in person, got that?"

MARY WAS IN a full blown panic. First Bill had showed up with the Portland Chief of Police and said he was being arrested. Then he had taken the men into his studio and let them remove a whole bunch of his computer stuff, leaving the disconnected wires dangling off the racks. His office looked like it had been attacked by a body snatcher that sucked out its life and left an empty carcass behind.

While the men were busy dismantling his studio, Bill had pulled her aside and asked her to do three things: first, call Dan Blossier, their attorney, and get him down to the police station; second, find a good bail bondsman to get him out of jail; and third, get hold of Darn Good Computer, the shop where he had sent his computer to be restored after the attack, and see if they had retained backup files.

Only one of the tasks had been easy. The computer store assured her they had everything backed up in case their service was needed again. But she'd been on the phone all afternoon working on the other two. Dan, the lawyer, had been in court and had not returned her calls. She did get to talk to his legal aid who said they'd need a twenty-five-thousand-dollar retainer to start looking into the case. Same with the bondsman. Bail hadn't even been set and he was already telling her what his percentage would be. They didn't have that kind of money. Other than a few thousand in savings, they didn't have any. Bill always insisted on giving it away. "It's the Lord's money," he contended. Well the Lord had never asked them to give so much; maybe He could give a little back.

The hardest part was explaining it to Angie. She depended on her father. His daily praises were her lifeblood. She had not taken it well.

"*Daaa, nooooo*," she squealed, squirming and reaching for him as he was escorted out. Mary had to grab her to keep her from falling off her chair. It was more important than ever that Mary get her husband out of jail quickly. If Angie were to drop into a depression, it could affect her physical health.

Fortunately, Rachel was still in town with Josh and wasn't due to be picked up until four. It was one less thing she had to think about. She would have time to calm down before explaining what had happened. Owing to the threat on her own life, Rachel would understand.

Mary had only herself to blame. If she hadn't agreed to let Bill start his latest series, none of this would have happened. She pretended to be strong, she actually wanted to be, but when push came to shove, she was mush. Her stomach fizzed, her hands trembled, and her eyes overflowed nonstop. She was leaving a trail of moist wadded-up tissues wherever she went.

For the moment the room was quiet. She was waiting on her call from the lawyer. There was nothing else to do but...she ran to the bedroom and fell on her knees, wondering why prayer wasn't her first thought, instead of her last.

Her elbows were on the bedspread, hands folded, tears streaming down her face. She looked up. "God, You can't do this," she cried. "I won't let you, hear me, I won't." The saliva in her throat was so thick her words came out garbled. She coughed to clear it away. "Bill's a good man, *uh-hem*. You know that, Lord. He didn't do anything wrong. He doesn't do the books, I do, *kuff*. I should be the one in jail, not him. Please get him out, Lord. Please, I beg You." She paused a moment lowering her eyes, her knotted hands pressing against her forehead so hard it left depressions in her skin. "We can't hire a lawyer, Lord, we can't even post bail. You've got our money. We gave it all to You. Please help, please." The tears streaming down her cheeks were dripping onto the bedspread, making it damp. She wadded up another tissue, blotting her eyes. Then it dawned on her. She stood, putting a hand to her breast to squelch the fluttering in her lungs, her breath coming in gulps. She fanned her face with her fingers. It was going to be alright. She knew what to do.

FIVE CARS PULLED UP in front of the Tantamoa 7-eleven as dusk gloomed the sky. The thick blanket of clouds made it darker than it should have been at six o'clock, but the rains had let up—at least for the moment. The store's green, white and orange logo reflected off the wet pavement as the cars rolled to a stop. The air smelled of decaying sewage. Marie was disappointed with the turnout, though she kept it to herself. It was hard to get people out when the sky threatened rain, but the leaders were all there, Donnie and Ron, and Barba and Dandy and Jeff and a dozen others, even Vic. No one asked about Josh, though he was notably absent.

Marie was standing over by Ron's burgundy Camry. They had their heads together, their voices hushed.

"I just don't like having to keep things from my roommate," Ron said.

"Really? All this time he's been hiding who he is from you, and you're worried about keeping secrets from *him*."

Ron leaned back on his car, his arms folded. "We've talked about this, Marie. I'd do the same if I were in his shoes. I can't imagine what it would be like to have Bill Best for a father. But it's obvious he and his dad don't get along. He's going to be really disappointed about not being in on this. He should be here."

Marie tucked a lock of brunette hair behind her ear and placed her hand on her purse. "I gave him a chance. I told him as clearly as possible that he didn't need to keep secrets from me, but he refused to come clean. He doesn't trust me, so I don't trust him. It's as simple as that."

"And you're absolutely certain he's Bill Best's son?"

She reached into the small bag and found a barrette which she used to pin her hair in place. "One-thousand percent. Vic said it, and he knows the family, but I know myself because his car's registered to a Joshua Best. I saw it with my own eyes."

Ron brought a hand up to scratch the side of his beard. "I still don't understand why you didn't confront him right then."

Marie smoothed the sides of her red skirt and adjusted her black leather belt. "I told you, because he's my ace in the hole. As long as he thinks he's fooling us, we can use him. We don't need him tonight, but the time's coming when we may, and then we'll have leverage, alright?"

Vic came over, wearing a brown leather airmen's jacket with a fleece collar and dark aviator glasses on a night when it was already too dark to see. With his short blond hair and mustache, he looked like a WWII pilot. "Hey guys, we gotta get going. I haven't got all night."

Marie smiled, the red gloss of her lips bright even in the dim light. "We'll talk about this later," she said to Ron. Then she took a step back and over the roof of Ron's car, addressed a gathering of about fifteen people. "Okay, guys, Victor's going to lead in his car and the rest of us will follow. Don't fall back or get out of line. If you don't make it through a stoplight, use your high beams to signal the person in front of you and we'll get the train to pull over. Okay? Let's roll."

The crowd dispersed and went to their cars in groups of twos and threes. Doors slammed and engines fired up. Vic climbed into his shiny black Cadillac XTS, and pulled out of the parking lot. The train rolled out behind him with their tires scrunching the granular puddles. They cruised through several town lights with minimal traffic, passing an old white church with a bell tower and illuminated cross. Not long after, they crossed the Watalong River and drove up alongside the tree farm of the man they were about to shame. Vic veered off at the juncture where the old logging road cut its way into the mountains. All five cars pulled in behind him. He got out, putting his sunglasses on, and dropped back to talk to Marie. He placed his hand on the roof of Ron's Camry and leaned in as she brought the window down.

"This is it. Bill's place is that way," he said, pointing back toward a gravel track that seemed to vanish into a black hole.

Marie tried to see where he was pointing, but it was too dark. She wrinkled her eyes. "Okay. You didn't have to stop, just go on and lead. We'll follow."

"No thanks. I'm a friend of the family. I can't afford to be seen."

"The deal is you show us where Mr. Best lives."

Vic straightened himself, shoving his hands into the pockets of his leather jacket. "And I have. I'm telling you this is where Bill lives, but

I'm not taking you to his front door." With that Vic went to his car, but he turned back before climbing in. "Good luck," he said. One side of his mustache rose as he smiled. He slid in behind the wheel and shut the door, his Cadillac pulling into the street leaving them to find Bill's house on their own.

"Unbelievable," Marie said.

"Friend of Bilbo Best," Ron said.

"Jerks of a feather. Got it."

Ron pulled his car around to where it faced a road that disappeared into a tunnel of darkness like a highway to nowhere. He waited for the other cars to form up behind and then pulled forward, slowly ascending into the Cascades.

It was rough going. The road was unfamiliar and the rain soaked gravel caused tires to slip. A deer and a fawn shot out of the woods to their right and bounded across the road. Ron slammed on his brakes, causing the whole train to come to an abrupt halt. He waited till his heart had time to quiet, then started up again.

If there had been a moon, at least the shadow of the trees would have been visible, but on a starless night like this, all they could see was the road directly in front of them. The track was full of potholes washed out by the rains, painting the sides of their cars with mud. They had driven at a snail's pace for about twenty minutes when they saw several red reflectors on what appeared to be a steel gate barring the road. Ron pulled his car to a stop and leaving the door open, got out, followed by Marie. They walked over to inspect what they were seeing. It was a barrier made of heavy gauge steel pipes. One side of the mountain rose up steeply, the other dropped off like a cliff. They could hear the roar of the Watalong River surging in the canyon below. Ron gave the gate a shake, but it held fast. There was no way around it, and no way to move forward.

Ron looked down the trail behind them. It was a one lane track with no place to turn around. They would have to back up single file all the way down the mountain. "Buggers!" he said.

TWENTY-FIVE

THE PARK BLOCKS were in full bloom. Dazzling displays of pink and red roses lined the walkways sending their perfume into the hearts of passersby, while Elms and Maples, with their domes of green, were painted on a canvas of blue like a modern Monet. It was a slice of Eden in the middle of the city, a respite for the weary. Emerging like bears from hibernation, the pathways were filled with joggers, and walkers, and sitters basking in the sun. Winter days in Portland were usually viewed in black-and-white so you learned to take advantage of those filmed in Technicolor.

Rachel made her way through the Park Blocks, the smell of the budding flowers lifting her spirits, though she tensed at the thought of seeing Josh. It had been two weeks since they'd spoken, but that was only because she wasn't taking his calls. Mary, who knew nothing of their falling out, had given her a ride into Portland and had asked her to update Josh on his father's situation. Bill was still in jail, but she was praying he'd be released that afternoon. The request had been sprung on Rachel as they drove into town, filling her with trepidation. She needed to call Josh to set something up, but lacked the strength, *help me Lord*. There was a park bench bathing in the sun just ahead. She went over and sat down, her golden hair sparkling in the rays of light that filtered through the trees. She removed her phone from the small knapsack she carried. Birds migrating up from the south were twittering in the branches overhead. She found the contact number and dialed and brought the phone to her ear. It rang, once…twice… three times and went to voice mail. "This is Josh, sorry I missed you,

you know what to do," and then a beep. Rachel hit the disconnect button and clutched the phone to her lap. Josh had to be aware of his father's arrest. The story had been the headline of every newspaper, social media site, and television broadcast for days. The arrest of a controversial figure like Bill Best was headline stuff, especially since Bill assumed a higher standard than those he criticized. "How Far the High and Mighty Have Fallen," one headline read. "Wild Bill Corralled by the Tax Marshal," read another. Surely Josh knew as much about his father's situation as she did. Rachel got up and headed for Cascades Coffee. Assuming he'd be there, a casual bumping into him would be easier than making a call.

VIC HAD BEEN observing Rachel's routine for the past few weeks. He sat in the shade of a giant oak wearing his aviator glasses and a baseball cap with the bill turned down. His T-shirt wrapped his torso like latex rubber. His denims were faded and his tennis shoes were suitably worn. Anyone seeing him would think him a typical collegian—but he didn't want to be noticed—he wanted to blend in.

He had the perfect site for surveillance. At the fringe of the Park Blocks, it was far enough back to be inconspicuous, but close enough to identify Rachel as she came and went. On more than one occasion she'd appeared in shorts and halter top, and with her ponytail bobbing behind her, had gone off jogging with some jock. Then one day she'd come back from her jaunt alone. Vic hadn't seen the man since. Hadn't seen Josh either, which surprised him because they used to meet for coffee several times a week, but apparently that had ceased too. All the better for him because he needed to catch Rachel when she was alone.

He pulled the baseball cap from his head and used an arm layered with curly blond hair to wipe the sweat from his brow. He flicked his phone to a weather map, checking the Doppler radar along the route. It looked to be clear sailing. He glanced up. She was crossing the road from one park to the next, the sun shimmering off her head like a golden crown. It was all coming together. He got up and followed at a discrete distance.

RON STOOD BACK, reading the banner one final time before taking it down. The Earth Day festival had been a resounding success, a daylong celebration of planet Earth and everything living on it. Thousands had shown up to enjoy the carnival atmosphere with bands, and jugglers, and puppeteers on stilts directing the movement of costumed actors on strings. But to Ron, and others of his ilk, it was about the community coming together to learn about supportable life systems and how important they were to Earth and its inhabitants. Over eighty sustainable businesses had displayed their wares, demonstrating Portland's commitment to saving the planet. But for some reason, they still hadn't gotten around to cleaning up the trash left behind. No one seemed to get that litter was as bad as any other pollution. He twisted the paper banner into a roll and stuffed it into his recycle bag.

The warmth of the day was balanced by a breeze off the Pacific Ocean. Ron paused, letting it cool his skin—and thanked Mother Earth for the air conditioning. Donnie was working another area, stooping over with his fine hair brushing the ground as he snatched up a piece of wet paper that wouldn't stick to his picker. Ron had recruited half a dozen helpers, including Marie, though she wasn't actually helping with the cleanup. She was busy dividing the area into parcels and assigning others to the task.

Ron stabbed a paper cup with his picker and discarded it in his bag. He just wished more people had a conscience. They'd left the trash, they should help clean it up. Like the blond dude in the baseball cap over by Montgomery Hall. All Ron had said was, "If you're not doing anything, how about lending a hand?" The jerk had ripped the sheet of paper he was holding and tossed the pieces into the wind. "Get lost," he'd said. A totally uncalled for response.

"Hey Ron," Marie called. She curled her fingers in, drawing him over. "I was just thinking about Josh. What's happening with him?"

Ron shrugged, his bottom lip protruding from his beard like a slice of pink watermelon. "Wish I knew. I hardly ever see him. He sleeps till noon, and I'm always out before then, and when I get back he's gone and doesn't get in until after the bars close."

251

"But you haven't mentioned anything about our trip out to his dad's place, right?"

"No, you said not to. I'm pretty sure everyone's avoiding him because you asked us not to mention it."

"Perfect. With the Earth Day celebrations behind us, it's time to start thinking about his dad again."

"What, are you kidding? He's in jail. Problem solved. Besides, if you'd brought Josh on the first trip, he would have unlocked the gate and this would be history." Ron saw a newspaper insert under the foot of a bench and went to pick it up.

"Maybe, but he's got to post bail sometime. I've been thinking about it. Right now, public sentiment is on our side. I think our chances of having an impact are better than ever. It was probably good we held off." Marie waited until Ron returned, his fingers sliding the flyer from his picker into the bag. "I think we should wait until June when it's warm. He'll be out by then for sure. And even if they put him away after that, I still want to shame him. You saw that podcast. He thinks we're of the devil. And his attitude about our planet, sucks. He needs to know you can't mess with Mother Nature. It will give him something to think about while in jail. June is only two weeks away, and it's the end of the school year. We can make it our last big blow-out. I'll bet we get a huge crowd."

"Sure, but at this point we don't even know if Josh is still on board, and without him, no one's going anywhere."

"He will be, I pretty much guarantee it. He's tried calling me, but I've been ignoring him. Most of his messages sound like he's had too much to drink. Poor boy, keeps saying how much he misses me. One call and I'll have him back on-side ready to go."

THE SWELLS ROSE fifteen feet high, washing over his bed. It was like he'd been thrown overboard and was clinging to a plank in the middle of the ocean, the storm raging on every side. *Help me Jesus!* Bedcovers and sheets were awash on the mattress as he rode the waves tossing to and fro. It was a dream that held him, yet it was real; he thought he was drowning. Water filled his mouth and nose, choking him. The currents tore at his clothes, spinning him around, dragging him down.

Then he was floating underwater, unable to move without resistance, stuck in a cube of green Jell-O. *Is this what it's like to die?* And he knew he was dead already, because he didn't deserve to live. The world hated him. Marie ignored him, Rachel loathed him, his father despised him, and his friends had rejected him. But the depths knew his pain, the inescapable horror of being ousted by humanity. In the solace of the deep he found comfort, like a babe in its mother's womb, *sweet, sweet, peace.* All he had to do was answer the siren's call.

MARY DROVE BILL through Tantamoa, stopping at the light next to Waynscott's Family Pharmacy. She'd been tentative about asking him to let her drive, but she assured him she'd grown fond of driving the old truck, and she had something she wanted him to see. Bill hadn't argued. He was just glad to be free.

She had already explained about why it took so long to come up with the bail. Bill had been arraigned the first day, at which time his bail had been set, but he'd spent four days waiting for Mary to come up with the cash. The IRS had placed a temporary freeze on their bank account so she didn't have the five-thousand good faith money for the bail bondsman, which he needed before he would put up the balance for Bill's release.

She had gone to the bank, but ran into a brick wall when she found they had no collateral. She had always assumed, as had Bill, that they would use their house, but in the bank's view, the home was the property of the U.S. Forest Service since they owned the land the cabin was on. But God is faithful. While pleading with God to free her husband, an idea had popped into her head. She had gone to Darn Good Computer and asked about using the backup file of Bill's email list to approach his listeners. The repair store not only arranged everything, but set up a GoFundMe page to accept donations, and his listeners, having just heard Bill mention his problem with the IRS, jumped in by the hundreds, giving enough to not only cover the bail in full without needing a bondsman, but their upcoming legal fees as well. Bless the Lord for that.

Mary swung the truck through the gate of the Christmas tree farm, the tires glopping through the mud as it rolled to a stop. She checked her phone. Rachel was supposed to text if she needed to be picked up. Otherwise it was assumed Josh would drive her home.

"Why are we stopping here?" Bill asked.

"You'll see." Mary climbed out and avoiding the mud track walked past the truck's crumpled fender and stopped, waiting for Bill to join her. She took his hand and they strolled together. The barn was coming along nicely. The frame was now complete and the roof on. Hammers and saws pounded and screeched with sawdust spewing into the air. The boards for the walls were being set in place.

Bill stopped for a minute taking it in. "Dang if that don't look good. I just hope I'll be around to see it finished." He looked at Mary. "I could get up to five years, you know."

Mary turned toward him taking both his hands in hers. "I have a feeling everything is going to be fine. You're the one who's always saying God is a God of miracles. Come on, I've got one to show you," she dropped one hand and led him around the corner to the open space where the acres of trees had been burned. "You know how you were worried about getting the trees planted before their roots started to grow. Well, God answered that prayer too."

As far as the eye could see, row upon row of new trees were already in the ground with green mats laid out around their bases. Mary waited for Bill to say something, but he didn't.

"People from the charities we support kept calling to see if there was anything they could do to help," she said, "and I thought about how you couldn't plant the trees while in jail so one thing led to another and look, they got everything done." She felt Bill's shoulders quake and thought she saw a tear forming in his eye, but that was silly. Bill never cried.

VIC FOLLOWED RACHEL at a safe distance until it occurred to him that to make his plan work, he needed to be inside the coffee shop before she arrived. It had taken some quick maneuvering but when the time came, he'd crossed the road to the retail side of the street. Then he'd powered up the sidewalk while keeping his head turned toward the buildings so she couldn't see his face. She had continued her stroll up the middle of the park, partially hidden behind the shrubbery and trees. He was reasonably sure she hadn't noticed him sneaking by. He was already seated toward the back of Cascades Coffee, when she took her place in line.

He kept his head down so that the brim of his cap covered his face until she was seated and waiting for her coffee. Then he got up, removed his hat, and casually strolled by her table, smiling courteously as he would at a complete stranger, and then stepped back into her field of view.

"Don't I know you?" he said, feigning surprise. "Sure, you're Josh's friend. I remember. You helped out that time he…you know, he was kind of messed up. That was nice of you to take care of him like that. Name's Vic," he pointed at himself and removed his shades so she could see him better. "And your name was, ah, just a second…he called you Rachel, that's it, Rachel. Fancy meeting you here. How have you been?"

Rachel stared at him blankly. "Yes, hi…ah…fine," she said coolly. She grabbed a napkin and pulled it into her lap. Her ponytail dropped over her shoulder as she looked down to make sure the napkin didn't fall to the floor.

"I was just picking up a few things, and I thought I'd grab a coffee before heading back, and here you are. Imagine that. Mind if I sit down?" Vic pulled a chair out and dropped into it without waiting for an answer. "Have you seen Josh lately? I was going to call and see if he wanted to get together while I'm in town, but I ran out of time."

"No. I haven't, actually." Beneath the table, Rachel was fidgeting with her napkin, twisting it into a rope and then unrolling it and spreading it out flat on her knees.

The barista behind the counter called Rachel's name. She started to get up but…

"No, no, no, let me get that. Least I can do. I'll be right back." Vic popped up and went to the serving counter, checking the three or four cups already there until he saw one bearing Rachel's name. It had a flower design melded onto the surface of the coffee. He looked back over his shoulder to see if she was watching. Her eyes darted away.

Vic strutted back to the table. "Sorry I messed up the pretty picture. It looked hot so I used one of those sticks to give it a stir. I didn't want you burning your lip."

Rachel reached out and took the cup, perturbed at the ruin of her art. She brought it to her mouth, blowing across its surface. "It's okay. I like those pictures, but you can't keep them." She took a small sip and set the cup down. "You're not getting one for yourself?"

Vic sat down and leaned forward with his arms folded on the table. "Already had mine. I was on the way out when I saw you sitting here."

Rachel nodded, smiling hesitantly, not anxious to get involved in a conversation with someone she didn't know. She glanced around hoping to see Josh, but he wasn't there.

"So what have you been up to?" he said.

"Not much. Mostly, all I do is study."

"You going to PSU?"

"No, I'm taking courses online at Northwestern."

"Nice school, you must be smart." Vic brought his arms up with his elbows on the table, knotting a fist into his open palm to rub his knuckles. His biceps looked like they might rip through the sleeves of his T-shirt. "I don't know anything about you. Tell me about yourself," he said.

"Not much to tell," Rachel said, lifting her cup to take another sip.

"Like, what's your major?"

"Psychology with an emphasis in counseling. I want to help people, especially those who can't afford a traditional counseling service."

"Uh-oh. Guess I'd better be careful what I say."

Rachel gave her wrist a flick letting the coffee swirl around in her cup, then raised it to her lips and drank a little more. She stared at the coffee, frowning. "Doesn't taste as good as usual," she said, sucking on her tongue. "Has kind of a salty aftertaste." She put the cup down.

"Don't worry, it's not like that. I just want to give people the tools they need to cope. Of course, from my perspective, that's Jesus."

Vic caught her staring at a young man across the room just getting up from his table. *Josh?* He was tall with dark hair and had the same physique, but as the man swiveled toward the door, he saw it was someone else. He had the feeling Rachel was thinking the same thing.

"Jesus, huh, that's interesting."

"I may change my major before I'm through," she said, drawing her eyes back to Vic. "But it's not something I'm in a hurry to do." She drank the remainder of her coffee and set the cup down. "I'm sorry," she said, "but I really have to be getting back. We're into finals week so I need to study."

Vic smiled, the bend in his moustache skewing his face. "Of course," he said. He stood and took a step back, making it easier for her to leave.

Rachel got up, but brushed the table with her thigh, rattling her cup. "Oh. Sorry, clumsy of me." She stepped forward, off-kilter, her balance impaired.

"Let me help," he said. He placed his arm around her waist and guided her toward the door.

"I don't know what's wrong with me. I feel dizzy."

"We'll get you outside. You just need a breath of fresh air." Vic was cautiously aware of the eyes following them, but they were looking at Rachel, not him. Men probably stared at her all the time.

He stepped outside feeling the weight of Rachel's body collapse against his own. He managed to swing her arm over his shoulder, but holding her that close was like wearing a blanket. They hadn't gone a dozen yards before his shirt became moist. Doing this in the heat of the afternoon probably wasn't the best idea.

She seemed to be fading fast. He'd hoped she'd be able to walk to his car on her own. He didn't have a lot of experience with Rufies, though he had used them with great success on two other occasions. It was going to be a long drive, so he'd stirred a little extra into Rachel's cup, maybe a bit too much. His car was around the corner. He'd make it. Her feet were moving like she was taking steps, but her body had gone limp.

"Whaaasszzz happenin to meeeeee?"

"It's alright. You're going to be fine. Just let me help you into the car."

Vic looked around. Thank God the street was empty. He propped her up while he fished in his pocket for the key. Getting her inside was harder than he'd imagined, but he hadn't expected her to pass out so quickly. He set her on the seat and brought her legs around. She looked lovely, like sleeping beauty. He closed the door.

He went around, tore the parking ticket from his windshield, and tossed it in the back, then slipped in and started the car. He turned the wheel to the left and slowly pulled away from the curb. His first job was to get out of the city. Then, once they were up I-5 beyond the rolling suburbs, he would find a remote exit where he could pull off—and get Rachel into the trunk.

TWENTY-SIX

CLOUDS WITH GOLD fringes festooned the sky. Through his window, Vic saw the sun descending in slow motion toward the horizon. They were too far inland to see its rays rippling on the water, but they were close enough to smell the seaweed and taste the salt. By his estimation they were only thirty minutes from the border. Vic had his window down, enjoying the feel of the cool air whipping his hair.

He backed his foot off the gas. He was like a horse picking up its pace as it approached the barn. Time to ease back on the reins. Getting pulled over for a ticket would not be smart.

Vic rubbed his eyes. He was weary of the drive. He pushed against the seat, raising his backside to improve the circulation in a leg that was feeling numb. They'd been on the road for four hours, but they were almost there. Once they crossed the border into Canada, much of the stress he felt would melt away. He could use the darkness to smuggle the girl into a motel.

He never used her name. Becoming too personal might inhibit his ability to do his job. Just looking at her made him regret his assignment. He hadn't considered how lovely she was—*such a shame*. He had promised Wessler he wouldn't hurt her. If it came down to it, her death would be quick and painless, and if not, he was starting to wonder if he shouldn't keep her for himself. For the first hour, while she still rode up front with him, he had talked to her just like she was conscious, though she couldn't respond. He was tempted to keep her up front with him all the way to Canada. He would have, if he could have convinced himself she'd stay asleep—the man who was paid to let them through wouldn't ask him to wake her—but there was just no telling. One of his other targets had awakened shortly after five the next morning; the second, not until afternoon. There was no way to be sure how long this one might be out, so he'd done the safe and responsible thing. He had pulled over just outside Castle Rock and moved the girl to the trunk, even though he found covering her mouth and binding her arms and legs with duct tape, distasteful.

TWO HUNDRED AND FIFTY miles south, Bill knelt atop a cliff that overlooked a lake shining cherry red in the light of the setting sun. The rock he placed his elbows on had probably been there when the Mayflower landed at Plymouth, its age commensurate with the way he felt. His shoulders sagged, the veins in his eyes throbbed, and his knees ached from planting them on the hard ground. He'd made the trek up that trail dozens of times before and never had he felt so exhausted.

What do you do when your life falls apart? His lawyer was confident they could beat this thing. They had recovered the backup copies of his hard drives and could demonstrate everything was exactly as Bill said it was, there was no reason for the government to pursue this any further. He was sure the charges would be dismissed. And since the anticipated indictments for arson and insurance fraud were contingent upon the tax evasion case, they too, would go away.

God had already restored his tree farm. A fresh crop of trees had been planted and the barn was almost finished. What was there to be so despondent about?

Josh, the one unresolved issue.

A pair of eagles circled over the water, their bodies silhouettes against the crimson sky. He'd been a good parent to at least one of those birds, saved its life by descending that cliff to rescue the eaglet after it had been abandoned—and he'd broken his own leg in the process—but what had he done for Josh? Darn well nothing. Dang it though, Josh was a bird of a different feather, more humming bird than eagle. No, Ted had been the eagle. Even Angie had more grit than Josh. How was he supposed to deal with that? How was Isaac supposed to deal with Jacob?

"That's me Lord; Isaac who loved his son Esau, the hunter, while his momma's boy Jacob, got the blessing. But dang it all Lord, it's hard. I loved both my sons, I did, it's just that Josh was…different. I brought Ted here and dedicated him to you, and I carried Joshua here as an infant, laid him right here on this very rock, even when Mary fought me on it and questioned my sanity, still I brought both my boys to this alter to lay them before You. Just as Abraham did with Isaac. I gave them to You Lord. And You took Ted. He was Yours, I had no right to complain, but now it seems I'm losing Josh too. Don't do it Lord, please. Not just for me, but for Mary. She loves you Lord. Why would you want to hurt her like that? Please, it's breaking her heart. At least let her know Josh is alright. And me Lord. I'm a screw-up of a father. You know that. I can't seem to do a darn thing right, but I'm trying Lord. Please. And thank you Lord for the way you got the people to plant those trees. I'm still in awe about that. And I'm still praying my lawyer is right, and that we'll get those charges dropped…"

Oh, taste and see that the Lord is good. Blessed is the man who trusts in Him!

"Really Lord, is that for me?"

Bill heard it before he saw it, the *eyeeeeeeee, eyeeeeeee, eyeeeeeee,* cry of the eagle. He got up from his knees and stood, turning away from the sun to see better, and instantly felt the *whoosh* of the bird with its seven-foot wingspan swing by, nearly knocking him off his feet. He raised his elbow protectively, feeling the wind in the eagle's wake. "Whoa! partner, what gives?" He turned and saw the eagle rising far overhead, turning to make a second dive. "Hey there, now, let's not be biting the hand that fed you. I'm the one who saved your life, remember?" he ducked as the eagle made a second pass, attempting to run him off. He saw the eagle climbing into the sky again. Then he heard the *eyeeeeeeee, eyeeeeeee, eyeeeeeee* and realized it wasn't coming from the bird, but from behind him on the cliff wall. *Of course. It's that time of year. I'll bet—*

Bill moved to the edge of the precipice, treading carefully because the overspray from the waterfall made the rocks slippery. The eagle mounted another attack. Bill got down on his belly. The bird wouldn't strike him, he knew that, but the closer he was to the ground, the better. He scooted to where he could get his head out over the lip of rock and look down. The nest was six foot across, but it was hard to see because of the cliff's overhang. The bird swooped and pulled away again, not coming close enough to hit Bill, but enough to put the fear of God into the average man. Bill edged about ten feet to the right where the outcrop was less pronounced. Sure enough, the nest was full of downy white feathers. They had eaglets. The bird was just protecting his young. A second eagle circling out over the lake dove into the water and came away with a trout in its talons. She'd want to get that meal to her babes. Bill scrambled to his feet.

I get the picture, Lord. Gotta take care of all the birds in the nest. The sun had dropped beyond the horizon, leaving a hazy pink dusk in the sky. Time to leave.

He raised his hand to shield his eyes, searching for the eagle. It had descended to a lower elevation, out over the water, flying straight for the cliff and its nest. "Okay, I got the message, I'm gone. You and your mate take care of those younglings. I got my own. I'm too old to climb down that cliff to take care of yours."

A HALF DOZEN beer signs shed light on the shadowy recesses of the bar, but they weren't bright enough for Josh to read by. He held the sheet of paper up, the glowing red neon of the Budweiser logo illuminating the page. Or maybe it was difficult to read because he'd used a pencil instead of a pen, or maybe because he'd had too much to drink. What other choice did he have? They were out of beer at the apartment and writing this kind of stuff required fortification.

It was quiet in the Cheerful Tortoise, but only because it was early. The revelry wouldn't begin until after nine and Josh planned to be gone by then. He pulled the sheet of lined notebook paper in close to see what he'd written. It was just a rough draft; he'd probably change it later, but it held the gist of what he wanted to say. Not a suicide note, per se, more a final farewell. It was time to go, no regrets. He didn't need Joseph to interpret the dream. Night after night the same vision, the surging water pounding him down until he felt release. That's just how it would be. His eyes scanned the page.

Hi guys, Mom, Dad, friends.

First I want to say please don't blame yourselves for my death. No one caused it, it's just the course of nature, the weak falling prey to the strong—but that's not really what this is about, is it? Perhaps a better illustration is the square peg in a round hole. That's how we describe something, or someone, that doesn't fit. That's me. I was born into a world of roundness, and I'm as square as they get.

The trouble is, when you try to drive a square peg into a round hole the corners get hammered off and that hurts. That's the pain I want release from. But don't worry, this isn't on you. This is about me. Well, not just me. I'm placing myself in the hands of God. (a few of you college friends may sneer at this, but sorry, I still believe in God). It's a feeling I can't seem to shake, so I guess I'll just have to take it with me to the grave. He cares for me. He doesn't want me to hurt like this. This why I believe He's calling me home.

By now you know I chose the river to carry me into the next life. Did you know the ancient Egyptians believed their god Mahaf, piloted a ferry across the river of death to deliver souls to the underworld? I was online looking for ways of escape when I found, much to my surprise, that the river of death is a common thread. Here's a little ditty from 'Goodnight Irene.' by Huddie Ledbetter and John Lomax.

Sometimes I live in the country
Sometimes I live in town
Sometimes I have a great notion
To jump in the river and drown.

I think that's cute, but also true. Sometimes you do get a great notion. Ted got a great notion to run the river, and while I can't say he wanted to die, daredevils often have a subliminal death wish.

263

Or how about this one called, 'River Blues,' by Robert Crumb.

I'm ready for the river, the shivery river,
The river that runs down to the sea
I'm gonna drown my troubles, and leave just some bubbles
To indicate what used to be.
I made my will, I wrote some notes,
I'm gonna keep walkin' 'til my straw hat floats...

You gotta love that—just sayin'. Fats Domino sang 'Going To The River' which hits pretty close, too.

I'm goin' to the river,
Gonna jump overboard and drown
Because the girl I love
She just done let me down.

No Marie, I'm not talking about you, you either Rachel, this is about me. Enough foolishness. Just know that I'm far happier now than I have ever been. Dad, Mom, I promise to say hi to Ted for you when I see him. Please try to understand.

Now, to one and all, I bid a fond, farewell.

Josh set his missive down but jerked it back when he saw the paper absorbing the water rings left on the table by his beer. He used a napkin to wipe the paper off and folded it into his wallet. His cellphone started to buzz. It was a text from Marie.

"Josh, where have you been? Sorry, my fault. I know you've left messages. I've been so busy with organizing Earth Day I haven't had time for anything else. But listen, we haven't forgotten about our rendezvous with Mr. Best. We were able to find out where he lives, so now we're planning a protest there and I want to make sure you're in on it. You're a valuable member of this team, Josh. We will be meeting at the

Cheerful Tortoise tonight at nine. Please try to be there. See you then. Marie."

Josh looked at his watch and raised his head just as Ron and Donnie came through the door. It would mean forgoing his departure for a few days, but why not? They were giving him a chance to deliver a final coup-de-grace to his father.

DOWN THE DARK hall of a building with no windows, in the depts of an undisclosed location, Cal stood inspecting the results of his work. He, of course, hadn't done anything personally, he'd hired the job done, but it was all the same. It was his idea, and to his credit. His NSA contact, Mr. Damshie, would agree. He could already see the presidential citation hanging on his office wall.

The screen in front of him glowed with long lines of data, not all of which were forged. The majority of the records, those entered by Bill, were legitimate, but the new entries totaled a hundred-and-seventy-six-thousand dollars' worth of untaxed income. *Bye, bye, Bill.*

"And you're sure no one will know?" Cal asked of the programmer he'd commissioned to add files to Bill Best's database.

"Not a chance. I've backdated the entries and removed every trace of data scheming. As far as anyone is concerned, these files have always existed."

Cal had no reason to doubt the man. He was a government contractor, and the government only used the best, or maybe it was the cheapest, but they wouldn't use someone who couldn't do the job. The fact that the man had contacts in the defense department, spoke volumes. "I want you to know the IRS is in your debt."

"Great, my taxes are due. I'll send them over to your office for approval," the man said with a smile.

"Only if you want an audit, least that's what my department does."

"Thanks, I'll pass. But no, really, it was my pleasure. I never liked this guy. I'm glad someone's finally found a way to shut him down."

"The IRS at your service," Cal said. "Help me load these on a cart.

The Justice Department is waiting for me to get these to them. They're the backbone of our case."

THEY HAD CROSSED the forty-ninth parallel, the dividing line between the U.S. and Canada, which made them now officially on Canadian soil. The sun was setting on the Peace Arch, the sixty-foot-tall emblem of American and Canadian solidarity, with both country's flags flying on top and the words, "Children of a Common Mother," inscribed on its face. Cars were forming up at the Canadian checkpoint ahead. Vic took his place in line. The building looked like an airport observation tower, or maybe a space port with giant panes of glass slanted outward under a domed ceiling. There were multiple drive-through lanes, only two of which had green lights indicating they were open. Vic had read how the wait times could be over an hour, but sometimes as little as fifteen minutes. It looked like they were lucky. The lines were short. The sign said, "Keep right," and, "Garder la droite." Vic chuckled to himself. It was something he would have to get used to. The Canadians had insisted on making the entire country bilingual.

The traffic moved steadily forward. Each car seemed to stop for about three minutes, just enough time for drivers to show their passports and answer a few questions. When his time came, he'd be ushered through without inspection. It was prearranged. He just had to remain in the first lane. Senator Wessler said the border guard in that booth was instructed not stop any black Cadillac's coming through that evening. Piece of cake.

Vic reached into the glove box for his passport and removed his wallet to get his driver's license. He wanted to be ready with his identification in hand. The red octagonal sign said "Stop" and "Arrêt." Only one car was ahead of him now, and it was pulling away. Vic rolled up to the window. He reached out and handed the border guard his documentation, just as he had seen others before him do. The man was all business, no smiles. He examined Vic's paperwork, and then turned to ask, "What's your citizenship?"

"Ah, American, born and raised in Portland." It wasn't the truth, but that's what his documents said. They also stated he was Carl Rove, an alias, but that didn't matter. Victor Damshie wasn't his real name either.

"Where do you currently live?"

"Same place, Portland."

"Where are you going in Canada?"

"Vancouver. I'm visiting a friend."

"How long do you plan to stay?"

"About a week, maybe less."

"What are you bringing into the country?"

"Not much, some clothes, a little food."

"What kind of food?"

"Cereal, coffee, a few bananas and oranges."

"Anything else?"

"No, that's everything."

"Okay," The man handed Vic his paperwork. "Please pull your car over to the left and park against that wall."

"Excuse me?"

"It's illegal to bring fresh fruits and vegetables across the border. Just pull over and go into the building and wait. Someone will come out and do a secondary inspection. Strictly routine, but they'll have to confiscate your produce."

"But...I. You do see I'm driving a black Caddy, right?"

"Park over there," he said, indicating the direction with a nod of his head. "You're holding up traffic. Go."

"What the...!" Vic eased his foot off the brake, rolling to the spot specified by the border guard. He put the car in park and sat thinking for a minute. The sky had grown dusky, but not dark enough to afford cover if he had to make a run for it. Poor choice. They'd be on him in minutes. But if he went inside, it would be over, unless...unless Wessler had someone inside as a backup. Maybe they'd just take his groceries and let him go. A car two spaces down was undergoing a similar search. The guard was asking the man to open his trunk.

Vic reached for the gun tucked under his seat, then found his jacket and slipped it on while checking his review mirror. The guard in the booth was already occupied with the next car in line. Wessler, son of a…bureaucrat, better pray they don't find your girl, I won't go down alone. Friggin' incompetent… The guard to his left had his head in the trunk of the car he was inspecting, riffling through its contents.

He could make a run for it, but he wouldn't get far. There were several police cars parked on the road ahead. Vic shoved the gun into his pants behind his back, the bump covered by his coat. He reached around the seat to grab the bananas and his bag of oranges. No one said anything about fruit being illegal. Driver's license and passport, that's what they said he needed, and they'd supplied both. And what the heck happened to the guard who was supposed to wave him through? He swung the door open and stepped out of the car, heading for the building.

Two agents in dark blue uniforms with large embroidered patches on their shoulders were sitting behind a counter. A third stood at a cabinet shuffling through files. Vic approached casually. Even if they took him into custody, he'd be out in a day. Wessler wouldn't risk leaving him there. He knew too much.

"They told me I can't take my fruit into Canada," he said as he dropped the oranges and bananas on the counter. "Sorry about that, I didn't know."

The officer leaned over and shoved the produce aside. "Please sit down. We'll be with you in a minute."

"My name is Carl Rove, on a diplomatic mission for the U.S. Senate. Anyone here connect with that?" He said it loud enough to be heard by everyone in the room in case Wessler had an inside man.

"I don't care if you're the Queen of England. Please, sit down."

Vic looked over at a row of chairs along the wall. He didn't have time for this.

The officer who had been outside doing an inspection came through the door and stood behind Vic, just off to his left.

"Any chance we can expedite this? Like I said, I'm on a diplomatic mission. I really have to be going."

The agent at the counter shook his head. "Sit down, please."

"For what?"

"Once you're sent in here, we have to do a search. That's the policy.

Now go sit down."

Vic inhaled through his nose and puffed it out audibly. He smiled raising one side of his moustache. So they were going to do a search. It was over. Wessler better get him out quick. "Sorry" he said. He reached for his weapon.

"GUN!" someone yelled.

TWENTY-SEVEN

PANDEMONIUM BROKE out with chairs scraping back as officers ducked behind their workstations, reaching for the silent alarm.

"Come on people. Relax. You got me, okay? I'm just trying to surrender my weapon. I give up." Vic started to back away. Game over. He would show them the girl, let them arrest him, and wait for Wessler to bail him out.

Over by the filing cabinet an officer dropped his hand like he was going for a weapon. Vic's response was automatic. His finger tightened around the trigger and his gun exploded, the bullet ricocheting off the filing cabinet leaving a deeply ingrained groove in the metal. *Crap!* Vic spun around but froze as fifty-thousand volts of electricity coursed through his body causing an involuntary muscle spasm that threw him to the ground.

The officer that had followed Vic into the building disengaged his Taser and stepped over Vic's twitching body to place him in cuffs. "Good thing I came in when I did," he said. "You guys want to help? My hands are shaking."

All three border guards, including the one who'd just dodged a bullet, raced around the barrier and grabbed Vic under the arms. They yanked him up, dragging him to a chair along the wall, and thrust him into it. The temperament was edgy; you don't discharge a firearm in a federal building without drawing ire.

Two officers with the Royal Canadian Mounted Police slammed through the door. Their simi-automatics were held at the ready, but they eased back when they saw the suspect in handcuffs surrounded by four border guards. Their navy blue uniforms were starched and pressed, a distinctive yellow stripe running down the legs of their pants. A gun lay on the floor a few feet away. "You got him?" one said. His weapon was held in both hands but pointed at the ground. "Are there others?"

"No, he came in alone, and I came in after. Didn't see anyone else." The guard's voice trilled with nervous excitement. "Never had to use my stun-gun before."

The second RCMP officer went to pick Vic's gun off the floor. She put on a pair of latex gloves but still held it by two fingers as she dropped it into a plastic bag. The broad black bill of her hat rode low on her forehead, its yellow band the same color as the stripe on her pants. "What happened?" she said.

The agent who first spoke with Vic looked at their prisoner, shaking his head. "He came in with a bag of fruit and dumped it on my desk. He wanted to leave, but I said he had to wait until we inspected his car, and then all hell broke loose. He went for his gun, shooting at Frank, and then Mike hit him with the Taser. Dimes to donuts he's holding a few bricks of cocaine."

The Cadillac's windshield was spattered with bugs, perhaps not as many as you'd see in the heat of summer, but enough to make the vehicle a speckled mess; the shiny black paint was coated with a thin layer of dust. Officer Jakes walked around the vehicle with a German Shepherd, letting out enough leash to let the dog sniff every part of the car, bumpers, fenders, doors, and undercarriage, but the dog gave no sign of sensing contraband. "Boy, that's a surprise. I could have sworn we'd find drugs."

Vic sat in the back of the RCMP cruiser locked behind a steel mesh that separated the front seat from the back. He could see they were going through his car, but his electrical bath had muddled his mind. His teeth were clamped tight and his tongue was thick as a wet sponge. "Don't touch her, she's my responsibility. Don't you touch her." But his words were as disoriented as his brain, and like his brain, were as coherent as mush.

One of the officers reached for the door and pulled it open. He went through a bag of food, dumping it onto the back seat, Shredded Wheat and Great Value coffee, then pulled out each piece of clothing, suits and shirts, shaking each item, feeling the seams for unusual lumps, and turning the pockets inside out. He stooped down and scooped everything from under the seat onto the carpet: a few potato chips, some lost coins, and a plastic coffee cup lid, but nothing illegal. While he was doing that, another officer was up front going through the glove box, panel pouches, and the console. *Nothing.* He hit the trunk release.

Officer Jakes was standing behind the car restraining the dog while the others did the search. He saw the trunk pop open and slid his finger under the lid to lift it the rest of the way. "Hey guys, you better come see this," he said.

Vic was taken handcuffed, riding in the back of the police cruiser to the RCMP headquarters in Surry, B.C. They'd wanted to question him, but either he was playing dumb, or his mind was still too confused to handle interrogation. After being processed, he'd spent the night in a holding cell with a stainless-steel toilet and thin mattress on a spring-wire cot. They weren't the most comfortable accommodations, but he managed to get a good night's sleep. As his thoughts began to untangle and his memory returned, he took stock of his predicament. It wasn't anything new. He'd been arrested before, and the charges were always dropped. The girl couldn't tell them anything. She wouldn't remember how she came to be in his car. His one call would be to Wessler who would build a diplomatic case for his release. Wessler had too much to lose by leaving him there. Besides, he should be happy. When Senator Powers realized how close he came to losing his daughter, he'd think twice about how he voted. Mission accomplished. He just had to wait them out. Hopefully, it wouldn't take long.

He was given a scant breakfast of scrambled eggs, toast and coffee, and around ten was hauled off to the room where he now sat. He didn't know he was in Surry, or that his case was being handled by the Major Crimes Unit of the RCMP, he knew only that he was being held against his will by a foreign government.

He was seated at a table in a room without windows with two men who introduced themselves as detectives Whitlock and Scone, adjuncts to the Missing Persons Unit, an odd situation they themselves had to admit. Usually Missing Person's handled cases where someone had been kidnapped and needed rescue. But in this case, they had the victim, and the alleged kidnapper already in custody. They just had to piece together the crime.

"I thought you Mounties wore red coats with flat brimmed hats." Vic said, trying to lighten the mood. His captors were dressed in regular business suits, but all the pictures he'd seen lining the hall as they brought him in were of officers in full regalia.

"You're not doing yourself any favors by not talking to us." Officer Whitlock leaned on the table, towering over Vic.

"I already told you, I have nothing to say." Vic imagined himself in the serge of the Mounted Police. He'd look right smart, his blond mustache under that brown flat brimmed Stetson, his buff body filling out that red jacket, those calf high boots covering his blue pants with that wicked yellow stripe.

"You kidnapped a young lady. That much we know. She was bound and gagged in the trunk of your car."

"One more time, I don't know what you're talking about."

"And you brought her across international lines from the U.S. into Canada. In the U.S. that's a federal offence under the jurisdiction of the FBI. We can turn you over to them if that's what you want, but trust me, you'll get much better treatment from us."

"I don't recognize your sovereignty over me. I'm a U.S. Citizen. I need to talk to the U.S. Consulate."

"Your consulate deals with lost passports, not human trafficking. Where did you pick up the girl?"

"What girl?"

"The girl we found tied up in the trunk of your car."

273

"I told you, I don't know anything about any girl. I demand to see the U.S. Consulate."

"And that's why you pulled a gun on our border guards."

"Again, I was taking it out to give it to them but it accidently fired."

"And you took aim on a federal agent."

"I'm not saying anything else."

"At least tell us the girl's name. She's in a hospital. It would be nice to have her medical history so she can get proper care."

"If you need her name, why not ask her?"

Detective Whitlock arched his back, relieving the pressure on his spine. "Believe me, as soon as she wakes up, we will."

THE LATTER PART of Spring was a beautiful time of year. It was the season when the trees showed their most prodigious growth, the buds breaking open and shooting out bright green sprouts, attaining new heights for the tree. But it was also a risky time of year because a late season frost could kill the buds and severely limit the tree's growth. This year it was warm and the newly planted trees were doing fine. Only about two percent had failed to take root. The rest were sending out shoots of bright green, showing they had accepted the transition to their new home. Bill was on a stepladder picking cones from a seven-foot Douglas fir in the section of trees that had survived the fire. It was grueling work because the cones were both prickly and covered with sap. He had already dumped more than a dozen cones into his sack from this one tree alone, and there were several hundred undamaged trees yet to be pruned. You had to get every cone because they blocked the growth of branches, leaving empty spaces where Christmas ornaments should be hung.

Part of him wanted to chuck the whole Christmas Tree farm idea and go back to being a journalist. *Nuts!* It was his podcasts that got him into this mess. The cancel culture was out to destroy his credibility. Who'd listen to a convicted felon? And a conviction for tax evasion would likely lead to charges of arson and insurance fraud. It was funny how things could turn around so fast. Yesterday it seemed he was home free; today it looked like he was jail bound. He wasn't guilty of anything, and yet earlier, when he'd spoken to his lawyer, he'd sensed the man's confidence wavering. Through discovery the lawyer had found that, according to the IRS, numerous unreported donations had been deleted from Bill's server, many of them substantial. The IRS had reportedly dredged up the missing files. Bill knew that was impossible, but the evidence was there, and supposedly, irrefutable. This was a lot more serious than he'd thought. The government was attempting to frame him. *God, are you really going to let evil win over good?* Bill plucked another cone and tossed it into his bag, his stomach curling with stress. If he ever climbed out from under the weight of all this, he should retire and spend his summer mornings on the lake with his fishing pole, or having coffee with Mary while the sun rose like yellow fire over the Cascades. Then again, he might be spending the next few years drinking watered down coffee in a facility where the inmates wore orange, and orange was definitely not his color. But this was wrong-headed thinking. God was still on the throne, though knowing God was in control didn't stop him from feeling anxious. He plucked another cone from the tree and tossed it into his bag. A witch's broom stemming from the trunk was buried deep in the needles. Ugly *sucker*, all those branches shooting out from a single knot. He had to remove it. Nobody wanted a misshapen tree. Bill heard the ringtone of his cell and tossed three more pinecones into his bag before pulling off his gloves. He reached into the pocket of his coveralls and brought the phone to his ear wondering who it could be since very few people knew his new number.

"You got Bill," he answered.

"Bill? It's Stan."

Bill stepped down off the ladder and began walking down a row of trees. "Senator Powers, what can I do for you?"

"That's Stan to you, Bill. My friends don't call me senator. Anyway I just wanted to talk to you about a couple of things. First, I have to compliment you on your recent series of podcasts. I'm sure it took courage, but people need to know what's coming, and they're having a powerful impact. And I deeply regret this fiasco with the IRS. I have no doubt there's a connection between what you said and what's going on. I want you to know I've called for an investigation into the matter."

"Thanks Stan, I appreciate it. I do seem to be attracting the wrong kind of attention, but I count my blessings. So far they've left my family alone, thank God. But I agree, people need to know where this is all heading." Bill stopped at a noble fir, reaching into a thick mass of branches. *Darn, another witch's broom.* He looked down the row, trying to mark the spot so he'd be able to come back and fix it later.

"Globalism is on the rise. Take it to the bank," Stan said. "Look, I know it's belated, and I should have called sooner, but I did want to say thanks. And thanks again for taking Rachel in. You're not the only one under pressure so having Rachel out of harms way means a lot. Speaking of which I haven't heard from her today. We were scheduled to talk this morning, but I've been leaving messages and she hasn't returned my calls. It's not like her. Frankly, I'm a bit concerned."

"That's odd. Yesterday, Mary dropped Rachel in the city to meet with Josh. She was supposed to text if she needed a ride and when she didn't we assumed Josh was bringing her home."

"So you haven't seen her?"

Bill paused, realizing his concern for his own well-being had resulted in negligence toward his charge. He wiped his chin, afraid of what might be coming next. "Mary and I went to bed early, though Mary did mention that she expected Rachel to be home soon, and I left early this morning so I haven't seen her today, but I'm sure she's there," but even as he said it, a tone let him know Mary was calling. "Hold on, Stan, I've got Mary on the other line. We'll get to the bottom of this." He swiped the answer icon, but before he could speak, heard Mary's voice coming through in a frantic soprano pitch. "Bill, have you seen Rachel? Angie and I were letting her sleep in but when I went to see if she wanted breakfast, she wasn't there…"

VANCOUVER GENERAL, with its seven-hundred and thirty-seven beds, was one of the largest hospitals in the country, and certainly the largest in the province of British Columbia. It had achieved remarkable growth, considering its humble beginning as a nine-bed tent servicing employees of the Canadian Pacific Railway.

Plain clothes officers Brad Whitlock and his partner Marty Scone stood outside Rachel's room talking with Doctor Hathaway, Chief Medical Toxicologist at VGH. Both men understood the demanding schedule the doctor maintained, and the inherent danger of pushing him too far with too many questions, but they needed answers, and Brad was determined to get them.

"Has there been any improvement at all Doc, any change to her condition?"

"You mean since this morning when you called? Gentlemen, I appreciate your need to talk to the patient, but nothing has changed and if it does, I promise you'll be the first to know."

"So she's still psychotic?"

"No, not psychotic, I don't know what she is. Physically, there's nothing wrong with her. Mentally, she's withdrawn. We ran a full tox panel, and like I said, she's lucky to be alive. She had enough Rohypnol in her system to kill a horse. How she even made it this far, I don't know, but I do know this; you need to prepare yourself. She may never be able to give you what you want."

"I hope you're wrong, Doc. She's not just a victim, she's our only witness. Our perp is denying any knowledge of her. He claims if she ended up in his trunk, someone else put her there, and without her testimony, we may not be able to prove otherwise."

"Well I hate to say it, but you should probably plan for the worst. Our patient's in a coma and…"

"Coma? But you said she's awake. She opened her eyes, right? Shortly after they brought her in."

"Yes, she is awake, but she's not aware of her surroundings. She's in what I would call a vegetative state. Her eyes open and close, she reacts to loud noise, but her response is involuntary, not true consciousness. I'm no expert in this field, I'm referring her to a neurologist for further diagnosis, but personally I feel the overdose of Rohypnol has affected her brain. If we're lucky, the effects will wear off over time, but there's no way of knowing how long that might take. She might snap out of it tomorrow or it could be years from now. In the meantime, we'll be transferring the patient to a long-term care facility. We can't do anything more for her here."

"Dang, doc, you sure are a harbinger of good news. We're going to let a kidnapper, and probably a rapist, walk just because our only witness can't talk. Can't you at least let us see her? You said yourself she's healthy. What's the harm?"

The doctor paused, frowning thoughtfully. "Alright, okay, but understand the risk. If you get her upset in any way, she could have an emotional break, and that would only prolong her recovery, and that's the last thing any of us wants."

Detectives Whitlock and Scone were ushered into a room brightly lit with florescent tubes and sun-filled windows. Doctor Hathaway gave them one final admonition to be gentle and turned to leave.

Rachel was lying on a hospital bed with the back raised. Tubes inserted into her veins led back to clear plastic bags hung from rolling stands. Monitors with LED displays kept track of her vital signs but none of that was necessary because Doctor Hathaway said there was nothing physically wrong with her. It was strictly hospital procedure. The TV was on but she wasn't watching the program. Her eyes stared off into space like they were looking at something no one else could see.

Detective Whitlock grunted, his cheeks pulling back like he was wounded and in pain. The girl in front of him looked like death. He grunted again and shook his head, then folded his hands. "Hi there. My name is Brad, and this is my partner Marty," he said in the softest voice possible. "We're detectives with the major crimes unit of the RCMP. Would it be all right if we asked you a few questions?"

But Rachel didn't answer. Her eyes were empty, void of recognition. She couldn't hear, see, or feel anything. She lay on the bed, stretched out like a sack of potatoes, dead to the outside world, but deep within—*deep, deep, deep*—there was a person inside the person, and that person silently watched a movie being played in the darkened theater of her mind.

Look now. There's a little girl running through a field of wildflowers. A little blond girl wearing a yellow cotton dress with a white ruffle apron. Look! Can you see it? Yes, black patent leather shoes and yellow turned down socks. Yes, that's right, and look, there's the yellow ribbon. As she skips through the turquoise sky, her long blond hair dances behind her like rays of sun. Oh, how pretty she is, skipping through the grass along the side of the hill. She comes to a patch of daisies. They wave at her, beckoning, promising to share her future. Ask one! Taking it up, rolling it between her thumb and finger, one by one she carefully plucks off the petals letting them float away gently on the breeze: "He loves me, he loves me not..."

TWENTY-EIGHT

BILL CLIMBED OUT of his truck and began walking through a subterranean parking lot on the periphery of PSU. It was in fact, the same lot where his son had parked the evening of his birthday, and where the car he'd received as a present was parked still. But Bill didn't know that, nor did he know as he walked the two blocks back to Portland State, that he would pass by an establishment with his son sitting inside enjoying his first beer of the day.

Bill had only visited the campus once, and that was when he and Mary had dropped Josh off to start the school year back in September. Bill had been given a tour, but the buildings with variant facades, were as dissimilar as the rocks along the Watalong, and he found himself spinning like a depolarized compass unable to find a bearing. He finally did what every man hates to do. He stopped to ask directions.

"Excuse me, there's a coffee shop around here somewhere, Cascades Coffee I think it's called. Do you happen to know where it is?" he asked of a girl with pink hair who was sitting on a cement bench organizing a dozen or more rings by trying different ones on different fingers.

The girl glanced up, her eyes narrowing as though she was looking into the sun. Her brows furrowed in. "You're him," she said.

"What?"

"You're that writer guy who thinks climate change is a hoax. Don't deny it. I'd know that face anywhere."

Bill shook his head, caught off guard by the recognition. He slid his hands into his pockets attempting to look nonchalant. "I'm not denying anything. I just need to find a coffee shop."

"It's at the other end of campus. You come to the Park Blocks and turn right then head up several blocks. It's on the left," she said, flicking her fingers as though shooing him away.

"Thanks," Bill said. He turned and sauntered off with his hands still in his pockets, evoking the image of a person without a care.

"You're destroying our planet, ya know?" she called after.

Bill turned to respond but the girl had gathered her rings and scampered off like someone in a hurry to be somewhere.

Bill traipsed across the open square noting the people he passed giving him a second glance. He wore his boots, but he always wore boots, and blue jeans, and a green flannel shirt. If he looked like a farmer, so what? That's what he was. He hadn't had time to change. Locating Rachel was the only thing that mattered now. His stomach roiled with anxiety. He'd be lucky to get thought all this without an ulcer.

The sky was blue, bedecked with cotton clouds and birds warbling in the trees. He stopped to roll up his sleeves. His flannel shirt was hot, but in his line of work long sleeves were necessary. Pinecones and prickly branches were constantly tearing at his skin.

"That's him!"

Bill looked up to see the girl with pink hair pointing his direction, though he looked back over his shoulder to see if she meant someone else. Suddenly he found himself surrounded by a dozen people, some holding signs that displayed his face. It was the wanted dead or alive poster his friend, Jack Palco, had told him about. He started to walk away but the group followed taking up the chant, "Bill, Bill you're a shill. Shame, shame, you're to blame. Oh, no, you must go."

It was hard to ignore, but you can't fight a mob, and any response would be incendiary. He turned onto the campus park, heading up the blocks in the direction the pink-haired girl said. The chanting grew louder as their numbers increased, the commotion drawing others like moths to a flame. By the time he reached Cascades Coffee there had to be at least thirty people, all chanting, "Oh, no, you must go," over and over again. He figured half of them didn't even know who he was.

He ducked into the store trying to purge the noise from his head, hoping the crowd wouldn't follow him inside. They didn't, but he could still hear their chanting as he scanned the tables. No Josh and no Rachel. *Now what?* He'd already been to Josh's apartment but though he'd pounded loud enough to wake the dead, no one had come to the door.

"Shame, shame, you're to blame. Oh, no, you must go!" Their cries were vibrating through the windows. The crowd outside looked like they wanted his head. He took a step back. "Is there another exit?" he asked of a girl standing at the bar holding a large paper cup to her lips. Steam was roiling up from the rim fogging her glasses. Hopefully, she wouldn't recognize him.

She nodded and without smiling said, "Down the hall past the restrooms. Bill took a calming breath and walked to the back of the building, watched by every eye in the place. He stepped into the clean blue air. Not a dissident in sight, though he could still hear their cries over the rooftops. He followed the alley keeping out of sight behind the buildings. Overfilled trashcans and the acrid smell of rotting produce accompanied his passage until the alley dumped onto a side street. He would have to take the long way around to avoid the urban plaza where he might be recognized again. The route would keep him on the main road but if he kept his eyes to the ground and headed straight for the parking lot, he should be able to make it without problem. His forehead blistered with drops of sweat. It was too hot for a long hike, but he wasn't about to cut across campus again. He began walking.

Marie was leading the choir. They kept up the chant, the street reverberating with their mantra in hopes of humiliating Bill when he reappeared. The window's glare had prevented them from seeing his escape. After a few minutes it became apparent that Bill was either sitting in a corner enjoying a cup of coffee, or that he'd snuck out another way. She grabbed Ron and had him check and found Bill was gone. She waved her arms at the group, calling a halt to the demonstration.

"Hey, people, it's hot out here, and Mr. Best's a coward. Ron says he skipped out the back."

A few cheers rippled through the crowd.

"But no worries, we're not letting him get away. He's a criminal, and he has to pay for his crimes. Tonight, we're gonna drive out and demonstrate right on his front lawn. Are you with me?"

Cries rose with fists raised and one man screaming, "Shame, shame, Bill's to blame!" which got the whole crowd going again. "Bill, Bill, you're a shill. Oh, no, you must go!"

"All right, all right." Marie held her hands raised with palms out in the universal sign of, stop. In the sun, her dark brunette hair looked like polished obsidian, her glossy red lips like two slices of candied apple. "Everybody pay close attention. We're going to meet tonight at the Seven-Eleven in Tantamoa. It's right on Main Street, easy to find. That's at six-thirty. I want every one of you to get on social media and get the word out. I want to see dozens of cars at the Seven-Eleven tonight. We're in this together. Let's show Mr. Bill Best how his backward ideas are hurting us. And for those of you who have been through this before, don't worry, this time we've got the combination so we won't be stopped at the gate."

The crowd's response was immediate, loud and vociferous, but their shouts slowly dissolved into murmurs as the people began to disburse. "Remember, six-thirty at the Tantamoa Seven-Eleven. Get the word out!" Marie shouted. Then she turned to Ron. "I can't believe he'd have the nerve to show his face around here, but this is perfect. Look at these people. They're pumped. All we have to do is get the message out to everyone."

Ron scratched his beard. "Yeah, okay, right, but what about Josh?"

"What about him? He's your responsibility." Marie was wearing a red halter top and shorts, but even dressed in scant few clothes, she gave off the faint odor of sour milk.

"Don't you think you're taking a big risk? You could have given him a little heads up, and made sure he's willing to help."

"He already agreed, you know that, and you gotta strike while the iron's hot, Ron. You saw those people. They're after blood. I can't let an opportunity like this pass by. Besides, it's June first, exactly when we said we'd go, and the weather's perfect."

"Right, gotcha, but you're risking it. If Josh, for whatever reason, decides he doesn't want to play along, you're going to have a lot of people really ticked off."

Marie swept a piece of lint from her red shorts and tried to wipe away a smudge. "Great, it's so hard keeping these things clean." Her eyes went back to Ron who was chewing his bottom lip. The hair of his beard stuck out like the quills of a porcupine. "That's up to you," she said. "You just make sure he's there."

"And how do I do that. By now he's probably sitting in the Cheerful Tortoise three sheets to the wind, and you know how it is when he gets like that, he can't talk, let alone walk."

Marie thought for a moment then looked off into a group of stragglers. "Donnie, come here." She gave a flick of her wrist, luring him in.

"What's up?" Donnie said. He shuffled over holding the hand of Dandy, the girl with the pink mane who'd identified Bill and started the protest. Donnie's rusty hair was hanging in his face. He tried to sweep it back but gravity pulled it down again.

"I need you to help Ron with a really important assignment. I need both of you to get over to the Cheerful Tortoise and pick up Josh. Bring him back here. If he's drunk, we have to fill him with coffee and get him sober. I'm going to get a group together to start attacking social media. We'll get the word out to everyone. We're going tonight. This is it. Good-bye, Bill Best."

BILL GLANCED AROUND the foyer of the Portland police station. Two people were at the counter talking to the desk sergeant. They looked homeless, like tent dwellers from one of the parks. Their clothes were unwashed and their hair unkempt and they reeked of body odor. The officer stepped back as they pressed in close to be heard.

"But they took my money," the woman said. Her face was the

color of cantaloupe and her hair was natty and gray. A heavy overcoat covered several layers of clothes. The officer turned away.

"They did. They went right into our tent and stole it," the man agreed. His hair too, was gray. His face was pockmarked and the back of his neck sunburned and deeply creased. He brought a hand up to his ear and cleaned it with his fingernail. "They took the whole kit and caboodle, all thirty-three dollars and fifty-two cents. Wait, no, I got some of the change here," he said reaching into a pocket that was frayed around the edges.

"All I can do is have you fill out a report," the sergeant reached for a clipboard with a pen linked to a beaded chain and slid it across the counter.

"Ain't you gonna arrest them?"

"Arrest who? Do you know who took your money?"

"No. That's why we're here."

The policeman rolled his eyes. "I can't make an arrest until we know who did what to whom. Just fill out the report and we'll take it from there."

Bill turned away and brought his phone out, dialing the number.

"Stan Powers." The response was quick, interrupting the first ring.

Bill walked a few feet away so he wouldn't be heard.

"Stan, this is Bill. I just wanted to call and update you." He glanced over his shoulder. The couple was arguing with the sergeant at the counter.

"Please. I still haven't heard from Rachel. I'm starting to worry."

"Stan, this is my screw-up. I take full responsibility. I was just… never mind, I won't make excuses. I think I may have found her, but it isn't necessarily good news."

The couple scooted down the counter letting the sergeant address the concerns of the next person in line. "You'll have to fill this out, Bett. My hands are shaky. I'm not even sure I remember how to write."

"Give it to me straight," Stan said. "If she's dead, I need to know."

"No, no, nothing like that, I just…I looked everywhere but I couldn't find either Rachel, or Josh. It's like they'd both disappeared, so I came here. I'm at the police station now. They say it's too soon

285

to file a missing person's report, but I ended up talking to a Detective Wilder. Turns out he got an interesting call this morning from the RCMP in Surry, B.C."

Bill kept a furtive eye on the couple. The woman looked flustered. "They want to know our address and phone number. We don't have either of those," she said.

"British Columbia?" Stan said.

Bill went back to his call. "Wait, let me finish. They called Detective Wilder to ask if anyone had filed a missing person's report for a girl roughly Rachel's age. They have one who showed up in British Columbia in a coma. Anyway the girl's unconscious, but she fits Rachel's description: tall, long blond hair, thin, pretty. They called Portland Police because the girl arrived in Canada with a man they now have in custody for trying to cross the border illegally. And his driver's license says he's from Portland, so they figure that's probably where the girl's from, too. Thank God it wasn't Josh, it was a Carl something-or-other, but they don't know who the girl is because she wasn't carrying any ID. Stan, I am so sorry. I don't know how this happened. I guess I wasn't watching her as close as I should. Anyway, the girl's being treated at Vancouver General and they'd really like to know who she is."

"Thank You, Lord. Thank You," Stan said. Then Bill heard him speaking to someone in his office. "Charlotte, get me on the next flight to Vancouver. Bill, can you have your police officer friend let them know I'm coming? Better yet, I'll call Detective Wilder myself. Portland missing persons. Got it. I'll touch base with him before I leave."

"You might want to wait and get a better description from the police in Surry. It might not be her," Bill said.

"It's her, I know it. I can't imagine Rachel in a coma. That's crazy, but there's got to be an explanation. Bill, I can't thank you enough. I'll call as soon as I learn anything."

Bill slipped his phone into his pocket and reached for his wallet. He removed two twenties and placed them on the clipboard in front of the indigent couple. "God bless you, folks. Have a nice day," he said. Then he turned and walked away.

TWENTY-NINE

THE MOON VANISHED into thin air like a white dinner plate disappearing under a magician's cloak. It slipped behind the clouds with a slight glow, only for a moment, and then was gone. The sky went dark, almost foreboding, with peals of thunder in the distance warning of a storm soon to come.

A car pulled into the yard, its lights spreading across what looked to be a drive-in movie theater with no empty spaces. Twenty or more vehicles were spread out around the house and double parked in the front yard. The protesters lowered their signs and moved aside as the driver threw his small Toyota into reverse, its wheels spinning on a bed of pine needles. The car backed up and came around heading down the gravel causeway in the opposite direction, hoping to park along the road. Josh watched it turn, its taillights looking like wavy red ribbons as it bounced over the ruts. The crowd filled back in and resumed chanting.

"THE TEMPERATURE'S RISING,
OUR PLANET WILL FRY,
CLIMATE DENIER,
PLEASE GO OFF AND DIE."

The incantation was drowning out the crickets and cicadas normally heard that time of year. And the fireflies, whose spiraling lamps could usually be seen reflecting off the lake, had been driven into the sawgrass to hide. Rolling thunder continued to follow flashes of light on the western horizon, but they were out over the ocean, too far away to portend immediate rain.

Some of the students began throwing water balloons at the side of the house while others raised their fists and cheered.

What? No! Better not be paint. Josh made his way around and was relieved to see the liquid was clear—*okay, just water*—but then wondered why he cared. They'd brought it upon themselves. They were criminals. He turned and went back to his place at the front, stumbling over fallen limbs and stones as he wound his way through the trees. It was supposed to be a peaceful demonstration; just a few people with signs. He hadn't thought so many would come, but that's how social media worked. One post was shared and then linked to others and voilà, all of a sudden they had a hundred people spread out across the front of the house with more arriving by the minute. Flashlights waved like light sabers cutting through the night. Josh took a hit off his bottle, the liquid burning his throat as it went down, and the crowd chanted:

"THE TEMPERATURE'S RISING,
OUR PLANET WILL FRY,
CLIMATE DENIER,
PLEASE GO OFF AND DIE."

That should scare them, Josh thought, wiping his lips on the sleeve of his hoodie, *You can't mess with Mother Nature without paying a price.*

The mob's leader was on a megaphone while his black-haired sidekick waved her hands frantically pointing to the rear of the cabin. "Some of you people go around back," the man screamed. "We don't want him escaping through a rear door. He has to be shamed."

Josh shrank back into the shadows, cloaked by a shroud of darkness where he couldn't be seen.

Every light in the cabin was on. Bill didn't want anyone sneaking into the house undetected. The two ceiling fans were also on, circulating the tension in the air. Bill sat down beside Mary on the couch, placing an arm across her shoulder. "It's nothing to worry about. They're just kids blowing off steam." He gazed out the windows at the flashlights waving in the dark. *Some people never get enough*, he thought. He hadn't told Mary about being harassed that morning, and he certainly wasn't going to tell her now. No point in feeding her fear.

"But how did they find us? We're supposed to be off the grid." Mary folded her hands in her lap, kneading her fingers. She looked at Bill, her forehead wrinkled with concern.

Bill took her hand and massaged her palm with his thumb and interlaced her fingers with his own. "The bigger question is, how did they get past the security gate? There's only one way up here and it's blocked by a metal bar that can't be moved unless you know the combination. Of course we're talking about college students. They probably got some computer nerd to crack the code. Anyway, I've already called and the police are on the way."

"But how did they find us?" Mary twisted around to face her husband. She pulled her hand back and began rubbing her fingers again, her eyes darting around the room. It was too warm to have a fire in the hearth, but the ambiance of the plank floors covered with carpets of American Indian design, the log walls old and yellow, and solid oak cases with hinged glass fronts filled with books, gave the space a feeling of serenity. She inhaled deeply taking the air in to calm her nerves, but the mantra of the mob outside calling for their deaths made her tranquility short lived.

"I don't know," Bill said, "but we'll find out. We've got half a dozen cameras out there. Every one of these kids is now being recorded. When the police start interviewing them someone will crack and we'll get the name of the organizers. And I can tell you this, I wouldn't want to be in their shoes when we do."

The chanting was growing louder and more intense. Bill looked at his watch and shook his head. He'd called Public Safety and was assured the police would be dispatched, but it seemed like they were taking their own sweet time.

A police cruiser was doing its best to find its way up the stretch of oiled road that once served as a conduit for logging trucks hauling their loads to sawmills at the base of the mountain. The path was serpentine. One moment the cruiser's lights were shooting out over the cliffs into nothingness and the next sweeping dense stands of two-hundred year old pine. A raccoon broke in front of the car but the driver braked before hitting the animal. The furry bandit trundled to the other side of the road and disappeared into the trees.

They had been summoned more than an hour ago but the road leading up to the cabin wasn't in their GPS and a half hour passed before they found it. Then the winding road carved into the side of the mountain was perilous, and ascending the steep slope at night, even in an emergency, took time. Their dashboard glowed with a digital display that gave dispatch instructions and kept the officers apprised of updates. The speaker on their two-way squawked. Dispatch was asking for their ETA. The house was under siege. The driver turned on his light-bar and stepped on the gas.

A rock the size of a fist flew through the window sending shards of broken glass onto a braided rug. It bounced off the plank floor and skidded over to Mary's foot, causing her to jump out of her seat.

"Okay, that's enough," Bill said. He had already lost one wife to the evil intents of unregenerate men. He would not lose another. He rose and crossed the room to his gun safe, dialing in the combination.

"Bill? What are you doing?"

Bill removed an ancient side-by-side shotgun from the steel cabinet. It was a beautiful piece. He held it up, the blue-black barrels shining in the light. The well-oiled plates were etched with scrolling designs and the wood stock was hand-carved with pictures of ducks flying out of a clump of reeds. He sniffed the oil used to clean the firearm and placed his thumb on the lever, snapping it open. "I'm just going to put the fear of God into them," he said. He reached up to the shelf and removed two twelve-gauge shells, sliding one into each chamber, and turned, heading for the door.

"Bill?"

"Don't worry, I'm not going to shoot anyone." He stepped out onto the porch. He was a big man. His presence alone was likely to intimidate a bunch of pajama boys like these, but with old Rusty in his arms, he figured they'd stand down pretty quick. His nose wrinkled at the smell, not the smell of pine, but another distinct smell—*gasoline?*—had to be coming from the shed where he'd parked his truck. He stomped out to the edge of the porch and pointed the smooth-bore high over everyone's heads, sending a round of buckshot into the air—*BOOM!* The explosion had the desired effect. The mob stopped chanting, lowering their signs. The air grew quiet.

Bill stood monolithic. The porch light at his back cast him in silhouette, a figure hard as stone. "You folks are trespassing on private property. I suggest you remove yourselves immediately."

No one moved.

"I mean now!" Bill fingered the second trigger and shot the sky once more and people scattered, some jumping into their cars and others retreating to the woods to find shelter behind rocks and trees.

Bill caught a glimpse of the police car's headlights as it rounded the last bend. The vehicle squeezed around the Toyota and braked to a stop. Its siren was whooping, its light-bar painting the cabin and the surrounding trees in bands of blue and red. A spotlight snapped on framing Bill in its beam. The doors flung open and the officers fell into position using the doors as shields while pointing their firearms at Bill.

"Lay the weapon down and get on your knees with your hands behind your head!"

Bill held old Rusty up, pointing the barrel into the air. "Wait a minute, officer I'm not…"

"Do it now!"

The spotlight's glare was blinding but Bill didn't have to see to know the policemen had their guns pointed at his chest. "Roger that." He brought the gun down slowly and laid it on the ground in front of him, kneeling as ordered.

The officers moved in, weaving through the cars with their guns trained on Bill. One came around behind, taking Bill's hands one at a time to lock them in cuffs. The other turned and yelled at the crowd. "The rest of you, stay where you are. No one try to leave."

"Really? Is this necessary?" Bill said, looking back over his shoulder.

The man with the megaphone ran over pointing at Bill. "Arrest that man. He's crazy. He ran out of his house and started shooting at us."

"I did no such thing." A hand reached under Bill's arm and he felt himself being raised. He stood. He was taller than the officer, and probably thirty pounds heavier, but he didn't resist. "This is crazy. I'm the one who called you. These guys are trespassing…"

"Just come with me, sir."

Bill felt a tug pulling him toward the police car. "Wait a darn minute. You got this all…" but the door swung open and Bill felt a hand on his head as he was pushed down onto the seat. "What the…? Am I under arrest? Seriously? On what charge?"

Mary stood behind the curtains watching in disbelief. *What are they doing?* She ran to the door, dashing outside, dodging around the parked cars to the police vehicle. "What's going on? Why is my husband in handcuffs?" She raked her hair over her shoulder and began twisting it into a rope.

The policeman closed the car door, locking Bill inside. "Sorry Ma'am. We heard a weapon discharge and caught this man holding a shotgun. We have to make sure no one's hurt. It's just protocol. The firearm's been secured, so if you'll just be patient we'll get this sorted out." He looked around and saw his fellow officer being harassed by the protestors. "Excuse me, I need to go assist my partner."

"Your freaking husband came out with guns blazing. He could have killed us all."

Mary recognized the man as the ringleader, the one she'd seen pointing at everyone, telling them what to do. He seemed older than the others, but it was hard to tell because his head was covered by a hoodie. His face was gaunt, with severe cheekbones covered by a goatee with forks along the sides, and his eyes were dark under a ridge of eyebrows that made them hard to read. His sweatshirt had a Portland State University logo on the front—*her son's school.* Her hand went to her face. *He wouldn't…* She glanced around the yard but, to her relief, didn't see Josh.

She turned back to the man and waggled a finger in his face, her eyes stern. "Now you listen here, my husband wouldn't shoot any-one..." She caught a spark of light off to her left. It looked like a fire-fly crashing into her house. Then she saw another coming from the right.

Josh caught it too. From his position in the woods he could see both ends of the cabin. It had grown dark while the protest was going on, the grey clouds melding into a solid black. Suddenly the walls of the building burst into flame. Fire licked up both sides of the house. *The balloons—gasoline—oh no, they didn't!* The incendiary liquid made the flames crackle and pop as they raced up the walls.

"*What the...*" Josh's eyebrows narrowed. *It's a peaceful demonstra-tion, not...* He watched as the fire reached the roof and exploded, the pine needles and shake shingles providing fuel for the flames. He saw his dad, locked in the police cruiser with his hands still cuffed behind him, banging his shoulder against the door. He could hear Bill's muf-fled cries as he desperately fought to escape.

Then Josh saw why. Seated in a wheelchair behind the window of her bedroom, a third person was agonizing over what was happening. Her body twisted back and forth, her arms whipping about errati-cally.

Josh threw himself into action. The pump house was twenty yards away. He began thrashing through brambles and tripping over stones, instantly sober over the thought of losing his sister. The latch was se-cured but he flipped it up and yanked the door open, tugging on both firehoses until they came free. He pulled his hoodie over his head, then placed one under each arm and ran into the yard, dropping one at the left side of the house and holding the other as he ran through the headlights of several cars that were now trying to leave. A car rolled forward, its tires crushing the hose, yanking it from his hands. Josh stumbled and dropped to his knees. He jumped up, frantically waving his arms. "Back up, back up! You're on the firehose!" The driver kept going, but it freed the hose and Josh took it up, continuing his thrust forward until he reached the two police officers. He glanced back and saw his mom over by the police car trying to talk to his father through the window. She tried pulling the door open but it was locked. He turned his back to them. "Take this," he said to one officer. "I dropped a second one over there," he said to the other. "Get them pointed at the fire. There'll be a kick when the water hits the nozzle, so hold on tight. I'll get it started."

He was running on adrenaline as he raced to the pump house again, looking over his shoulder to make sure the flames hadn't yet approached Angie's room. The cars had been rolling over the hose in their bid to escape but were bunched up now unable to move. Acting on training drilled into him by his father, he hit the electric switch starting the pump and waited until it drew water from the lake. When he felt the pipes shaking from the pent up force, he cranked the handle, opening the valve. The hoses filled, growing fat foot by foot, as the water raced to the nozzles. The police officers felt the trembling as it came to a head and blew out. They pointed their water cannons at the flames dousing the fire up and down both walls.

Cars were scrambling to exit but there was a logjam at the entrance because they had to squeeze between the police car and the white Toyota. Mary heard Bill's muffled voice coming through the door. "Get Angie!" he cried.

She turned and looked back at the house in horror. How could she have forgotten Angie? The two policemen were saturating her home with water. She couldn't see through the windows. Was Angie buried in all that smoke? The police officers were busy. It was up to her. She took off running.

The first cars out were wary of driving too fast, the road was narrow with tight curves, slowing traffic to a crawl. A burgundy Camry pulled up beside Josh and a door flew open. "Get in!" he heard Ron scream. Marie was holding the door, but Josh slammed it shut. "No way. My sister's in there," he yelled back, and took off running.

All his life he'd been a loser, but Marie had made him feel flat out pathetic. The gin had given him courage to speak his heart, and drunk or not, he would never forget her words. "Josh, I'm sorry if I gave you the wrong idea. I mean, I like you, you're a really sweet guy, but I can't love you, I'm gay. I'm with Barba. She's been my lover since we were in high school." —*Sucker!*

Josh sped around the back of the house and flew through the door of his mom's tropical cabana room, hoping she still hadn't seen him— please, Lord. It wouldn't change what he planned to do, but he'd rather not have her know he was a part of this. He wanted her to remember him fondly.

The room was full of smoke. He waved his hand in front of his face, coughing. His lungs felt on fire as he tried to breathe. He pulled his shirt up to cover his mouth. The water hitting the walls outside sounded like horses galloping across the desert, but beneath that was the sound of Angie's moaning. He rushed to her room and found her writhing, her body spasmodic, her throat gasping for air. Grabbing the handles of her wheelchair he spun her around and headed out the back again, tears forming in his eyes from the burning. He held his breath until he was outside and in the clear.

He coughed, *kuff, kuff,* then wiped his mouth and stooped over close to Angie's ear.

"Angie, you alright?" She was coughing, but breathing. It was all he needed to know. "Please try to understand. I didn't do this. No matter what they say, this wasn't me. I love you, girl, but I have to go, forever. I won't get to see you again."

He kissed her cheek and pushed her chair around the corner. Several people were standing behind the policeman turned fireman, opting to stay and watch the cabin burn rather than leave. Josh jammed the wheelchair into their midst. "Get her to her mother. She almost died in there!" He pulled his hoodie over his head and took off for the woods, ducking behind the trees and bramble to stay out of sight. Lightning was still flickering on the horizon, giving him flashes of light by which to see as he stumbled his way down to the lake.

Mary was frantic, unable to squeeze through the line of cars trying to leave. They were bumper to bumper blocking her way. She tried to go around but the train seemed endless. Random vehicles were coming in at odd angles, jockeying for a place in line. She was holding her hands to her face pacing back and forth, when off to her left a young man rolled Angie around the corner. "Oh my God, thank you, thank you, thank you." She climbed over the hood of the nearest car, ignoring the horn blasts—"Crazy lady!"—and rushed over to the man, hugging him like he was some kind of hero. "Thank you," she said again and again. "How can I ever thank you?"

"Think nothing of it," the boy said. He turned, and headed back to his friends who were now climbing into their car, getting ready to leave.

Mary dropped to her knees, wrapping her arms around Angie, her sobs getting in the way of the words she wanted to say.

Josh found the canoe upside down, the way his father kept it stored. Taking hold of the edge, he tried to turn it over, but it was too heavy. His bottle was over by the pump. Liquid strength, that's what he needed, or was he too drunk already? Staying low, he snuck up behind the box and grabbed the bottle off the stump where he'd left it, and then stole back down to the lake. It would be hard getting that canoe turned over by himself, but he had to. Bringing the bottle to his lips he took several long swallows to set the mood right. Lightning flickered in the sky. He got down on his knees and put the bottle aside, rolling onto his back. With his feet up under the hull he used all his strength to push the boat over. It flipped and landed on its bottom with a thud. *Excellent!* Now he just had to get it in the water. Planting a shoulder against the stern, he pushed, *gurrrrrrr*, and was able to move it forward a foot. *Great, only ten more feet to go.* He took a breath and did it again, one foot at a time until he reached the water. He was panting, his forehead beaded with sweat, but he made several more thrusts until the bow of the canoe was floating free. He went back for his bottle and stepped into the water, dragging the boat with him out into the lake. Wet up to his waist, he crawled over the edge and fell inside. The fire looked to be out, at least he didn't see any flames, just a gray vapid smoke wafting up through the trees.

He lay on his back watching as sparks of lightning illuminated the sky, the rumble of thunder like the voice of God.

You know I gotta do this, don't you? I really have no choice. There's nothing for me here—I don't belong.

He took another drink from his bottle and lay his arm across his forehead, resting like a passenger on a ferry captained by the Egyptian god Mahaf. They were on their way to the other side.

"God, I'm still trying to figure this out, you know. I mean, I wasn't expecting them to do that. That's not what I wanted. It just got out of hand…and Angie—you know I'd never hurt her. But burn the house? See God, he'll never understand. It's better this way. He hates me anyway. I'm no good. I can't face him anymore. If I thought for one minute we could ever treat each other with mutual respect, maybe, just maybe, then I'd consider another way." Josh held the bottle over his mouth until the last drop touched his tongue, and then flung it into the lake, *kerplunk.* Not even a freekin' star to look at, just the cold empty void of space. "You don't even know what I'm talking about, do You? Father, Son, one in perfect union. How could You? How would You like it if your Son was a wimp? Huh, *huh?* Jesus, what if Your father never thought You were good enough? What I want, all I want, is a father who respects me…Why would You deny me that?"

The canoe hit a sarsen, the turbulent waters sounding like a hundred thundering hoofs. He had been drifting on the current of the lake's one-way flow, and had entered the river's mouth and was rushing toward the rapids. He rolled over and got to his knees. All around him the waves were crashing on the rocks, whitewater foaming in their wake. The canoe was bouncing up and down like a roller coaster. It was too late to turn back. He was committed. *God I don't want to die, but I don't want to live like this.* The canoe hit the falls and went over, the bow heading straight down flipping him out like a stone from a catapult. *God, into your hands I commit my spirit.* He flew through the air headlong into a boulder, crushing his skull—and it was over.

THIRTY

S TAN BOARDED Air Canada flight 8041 leaving Chicago
O'Hare at 4:45 heading west into the darkness, or so it felt
four and a half hours later when his plane touched down in
Vancouver. He folded his newspaper and slipped it into his briefcase.

Through the porthole he could see the sun dropping below the
horizon, its hoary head disappearing into the haze, completing another
twenty-four hour cycle. Twenty-four hours in which thousands of
people died: through war, through famine, through poor health and
disease, but Rachel wouldn't die. This he knew. She was on the other
side of the fulcrum, the side in which thousands were also born to
take their place. She would not be added to the tally of those who
throughout history had lost their battle with the forces of darkness,
because God had saved her. He had taken her from being a waif,
homeless on the streets of Chicago, to the life she now lived with her
father. And God was not capricious. He had brought them together;
He would not tear them apart. Stan ceased his ruminations with the
final bump of the plane as it came to a stop at the gate.

He was traveling light. The only suit of clothes he'd brought was
on his back, a few changes of underwear and socks, a different tie,
and a pair of pajamas were in the duffel at his feet. She was resting
comfortably in a hospital, or so he'd been told; it wasn't likely he'd
be leaving with her that evening, but he hoped to make his stay in
Canada as short as possible. And he wasn't leaving without her. He
would wait for her discharge, and board the next flight for home.

There was no longer any doubt that the girl picked up at the

Canadian border was his daughter. The physical description was a match and a conference call with her doctor confirmed that at one time or another both the patient's kidneys had been removed. That report alone put to rest any uncertainty. The good kidney Rachel enjoyed now was one of his own, a donation he'd made, at least in part, to make up for all the years he'd missed caring for her as a father. But it was the picture they'd texted that provided absolute proof of her identity. It was Rachel, no doubt about it, and yet it wasn't. The picture looked more like a doll, or a puppet made in the image of Rachel, a rubberized effigy of a living human being.

Stan rose from his seat and began the slow shuffle with the long line of travelers disembarking, trying to keep the pressure off his damaged leg while holding his briefcase in one hand and his duffel in the other. *Why does it always sound like you're being sucked into a vacuum as you leave an airplane?*

"Thank you for choosing Air Canada, we hope you enjoyed your flight," the attendant said as he exited the forward door. The warm air in the aerobridge helped relieve his tension. He joined the lemmings in their march to the terminal.

If he'd thought finding his escort would be difficult, he was wrong. The two men in dark suits standing at the entrance to Canada Customs might as well have had signs around their necks saying, "Federal Agents." One had dark curly hair, the other was bald with thick-rimmed glasses and a goatee. Both stood erect with their hands folded in front of their belts. Stan's fellow passengers were lining up to have their bags inspected, but he was hustled off to the side and given VIP clearance. He was a guest of the Royal Canadian Mounted Police, who had taken the liberty of clearing him with the U.S. consulate. As a U.S. Senator, here on official business, he was granted the status of a diplomat.

"Brad Whitlock," the man with dark curly hair said, extending his hand. "And this is my partner, Marty Scone. We sure appreciate your coming so quickly."

"My pleasure," Stan said, shaking the hand offered, and then Marty's in turn. "Wild horses couldn't have kept me away."

"If you'll just come this way, we have a car waiting." The three men began walking toward an exit used by pilots and members of the crew. "So tell me Senator, how was your flight?" Brad said, as they breezed through Customs.

"Couldn't have been better. First time on Air Canada, but the service was great. And I appreciate your picking up the tab, though it really wasn't necessary."

"Nonsense, your daughter is the victim in a case we're working, and we need your help. The least the Crown can do is cover your expenses." The automatic doors closed, leaving them standing in a carport surrounded by the nauseous smell of bus fumes.

"About that. You said you'd fill me in when I got here. I don't know anything other than my daughter was brought here by some man from Portland and was found unconscious in his car."

They approached a black Chevrolet Suburban, nondescript on the outside, but a fully loaded emergency task force vehicle within. Marty, his bald head shiny in the parking garage lights, held the door open allowing Stan to toss his briefcase and duffel on the backseat before climbing in.

Brad took the passenger seat while Marty got behind the wheel and started the engine. It was dusk, dark to the east, but with a thin ribbon of purple still waffling on the western skyline. They pulled into a stream of red taillights, Marty using his blinker to squeeze them into the emergency lane to avoid airport traffic.

Detective Whitlock turned to look back over his shoulder, his face darkened by shadows. "It's not that we're keeping secrets, but it is an ongoing investigation, so there's only so much we can say. I'll tell you as much as I can on the way over, only we need to make a stop before we take you to the hospital. It's kind of why we're paying your ticket."

Stan reached for his briefcase, wondering if he'd heard right. He pulled it into his lap. "How long a stop? I really am anxious to see my daughter."

"The guy who brought your daughter up here is in custody," Brad said, ignoring the question. "We're holding him on a weapons charge."

"And for trying to enter the country illegally," Marty added, his dark rimmed glasses framed in the rearview mirror.

"And the illegal entry, but in today's climate, illegal border crossings are so common they hardly amount to more than a slap on the wrist. We really want to nail him for what he did to your daughter."

Stan's pulse quickened, his hands moist, sliding on the leather of his briefcase. "And what was that?" He scooted forward an inch, making sure not to miss anything.

Detective Whitlock paused a moment. "Your daughter isn't unconscious, at least not per-se. She's non-responsive. To use her doctor's words, she's in a vegetative state, like a deep coma, but with her eyes open."

Stan gripped the briefcase, holding on tight. *A vegetable, but no—God why?* Brad was staring at him, his expression obscured by the vehicle's dark interior. "Vegetative state, as in brain dead?"

"No, not quite. Doctor Hathaway does believe she's suffered some cerebral impairment, but to what extent he's not sure. He believes there's a good chance she'll snap out of it, but there's also the possibility she won't."

Won't? Stan's head whirled in confusion. He had come expecting to wait until Rachel regained consciousness, but—this wasn't God's plan, couldn't be. "Do you have any idea how she got that way?"

"Well, yes and no. There's no easy way to say this so I'm just going to say it. Your daughter was given a large dose of Rohypnol; it's a date rape drug given to girls to relax their inhibitions. It allows a perpetrator to take advantage of his victim, but it usually wears off without causing any long term damage, but Doctor Hathaway says the amount given your daughter was excessive."

No, no, no. Stan was shaking his head. "So you're saying my daughter was raped."

"Not necessarily. We don't know that. We weren't allowed to do a rape kit without the victim's consent, and since your daughter couldn't give us permission we have yet to see any evidence of that."

Stan took a breath and let it out slowly. His gut felt hollow. He wished he'd eaten something on the plane. He sank back in his seat, bringing his briefcase up and wrapping his arms around it like a security blanket, troubled that he, an ex-Navy SEAL, holder of the Trident and Purple Heart, should feel so helpless. *Pain is weakness leaving the body*, he reminded himself. He hadn't felt this way since the day he lay in a military field hospital being told he might never walk again.

"Anyway," Detective Whitlock continued, "we suspect the man who assaulted your daughter gave her the drug, and then taped her hands and feet and put her in the trunk of his car and drove her across the border into Canada. But of course he claims he didn't, and we have no actual proof that he did."

"But you found Rachel in his car. How much proof do you need?"

"You're thinking like us, not like a prosecutor. Finding her in his car doesn't actually prove he's the one who put her there. Our Crown Attorney doesn't want to prosecute a case he can't win. That's why we're so desperate to have your daughter testify, and why we're hoping when she sees you, she'll wake up, but we can't count on that. Before we take you to see your daughter we want to swing by and introduce you to the perpetrator..."

"Wait a minute. I came to see Rachel, not her assailant. I need..."

"I know you did, and you will, but this is important. The perp is scheduled for arraignment tomorrow. Right now we're only holding him on the two lesser charges, one for pulling a gun on a customs agent, which he claims he only did to hand it over, and the attempted illegal entry. If we can't charge him with kidnapping or trafficking or some other major crime, he'll probably make bail and disappear back across the border. We're hoping to have you talk to him, introduce yourself as Rachel's father, and catch him off guard. I think the man's a sociopath, and sociopaths are born liars. They like to make it up as they go and genuinely believe what they say, which is why he shows no remorse or guilt. He doesn't feel he's done anything wrong. He's probably aching for a chance to defend himself. We just want you to get him talking. The rest is up to him."

"You want me to politely entertain the sociopath that brutalized my daughter, is that it?"

Brad nodded grimly, his mouth turned down at the corners. "Sounds about right. Think of it this way. You'll be helping us put this animal in a cage where he belongs."

Stan was ushered into a room painted beige with a gray metal table and chairs. He had witnessed evil on the battlefield, where whole villages were slaughtered in the name of god. In his soup kitchen, where he spent his off hours feeding the poor, bumping heads with the dregs of society came with the territory. He had seen a man die with a knife in his gut from someone who wanted his cigarettes, seen a woman bleed to death after cutting her own womb open to rid herself of a child she didn't want, and he'd seen dozens of people—including Rachel's mother—die from overdosing themselves on opioids. He had run for a seat in the senate to see if there wasn't some way to end the madness. But the heart of man was desperately wicked—and the world was forever turning, and people forever dying. There would be no end.

He could feel his fingers trembling, his blood pressure rising through the roof. He paced back and forth wondering what to say to a man who had drugged and kidnapped and maybe even raped his little girl. He looked up at the camera. They were being recorded. He wiped his hands on his pants. He knew something the detectives didn't. It was Mark Wessler who pulled him aside making veiled threats every time they butted heads. Getting Mr. Rove to confess was one thing. Getting him to give up who he was working for, was another. He turned at the sound of voices.

The metal door squeaked open and the same two detectives he'd already met walked in. They looked confused. Brad pulled a chair back and sat down, his fingers drumming the table, Marty remained standing. "I'm afraid we have some bad news," Brad said.

Stan felt goosebumps rise on his arms. *God, don't let it be Rachel.*

"We can't produce Carl Rove," Marty said. He removed his glasses and took a tissue from his pocket to wipe the lens. "Your FBI came in earlier today and took over the case," he said, squinting. "The kidnapping happened in the U.S. so they claimed jurisdiction. Apparently, they had extradition papers ready to go, and even a signed release from our Crown Attorney. All they're giving us is the illegal crossing and weapons charge, which they say we can prosecute after they're through with their case," Marty slipped his glasses back on, "which means probably never. Frankly, this is embarrassing. I really don't know what to say, other than you're welcome to stay in our country as long as you need."

Stan rode to the hospital with two very despondent detectives. They had gambled the Crown's money on the hope of prosecuting Carl Rove, and lost. The Canadians would miss the privilege of taking Carl to court, but they had the consolation of knowing any sentence imposed by a U.S. judge would probably trump one levied in Canada.

Stan appreciated the effort, but he hadn't come here to convict Carl, or anyone else, he had come to collect Rachel and take her home. For him, the ride to the hospital was filled with apprehension. He couldn't imagine Rachel in a vegetive state, and his heart groaned over the thought that she might have been raped. But the most difficult issue he faced was the realization that he had caused all this by refusing to yield his vote. But how could he? He was caught between the devil and the deep blue sea. His stomach churned.

Marty pulled into a parking space reserved for emergency vehicles. "It's a good thing you came when you did, Senator. They're talking about transferring your daughter to an institution for long term care and, believe me, most of the residents there are crazy. I don't think it's the best place for your daughter to convalesce."

"That's not going to happen," Stan said. "I plan on taking her back with me tomorrow." He opened the door and stepped out. The parking lot was bathed in a purple darkness; the light from the hospital windows rising up like a checkerboard standing on end.

They rode the elevator in silence, their hands folded, their eyes locked on the stainless-steel doors as the numbers in the digital display rose with the passing of each floor. There wasn't much to say. Stan shifted his weight to ease the pressure on his bad leg, but he was lost in thought. A little more than a year ago he'd met his daughter in a hospital just like this. She was in need of a kidney but was refusing to take his because she was convinced he had given her mother the overdose that led to her death. He hadn't, but it took a whole lot of convincing to get her to accept his donation. Only now he was facing losing her again, because of another overdose, one his actions had led to, and he had nothing left to give.

The doors opened. "You need to be prepared for what you're going to see." Marty said, as they led Stan limping down the hall to Rachel's room. Detectives Whitlock and Scone stepped aside to let Stan go in first.

The hardware was the same, same generic LED displays, and tubes and racks and multifunction bed, but the patient was totally different. Rachel sat propped up on pillows staring out into space. Her eyes were open, but they were vacuous and empty. There was nothing in them that suggested life—*people die with their eyes open*—but she was too flush to be dead. He slipped over and gently took her hand, but she offered no sign of recognition, though the warmth of her touch was a blessing. He leaned in to kiss her cheek and whisper in her ear. "Rachel, it's me, it's your dad. Can you hear me? Blink if you hear me."

But Rachel didn't. Her ears were no longer tuned to the frequency of his voice. She reclined on the bed in a world of her own, staring at images no one else could see. The light, bouncing off objects in the room, was received by her pupils and processed, and millions of pictures were sent down the optic nerve to her brain, but there they stopped. The images were absorbed by darkness. She was unable to recognize familiar things. Instead she saw things that did not exist. Inside the clockwork of her brain other images formed: random thoughts, mere flashes of memory, electrical pulses that created momentary pictures— a summer day, a little girl picking flowers. Then she saw a face. It was the face, that face with a twisted smile, that kept her running back into the deeper recesses of her mind afraid to come out.

THIRTY-ONE

ALL UP THE WATALONG you could hear the sound of trout skipping through the water, not with human ears, but with those of insects flitting away to keep from becoming breakfast. He didn't hear the trout, but he thought he might have heard the voice of God—not in the churning of the water, or buzzing of the flies, but in a feeling that wrested his soul. The morning sun beat down hard on the rocks where he sat contemplating the existence or nonexistence of a super-intelligent being that moved men around like pawns on a chessboard. He didn't buy it. It was as if he'd arrived there transported from some other planet, not by the hand of some potter molding clay, but that's the thing about life, you can't know who you are until you find yourself.

He picked himself up and headed across the shallows, tripping over stones and moss-covered rocks till he reached a bleached log stuck in a sandbar on the other side. He pulled himself onto the shore and climbed up the embankment to the highway. He could see the roofs of the buildings—the spiraling church tower, and the flat gravel top of the Albertson' grocery—in the town below, shining in the light like a city cut out of a hole in the forest. He stuck out his thumb, just another wayfaring stranger going nowhere on the road of life.

IT WAS AFTER ten before Bill got a contractor on site to look at the damage done to his roof. The walls, made of heavy log construction, had survived—*thank God*. They would require a power washing, to get rid of the charred soot, and there were a few spots that might need a patch, but overall the fire had licked up the gasoline and left the wood intact. It was the pine-needle covered roof that went up like tinder as the flames swept across, leaving large holes in the plywood substructure and gaps in the rafters. The repair estimate was eighteen-thousand.

For once he was glad they'd put him in that police car. Filing a second insurance claim in so short a period of time would require an investigation, but they couldn't accuse him of arson when the fire was started while he was locked away. But it was arson, of that there was no doubt, probably started by the same protestors who torched his trees. It wasn't that long ago that activists had burned half the city of Portland. *What's with these guys and fires?*

Three men were on the roof tugging blue plastic tarps over the cabin's crown. Rain was in the weekly forecast, as it always was. The last thing Bill needed now was water getting into the house. Once the crew got the tarps buttoned down, they would leave. The roofer had other jobs waiting and wouldn't be able to start on Bill's repairs for another week.

Bill stood back taking it all in. His domain was in the middle of a forest primeval, untouched by man except the one small clearing where the house sat. It was supposed to be a sanctuary, but not anymore. He was confronting forces of darkness from which he could no longer hide.

He propped his ladder against a tree and bounced it against the trunk to make sure it was stable before starting to climb. Security at his place had been a priority ever since he'd begun receiving threats years ago. He'd often wondered if it was worth the expense, since the digital recorders had never been needed—until now. He opened the back of the aluminum box that protected the camera from the weather. Sliding the camera out, he removed the memory card and slipped it into his pocket. It was the fourth such card he'd retrieved, with two more to go. He wasn't particularly interested in identifying everyone, but arson was a crime, and those who torched his house should pay. If justice were to be served, they'd also find those who had burned his tree lot, or at least the two leaders, the ones giving orders—Mary had described one as a man in a hoodie with a dark goatee, and the other as a woman with short black hair and a red dress. Bill had already scheduled a time to turn everything over to the police for review. From there they would hone in on the sharpest images and round up the culprits. The minor players would be interviewed and threatened by the police to give up the names of those that actually mattered.

Aside from all this, something else troubled Bill. He had taken Mary and Angie into town and set them up in the Watalong Lodge, a place popular with fishermen and hunters because it had rough wood floors that allowed them to traffic in boots. It was the only hotel in Tantamoa and he wanted his family close by, but he didn't join them. He would be staying at the house in case someone showed up to finish what they started.

This morning, awake before dawn, he'd felt the sudden urge to hike to the top of the falls before the sun rose so he could thank God properly for delivering his family from harm, and especially for sending someone inside to save Angie. And for the mystery man who'd found the hoses and saved his house from burning to the ground as it would have if the police had merely called the fire department and waited for them to arrive. But after getting fully dressed and brewing his coffee and heading down to the patch of ground where his canoe was stored, he'd found it missing. It had been there the day before, and he was pretty darn sure the protestors, in their rush to leave, hadn't taken it with them—it was much too heavy to carry and would take a truck to move—but it was gone. He'd never had trouble with any of the folks that stayed in the campground at the other end of the lake, but the only conclusion he could draw was that someone had seen him out fishing and decided that the old hand-carved Chinook was a beauty worth stealing. He should have kept it chained, but he couldn't imagine someone wanting it that bad. He had called the Park Ranger's office and asked them to keep an eye out for it. No description was needed. They knew exactly what to look for.

Bill turned as he caught a figure approaching from behind.

"We'll be takin' off now," Harold said, slipping his glove off to shake Bill's hand. "She should hold pretty tight and I don't 'spect any leakage, but call me if somethin' should sprout." He looked down and spat a wad of Red Man onto the ground, barely missing his boot. "I should be back at it next week, but it might be a bit longer iffin we gets held up by rain." His gums oozed with the brown syrup of his chewing tobacco. He pushed his soiled baseball cap back on his forehead, curls of thick gray hair flipping out from beneath.

"Just do your best," Bill said. "I've got my wife and daughter staying in a hotel." Bill's phone trilled. He pulled it out and checked the display. "I have to take this," he said.

"Shore, call me if you need me," Harold walked off with his boots dragging trails through the pine needles on his way to a crew-cab pickup already loaded with his men.

"You got Bill," Bill said into the phone.

"Bill, it's Stan."

"Yes, Stan. *Ouch*, I'm sorry, I was supposed to stay in touch. Things just went crazy around here. How was your trip? Was it your daughter? How is she?"

"It was, and there's a real story to tell, but the main thing is she's been released from the hospital and I'm heading your way. The doctor suggested I don't return to Chicago, at least not yet. He thinks Rachel will recover better surrounded by her most recent memories."

"So, she's okay?"

"Kinda, maybe, we're not sure. We've had several developments in the last twenty-four hours. I'll fill you in on the details when I see you."

"Okay, but when I said it had gone crazy around here, I meant it. I'm trying to get repairs done to my house," Bill turned to look at the damage and saw Harold and his crew pulling away, "so I probably won't be able to see you until tomorrow."

"No, that's fine. I promised to let you know when I heard something. Thank God she wasn't molested. At first they thought she might have been, but I had them do a rape kit and it came back negative."

"But she's in a coma?"

"I'll explain all that when I get there. We're leaving on a Delta flight at one and should be in Portland around four."

"Sounds good. I'd love to have you stay with us but we had a fire at our house last night."

"Fire? Again? You're kidding. What happened? Was anyone hurt?"

"No, we're fine and the damage wasn't nearly as bad as it could have been. The good news is that we'll catch who did it this time. I have cameras installed around the property, which I'm turning over to the police this afternoon. But while I'm staying here to watch over things, I've got Mary and Angie in a lodge forty minutes away."

"In a lodge? Where? You think they have vacancies?"

"*Um*, not sure. They stay pretty full year 'round, but you never know, they might, but listen, this isn't the kind of place where a senator stays. It's rustic. I'm not sure you'd be comfortable there."

"Then you don't know me. I used to live upstairs over a food kitchen in the poorest part of Chicago. My favorite pastime was counting how many cockroaches I could kill in a night. I'm sure it will be fine. What's it called?"

"The Watalong Lodge, but like I say, it's three star. Don't say I didn't warn you."

STAN DROVE THROUGH Tantamoa looking for the fishing lodge as described by Bill. The buildings were antiquated with false facades that reminded him of the cow-towns in westerns he'd seen on TV. The hotel was supposed to be on the right heading out of town. "Can't miss it," Bill had said, but with the forest closing in ahead, there wasn't much town left to see. He had Rachel sitting beside him, strapped in by a seatbelt, looking lovely in everything but her eyes, which seemed to bulge in her transfixed state.

Stan wiped his forehead. It had to be in the high eighties, but the humidity made it seem worse, and the car's air conditioner had a faulty switch that wouldn't engage, something he didn't realize until they were already on the highway, stuck in traffic. He'd chosen a late model Caravan to give Rachel plenty of room, but the new car smell was lost in the rush of air pouring in through the windows. He shouldn't have worn a suit. He had two options: to arrive smelling like a gym locker with damp, wrinkled clothes sticking to his body, or to arrive with his hair looking like it had been whipped by an eggbeater. The latter was preferable so he left the window open. The rush of air was deceptive. Rather than cooling, it intensified the heat the way wind from a bellows increases the blast of a furnace.

Stan stopped at the intersection, waiting for the light to change. It couldn't be much further; the last building on the edge of town was just a few blocks ahead. He was looking forward to the air-conditioned comfort of the lodge, though when he'd called to make a reservation, the only room they'd had was a single with a full size bed. He took it because he wanted to stay close to Bill's family. In their phone calls, Rachel had mentioned her friendship with Bill's son. Stan was hoping if he could get the two together, the memory might snap her out of her stupor.

He yawned and shifted his weight to ease the pressure on his back. He had spent the night in the hospital with Rachel, letting the reality of what he was facing settle in as the hours passed. The doctor had said the trance was caused by the inordinate amount of Rohypnol in her system. The early prognosis had been that, given time for the drug to wear off, she would recover. One day she would just wake up, like sleeping beauty from a dream.

To their amazement they had subsequently discovered that her reflex mechanisms worked fine when utilized. If you tried to stand her up she would comply, but she would stay there until you took her hand and led her away, then she would follow. If you made frequent trips to the bathroom, she would relieve herself; however, she was just as likely to wet the bed if you waited too long. But she was ambulatory. A blessing, however small, was still a blessing and Stan counted Rachel's mobility as such. All her motor functions were intact, the things that ran on instinct. If you put food in her mouth she would chew and swallow. She could sip liquids. But her mind remained locked. There was no communication. She refused to speak, and while her doctor was certain she could hear, she never appeared to listen. Unless moved by someone, she would sit for hours staring off into space as though mind-linked with an alien life form on some far distant planet.

Stan looked over at his daughter, beautiful in the worst of times.

311

It made him uncomfortable to think they would be sharing the same bed, and not only that, he would be responsible for changing her diaper and giving her a bath. He didn't fear temptation; he would never take advantage of his daughter, but handling the nude body of a beautiful woman was bound to conjure improper thoughts, even if he rebuked them. There was a reason the Bible forbade uncovering the nakedness of a close relative.

The building was white and clean with multicolored flowers blooming in the garden and fresh cut grass. He caught the scrolling woodwork of the sign as it swept by: Tantamoa Convalescent Home.

Stan pulled to the curb, braking hard with his hand outstretched to catch Rachel as the tires skidded to a stop. Dust flew by settling on the paint of the van. Rachel seemed unfazed. Looking back over his shoulder, he threw the van into reverse, backing up till he was even with the driveway, and pulled in. If that wasn't God, what was? One minute he's concerned about how to best care for Rachel and the next God leads him to a convalescent home, less than a block from where he'll be staying. He hoped they wouldn't mind taking in a short-term guest.

He came around the van, his hairline beaded with sweat, chiding himself for complaining when the deserts of Iraq were hotter by twenty degrees. He took Rachel by the hand and led her into the lobby, immediately relieved to feel the room's air conditioning.

"Good afternoon, how can I help you?" he heard as he entered.

The woman was tall, mid-fiftyish, with her light brown hair swept back in a high bun. Her business suit was beige, which she wore with white sneakers. It was hard to tell if she was a nurse, or an administrator. Didn't matter. The sign said this was a skilled nursing facility, which was exactly what he needed.

"Hi. I was wondering…ah, this is kind of hard to explain. My daughter experienced a severe trauma and it's sent her into a shell. She's fully functional. And by that I mean she can walk and sit down, eat and relieve herself, but she doesn't talk or acknowledge that she hears anything, so she needs constant supervision. I need a place for her to stay until she comes out of it. And that could be anytime, because it

312

only happened recently, but no one knows for sure. I was wondering if you could take her in and watch her overnight, but then let me pick her up during the day. I want to take her around and introduce her to familiar sights. They say if she sees something that jogs her memory, it might snap her out of it. Is that something you can do?"

"Interesting. Yes, it's a bit unusual. Most of our residents are here for long term palliative care, but we already have one amnesia patient and several with Alzheimer's and dementia. Actually, we provide care for just about anyone who needs it. And we have a full nursing staff on site. When were you thinking of starting?"

"I was hoping, now."

As Stan anticipated, he'd found the lodge just a block and a half from where he left Rachel. God, thank You for opening doors I can't see. It was everything Bill had said, clean but simple no frill furnishings, with floors that looked like they'd been trampled on since the eighteen-hundreds.

He had gone straight to his room and tossed his duffel onto a chair. Removing his toiletries, he placed them on the sink in a bathroom hardly big enough to turn around in without bumping the toilet. After being up all night watching over Rachel, the bed sucked him in like a magnet. He laid his suit coat over the arm of the chair, loosened his tie and kicked off his shoes. His head barely hit the pillow before he was asleep.

It took a minute for him to realize someone was pounding on his door.

His head fought to clear the fog. "Alright, alright, I'm coming. Give me a second." He pulled himself from the bed and stood, raking his hands through his hair as he reluctantly limped to the door. It wasn't locked. He had half a mind just to say, come in, but decided it was best not to invite strangers.

He cracked the door open, peering out and saw Bill standing on the other side with Mary and Angie.

"Front desk said you'd checked in. I got done filling out my police report and swung by to see my family. We're heading out to get something to eat. Grab Rachel and join us. They got a great fish restaurant just down the block, best trout this side of the Rockies."

Stan tried to catch his breath. His slumber had been deep but, he looked at his watch, he didn't regret Bill waking him. If he'd slept any longer he might have woken up at three in the morning unable to sleep. "Sounds great," he said. "I haven't had dinner. Ah, but Rachel's not with me; I checked her into a convalescent home here in town. She's still recuperating. Hi Mary, nice to see you again. You too Angie."

Angie pushed her hands together twisting them inside out and giggled.

Bill craned his neck to look around the room. "Looks like you got yourself a real matchbox here."

"It was the last room they had, but it's alright." Stan ducked back inside and picked up his shoes, slipping them on. "Glad I found a place for Rachel to stay though, it would have taken a shoehorn to get the two of us in here together."

They stepped out into the hall and headed toward the elevator with Bill rolling Angie in her chair as they passed the laundry. The steam escaping the door was thick with humidity. Exiting at the first floor, they went out the front, turning right, down a cracked, weed infested cement sidewalk. The back of the hotel fed right onto the Watalong and you could hear the rushing water and smell the damp algae covered rocks that lined the shore.

"The restaurant is next to Tantamoa Bait and Tackle. They're both owned by the same family. They sell fishing gear to folks who catch the fish, then they offer to buy the fish so the restaurant always has a fresh supply, which is why it's called the Hook and Cook, but they sure know how to grill trout. Been doing it for more than forty years in the same location. So tell me, how is Rachel? What's the story?"

Stan arched his back. He had carried a hundred-and-twenty pound pack across desert sands, into jungles, and through rivers, but none of that compared to the weight he felt now. "Pretty tragic, if you ask me. My daughter got picked up by a guy who lives in Portland. I don't know anything about him other than the FBI came in and grabbed him up, so it's likely he was wanted for other things too, but I can't confirm that. They found Rachel bound in the trunk of his car when he tried to cross the border into Canada. And of course, I've got to believe this has everything to do with the threat made on Rachel's life."

Mary's head swung around, eyes wide with concern. "Oh no, poor Rachel."

"Thankfully, she wasn't hurt, at least not physically, but she suffered mental trauma and it has her dazed. She doesn't recognize me, or anyone, doesn't respond to noise, can't communicate, she just walks around like a zombie oblivious to the world around her."

"Oh Lord, that's awful. Is there anything...What can we do to help?" Mary pulled her hair to the front and began coiling it around her finger.

"Nothing. The convalescent home is taking care of her. The doctor in Canada said she could snap out of it but there's no way of knowing." Stan continued walking, the pain of his leg festering again. Angie's wheelchair was clacking on the pavement; the overcast sky looked like galvanized tin.

Stan felt his blood surging. "And I'll tell you honestly, I want to cut off the man's gonads and shove them down his throat, but Jesus says I have to forgive, so that's what I'm trying to do."

Bill shook his head. "Good luck with that. I'm not sure I could." He reached for the restaurant's screen door, holding it open as they stepped into a room that smelled of smoke and deep-fried grease. The paneled walls were covered in plaques of taxidermied trout and bass, some two feet long, looking like they were jumping out of the water to catch mosquitoes in a perpetual state of bliss.

Bill found a table for four and pulled a chair out making space for Angie's wheelchair as they sat down. Against the wall, an old Wurlitzer playing Hank Williams burbled with colored lights. Just what you'd expect in an old logging town turned popular fishing destination. Stan plucked up a napkin and blotted his forehead. "I think we better change the subject before I get angry and ruin the evening. You never said what caused your fire. And I know it wasn't your cooking," he said, winking at Mary.

"We were targeted by a bunch of tree-hugging college punks who took exception to some articles I wrote long ago," Bill said.

"My God, has the world gone crazy? It's not enough you're accused of tax evasion, but now they want to burn down your house, not to mention your tree farm. And me, little over a year ago they tried to stop me from getting elected by accusing me of having sex with a prostitute. And my daughter, this whole thing with her is about my refusal to regulate crypto-currencies. It's insane."

"Cryptocurrency?" Mary looked confused. "I thought that was play money, not something real."

"Oh, it's very real," Stan rejoined, "but the beauty of it is that it's unregulated, so there's no government interference. Your transactions are private and your profits are encrypted and stored in digital vaults where the government can't touch them. But, of course, the government doesn't like this. I sit on a Senate sub-committee that's looking at ways to get control of the cryptocurrency market. And, of course, they want to establish a U.S. digital dollar, one to be used by all citizens for everyday transactions, and eventually to be rolled into a world currency, and we know where that leads. Up till now I've been successful in keeping the committee from moving forward, but that's when I started getting veiled threats about Rachel, and that's when I came to you, because I thought maybe it wouldn't hurt to expose what they're doing…"

Bill pounded the table with his fist hard enough to make the silverware rattle. "Crud, Stan, I am so sorry. I let down my guard."

But Stan waved him off. "No, no, don't go there. This is on me."

"No it's not. It's not on either of us. We just stepped into the viper's nest. We're not responsible for the evil that resides in the hearts of others. We fight the good fight and sometimes we get wounded—but ultimately we win. That's what the Good Book says."

"Spiritual warfare? I get it. So you think this is Satan's response to our coming against him."

"Don't know. What do you think?" Bill's phone began trilling. "Excuse me," he said. He pulled his phone from his pocket and brought it to his ear. "You got Bill."

"Bill, Jim Bartolo, over at the park ranger's office."

"Hey Jim, what's up?"

"A couple of guys fishing the Watalong came in and told us about a canoe they found at the base of the upper falls. We thought it might be yours so we went to check it out. It was. It had gone over nose first and got jammed up against the rocks. It was pinned in pretty good. Took four of us to get it out."

Bill's eyes went to Mary, then to Stan. "You didn't have to do that, Jim, but I appreciate it. Thank you. Okay with you if I swing by tomorrow and pick it up?"

"Wait, let me finish. We found a wallet jammed up under the seat. It belonged to your son."

"My son? Josh?"

"Yes, and there's something else…"

THIRTY-TWO

BILL HUNG UP THE PHONE, staring out the window, stalling. What could he say?—a suicide note? Come on, that's not Josh—*a little troubled maybe, but not suicidal.*

"Bill? Who was it?" Mary said.

Bill brought his head around. "It was the ranger at the campground. I didn't have a chance to tell you, but my canoe went missing and I thought it was stolen, but the rangers found it."

"Well, that's good, isn't it? Why the drawn face?"

"Was it damaged?" Stan asked.

Angie's elbow flung out, but Stan caught it before it hit him. He gently placed it back in her lap.

Bill's bottom lip puckered. He shook his head. "No, the only way to damage that ol' beast is with a chainsaw."

"What, then?"

He took a deep breath, exhaling audibly through his nose. "It looks like maybe Josh took it. He rode it over the falls."

Mary's face stiffened, tension forming around her eyes. "Noooo, no, don't you dare say that."

Bill reached for her hand... "They don't know anything yet. Josh wasn't found," ...and made the decision to leave the note out of it. Better she think it an accident, than know her son wanted to end his own life.

Mary pulled her hand free and grabbed a napkin, wadding it in her fist.

Bill picked up his spoon, rubbing the bowl with his thumb. "It's

318

too late to do anything tonight," he said, setting the spoon down with a *clack*. "They're putting together a search party first thing in the morning. We're going to comb through every nook and cranny from the lake, to the sand washes outside Tantamoa." Bill placed his hand on Mary's forearm and felt her trembling. "Mary, honey, let's not jump to any conclusions. He could have gotten out anywhere along the lake and just got careless and let the canoe drift away. It could easily have gone over the falls by itself. Trust me. I don't believe God's going to let that river have both our sons."

Mary looked up, her eyes glistening, starting to brim. She shook her head. "No, noooo, don't you dare try to placate me," she said, pushing him away. "I'm not stupid. Josh hated that canoe. He wouldn't take it anywhere. And if he just got out, he'd be back by now, and they wouldn't be doing a search."

Angie twisted in her wheelchair, writhing like she wanted out. "*Joooossshhmmmom*"

Bill stared straight ahead. The jukebox was bubbling with color, the music a low country boil, and the fish, those blasted fish on the walls with their mouths gaping open and tails flapping, were grinning at him—*Don't worry, be happy.*

The darkness that night was too great for Bill to sleep, not the absence of light, but a darkness of the soul. He lay on his back staring at the ceiling. If trouble had come, the responsibility was his, and his alone. And if Mary ever read that accursed suicide note, she would know it too.

She lay on her side, her knees pulled up in a fetal position. He could hear her muted sobs. He wanted to be a comfort, to roll over and place a hand on her shoulder, but every time he tried, she'd stiffen, and then push him away. It was like she could read his thoughts, putting the blame squarely on his shoulders. He had finally gone too far, and now there were repercussions. With her two sons gone and him in jail, Mary would be alone to care for Angie. *Why would You do that, Lord?* He could handle doing time. The Apostle Paul called himself a prisoner for the sake of the gospel. Bill could do that, if called upon. But he wasn't necessarily being imprisoned for preaching Jesus, though he was being persecuted for what he believed, so maybe he was. Christians were called to suffer for Christ, but the newspapers would spin it like he was cheating the government, certainly not a Christ like behavior. His testimony would be tarnished forever. And *why, why, why*, would Josh want to kill himself?

The ranger had found the letter while going through Josh's wallet for a name to contact. He didn't share what it said, he would let them read it in private, but he did say Josh's swan-dive over the falls appeared to have been deliberate. Part of Bill wanted to get that note and rip it up before anyone else, including himself, had a chance to read it. He didn't need his failings as a father forever immortalized, but the other part yearned to know—*why*.

Angie, too, was restless. Bill could hear her moaning in the other bed. He wished he could have removed her from the room before anything was said, but the situation had evolved beyond his control. He brought his watch up over his head for the umpteenth time. *Four.* They'd agreed to not get up until five. The ranger's office didn't open till seven, but he couldn't force himself to stay in bed any longer. He rolled over and swung his feet around to stand.

Mary reached for a tissue on the nightstand and used it to wipe her nose, discarding it on the pile of six or seven already there. "I can't sleep either," she said.

"I was just thinking of taking a walk to clear my head."

"I've been praying. All night long. Crying out to God and I think He spoke to me. I think we'll see Josh again. I think that's what He said."

"But you're crying."

"I know," she said softly. "I can't help myself."

They collected Stan, who elected to leave Rachel in the convalescent home for the day. Mary insisted on coming and that meant Angie was coming too, so they piled into the van because they couldn't all fit in Bill's truck. *Better this way*, Bill thought. He wasn't coming back with them anyway. Whatever the outcome, he planned to paddle the canoe back to the cabin. Stan could drive the ladies back to the hotel and then swing by the cabin to pick him up. No one mentioned what they might do if Josh's body were found washed up on the rocks.

Stan and Bill rode up front, with Mary and Angie in the back. The road ahead was blue, lit only by the twin beams of the headlights, the sky dark and threatening rain. They passed the logging road to Bill's cabin and continued on up the highway. The gravel road veered off to the right, leading to the south end of the lake. The paved road headed up through the mountains to the north where vacationers had access to High Ridge State Park, and the Campground.

They rode in silence, their headlights sweeping the road illuminating the early morning insects that splatted against the van's paint. Spots of rain started to appear on the glass. Stan turned the windshield wipers on intermittent. "Going to be a lot harder to search if it rains." *The only easy day, was yesterday*, the SEAL axiom stuck in his head.

"Wetter maybe, not harder. I've fished that river top to bottom in five hours, and that's with stopping to tie and cast my fly. Get half a dozen men on it and we shouldn't have a problem. We'll probably find Josh lying injured on some sandbank, but hopefully not too bad."

Or find his body, Stan thought. He saw a sign that read High Ridge Ranger Station and pulled off. He looked at his watch. It was only a quarter to, but a light was on inside the building.

The men climbed out. Bill went around back and opened the van's rear hatch to remove Angie's wheelchair. Then he brought it up alongside the sliding side door, and unhitched her seatbelt. Placing his arms under her legs and around her back, he lifted her out and into the chair. Mary waited and crawled out after.

The quartet moved in unison to the front of the building. They turned aside at the steps and followed Bill around to the handicap ramp.

A ranger stepped out and held the door as everyone filed in. He wore the typical kaki brown shirt and dark olive green pants with a patch on his shoulder that said Oregon State Parks and a gold badge that said State Park Ranger. "Good to see you, Jim." Bill said as he rolled Angie inside.

"You too. I only wish it were under better circumstances." Jim doffed his Smokey the Bear hat and closed the door behind them.

Bill checked to see where Mary had gone. She was on the other side of the room, occupied with a topographical map of the Watalong Valley, the gorge through which the river flowed. He leaned in and lowered his voice. "Can I get that letter from you, Jim? I haven't told Mary about it yet."

Jim nodded and reached under the counter. He brought it out and handed it discretely to Bill who carefully folded the damp sheet of water-stained paper and slipped it into his pocket.

"Thanks, appreciate it. So what's the plan?"

Jim looked around and motioned to the man seated at a desk behind him, who picked up several stakes with red flags stapled to them and came to the counter. The man was dressed in the same uniform as Jim but instead of the brown flat brimmed hat wore an olive green baseball cap with the state park's tree, mountain and lake crest. "Bill, this is Ranger Norfolk, he'll be spearheading the operation."

"We've met," Bill said, shaking Ed Norfolk's hand. "But let me continue the introductions on around. This is my daughter Angie, and this is my wife Mary." Mary looked up from the map with a thin smile and glassy eyes and nodded. A tissue was wadded in her hand. "And this is my good friend Senator Stan Powers from the state of Illinois."

"It's an honor." Ed said.

"The Senator will be joining us in the search, but if it's alright I'd like it if the ladies could stay here. Mary will take care of Angie so they won't be in the way. How soon do you think we can get started?"

"Soon as everyone arrives. The women are fine, your wife can sit at my desk and help man the radio while Jim deals with campsite issues. Now what about you, Senator?"

"Stan. Please. What about me?"

"You can't go out like that, dressed in slacks, and especially wearing dress shoes. I won't be responsible for your slipping and falling in. What size shoe do you wear?"

"Usually nine and a half, but I'm former navy, born on the water, a little shoe leather won't slow me down."

"Jim, can you grab my waders? They'll fit. I'll be searching the lower end where it's less rocky and not so steep so I won't need them. Bill, I see you're wearing corks but if your waders are in your car I recommend you put them on."

"Sorry, we stayed in Tantamoa last night. What you see is what you get."

Ed looked out the window and saw a truck pulling up outside. "Okay, everyone's here." Jim came out of the back with a pair of hip-waders and a stack of hard-hats. "Everyone needs a helmet," Ed said, "and keep the chin strap on. I don't want them floating away if you fall in."

Stan began pulling on his waders as three men clomped through the door fully decked out in fishing boots and tin hats. Two of the men had ropes coiled over their shoulders. It was obvious they'd done this before.

"Okay, guys, introductions. Jack, Charlie, Sam," Ed said, indicating the three men. "These are my regular volunteers. We lose children up here at least once or twice a year, so they're familiar with the territory. Guys, this is Bill, and this is Stan."

"We know Charlie. He volunteers at our tree farm every year. Gives hayrides for the kids."

"I read about your other son." Sam said sticking out his hand for Bill to shake. "Terrible tragedy. Know it was years ago, but I imagine it still hurts. Don' worry, if your boy's out there, we'll find him."

"Right. Okay," Ed continued. "We're going out as three, two-man teams. It's twelve miles from the lake down to the bottom of the mountain," Ed moved forward, jostling them over to the map where Mary was standing, their close proximity nudging her aside. "Two guys, Jack and Sam are going to start up here." Ed pointed at the north end of the lake. "I'll drive Bill and Stan four miles down to about here," he said, pointing further down, "and let them off. Here's a red flag, guys. Plant it where you start, make it secure, but make sure it's visible so when the first team reaches it, they'll know they've covered the distance. I'll take Charlie with me. We'll drive four more miles down and do the same at our starting point. I have three sets of walkie-talkies, one per team. They're all tuned to our emergency channel so stay in touch and let us know if you need help. That's about it. Let's mount up."

323

THIRTY-THREE

T HE SCREEN DOOR slammed behind Jack and Sam, who went out first. They had to walk the lakeshore for an extra half mile to get to the mouth of the river, but it was flat and easy-going, though the thick clouds made it darker than it should have been at that time of the morning.

Bill turned to Mary and gave her a hug, kissing the top of her head.

She brought a hand up and placed it on his shoulder, still clinging to her wadded tissue, and for the first time since receiving the news, Bill felt her soften.

"Bring my son home safe," she said.

Bill took a breath and nodded. Hopefully, they'd find Josh alive— no, they *would* find Josh alive, he was sure of it. God wouldn't take both his sons...but then he thought again about all the mothers who'd lost both sons to war—and wasn't that what this was, spiritual warfare? He walked over to Angie, sweeping his hands over the top of her head. "I'm going to go find your brother. I need you to be brave and take care of Mom for me," he said, tossing her hair. "She's not feeling too good this morning."

Angie looked up, her broad face grinning ear to ear. "Yaaassssss," she said. It was all the encouragement Bill needed.

Ranger Ed drove Bill and Stan to their drop-off point, with the wind pummeling them, trying to push them off the road. The rain had begun to fall in a steady drizzle. Ed's windshield wipers clacked back and forth.

"Lovely day for a walk in the park, 'eh boys?"

Bill sat in the back of the crew cab with his knees scrunched under his chin. If there was a silver lining to this cloud, it was that he'd got the roofer out in time to seal up his house. His other clouds weren't as bright, like how he was about to lose his freedom for a lie, and how even if they found Josh alive, he might end up in jail without being given the chance to reconcile.

"Okay, guys. You probably got the roughest section, but Sam's got a bad knee and Jack's getting on in years. I have to do the bottom section so I can drive back and pick you guys up, but you know the terrain Bill. Senator, your military experience speaks for itself. I'm confident you'll do fine. Each of you should take one side of the river so you don't miss anything. And be sure to go deep into any brush, logjams and fallen trees. We found one kid buried in some brush, forced back by the water so he couldn't crawl out, but he was alive. Good luck."

Bill and Stan climbed out, Stan with the walkie-talkie in one of the upper pockets of his hip-waders. Bill carried the tire iron from Stan's rental. He'd not forgotten Ted's foot caught in the cleft of a rock. If it happened again, he wanted something to pry Josh free.

They hiked down the steep incline to the river, Stan obviously favoring one leg over the other. Bill wanted to say something, but let it go. Dirt and pebbles slid under their feet. The sound of the water pounding over the rocks was deafening. Lightning exploded overhead with the cannon-fire of thunder echoing through the gorge. Bill held out his hand and felt the rain as it began to pour. *Really?*—"Come on, give us a break!"

"The only easy day, was yesterday," Stan shouted above the din. "It's something we said in the service. I've got the waders on. I'm going to cross to the other side."

"Suit yourself," Bill said knowing in a few minutes he was going to look like he'd jumped in the river anyway. "I'll plant the flag."

They waved at each other from opposite banks, and Stan gave a military hand signal to move forward.

The shore was thick with brambles, forcing them into the water where the current threatened to sweep them away. Bill used to fish this river many moons ago, but even though he'd recently started fishing again, it was a place he still avoided. Looking out over the lake brought a sense of peace. The river, with its volume of water—tons per second—crashing over boulders and rocks, was just plain menacing. He yanked his foot out of the current's swell and plowed forward. It was spring, when the mountain runoff was at its highest.

The mist rising from the water made it difficult to see, but he could make out Stan on the other side, using what looked like a kayak paddle to probe a blackberry thicket, making sure it was empty. He checked his watch, splattered with fat drops of rain. An hour had passed but they'd covered less than a mile. *God. Please, I'm begging You. Try me, punish me, do anything You want to me, but don't do this to Mary.*

The water continued pushing him forward, but he kept his footing sure. He planted one foot at a time, the way he had when fly-fishing years before; only the water was shallower then. The river was up to his waist, making it near impossible to lift a foot without losing his balance. Stan was in the two-foot shallows. He brought a hand up, cupping his mouth. "You okay?" he shouted over the pounding surf.

"Yeah," Bill yelled back. "But I'm in a bit too deep. I got to get out of this hole or I'll be sucked downriver."

Stan looked around and found a rock with a reasonably flat surface. He climbed up with the water rushing over his feet, and flipping his paddle around, held the handle out to Bill.

Bill grabbed on and Stan began pulling him in. "Where did you get this?" Bill shouted as he dropped to his knees and crawled onto the shore.

"Up there. I was looking into a tangle of brush and it was stuck inside."

"This is from our canoe. See, J.B., those are Josh's initials. He carved them there as a boy. Did you see anything else?"

"No, sorry, and I looked really good. I even called out his name."

Bill had to travel upstream to get to where it was shallow enough to cross back over to the other side again. He saw Stan on the opposite bank, his metal hat bright against the dark water. He was a good distance ahead of him now. Moving quickly, he started back down, covering ground he'd already explored till he'd caught up and passed him again.

And then, there it was. He paused, taking in its slick gray surface—*the sarcophagus.* The wind raged, the thunder boomed, and the sky exploded with light. Bill stood frozen. He could go around, he could avoid it altogether, but something made him climb up on it, if for no other reason than to exude ascendancy. He stood on the crest of the boulder, looking at the sky, wondering if Ted's last sight looking up from his watery grave was something like this. The trees along the riverbank were swaying in the wind. The river squeezed through the three-foot wide gap with a force as strong as the pull of gravity. If he'd had a stick of dynamite he'd have jammed it down the throat of that crack and blown the rock to smithereens. He edged forward and stooped to strike the jagged outcrop with his tire-iron but the steel rod bounced back ringing in his ears. He stared at his hand, stinging from the blow. The lip of the wedge was unbroken.

"What's wrong?" Stan said as he came up from behind.

Bill's neck craned around, startled by the intrusion. His hand with the tire iron lowered, his jaw, clenched tight, relaxed. The rain pinged off his tin hat. "This is where it happened," he said. "It's where Ted died, his foot caught right there in that crack."

Stan stepped forward, inching out over the lip of the boulder to see.

"I was so stupid, I blamed Josh, when I knew deep in my soul that Josh would never have been there if it wasn't for Ted. And now I may lose Josh too. You think God is punishing me for my foolishness?"

"Let's just hope and pray Josh is okay. We still have a long way to go."

A quarter-mile downriver lightning struck a tree splitting the giant ponderosa down the middle causing half to fall into the river. The thunder was so close it was instantaneous, booming like a cannon in their ears. Stan felt the ground shake as the soundwave thumped his back pushing him off the rock. Bill reached out and Stan caught his hand, but by then he was freefalling with his paddle waving in the air. The weight pulled Bill off balance. Bill watched the tire iron fall into the vacuum as his momentum carried him forward, following Stan in. *Whafummp* They were spinning like unmanned rafts, swirling on the current. The river had no bottom. Bill heard the radio squawking in Stan's pocket. "I think we need to call off the search until this front passes," Ed's voice said. Stan used the paddle to turn himself around till he was sliding downriver feet first. He reached out and caught Bill's mackinaw and pulled him around. "Get your feet up and kick that tree and grab onto a limb, it'll stop us."

"I repeat, we're calling off the search until the storm passes," the radio garbled. "Do you copy?"

Bill and Stan glommed on and used the branches to pull themselves out of the water until they were standing on the flat surface of the split tree.

Stan began wiping the water from his arms. "Man that water's cold."

"It's the spring runoff. The snow melting on Mount Hood comes straight here. Pure ice water."

Stan went for the radio in his pocket, looking at Bill. "You quitting?"

Bill shook his head, "Not in this lifetime."

Stan pushed the mike button, water dripping from his chin. "Not an option. No man left behind," he said. He tried sweeping his hand across the top of his head to wring out his hair but his tin bucket got in the way. "It's a military thing. Both you other teams plant a flag where you leave off and Bill and I will cover the rest."

There was muffled conversation at the other end and then Ed's voice crackled again. "Team one says they're almost finished, so they'll continue. It's only a drizzle down here. I was worried about the lightning I see up at your end. But if you're good, we're down in the shallows, so we'll finish up too. How much you guys got left?"

"About a mile. You can pick us up where you left your flag. I take it no one's had any luck."

"Not so far, but we're not done yet. We've still got a bit of riverfront to cover. After that we have to hike four miles back to the truck, I figure we'll be another hour."

"Same here."

"Alright. You guys take care."

"Copy that."

At four o'clock the rains retreated. The darker clouds moved out over the ocean and those that remained had light in their creases. Only scattered drops pinged off the tin hats of the crew, with some residual spattering in the puddles at their feet. The teams met outside the ranger station for a final debrief. Bill and Stan were the only ones soaked to the bone, but they'd had a little time to dry while waiting for their ride. Each team assured the others that they had been thorough in their search, but Josh had not been found, either alive or dead. Bill thanked everyone for their help and promised each of them a free Christmas tree if they wanted to stop by his farm next season.

Through the window, Mary spotted the group huddled around the ranger's pickup and flung open the door rushing outside. She thrust herself into the circle. "What did you find? Do you have him? Is he alright?"

"I'm sorry, we came up empty," Ed said. He removed his helmet and held it over his chest with a hand.

"It's good news, hon," Bill said. "If Josh had died on that river, we would have found his body. The fact that we didn't tells me he's alive. Come on, let's go back inside." He put his arm around her shoulder, guiding her toward the door.

"God told me we'll see him again. He told me...I'm sure of it."

In another life perhaps, Bill thought, but then—*oh ye of little faith,* he rebuked himself.

They clambered inside where Stan was laying his waders over the counter, returning them. He plopped his tin construction hat and the walkie-talkie on top of the pile and went to squeeze his wet socks into dry loafers.

Bill unhitched his helmet and turned it in, then went and got

Angie and brought her over to Mary. "Listen, I need to get the canoe back home," he said, glancing over at Stan. "You think you could drive the ladies back to the hotel, and then pick me up at the cabin and bring me back down so I can get my truck?"

"You want me to tag along? Mary can drive the van back around and pick us both up."

"No, I need to be alone. I need time to think."

The wind had died, eerily, like the calm one feels in the eye of the storm. Bill was in the canoe, coasting on a surface smooth and clear as a sheet of glass. He only had the one paddle found by Stan, but it was all he needed.

The sky was clear, the five o'clock sun breaking through the remaining clouds like a knife cutting through butter. Bill brought his paddle to the other side to make a course correction, the runoff dimpling the surface of the water.

It was cold on the lake, the evening air eating through his water-soaked clothes. His chin quivered. It would take Stan at least two hours to drop the ladies off and drive back to the cabin. Bill veered off course, gliding up the inlet toward the falls. Then he went another mile till the sun dipped below the horizon. The world was rapidly changing. Culture, traditions, and laws that had stood for centuries were under attack. The Bible said the mystery of iniquity was already at work. Both he and Stan had come against it and suddenly both had children at risk. *Coincidence?* Not likely. He was facing so many trials, some in the courtroom, some in the spiritual realm, it was hard keeping track. Job, who lost everything, had said it best. *The Lord gives, and the Lord takes away, blessed be the name of the Lord.* He needed to get down on his knees and pray.

Bill picked up speed, forcing the canoe forward one stroke at a time until he was about halfway up the inlet and approaching the shore. He gave his paddle a few extra hard draws, sliding the canoe up on a sandy beach. The trail was moist from the rain, the wet ferns soaking his legs as he passed, his damp clothes sticking to his body. He came to the base of the sixty-foot waterfall but didn't stop to appreciate its majesty. Instead, he continued up the side of the hill, traversing across beds of loose shale that avalanched down the mountain under his feet. It took only ten minutes to reach the summit, even with pausing several times to catch his breath. He stopped with his hands on his knees, realizing he wasn't in as good of shape as he used to be, then straightened himself and looked out over God's creation. To his right, he could see the lake, purple as amethyst in the waning light. To his left he saw the Cascades with the sun behind them glowing like they were on fire. The trees in the shadows were shades of ocean green. *I will lift up mine eyes unto the hills, from whence comes my help! My help comes from the Lord, maker of heaven and earth.*

He turned to look at his altar, the rock where he'd brought Ted and Josh when they were babies and offered them up to God the way Abraham had with Isaac. He would never let Mary know his thoughts, but he knew if God wanted them back, they were His, but he was here to pray against that idea. And while he was at it, he needed to pray for protection for himself.

Gideon had faced an innumerable army of Midianites and staved them off with three-hundred men, Jehoshaphat faced the armies of Ammon, Moab and Mount Seir and cried, "We have no power against this great multitude, nor do we know what to do, but our eyes are upon You," and they fled before him. When the Rabshakeh of the king of Assyria came against Israel, Hezekiah prayed and the angel of the Lord killed one-hundred and eighty-five-thousand of them before breakfast. If God could do that, He could drive off a few demons. The main thing to realize, was that the battle was the Lord's. Bill stared off into the horizon, the Cascades a silhouette against the glow of heaven. In the eyes of the world, his situation was hopeless, but nothing was impossible with God.

THIRTY-FOUR

"TELL ME ABOUT your God."

"What would you like to know?"

"Well for starters, who is He?"

"He's the God of all creation, the God who made me, and then turned me loose to decide for myself whether or not I wanted to follow Him."

"Okay, stop. So you believe this God of yours made you out of, what—dust?"

"Maybe. I don't know exactly how He did it, and frankly, I don't care; I just know He did."

"I don't buy it."

"So how do you think we got here?"

"I don't know. I kinda feel like I was dropped here by a spaceship from another planet."

"A perfectly normal feeling for someone in your predicament. But you see, if you believe that, then you believe in evolution."

"Not necessarily."

"Oh yes, because see, if there's no God, all life had to come from nothing, and then that nothing had to become something, and whether that nothing-to-something started here or on some other planet is immaterial. Either God made us, or we evolved, period. And since we could never have evolved, then there has to be a God."

"Never is a pretty strong word."

"True, but then, truth is always strong. Look, I know I'm just an M.D., but this is my hobbyhorse. I've spent the past two decades studying this subject. I could spend years trying to teach you what I've learned, but it would be pointless unless you want to believe. Most modern scientists know evolution doesn't work, but they choose to believe it anyway because they don't want to believe in God. It's the same with you. If you want to believe, I can give you a thousand good reasons, but if you don't we're just wasting our time."

"Maybe, but humor me. Tell me why evolution doesn't work."

"I can't, neither of us has that much time... Okay look, in a nutshell, the whole thing is based on mutations taking place in our DNA. Kind of like small mistakes that occur during replication where the new strand comes out slightly different than before. Now these mistakes, or accidents, can account for a lot of things, but you can't have a lot of accidents create extremely complex perfectly designed machines. It doesn't work that way. Complex machines come by design. Ask yourself why you have taste buds on your tongue, or at all for that matter? Accidents, without design or purpose, can't accomplish that. Taste buds on a tongue mean some intelligent designer said, if the tongue is going to be used to help people chew, then I need to put taste buds there so they can enjoy what they eat. By the way, butterflies have taste buds too, only they're on their feet. I guess the all-knowing all-thinking accident thought butterflies should be able to taste too. Why are your teeth perfectly matched, and how did they get in your mouth? They're just bone, yet they're different than every other bone in your body. If everything happened by accident, why don't you have a tibia in your mouth instead of thirty-two perfectly balanced teeth? When these accidents were happening how did you end up with two arms, with perfectly matched hands and fingers, instead of an arm on one side and a wing with feathers on the other? How did you end up with an eye with so many highly complex parts; like the iris, the pupil, the cornea, and the retina? Each part would have had to evolve separately through bazillions of accidents and still fit and work perfectly together. And then, accidentally, without thought, or purpose, accidentally evolve an optic nerve at the back of the eye that accidently worked its way to the back of the brain to deliver pictures to your visual cortex. And don't get me started on the brain or we'll be here all night. The point is, we're not here by accident."

IT WASN'T SO MUCH the river itself, but the time of year. After a good year of snow, the lake, and the Watalong that flowed from it, were known to flood their banks, in spite of Global Warming. Bill guffawed, last year they'd seen more snow on the mountain than in the past decade. Ski operators were thrilled until it ended with an early spring, which now had every river from the Watalong to the Columbia overflowing.

He picked his way along the left side of the upper gorge, slowly probing the blackberry thickets and dismantling driftwood jams for any sign of Josh's passing. It wasn't that he didn't trust Sam and Jake, he was confident they had done their best, but as Ranger Norfolk said, Jake was getting old and Sam had a bad knee. He just wanted to make another pass to be sure nothing was missed.

A fallen tree stripped of its bark and bleached by the sun was jammed into a crevice formed by two rocks. The water folding over the smooth yellow trunk was clear as crystal but the angle at which the tree jutted out created a hollow space where the water pooled swirling underneath. *Dang it all.* Today the sun was shining, today he had worn his hip-waders, and today he was hoping to stay dry. But he'd vowed to leave no stone unturned. Dang!

Bill unbuttoned his plaid flannel shirt. He didn't regret not calling his friend, Senator Powers, the man had to spend time with his daughter, but right about now he sure could use the help. He hung the shirt on a broken limb. Unless, God forbid, he fell in again, the waders would keep his bottom half dry. He put a hand against the log and stretched his arm under the water as far as it would go, waving his hand around to feel for anything other than rocks. His heart started to pound as he tugged on an object until it came loose. He pulled it back, bringing a torrent of dirt and debris with him as he pulled it from the water and held it up to the sun. It was exactly what he thought it was—an old tennis shoe—just not one belonging to Josh. The rubber sole was intact, but the canvas was decomposed and falling apart. Had to have been there more than a year. He tossed it up on the shore where the campground maintenance crew would find it. At least his shirt didn't get wet. He took it from the limb and slipped it over his shoulders again.

Leaving a note explaining his absence to Mary, he had risen before first light and had taken the Chinook, paddling five miles to the campground so he could be there at dawn. God was going to help him find his son, he believed that, but in spite of casting out all doubt, he still couldn't sleep. It would be a long day.

He envied Mary. Somewhere along the way she'd latched on to the promise she'd been given and had slept soundly. Her soft purring niggled him as he rolled and kicked off the sheets, and turned, and pulled them back on; listening to the call of an owl down in the cove and a mouse skittering along the baseboards.

He didn't count it unbelief to be out there. It was more like the unction of God calling him to do something more. Since there wasn't anything else he could do, this had to be it. If he didn't find what he was looking for in the upper rapids, he would search the lower sandbars as well. He would either find Josh dead, or by the end of the day, know with absolute certainty he was alive.

"Alright God? I'm doing my part, but You have to help." He moved a tree branch that had come down with leaves still on it. The whitewater chopped with such ferocity, he had to stop to maintain his balance. Sun sliced the water into shards of yellow, white, and gold.

"The thing is, God, I fully expect You to bring Josh back alive, that's not the problem. The problem is I want him back as a son, not like it was before." Bill sloshed around a boulder where the water was deep enough to flow over the top of his hip-waders. He clung to the rock and managed to inch back up to the shallows, with only a trickle of water seeping in. He felt its icy chill, but his body temperature quickly made it warm. "And You don't have to tell me I'm the problem. I get it, *weakness*, never could understand it, probably never will. Hard enough in a woman, but in a man? *Blessed are the meek for they shall inherit the earth.* I know, I know, but it doesn't make it easier to relate…okay, I did feel helpless when I couldn't get to Angie—but that fire might have killed her—and that was helpless, not hopeless, is that how Josh feels? *But God has chosen the foolish things of the world to confound the wise; and God has chosen the weak things of the world to confound the strong.* Seriously? Bill's eyes looked to the sky, a field of blue with castle white clouds. "What? You want me weak? *Why?* Was Moses weak? Was David? I still want Josh back, but endowing him with a little backbone might help."

He wished he'd gotten a chance to read the letter. He'd tried to remove it from his pocket but his swim in the river had turned the paper to mush and it came out in pieces. The few penciled words that remained were all but washed away. What if the note had brought forgiveness? *When I am weak, then I am strong.* Stop it!

A half-circle basin formed by stones was covered in leaves. Bill grabbed a stick and began swirling it around to peer down into the water. Multi-colored rocks, buffs and whites, grays and browns, rested on the bottom—then the flicker of a dark shadow. WOAH! Bill jumped back as a trout leapt out of the pool. It landed flopping on the rocks until it slithered off into the water and disappeared again. Bill's heart was pounding.

He leaned on a rock, looking at the opposite bank, breathing hard. The other side looked foreign, a whole new adventure waiting for him to explore on his way back up, but... He stood to get a better look. It was the other paddle backed against a line of rocks under leaves and broken limbs—and they'd missed it!

STAN HELD RACHEL'S hand, guiding her across the courtyard. He had to credit the staff at the hospice. They'd done a fine job of getting her ready. Her outfit, a sleeveless yellow blouse and blue jeans with her hair done up in a ponytail, made her appear perky, in fact, almost normal, which was just the way he wanted her to look in case they happened upon someone she knew. He'd done his best too. His slacks had become ruined in the river, and Bill's clothes were too big for him to wear, so he'd started the day by shopping for a pair of jeans that fit. His new shoes were sneakers, and his shirt was dark green with a subtle pinecone print. *How very Oregonian*, he'd thought upon seeing himself in the mirror.

He turned up the Park Blocks heading toward Cascades Coffee hoping Rachel might recognize something: a friend, a monument, or simply a flower from one of the many gardens, anything that might cause her to wake up and say, "Hey, I've been here before."

He'd learned about the coffee shop from Mary at dinner. It had been a weary affair with little conversation. Everyone at the table was exhausted. The men had showered, and changed into clean, dry clothes, but they were feeling spent. Bill's clothes were too big for Stan, but he'd worn them gratefully because at that point he didn't have anything else. Mary, resting on God's promise that she would see her son again, was serene. Angie, though assured her brother would be found, remained anxious. She would moan and her arms would come out swinging wildly. Bill was constantly placing them back in her lap. Rachel wasn't calm or subdued. Rachel wasn't anything. Deep in her mind she was picking daisies, but to the outside world she just sat and stared at the wall. Stan had noted how both he and Bill now had daughters they had to feed by hand. He wondered if Bill thought it was coincidence, or Satan replicating the hurt he inflicted on people.

Stan paused outside the coffee shop, turning Rachel every which way, letting her take in the sights, hoping something might register on her brain and get it functioning again, but she remained oblivious. He took Rachel by the hand and led her inside. Only two tables were occupied, one by a tattooed construction worker wearing a day-glo orange hardhat, and the other by a girl with pink hair. Neither were Rachel's type. Stan's hope that Rachel might bump into a familiar face was fading, particularly with respect to Josh.

"Rachel?" the pink-haired girl waved as they entered. Stan did a doubletake. The girl got up and rushed over. "Where have you been? I thought maybe you'd flown back to Chicago." She stepped forward throwing her arms around Rachel, her purple fingernails splayed out on Rachel's back. Then she stopped, loosening her embrace, and looked at Rachel again. "Are you alright?" The pink mophead stepped back and brought a hand up to cover her mouth.

"Hi, my name is Stan Powers. I'm Rachel's father," Stan said holding out his hand.

The girl took it warily. "Dandy," she said. "What happened to her? Hey, you're that senator guy, her father, the one I called. You wouldn't talk to me." She glanced at Rachel. "Oh no, you didn't."

"Didn't what?"

"You messed with her mind, didn't you? You, you…"

Stan looked askance. "What? No, what are you talking about? Rachel's my daughter for Pete's sake, but someone did do something and now she's withdrawn and refuses to talk about it. Look, can we sit down. I'll explain everything."

Dandy put a purple nail to her mouth and went back to her table. Stan noted the rings that covered her fingers like totems on poles.

Stan pulled a chair out for Rachel, then one for himself and sat down.

"Looks like she's had a lobotomy," Dandy said, staring at Rachel's face while chewing on her bottom lip. She took her rings off one at a time and laid them on the table in a straight line, flexing her fingers.

Stan took Rachel's hand, feeling its soft warmth, then looked at Dandy. "I was hoping if Rachel saw someone she recognized, someone like you, it would jog her memory, and she'd wake up. Unfortunately, it doesn't seem to be working."

"You said you'd tell me what happened."

"Right. It's like I said, she suffered a trauma. Some lunatic grabbed her and tied her up and stuffed her in his car and tried to take her to Canada. Thankfully, he didn't make it and got stopped at the border…"

Dandy's mouth dropped open, her eyes narrowing, her head slowly wagging back and forth.

"What? You know something? You need to tell me."

Dandy started slipping her rings on her fingers again with her eyes looking down. "There was this guy, creepy dude, and he had a strong interest in Rachel. And by strong, I mean unnatural. We made a deal with him. He was supposed to show us where this conservative dude, Bill Best lived…" she stopped like she was revealing something she shouldn't, but then continued, "…We wanted to do a shout-down at his house, but no one knew where he lived. But this guy did and he said he'd take us if we'd keep an eye on Rachel for him, and we said we would, so he took us out there but he didn't tell us the dude had a locked security gate, so we had to turn around and go back, and then we decided not to help him. But then Rachel disappeared, and I feared the worst and here she is. Get the connection?"

Stan nodded. "Guy name of Carl Rove, right?"

Dandy shook her head. "No this was Victor something-or-other. I forget the last name, but his first name was definitely Victor."

Stan reached into his shirt pocket for the booking sheet he'd received from the RCMP. He unfolded it and spread it out on the table so that Carl Rove's photo was front and center in glorious black-and-white.

Dandy was still slipping her rings back on, but as the photo slid into view, she popped out of her chair dropping one ring clattering to the floor. "That's him." She cried.

BILL HAD FISHED the paddle out of the water and found the initials Ted had carved as a young boy, verifying its ownership. He'd carried it with him all the way down and up again until he finished the loop and was back where he started that morning. Then he'd taken the road and bypassed the four miles he and Stan had covered, and started again doing the bottom four mile section. It was late afternoon. The sun on his back made his flannel shirt feel like an electric blanket. He still had to go back up the other side to be able to say he'd checked every inch of the river himself. His legs ached from fighting the current and his back was tired from so much bending over. He wasn't a quitter, but he sure felt like giving up. He was scouring the last gravelly beach when something caught his eye. There were foot tracks in the sand along the river's edge. They could have been anyone's, but they sure weren't made by Ranger Norfolk or Charlie. They had both worn boots, and these prints were left by tennis shoes; shoes very close to the size worn by Josh. He circled the area, being careful not to pollute the sand with tracks of his own. Standing at the water's edge, he could see where they disappeared into the river. He crossed over and saw again where they came out on the other side. There seemed to be quite a few at the base of a beached log, but they were on top of each other so it was hard to tell. He could easily see the brush broken and soil disturbed where the person had climbed back up to the road. But he didn't find any tracks coming down from the road to the water.

Bill waded back across. It wasn't likely the prints were left by Josh. It would have been nearly impossible for a body to have floated down the river this far without getting snagged on something, and especially without a floatation device. At this point the river was too broad and shallow. You could see the rocks shining like gold coins on the bottom all the way across. The water was less than two feet deep.

Then Bill saw it. Right at the river's edge, where the water lapped and foamed in tiny white bubbles, there was a one-inch ridge where dirt and sand had built up against an object of some kind, and the ridge was in the shape of a body. Bill took a closer look. He wasn't imagining it. He could even make out a lesser ridge inside the first where silt had built up under the person's arm...and a spoon indentation where the head had rested on a sandy pillow. Someone had lain there—half in the water—and lain there for several hours. Why would anyone do that unless—unless they were unconscious! And it occurred to him that he now knew what Mary had already taken for granted. Josh was alive!

THIRTY-FIVE

I T WAS JULY, past the summer solstice and the days were long and unbearably hot, but Bill tried to make the most of each one. He didn't know how many he might have as a free man. His trial was bearing down on him and to make matters worse, there was still no word from Josh. They were struggling to hold onto the assertion that their son would be found alive. Ranger Norfolk had reminded Bill that people pulled underwater could be held down by the surge, sometimes not resurfacing for months, particularly during high-water season. Rachel remained unresponsive. Stan continued taking her to Cascades Coffee hoping she might recognize someone, or that Josh might stumble in letting everyone know he'd survived. Bill spent his days consoling Mary and preparing her for what could be a long separation.

The day finally came, not so much because the Constitution guaranteed Bill a speedy trial, but because Cal couldn't wait to see Bill in jail, or rather, couldn't wait to receive a pat on the back from the President of the United States. Torrents of rain pummeled the ground, the wind driving the waves into the seawall along the Oregon coast, the sky dark except for the lightening blooming inside the clouds. Bill cinched his belt and slid his tie up under his buttoned collar. The darkness outside his window was foreboding. *Boomcrackleroar* went the thunder. It was Satan's game, but God's to win. Bill was just a token on the board.

Mary slipped into their bedroom and came up behind him, placing her arms around his waist with her head resting against his shoulder.

"I'm not going to let them take you," she said.

Bill unlaced her fingers and turned around to face her. "You may not have a choice," he said.

"No, I'm not hearing that." Her eyes were moist and veined in red; it hurt Bill to know she'd been crying. "Losing you and Josh and Ted would be too much to bear and God wouldn't do that. He's promised not to give us more than we can handle. You're coming home with me tonight, Bill Best. You hear me? There's only so much a woman can take."

"I'll do my Best, pun intended. The rest is up to God." Bill broke free and went to the bed, sitting down to slip on his shoes. "My lawyer is preparing me for the worst. He says our case is flimsy. They say their expert witnesses can prove I deleted files that I know were never there. And what have I got? Just my word."

"Your word and God," she reminded him. "Don't you dare get negative on me. I need your strength, now more than ever."

"Yeah, well God's been dealing with me about that. I get the feeling he wants me to be weak sometimes, and that's pretty much how I feel right now." Bill stood. He was wearing his only suit, the one he wore to church each week, and on Christmas and Easter. The wool was navy blue, his red silk tie standing brightly off his white shirt, his shoes black and shiny. His face was clean shaven, his chestnut hair neatly combed.

"You look good. I can't imagine anyone wanting to convict you."

"I just might be the best dressed man in jail."

"That's not funny," she said.

They drove to the Multnomah County Court House in Bill's old truck with the fenders rattling and the windshield wipers flapping against the summer rain. Mary was wearing a blue polyester pullover that had a silky sheen, but even though they'd used an umbrella, drops of water still spotted her dress, and Bill's suit was wet on the shoulders where he was exposed to the rain as he held the umbrella over Mary's head. Their wardrobe, upscale against the backdrop of the beat-up old truck, made them look like the Beverly Hillbillies driving to a black-tie soiree.

The courthouse ran alongside the downtown Plaza Blocks, just a short distance from the Willamette River, where street parking was virtually non-existent. Bill circled the area but finally gave up and pulled into the metropolitan garage adjacent to the court, knowing he and Mary would get soaked crossing the street. If this was to be his last day of freedom, the least the Lord could do was make it nice. He helped Mary out of the truck and held her hand as they splashed through the puddles, running across the road and into the building. Their umbrella was dripping water on the tiles as they stepped inside. *Boom!* Thunder shook the windows.

His lawyer was there to greet them, along with a gaggle of reporters who surrounded Bill with questions, the strobes of their cameras blinding them more than the lightening.

"Do you deny refusing to pay your taxes?"

"Care to comment on why a charitable organization you allegedly give money to, turned you in?"

"Are you planning to shut down your 501-c3?"

The lawyer took Bill's arm and pulled him inside the courtroom with Bill using his coat to shield Mary from the cameras. To his surprise, the place was packed. What happened to social distancing? They originally thought the trial would be virtual, but Mr. Moody had insisted on making it public and inviting the press. Mr. Moody represented the government, and they made the rules.

Heads swung around as they entered. Bill recognized many of the faces. Stan had made it into town on his own, choosing to leave Rachel in the convalescent home for the day. Angie too was missing as they had elected to leave her with their pastor's wife, but the minister himself was there, as were several prayer warriors from the church, representatives from the various charities he supported, and even a few of those who regularly gave to his podcast. Among those he didn't recognize were about a dozen masked faces that looked like they wanted him convicted and hung from a tree in the park. He might not have known them, but he knew their intent. He figured at least some of them were present when his house was set on fire.

Mary was removed from Bill and asked to sit with Stan while Bill was taken up front to the defense table. He turned as he sat down, giving her one last wink to exude confidence. Then it began.

A bailiff walked to the center of the room and announced, "Oyez. Oyez. Multnomah County Court is now in session, the honorable Judge Maynard Smith presiding. All rise."

The room shuffled to its feet and remained standing as a tall, bespectacled man in flowing black robes took a seat behind the bench. He removed his glasses and rubbed his eyes and put them back on before taking a sheaf of papers from the bailiff. "The United States vs. William Best. Alright, then," he said looking up, "is everyone present?"

"All present," the bailiff said.

Bill thought he had prepared himself for what was coming, but sitting quietly while one witness after another defamed his character was torment, especially knowing it was all nonsense. He had always paid his taxes, and because he answered to God, had diligently accounted for every penny. Several low-level employees had gone on-and-on about minor discrepancies which could be easily explained. In each case, his lawyer took them apart on cross. The judge at the bench seemed disinterested, if not completely bored, as though he understood such arguments were made to attack Bill's character, and had little to do with his guilt or innocence. At one point he removed his glasses and held them up to the light as though looking for a smudge, then wiped them with a Kleenex before asking the opposing counsel if he could move things along. The jury, too, looked half asleep.

It was after lunch before the prosecution was ready to wrap up their case. They had already presented the damming testimony of their expert witness. The man had been introduced as a private contractor who held security clearance with several federal agencies, including the FBI, the NSA, the IRS and Homeland Security. His forte was digging into criminal cases and dredging up computer files long thought expunged by terrorists, hackers, spies, and money launderers. His credentials were impeccable. Under oath, he swore to having found many such files on the servers belonging to Mr. William Best.

Bill and Mary had toyed with their lunch, their forks moving the food around on their plates, neither one able to eat, though their lawyer encouraged them not to lose hope. He had learned that the judge had recently been audited by the IRS, and didn't much care for the institution, though he refused to recuse himself and vowed to remain impartial.

The prosecution's last witness was Calvin himself. They had saved his testimony in hope of going out with a bang. Bill sat up straight when the prosecutor called Mr. Moody to the stand. His stomach, already in knots, tightened even more. This was the man who ransacked his office to get at his servers, the same man who threatened to put him away. The falsified data had to have come from him.

"And can you tell the court what transpired on that day."

"Certainly." Cal leaned forward lacing his pudgy fingers around his bulging stomach. "Our forensic expert, who you just heard from, came to me and said he had uncovered dozens of files that had been deleted from the servers we subpoenaed."

"And what was contained in these files?"

"Donations. Mr. Best apparently lives on donations made by his constituents. Some of it he uses for operating expenses. He does a pretty fair job of reporting these. Some he gives to the various charities he supports. But the bulk he siphons off for himself."

"And by bulk you mean—"

"One-hundred and seventy-six thousand dollars. And that's on top of the three-hundred thousand he claims as income."

Gasps were heard around the courtroom as heads spun around gawking at Bill.

Bill leaned into his lawyer. "That's ridiculous. Nothing like that ever happened." But his lawyer placed a hand on Bill's forearm. "He's just trying to rattle you. Try not to react."

"Were you able t++o trace any of these back to their source for verification?"

"No sir. Mr. Best is clever. He only deleted cash donations, where there was no record of money changing hands."

"Cash? Can you explain why anyone would send cash? This is supposed to be a charity. Wouldn't people want a receipt so they can deduct their gift from their taxes?"

"People use cash for a lot of reasons, but mostly for laundering money…"

"Objection." Bill's lawyer jumped to his feet. "Assumes facts not in evidence."

"Sustained," the judge retorted. "The witness will refrain from making statements outside the purview of this case."

The lawyer leaned into Bill's ear. "He's trying to broaden his scope. He wants the jurors to see you as part of organized crime."

Bill closed his eyes and slumped into his chair. *God help me.*

The doors at the back of the courtroom opened and a clerk quietly made his way forward to hand Bill's lawyer a note, who read it nodding, his eyes widening appreciatively.

"Would the defense like to cross-examine the witness?" the Judge said.

Joe rose to his feet. "Your honor, the defense would like to request a brief recess."

"Dare I ask why?"

"It looks like some new information has come to light which requires our immediate attention."

The judge looked at his watch then back at the lawyer. "Is this information crucial to your cross examination?"

"Yes, your honor, I believe it is."

"Alright then. The court will be in recess for fifteen-minutes." He brought his gavel down with a *bang!*

Bill looked at his lawyer expectantly.

The man leaned in and handed Bill the note. "I don't know what it is, but I have to take it seriously. Go out and talk to Mary. Better yet, pray. I've got to go. I've only got fifteen-minutes to figure this out." He got up and left, leaving Bill to decipher the note for himself.

The witness is lying. I have proof. Meet me outside, now! the note read.

As expected, the judge returned to his bench precisely fifteen-minutes after they'd adjourned. But Bill and his lawyer were primed and waiting.

Judge Smith pulled his glasses forward looking over the frames. "Is the defense ready to proceed with its cross?"

"We are, your Honor."

"Alright then. Mister Moody, would you please retake the stand?"

Cal got up from his seat and shuffled to the front, his belly bulging over his belt. Judge Smith leaned over and admonished him. "You understand that you are still under oath, Mr. Moody?"

"I do, your honor."

"Very well, proceed."

Bill's defense counsel stood, his eyes locked directly on Cal's as he approached. "Mr. Moody, is it your testimony that the servers you acquired from Mr. Best's house contained deleted files that showed more than one-hundred and fifty-thousand dollars in unreported donations?"

"One-hundred and, *wheeze*, seventy-six thousand, yes." Cal reached for his pocket and removed an inhaler. "Excuse me," he said, sucking in the chemicals that were to him, the breath of life.

"That's alright, take your time." The lawyer waited until Cal appeared to be breathing freely, and resumed. "And is it your contention that the files you uncovered were always there, but were supposedly deleted by Mr. William Best."

"What do you mean? Of course they were there. We found them, didn't we?"

"Yes or no, Mr. Moody. Is it your contention that there were files on Mr. Best's servers that existed prior to his having deleted them?"

"Yes, but nothing is ever really deleted. There are always backup files buried deep in the software's architecture."

"Your honor, would you instruct the witness to answer, yes or no."

The judge leaned over his bench to look down on Cal. "Mr. Moody, unless instructed otherwise, please limit your answer to a simple, yes or no."

"What if I told you we examined backup copies of the same servers you have in your possession and found no such deletions exist."

"What backup files? We took the servers from William Best's home. All of them."

"Not all, Mr. Moody. Copies of the discs had been previously sent to a shop here in Portland where they have since been examined by an independent analyst whose testimony you'll hear in a moment. Suffice to say, there were no such deletions found…"

"Objection!" The prosecuting attorney was on his feet. "Now counsel is testifying for the defense."

"Sustained. Do you have a question for the witness?"

"Yes, your honor. My apologies." The lawyer strode a few paces looking down as though reading his notes, then spun around to glare at the plaintiff. "Mr. Moody, have you ever either directly or indirectly, tampered with the data on Mr. Best's servers?"

"No, of cours…"

"Objection!" The prosecutor was on his feet again. "Mr. Moody is not on trial here."

"Your honor, the defense would like to submit into evidence the following recordings made January 26th, and March 11th, respectively. He walked over and placed a small recorder on the bench in front of the judge. I'll draw the connection if you allow me to proceed."

"Objection overruled. Let's see where this is going, but Mr. Blossier, I caution you to get there quickly."

"Yes, your honor." Joe turned and addressed Cal again. "Mr. Moody, do you recognize the man sitting in the back row of the courtroom?" He swung his arm around and pointed at the man he'd just had a meeting with, who had slipped in after the break.

Cal shriveled, drawing back as he grabbed his inhaler again, visibly shaken.

"Answer the question, please."

"Ah…yes, I guess."

"And can you give us his name?"

"That's ah, Steve DeMarko."

"And didn't you recently fire Mr. DeMarko because he wouldn't falsify evidence against Mr. Best?"

"No…I mean it's not like that…"

"Careful, Mr. Moody. You're still under oath. Mr. DeMarko will give his testimony in a minute. Do you remember telling him that you were going to plant data on Bill's servers just to get a conviction?"

"It wasn't like that, we were just messing around."

Joe turned to face the judge again. "With the court's indulgence, I would like to play the submitted recordings."

"Objection, once again, Mr. Moody is not on trial."

But Bill's lawyer assailed the prosecutor with a glare hot enough to melt steel. "Mr. Moody opened the door when he said he had not trifled with Mr. Best's computer. The recordings clearly show that Mr. Moody has perjured himself. It is, in fact, he who is guilty of committing a criminal act."

"I'll allow," the judge said.

THE SUN HAD broken through the clouds spreading rays of yellow and magenta light on the hills to the east. Bill had dressed down, sporting a flannel shirt and jeans as they drove to his favorite barbecue pit where the meat was basted in a thick coating of sauce and roasted over an open fire. Dinner should have been a celebration. The charges against Bill had been summarily dismissed—thank God for the forthright honesty of Steve DeMarko—and Calvin Moody taken into custody on a charge of perjury with numerous other charges pending further investigation.

"It wasn't me, it was the NSA," Cal whined as they took him away. "I'm a patriot serving my country, doing my job. Don't you see? I'm the victim here. I was following orders."

Bill swirled his baked beans around on his plate, but didn't take a bite. Their trials were far from over. Rachel was still in a convalescent home, her mind a million miles away, and Josh was still missing with no clue as to his whereabouts. Mary remained vocal about her belief that she would see her son again, and Bill refrained from suggesting that it might be in heaven when they were reunited with Ted. At least their lawyer assured them that the possibility of Bill being charged with arson was off the table. Without motive, they had no case. The same went for the insurance fraud. Bill wouldn't be serving any jail time, but he somehow felt like he was already in prison.

A reminder of the wickedness of man sat in the middle of the table. The court retained the original recording, but Steve had sent a digital file to Bill's phone. He reached over and hit the play button again.

"They want us to find something on this guy, even if we have to make it up…"

"You're not going to bring this guy down for tax evasion. He's the epitome of honest."

"Steve…"

"Yes?"

"You're fired!"

"Excuse me?"

"…I didn't say you had to find something big, just something we can use. The powers that be want this guy out of the picture…" "…I'll bet there's a ton of cash he doesn't report. Anyway, it doesn't matter, once I have his servers, I can add files for donations that never existed, files he never reported, making him guilty of tax fraud…"

The powers that be want this guy out of the picture, Bill thought. How was he supposed to celebrate when the government of the country he loved was bent on destroying him? He looked over at Mary. She smiled back, though faintly, as if to say she knew their battle wasn't with men. They were fighting principalities, and powers. *Be sober, be vigilant, for your adversary the devil walks about like a roaring lion seeking whom he may devour.* Sometimes Bill wished he didn't know his Bible so well.

The mood around the table was subdued, each considering what the revelations of the day meant, and how to respond.

Mary finally broke the silence. "Penny for your thoughts," she said.

"Greater is He that is in me, than he that is in the world," Bill replied. Then he shoved his fork into a steaming pile of pulled pork and took a bite.

THIRTY-SIX

I THINK I MUST have been religious once."

"Interesting. What makes you say that?"

"Just a feeling."

"Oh now, it must be more than that."

"I don't know. There's a part of me on the inside that says I was, but outside I'm not so sure."

"It's what I told you about the nature of man and free will. It's human nature to resist God."

"Right, well, I appreciate your spending so much time with me these past few weeks, I do, but it begs another question."

"Okay, shoot."

"If God made everything, who made God?"

"Ah, that one. Oldest question in the book. The problem is you think God is like you, but He isn't. He's infinitely bigger. Scripture says He holds the universe in the palm of His hand, and that's big. In terms of who God is, you're just a grub, only you're immensely smaller than that. But for sake of illustration I'll use it as an example. Go out in the garden and find me a snail or slug. Look at it and tell me if you think that slug can comprehend you and your ability to create. Your mind can design and build computers and, in case you still think you came from there, interplanetary spaceships, and microscopes to explore the microcosms and telescopes that explore the stars. But the slug can't understand any of this. To the slug, you're a god. The God I worship is so much bigger than I am, to Him I'm like a slug. I couldn't begin to comprehend Him. I can only know what He tells me about Himself

351

in His Word."

"But who made Him?"

"Hold on, I'm getting to that. God, having a mind, if you can call it that, so vastly bigger than our own, created everything, including all the known properties of our universe. Take time for instance. Time is a physical property. Inside time, everything is linear. Everything has a start point and an end point, a beginning and an end. But God, since he was before time and created the physical property of time, doesn't live inside time. In other words, in God's world there is no beginning or end, He just is. We can't conceive of such because we're limited by our experience, and in our world everything has a beginning and an end. To see it from God's perspective you have to step outside the box. God never had a beginning because beginning is something He invented. Beginning didn't exist until He made it so."

"See, that's what I mean. I must have been religious because deep inside I know all this. I just don't know how I know."

IT HAD TAKEN the Portland Police several weeks to round up those responsible for the firebombing of the Best's cabin. They had photos of those who threw the gas-filled balloons and those who lit the matches. Threatened with arrest for obstructing justice and the possibility of going to jail, their fellow insurgents verified their identities and gave them up without hesitation.

Mary had seen the fires being started, but not the faces of the arsonists themselves. Still, she described the ringleaders so well the police were able to identify them from the photos without secondary verification. They had Marie Boshinko and Jeremy Landers, who turned out to be an instructor at the university, in custody. All they needed Mary to do was come in and point them out in a line-up.

Bill pulled his pickup into visitor parking and got out, the steel door sounding like the lid of a garbage bin slamming shut. He hefted the wheelchair from the truck's bed and came around to hold the door for his wife, helping her out and then lifted Angie into her chair. He was remiss on his promise to get Mary a new car to replace the one they'd given Josh. She'd never liked riding around in the truck, but so far, she hadn't complained. With their lives topsy-turvy the way they were, it wasn't the best time to go car shopping.

They approached the doors at the front of the building and wheeled Angie inside, rolling her up to the counter. "We're supposed to ask for Sergeant Mandy," Bill said to the woman standing at the desk.

The officer stood back, reaching for an intercom phone. "What did you say your name was?" she asked as she keyed in a number. She wore a midnight blue uniform with a single gold chevron and a blue and gold arm patch that read, Bureau of Police—Portland.

"Bill Best. I'm here with Mary Best. They asked her to come and identify a few suspects in a line-up."

"Hi Mandy, there's someone here to see you…That's right, Mary Best."

Bill wondered if Mandy was a first name, or last.

"She'll be right with you," the lady said and then went back to doing whatever it was she was doing before they came in.

Bill took Mary's hand. "You sure you're okay with this?"

Mary nodded. "We'll be looking through one-way glass so they won't be able to see me."

"Yes, but after. If you identify them, and they go to trial, you'll be called as a witness."

Mary looked Bill in the eye. "Not if we show mercy. Besides, I don't want to think about that. Right now, the only thing I care about is getting Josh back. He's alive, I just don't know why he hasn't called or tried to reach us."

"He's in God's hands. All we can do is pray."

A door to the back opened and a woman stood in the gap, wearing the same uniform as the woman at the desk, only she had three gold chevrons, indicating her rank as sergeant. She was thirtyish with short cropped brown hair and dark eyes. "Mrs. Best," she said to Mary, holding out her hand. "I'm Sergeant Mandy."

Answers that question, Bill thought.

"First name also Mandy, so I'm Mandy, Mandy. My parents thought it was cute."

Or not, Bill retracted.

"If you'd like to come this way. Are you with Mrs. Best?" she said, addressing Bill.

"I'm her husband, just here for moral support, but it was my house that got burned too."

"Alright, you can come back, but once we enter the room, I ask that you refrain from talking. No coaxing, no comment, no anything. They'll have lawyers present and you don't want to give them a reason to have the identification thrown out. You'll be looking at two line-ups, one male and one female. If you don't recognize the people you saw, just be honest and say so. No pressure, all right?" She held the door for them, and then squeezed in front to lead the procession. They moved down a long hall passing rows of desks. Officers were either on the phone, or talking to victims of crimes. Virtually all the desks were littered with stacks of paper. Mandy led them into a darkened room and had them face a window with the curtain closed. A man with a briefcase was already there but he didn't bother introducing himself. He stood back, playing the silent observer. Mandy reached for a micro-phone. "Are we ready in there?"

"Good to go," came the response.

Mandy reached for a rod and drew the curtain back.

It took less than a minute for Mary to identify the man. He had shaved his goatee to look different, but his jaw was lighter where the beard had been because his skin hadn't tanned, leaving a perfect pattern of the flames that had decorated the sides of his cheek. Most of all, she recognized his eyes; dark and brooding with thick eyebrows and lashes. "Number four," she said.

"Are you sure? Take your time. We're not in a hurry."

"Can I ask him to say something for me?"

"Absolutely."

"Have him say, 'That man tried to kill us.'"

Mandy went to the mike. "Could you have number four say, 'that man tried to kill us?'"

Mary waited for the man to repeat the phrase and then said, "Number four. That's him. One hundred-percent."

Mandy went to the mike. "Alright, that's good. You can bring the next group in." She reached over and closed the curtain again. "I want to thank you for your help," she said and turned to the man with the briefcase. "Mr. Boden, are you representing both of the accused?"

"I am."

"Alright, then. Stay with us. We'll be done shortly."

They went through the same process with Marie and, while it took Mary a little longer because all the girls had short dark hair, by the end she was certain she had picked the right one.

Mandy ushered Bill, Mary and Angie out of the room and down the hall again. "I really appreciate your coming. It makes our job so much easier when people cooperate with the police."

"So what happens next?" Bill asked.

"They'll be arraigned and then go before a judge to set bail, which they'll likely make since neither of them has a criminal record. But don't worry, when it goes to trial I'm sure we'll get a conviction. We have them on camera and we have several of their friends willing to testify that these two told them to bring gas-filled balloons. And with your testimony on top of that, they're done."

"Will they serve time?"

"I can't say. Judges are all over the place on that, but even if they don't, their felony convictions will follow them the rest of their lives. The teacher will likely forfeit his job and the girl will be expelled. Makes life a little harder."

"Do they have to be charged with a felony?"

"That's up to the district attorney. He could plead it down to a misdemeanor, but I doubt he will. We have far too many protests where characters like these encourage throwing paint balloons at our officers, if not bricks and stones. He'll most likely want to make an example of them."

"But he can plead it down if he wants to, right?"

"I suppose so, why?"

Bill looked at Mary waiting for her nod, and when she smiled, turned back to Sergeant Mandy. "This was a personal attack on me and my family. They claim to hate me and everything I stand for, but these kids don't know me. They hate me for what they think I believe.

But, uh, we're Christians, and the Bible says we're to forgive others just as our Father in Heaven forgives us. So we've decided to try and show a little mercy. I run a small farm outside the city, which I believe they also burned. If I can get the district attorney to agree to community service, I'd like to negotiate reducing the charge to a misdemeanor in exchange for their agreeing to work with me for the summer. I think once they get to know me they might not hate me so much, and while we may never see eye-to-eye on everything, maybe we can at least learn to get along."

MOST OF THE elderly patrons of Tantamoa Convalescent Home gravitated to the common room where folks could sit and talk and enjoy one another's company. Those still cognizant knew why they were there. They were waiting to die, left by well-meaning relatives whose busy lives didn't allow them time to care for an aging parent. But that was okay, they had friends. There was always a card game to play, or movie to watch, and once in a while they even received a visit from one of their estranged kin.

Ellen was knitting, though she didn't know exactly what she was trying to make, but she would figure it out before she was through. Johnson was reading the same dog-eared golf magazine he read every day. Oglethorpe was shuffling cards trying to get a game going with the same suckers he'd beaten yesterday and would probably beat again today.

Stan sat beside Rachel, trying to politely ignore Margret, the woman on his left, who, by his recollection, was asking for the fifth time if he'd had the chance to meet her daughter because she was single and would make a good wife. In the game room Stan could hear a choral group singing *Chattanooga Choo Choo* around the old upright piano, and the clack of ping-pong balls bouncing against a table. Obviously someone was spry enough to play the game. He'd had several good conversations with lucid folk who had taken an interest in Rachel and wanted to know why she was there, her being so young and all. Ingrid had brought him a newspaper which he was trying to read, but he was having trouble concentrating over Margret's questions about whether or not he was married and if he'd had the chance to meet her daughter.

The story was third page news with a one column mugshot of a man no one seemed to know. Stan recognized him immediately. It was the man the RCMP had identified as Carl Rove, but the pink-haired girl had called Victor. The headline read: "Mystery Man Found Dead in Gallup New Mexico." The story went on to say how the man was found shot to death in the Sunset Motel outside of Gallup, in what appeared to be an execution. In trying to identify the deceased, the Gallup Police had submitted his photo and fingerprints to a nationwide database and were surprised to find him wanted in eleven states on charges ranging from kidnap to murder, apparently committed under a collection of names including those of Carl Rove and Victor Damshie. Stan was debating whether or not to read the article to Rachel. The incident could have the effect of jogging her memory. That was the positive side, but the negative was that it might also summon the horrors of what she'd been through, driving her further into her shell.

"I'M GLAD YOU'RE still here. I thought you might have left."

"I do have other patients, but sit down, I have a few minutes."

"All this stuff you've been telling me about God. I don't know why, but deep down, I believe it. That's why I think I must have been religious. It's inside me, you know?"

"Alright."

"But if that's true. There's more to the story, isn't there?"

"Right, the Jesus part."

"See, I knew you'd eventually get around to that."

"Actually, I didn't. You did."

"Whatever."

"It's the best part of the story, because as big as He is, and as infinitely small as we are, God chose not to ignore us or leave us to our own devices. Think of us as ants. We create civilizations, or colonies, and we honor our queen, and store up food, and protect our territory, go to war with other ant colonies and sometimes we get into places we don't belong. Now God could just step on us, or use bait traps to wipe us out, but instead He chose to become one of us. He said, these ants can't help themselves, it's their nature to get in My pantry, just as it's their nature to war against themselves. I'm going to become one of them and because it's their nature to build, but also to destroy, they'll end up destroying Me. But because I made them in the first place and hold the power over life and death, I'll come back from the dead and promise any of those who choose to follow Me, that I'll transform them into My image and bring them to live with Me. All they have to do is believe that I have the power to save them. It's a poor illustration, but that's what Jesus did. You've screwed up your whole life. You're so messed up you don't know who you are, or what you've done, but there's hope. All you have to do is trust Jesus—wait, where are you going?"

"To tell the truth, I don't know, but it suddenly dawned on me that there's someplace I have to be."

It became clear, as he walked down the hall, that he'd lost his mind. But he'd known that from the moment he'd awakened on that sandbank without any knowledge of who he was or where he belonged. He just knew he didn't belong here. He was needed somewhere else. He just didn't know where that was.

> "Rape, kidnap and murder are among the charges the unknown assailant was being sought for. It is hoped the perpetrator's demise will bring closure to those affected by a crime spree that stretched from 2015 to the present. One thing we know for certain, whoever this mystery man is, he won't hurt anyone ever again."

Stan finished reading the article. He folded the paper, setting it on the couch beside him. Rachel looked blank. He didn't think she'd respond, but it was worth a try.

A young man was moving down the hall, looking dazed. Dr. Murphy stepped out of his office, starting after him.

The projector inside Rachel's darkened theater whirred to life. A light began to shine, low at first but gaining slowly in brightness as images formed—a man lying on slab, cold and lifeless, a face, eyes open but unmoving, a body frozen in time and space. *He won't hurt anyone again.* The seconds passed and other pictures appeared on the screen; a little girl with blond flowing hair was sitting in a field of flowers. In her hand she held the remnants of a daisy from which the petals had been plucked. The little girl watched as the last petal, born on a ribbon of warm summer air, was lifted up and carried away. Smiling now, Rachel stood in gleeful excitement clasping her hands together. "He loves me," she cried, "He loves me!"

Stan pushed off his good leg, jumping to his feet. "Rachel!"

The boy stared at Rachel as he passed by with Doctor Murphy quick on his heels. "Where are you going, son?"

"Josh?" Rachel reached out to take his arm.

"Who?" the doctor said, spinning around.

"Rachel, you're back." Stan grabbed his daughter, breaking her grip on Josh as he smothered her in his arms.

Josh kept pushing forward till he was out the door.

THIRTY-SEVEN

MAN HAS NEVER understood the mystery of migration; birds that travel thousands of miles without a compass knowing exactly where they're going without having been there before. Josh was a migrant bird. He went out on the highway and stuck out his thumb and took a ride from the first vehicle that stopped. They were heading for High Ridge with a canoe mounted on the roof of a vintage Winnebago that creaked and wheezed and spewed diesel fumes as it rolled down the road. Three fully inflated tractor tire inner-tubes were strapped to the top and bicycles hung from a rack slotted into a trailer hitch in back.

They pulled him inside and welcomed him like family, offering him Coca-Cola and Dorito Chips while two kids on the floor wrestled with the family poodle, messing up the game of Scrabble they'd been playing.

She had called him Josh, the tremor of her voice sending a chill up his spine, not one of fear, but of discovery. She knew who he was. He should have stopped, but something compelled him to keep moving. Her name was Rachel. He'd heard the man say it, but something deep inside him knew it to be true, but it was unclear how he knew.

The RV took a sweeping bend to the left and Josh saw the place where he had crawled out of the river, the sandbar, the bleached log, the embankment. He had the sudden urge to make them stop so he could explore this place of beginnings, but he'd already done that— hadn't he? And by the time he got his thoughts sorted out they were already long past.

"So, what's your name?" The driver looked over his shoulder, making introductions. The man had a receding hairline that left his forehead bald, but the rest of his hair hung behind his back in a long ponytail. He had a full beard and sunglasses and looked like a Peter Pan hippy that never grew up. A peace symbol, braided into a long hemp macramé, hung from the rearview mirror.

"Josh," he said without hesitation, because the girl had said it and he knew it was true.

"Josh, I'm Mike and this is my partner Carla." The man pointed at the woman in the passenger seat. She had her feet balled up under her, standing on the seat like a chipmunk. Her long Indian print dress slid over her knees, covering her toes. The dress was a sleeveless pullover, but she wore an aqua T-shirt underneath that covered her shoulders. Several strings of turquoise jewelry were strung around her neck. Her hair was sandy brown and braided, hanging down below her waist.

"Nice to meet you, Josh," Carla said.

"So Josh, where you headed?"

"No place in particular. I'm just traveling, out to see the world." Josh said it because he didn't really know where he was going, but also because he thought it was the kind of thing a couple of hippy throwbacks would want to hear.

"Right on, man. Right on. This road goes through Mt. Hood National Forest, but we're stopping off at the campground for a few days. Carla needs time to complete a few orders."

Josh must have looked perplexed because Carla chimed in and said, "We have an online business. We travel around and when we come to a big city we stock up on beads and gemstones and head to a campground to make necklaces and bracelets to fulfil orders."

"You make a living doing that?"

Mike's sunglasses appeared in the rearview mirror. "We're not getting rich, but we get by. Carla has built up quite a following over the years, so most of our orders are repeat business. And she's always creating new designs which I take pictures of and post on our website."

"And I homeschool the kids while we travel," Carla interjected.

They passed a gravel road that angled off to the right, heading up into a heavily wooded mountain. It looked vaguely familiar. Pictures, images, pieces of a puzzle, all meaningless by themselves, but together...

"Make yourself comfortable," Mike said. "I'm going to slip into some music and zone out for a while. I'll see you when I resurface." And for the next seven minutes the Winnebago slid through the deep green forest to the tune of Neil Young singing, "Cowgirl in the Sand." Josh had never heard of Neil Young but whoever he was, he played a rabid guitar. Mike and Carla had fired up a joint and were passing it back and forth, the cloud of smoke filling the front section of the van, but when they passed it to Josh, he waved it off. He couldn't remember ever doing drugs, though he knew what they were. He wondered if he drank alcohol, but he couldn't remember that either. Mike kept the volume high, the tin walls pulsing with sound while his head be-bopped back and forth in time with the music. When it was over, Josh felt like his ears needed realignment. *Poor guy will be deaf by the time he's fifty.* Mike slipped another CD, The Doors, "Light My Fire," into the deck and the music played on.

They bumped and bounced into the campground, rolling to a stop in front of the ranger station. "This is as far as we go," Mike said.

"I appreciate your giving me a lift," Josh responded. "A lot of folks wouldn't do that the way things are out there."

"We always try to help when we can," Carla said.

"And I never worry about trouble," Mike reached under the dash for a revolver which he held up for Josh to see.

So much for peace, love and flowers, Josh thought. "All right, well, once again thanks for the ride." Josh hopped down. "Maybe we'll see you again sometime." Josh waved and backed up, taking a path through the trees away from the ranger station.

Now where? He had come this far on instinct and so far it felt right, but there was no little voice in his head telling him where to go from here. He kept to the trail, walking down to the lake. He knew this lake, or at least it seemed familiar. A bluebird warbled in a branch overhead. Josh glanced up. "You got any ideas?" but the bird took flight without offering advice.

362

He kept to the path and a half-mile later found where the lake fed into a river. To his left the water became a torrent, sluicing off downstream in a flow of whitewater rapids. The trail had ended, and while he could see where it resumed on the other side, the only way across was to step in and get wet, but something held him back. It took him a minute to realize what it was. He was afraid, but of what? There was nothing to be afraid of. It was just water. At the top end, where the water formed into the river, the lake was shallow. Joshua crossed the Jordan to the Promised Land. *Have I not commanded you be strong and courageous?* Now, how did he know that? He pulled off his tennis shoes and rolled up the legs of his pants and stepped into the water. *Burrrrrrrr.* He trod his way, splashing against the current, almost slipping on a rock that went sideways under his foot, but he made it to the other side. *Nothing to fear but fear itself*, he decided.

He tiptoed to the trunk of a fallen tree and sat down, waiting for his feet to dry before putting his shoes back on. He was committed to the trail now, but for what reason he didn't know—and then he did. Far out across the lake he saw them, two eagles, no wait, three, four, five, but three of them were smaller than the first two. A family. That's where he was supposed to go! *Who satisfies your desires with good things so that your youth is renewed like the eagles.* He remembered that—from the Bible. See he *was* religious, he knew it. No, not religious, religion was man's attempt to reach God, he was Christian—Christianity was God's attempt to reach man. He knew all of this. *But they that wait upon the LORD shall renew their strength; they shall mount up with wings as eagles; they shall run, and not be weary; they shall walk, and not faint.* Yes, yes, yes.

He wiped his feet, brushing off the dirt, and pulled on his socks and shoes and took off running. He had an appointment with God! Running, and running, and running, over rocks and roots and small inlets of water steeped in moss and mosquitoes. He only got about a mile before his breathing gave out. He had to stop with his hand braced against a tree, sucking in air. His lungs were on fire. Perhaps a more measured approach. He'd still get there. *They shall mount up with wings as eagles; they shall run, and not be weary; they shall walk, and not faint.* He took off again, walking this time, but at a good clip. The sun was dipping into the valley beyond the lake, the sky looking pink at its passing. He was determined not to miss his appointment.

The wooded path was easy to follow, though he had to keep using fallen moss-covered deadwood to cross stagnant pools where the water backed up and the eelgrass rotted to an oily purple infested with water striders and frogs. Ponderosa pine, blackberry bramble, Douglas fir, milkweed, sword fern, huckleberry, bracken fern, deer fern, and dogbane, he was able to identify the flora along the trail with ease, which was heartening. It had to be his upbringing. Someone, father, mother, had taught him the foliage of the area, and that meant he had parents, no, he had loving parents, because someone had taken the time to teach him about the forest and its ecosystem, and that's what loving parents do. Someone cared about him, someone loved him, someone had showed him all these incredible things.

He turned a corner and saw where a river fell out of the mountains, feeding the lake. Three black-tailed deer that had come down to the water to hydrate, bolted in front of him. He froze, waiting until they disappeared, bounding into the bush. He caught his breath and followed the river up into the growing shadow of the forest, the tree limbs turning grey in the glooming dusk. He passed a sign with large red letters that said, "no trespassing," but kept going. Something told him he'd seen that sign before. He checked the sky and saw the eagles still circling overhead, their wings spread like sails, catching the evening breeze.

Josh heard it before he saw it, but coming around a giant ponderosa into a vale of ferns, he found himself standing in front of a magnificent waterfall. The river gushed over a cliff sixty-feet above, and fell pounding on the rocks below with a thunderous roar, sending up a spray that looked like smoke. And out of that vapor the gray walls rose, slick and wet, ascending to a crag on the side of a cliff where there was a nest—the eagle's nest! Was that what he'd come to see? *Does the eagle mount up at thy command, and make her nest on high?* That's it, right God?

It was another proof that he'd had loving parents. So many verses had popped into his head over the past few days he was quoting scriptures he didn't know he knew. Someone had to have taught him those verses. *Thy word have I hid in my heart that I might not sin against Thee.* See, like that. And dozens more, which begged the question, where were they? He remembered waking up on a sandbar with his legs in the water and his head in the sand, wondering if he'd been born there, or had been left there to die. His head had felt like a bomb about to explode. He had three choices: finish the job for whoever had left him there, seek God to see if He could be found, or deny God's existence and live life on his own terms. He'd crawled to the top of the embankment, determined to let fate have its way. The nursing home was just a detour to find relief from his pain, the physical kind, not spiritual. It was the Bible on Dr. Murphy's desk that made him start asking questions. Dr. Murphy had found a lump the size of an egg on his head and suggested God was trying to knock some sense into him. *Maybe.*

Josh looked back down the gauntlet of trees that lined the river all the way to the lake, but he couldn't see the body of water itself. He'd need a higher elevation for that, a place to soar with the eagles. The wall along the side of the falls was practically vertical and broken into shards of shale. A difficult climb, but he could see where others had done it, so it was possible. He started up the side traversing diagonally across the mountain, determined to reach a place where he could see out over the lake. His foot slipped, sending several pounds of shale crashing to the bottom in a plume of dust. He froze against the wall, his heart pounding as he looked down, imagining himself falling with those rocks. *The only thing to fear is fear itself.* Roosevelt said that, a man in a wheelchair. *If he can do it, so can I.* He relaxed and loosened his grip, and kept going, finally coming to a switchback where the incline leveled out allowing him to stand and look out over God's country. The whole landscape was before him. The lake below, indigo blue, sat like a drop of water in the palm of God's hand. The forest, spreading out toward the ocean, was a carpet of deep green in the fading light. The sun, just barely a sliver on the horizon, shed rays of peach and pink and yellow. And the cumulus clouds were fringed with gold.

"God is this why You brought me here, to show me Your creation? God, You are beautiful. Reveal Yourself to me." And his eyes began to water, though it didn't make sense, because he wasn't sad. He was, in fact, happy. Looking back over his shoulder he saw he was almost to the top. He needed to complete his mission.

He moved along a track set at the beginning of time when the moon and stars were just being formed. The earth in all its glory was set in motion, spinning like a top as it turned east to west bringing light, followed by darkness, but always returning to light again, world without end. As he stepped up over the last ridge, he saw a rock old as the planet itself and a man bowed down to the Maker of all things with his hands lifted to Heaven crying out, "God, I miss my son!"

And in a microsecond of time all the memories through all the years, the good, the bad and the ugly, came flooding back—and the wandering prodigal saw the pig-slop he'd been eating, and the fatted calf, and himself, unworthy—but coming home.

EPILOGUE

ROLL THE BALL, roll it slowly. Once God sets a ball in motion it just keeps rolling. East, forever pushing toward the sun, brings light. West chases east, dragging the world into darkness again. It follows a course set out at the beginning of time. And will continue until time comes to an end. But look up. Standing on the mountain as you roll toward the light with the sun breaking over the curvature of the earth—you just might catch a glimpse of Heaven.

Thirty-six months later

THE WORLD HAD not ended, nor had the apocalypse come. For most, it was business as usual. Everything was new, though everything remained the same. Technology continued to race forward convincing Bill they were closer to the return of Christ every day, particularly with respect to man's slide into the moral abyss. Imagine a law being passed that made it legal for men and boys to engage in sex as long as it was consensual. More churches were closing, so many Bill had lost count. How could they continue when their offerings were being taxed, as was the church property itself? And while the markets were still producing gains for investors, the profits taken had less value due to skyrocketing inflation, and the national debt was beyond measure. More and more the buzz was that it was time for world leaders to yield control to a central authority.

But none of that exceeded what Bill was able to handle. It was the fulfillment of Bible prophecy. So it wasn't the depravity, or technology, or the great falling away that drove him over the edge, it was the complete stripping away of his freedoms. Bill was born free and, good Lord willing, he would die free.

Like most things, it had come subtly, sneaking up on the world without fanfare or reason. It was, after all, just a way of keeping us safe. A health passport was nothing more than a tool to be used to make sure everyone acted responsibility. No one was forcing anyone to take the vaccine, but if you wanted to travel, you needed to show you were fully protected.

When it was first introduced, Bill issued a warning. It was based on the same platform as the social credit system China used to keep its citizens in line. Behave and do what you're told, and you'll live long and prosper. Buck the government and have your privileges taken away. In China, that included all areas of life. In America, it was just a way of making sure you weren't going to infect anyone else. People who had taken the vaccine shouldn't be required to sit on an airplane next to someone who might carry a disease. But it didn't take long for retailers and restaurants and movie theaters and sporting events to jump onboard. Can't show your health passport, you're money isn't good here. Can't prove you're socially responsible, please stay at home. By then, there was little to distinguish America's health passport from China's social credit system. Do what your government wants, and you'll live long and prosper. Buck the government and have your privileges taken away. Thus it had begun, and thus it had expanded into all walks of life. Post too many dissenting tweets, and see your kid's university applications rejected. Speak out against party politics and find the promotion you've worked for, given to someone else. Take exception to the government's printing of money, have your loan application denied. Once the banks were involved, your credit was worthless until you towed the line. Inch upon inch, mile upon mile, people's right to speak out about what they believed, or against that with which they disagreed, was diminished. And now they were talking about making the passport a chip to be inserted into your wrist. How long would it be before you couldn't buy or sell without the mark or number of the beast?

Bill had never fully understood what James, the half-brother of Christ, meant when he said, "...count it all joy when you fall into various trials." He would have thought facing so many trials would wear him down, but instead, he felt lifted up. There was an inexplicable peace in knowing God was working all things to His good pleasure. The reign of Satan would only last until Christ stepped in to take His rightful place on the throne. Bill's job was to endure to the end, and for that he had but one option. Figuratively speaking, he'd been flying under the radar for most of his life. Today he would make it a reality. It was time to leave.

ONE SUMMER MORNING the skin of the lake was so taut it looked like a sheet of gray steel, blemished only where water-striders dimpled its surface. The sun was still behind the mountain, but the promise of its coming made it light enough to see. Bill brought his pole back and flung the tip forward. In the stillness you could hear the *whirr* of the line running out and the *plunk* as the weight broke the water.

They had risen at four a.m., earlier than normal, but this was a special day, and they only had an hour. The others would be waiting.

Bill reeled the line in, hoping to attract a Largemouth bass to his shimmering lure, but he came up empty. "Drat, they're just not biting this morning. Guess we'd better pack it in, or we'll miss the sunrise."

"I was hoping for a chance to show you up again but...wait a minute, *wait a minute*, got you, you son of a gun." Josh snapped his rod back, setting the hook. "And dang, she's a beaut. Stuff that in your ol' pork-pie hat," he said, reeling the fighting fish in. "Looky that." He brought the fish into the hull of the old Chinook and set it flopping on the bottom. "Got to be at least sixteen inches."

"Dang you, that's the one I was after." Bill picked up the line and handed it to this son. "Alright let's get a picture." The fish was whacking back and forth as Josh held it suspended in the air. Bill brought his phone up and took the photo, the automatic flash engaging in the low light, blinding Josh and his catch. Then he leaned in with a pair of pliers and worked the hook out of the fish's mouth and set it free. The

369

slick green scales of the bass disappeared beneath the dark blue surface of the water.

Bill smiled as both men brought their poles inside the canoe. Josh took a position in the back and began to paddle. He stroked until they were coming up fast on the shore and then held the paddle aloft, letting the Chinook slide up on the sand like a beached whale.

Bill jumped out and pulled the canoe further up onshore, making sure the river's current didn't carry it away. Josh hopped out after, leaving their fishing gear behind to be found by someone else.

They started up the trail following the course of the river through the dusky woods where towhees, and buntings and grosbeaks were just waking the morning with song. An edge of light hovered over the eastern horizon. Both men saw it and picked up their pace. The thunder of the falls greeted them as they stepped into the meadow where ferns and huckleberry grew. The mist off the rocks cooled the perspiration they'd acquired on their heated walk. Above them, morning clouds were turning scarlet and magenta.

"Think we'll make it?" Josh said as they pushed onto the trail.

"We'll make it, unless you slow me down."

"No chance of that."

The waterfall cascaded over the rocks, white as a wedding veil. Seven months earlier, when he'd received the news, Bill had determined to cut a trail into the side of that mountain. It was seven months of backbreaking labor that now paid off in the ease with which they ascended the slope.

As they came up over the top, Bill looked out over the plateau where the river flowed from the snows melting on the sides of the mountains. In the distance he could see a spark of light reflecting off the window of a blue-and-white six-passenger Airbus that sat with its rotors slowly turning, awaiting their arrival. The helicopter was there as a favor to Senator Powers. Its owner, Matt Meginnis, a generous donor to Stan's political campaign and close personal friend, would be their pilot.

Stan had fulfilled his mission. His investigation into Senator Wessler had stalled and was going nowhere. He couldn't prove it was

Mark who commissioned the assault on Rachel, and congress lacked the will to investigate a senor committee member. Mark Wessler was bulletproof. It mattered little anyway. The Senate was in shambles. No longer an autonomous legislative body, it had become a rubber stamp for the whims of a President who had campaigned on bringing the United States into the global community. Stan had tried to stave it off, but it was hopeless. There was nothing more he could do.

As for Bill, he had fought the government over his right to lease his five-hundred acres of forest—and lost. There was nothing for him here. They would be leaving the land they loved and taking up residence in a new country. If technology was the bane of freedom, he would go where technology had yet to take root and thrive.

The rest of the group was waiting as Bill and Josh crested the hill. Mary approached and took him by the shoulders, planting a kiss on his cheek. "Glad you made it."

"Wouldn't miss it for the world." Bill turned to address his fellow travelers. "Come on guys, gather 'round. We want to be standing right here when it happens. Sunrise only lasts a few seconds, and we can't keep our ride waiting forever."

Rachel disappeared into the tent and reappeared cradling a squirming blanket. Josh took his place at her side as everyone formed a circle around Abraham's rock.

"How you doing this morning, Mrs. Best?" he said, his hand coming up behind her hair to massage her back. Her white muslin dress nearly touched the ground, a wreath of daisies pinned to her head.

"Just fine, Mr. Best."

"Have I told you today that I love you?" He leaned in kissing her cheek and folded back the blanket to see the rosebud face of their child.

"Yes, but you can always say it again."

The sun broke over the mountain with yellow rays of light so blindingly brilliant it felt like someone had opened a door to heaven. In the valley below, the lake looked green, the trees chartreuse, and the clouds like spun gold. The eagles circling overhead formed an ethereal crown.

"Behold the dawn of a new day," Bill said.

TWO-THOUSAND MILES south on a similar cliff overlooking the Pacific Ocean, Lonnie Striker, missionary to the Sierra Madre del Sur, stood with his hands raised to God. He heard the scarlet macaw delivering its morning wake-up call, the sound of tributaries coming together and pouring over the falls, the wind channeling up the coast bending and whipping the trees. The sun was just cresting the mountains to the east, its red glow slicing through the tropical forest like a hot machete. He wondered if Bill was observing that same sun. They were scheduled to leave at dawn's first light, following the dedication. Lord willing, they would be standing together side-by-side to watch the sun as it set.

It was something Lonnie looked forward to. He hadn't seen Bill since his wedding but, like old friends, they'd kept in touch. Those had been tumultuous times, bringing down the Estrada cartel and its child trafficking ring, but nothing compared to what was going on today. He got only scant bits of news from a weekly paper, but Bill wouldn't relocate and continue his podcasts from Posada if it hadn't gotten really bad.

They continued to pray for Christ's soon return, but if forced to carry on, Lonnie had devised good cover. He had negotiated the purchase of a small coffee plantation where Bill and his family, and a U.S. Senator he had yet to meet, would cultivate beans and sell them through an off-the-grid wholesaler who still traded in pesos, not cryptocurrency. With God's help, they might avoid detection for years.

Lonnie took a deep breath, taking in the sultry air. He could smell the salt rising up from the ocean and see the moon still hanging like a shiny silver coin over the waves. A donkey being hitched to a cart, brayed down in the village. On the outskirts, an ever growing number of tents were blooming like multicolored flowers. Every day, more believers from the United States were making their way down to the Sierra Madre del Sur to await the return of Christ. In a unique way, it resembled the Underground Railroad used by slaves to find freedom in Canada, only now they were heading south to Mexico to avoid persecution. Who would have thought they'd be seeking a place where internet signals were weak, and computers few and far between? He watched the glow of the red sun as it rose over the jungle. It was a day the Lord had made, and he would rejoice and be glad in it.

BILL DREW IN A BREATH of that same air, though less sultry at his elevation. "This sun we see rising over Oregon's Mount Hood, we'll see setting over Posada this evening. Glory to God! I have a verse I want to read." Bill reached to pick up the Bible he had set on the rock and turned to Genesis 8:22.

> "While earth remains,
> seedtime and harvest,
> cold and heat,
> winter and summer,
> and day and night,
> shall not cease."

He closed the Book and set it down. "That was God's promise to Noah, and it's God's promise to us. No matter how bad it gets, the world isn't going to end until He comes to make it anew." Bill glanced around, his eyes burning. He had to swallow the mucus in his throat to keep his emotions from showing. But why? His son was there, married to the daughter of his friend, and they'd given him a namesake. There was reason to rejoice. Why the mask? *The meek shall inherit the earth.*

"You know, I was just thinking," he said. "I've always called this Abraham's rock." *Sniff.* He wiped his cheek with a red mackinaw sleeve. "And when you think about it, we're like Abraham, called by God to go to an unfamiliar place. I'm sure he was filled with uncertainty, too, but like us, he knew God was faithful." Bill raised his hands, choking down his phlegm, and in a deep baritone voice, began to sing one of the grand old hymns of the faith:

> "Great is thy faithfulness, Oh God my Father,
> There is no shadow of turning with Thee,
> Thou changes not, thy compassions they fail not,
> As Thou has been, Thou forever will be."

Mary's eyes glistened as she joined him in raising her hands, along with Stan, and Rachel too, though she kept one arm snuggling her baby to her breast, and Josh with his right arm around her waist lifted his other to heaven; even Angie sang in sweet discordant harmony.

"Summer and winter, springtime and harvest,
Sun moon and stars in their courses above,
Join with all nature in manifold witness,
To Thy great faithfulness, mercy and love…"

Bill turned and received the bundle from Rachel raising it high in the air—and there at the top of the world, with the sun and moon and earth and sky blessing the God of Heaven, the family joined hands to celebrate the christening of little, William Christian Best.

Bill struggled to hold back but it was pointless; the rapture of the moment was too great. His eyes burst into a river as powerful and forceful as the Watalong.

Real men don't cry, he thought. *But maybe sometimes—they do.*

Novels by Keith R. Clemons:

If I Should Die

Above the Stars

These Little Ones

Angel in the Alley

Mohamed's Moon

Mohamed's Song

Stretching Heaven

One Pair of Shoes

On Solid Ground

While Earth Remains

Available at: www.keithclemons.com

Origin of Characters in this book

Bill Best

The character Bill Best previously appeared in two other novels, *If I Should Die*, where Bill rushed in to save the life of his wife Laurie and reconnect her with their daughter Angie, and *These Little Ones*, where Bill joined forces with Missionary Lonnie Striker in bringing down the Estrada cartel and its child trafficking ring.

Stan and Rachel Powers

Stan and Rachel together appeared in *One Pair of Shoes* and *On Solid Ground*, where after a lifetime of separation, and lives going opposite directions, they were finally brought together by a series of miraculous events.

Lonnie Striker

Lonnie first appeared in *Above The Stars,* where he temporarily left his post as a missionary in the Sierra Madre del Sur to run a film company left to him by his father, and then in the sequel, *These Little Ones* where he solicited the help of Bill Best to retrieve the children taken from his orphanage by the Estrada cartel.